DARE MIGHTY THINGS

DARE
MIGHTY
THINGS

HEATHER KACZYNSKI

HARPER TEEN
An Imprint of HarperCollinsPublishers

To Rosie, who is my dream come true

HarperTeen is an imprint of HarperCollins Publishers.

Dare Mighty Things
Copyright © 2017 by Heather Kaczynski
All rights reserved. Printed in the United States of America. No part of this book
may be used or reproduced in any manner whatsoever without written permission
except in the case of brief quotations embodied in critical articles and reviews. For
information address HarperCollins Children's Books, a division of HarperCollins
Publishers, 195 Broadway, New York, NY 10007.
www.epicreads.com

Library of Congress Control Number: 2017943433
ISBN 978-0-06-247986-0

Typography by Sarah Nichole Kaufman
17 18 19 20 21   PC/LSCH   10 9 8 7 6 5 4 3 2 1
❖
First Edition

Far better it is to dare mighty things, to win glorious triumphs, even though checkered by failure, than to take rank with those timid spirits who neither enjoy much nor suffer much, because they live in the gray twilight that knows neither victory nor defeat.

—THEODORE ROOSEVELT

ONE

A MODERATELY INTELLIGENT robot could do my job. Obviously, letting a seventeen-year-old intern anywhere near actual rockets would be irresponsible, but still—NASA was vastly underutilizing my skills.

Not that I was complaining. Because, come on—*NASA*. I'd mop the floors as long as they let me stay. I mean, this was where they built the rockets that took men to the moon. Not that you could tell by the bland cubicles, the water-stained ceiling tiles, and the dead insects collecting in the light fixtures of this fifty-year-old building. My dad, who was working two floors above, said that NASA's glory days were behind it. But maybe one day there'd be funding and real history being made again. That was my hope, anyway.

I'd grown up in Huntsville, a town nicknamed Rocket City, whose history was so entwined with spaceflight that the two were nearly inseparable. A life-size model of the rocket that took us to the moon jutted out of the landscape like a compass rose, a landmark visible all over town. I'd grown up believing the impossible was possible. There hadn't been any other path for me but NASA.

I'd worked hard to get here, beating out dozens of my fellow high school juniors desperate to pad their résumés. But "here" ended up being a cubicle in the legal department of NASA's Marshall Space Flight Center, doing mindless data entry for zero dollars an hour. Sure, I'd made it inside the building, but it was boring. And I hated being bored.

To keep my brain from melting, I listened to Beethoven in one ear, memorizing his piano sonatas so I'd be prepared to kick ass at youth orchestra auditions come fall.

"Hey, kid!" My coworker Andre, a paralegal who liked bossing me around because I was just a high school intern, came marching toward me. His features were all contorted, like he smelled something rotten. I braced myself. Andre didn't exactly like me, not since that little incident where I'd corrected his math at a staff meeting. In front of our boss. And the whole department.

He jabbed his thumb vaguely over his shoulder. "Big boss wants to see you. And you'd better take that thing out of your ear."

Hesitant, I slipped out of my chair and popped out my earbud, suspicious that maybe this was Andre's idea of a prank. Still, it'd be an excuse to stretch my legs.

I found Mr. Finley standing outside his office, shaking hands with a large man shaped like a refrigerator, surrounded by an entourage of serious-faced people in suits.

The man had the air of a politician, but it wasn't anybody I recognized. A younger guy, about my age, stood beside the man, dark blond hair gelled to perfection—comb marks still evident—wearing the same serious face as everyone else. I wondered if he was an intern, like me.

Luckily Mr. Finley spotted me before I had the chance to stand awkwardly off to the side for too long. "Ah! Miss Gupta! Let me introduce you to Ambassador Otor Kereselidze, the Georgian ambassador to the United Nations. This is one of our most promising young interns, Miss Cassandra Gupta. Her father is in propulsion engineering."

The ambassador smiled broadly and offered his impressively large hand to shake. While my hand was engulfed in his, I smiled beatifically while mentally trying to place the country of Georgia on a map. The closest I got was "somewhere between Russia and Germany."

"Good, good, very good," said the ambassador, his vaguely Russian accent thick but clear. He didn't care who I was in the least; he was just being polite. He clapped a hand on the shoulder of the younger guy beside him. "This is my son, Luka. About the same age, yes? Interested in space as well."

The blond guy with the gelled hair surveyed me coolly and

gave a nod. I did the same, wondering what this was all about.

"Ambassador Kereselidze was just taking a brief tour of our facilities," Mr. Finley explained to me. He turned back to the other man. "It was an honor to meet you, Ambassador."

"Please, the honor is all mine. My son is very passionate about space! I hope that one day, our countries can work together to return to the stars." He gave a photo op–worthy smile.

Luka didn't. His eyes lingered on me with distaste, like he couldn't understand why I was even there.

The entourage filed out the door, and when they were gone Mr. Finley turned to me. "I'm glad you got a chance to meet him. Georgia doesn't have a space program, of course, but it's always smart to be on good terms with politicians, especially these days. Come on, let's go to my office."

He led me down the hall and through the twisting cubicle maze while I mentally reviewed what he could possibly want to talk to me about. When we reached his office, he held open the door for me, ushered for me to sit, and closed the door behind us with a heavy, permanent-sounding thud. A walnut desk large enough for my whole family to eat dinner on filled the space between us. Framed degrees dotted the wall on the space above his head.

I knotted my fingers together in my lap.

Mr. Finley leaned his forearms onto the desk, peering at me through glasses that reflected a bar of light from the overhead fluorescent. "Sorry about taking you away from your work," he said. "I'll try to keep this short."

"It's no problem," I said, shaking my head a little too hard. He couldn't know how grateful I was not to be back at my desk right now. "I can catch up pretty easily."

Too late, I realized how conceited that sounded. I started to correct myself, but Mr. Finley was laughing. "I know, believe me. Doing rote work for the legal department is below your skill set. But we all have to start somewhere."

I nodded vigorously, my face hot.

"You will go on to do something remarkable, I'm sure," Mr. Finley said. "Which is part of the reason I asked you here today."

Mr. Finley hesitated, fidgeting with a ring on his knuckle. "I'll just get to the point. Our friends at JSC are hosting an . . . experimental program. It's going to be kept under the radar for now, so don't mention this to anyone but your parents." He paused, leveling a gaze at me over his glasses. "This is a chance to go into space, Cassandra."

At Johnson Space Center? Where they trained astronauts? My chest contracted in nervous anticipation.

"Most of the team has already been chosen, but for this particular expedition there is a need for someone younger than our current crop of astronauts. There is one slot for an exceptionally intelligent, intensely motivated, and physically fit young person. Nominations are awarded only through personal recommendation of NASA personnel. And I'd like to submit your name for consideration." He peered at me over his glasses. "But first, I wanted to make sure this is something that you would be interested in."

"Are . . . are you joking with me, sir?"

Mr. Finley restrained a smile. "No, I assure you I'm quite serious. But make no mistake. This is a competition; it will be difficult. My recommendation is no guarantee you'll be accepted. And though the other competitors will be young people as well, you will be the youngest. You'll turn eighteen on August first, isn't that correct?" He picked up a file and squinted at it, checking his facts.

I nodded. "Yes, sir."

"Then you'll get in just under the wire. However, we'll still need your parents to sign off on this before I can send in your recommendation."

I molded my expression into something I hoped was very mature and adultlike. "Yes, sir. I don't believe my parents will object."

This couldn't be real life. I peered at the calendar behind Mr. Finley's head, just to make sure it wasn't April Fools'. "Not to seem ungrateful, but aren't there plenty of more experienced people? Air force pilots? Engineers? Adults?"

"Of course they need people who actually know how to operate a spacecraft," Mr. Finley said. "But the requirements for this mission are unique. I don't know more than that, unfortunately—just that this competition is only open to gifted individuals between the ages of eighteen and twenty-five. I know you don't turn eighteen until August—but they'll make an exception, if you choose to go. And it's a once in a lifetime opportunity. I won't lie that your designer genetics play a part in this, though you certainly aren't the only enhanced individual who will be there. But you are also very intelligent, very driven. Your résumé just to get this internship was quite impressive."

"Thank you, sir."

"I have to say I'm a little reluctant to even let you go, as I was hoping we could keep you around this office permanently. Our percentage of data entry errors has decreased dramatically since you've come aboard. Not to mention the money we've saved since you caught that payroll discrepancy." Mr. Finley's eyes twinkled.

I shuddered. Working in the legal office *full-time*? Doing *data entry*? "What kind of mission is it?"

He leaned back in his chair and crossed his arms. "All I know is that it is an unprecedented mission of exploration. I know you're smart enough to understand that unprecedented means dangerous."

"It's the best kind of dangerous, sir." The chance to see something no human had ever seen? To go somewhere humans had never gone?

He chuckled. "So, what do you say? I'd have to let them know by tomorrow."

I wanted to jump out of my chair and scream "Yes! Yes!" and shake him until his glasses fell off, but that would probably mean I'd be marked psychologically unfit for space. Instead I forced calm into my voice. "What would I have to do?"

"Don't feel like you have to make your decision right away. Sleep on it."

"No!" I said, too forcefully. "I mean, thank you, I don't need to think about it. I accept. What do I need to do?"

He smiled and leaned over the desk. "I know you're athletic. Make sure you're at the top of your game. If they accept you, of course, that means you'll miss your senior year of high school. The first few months, at least, even if you aren't selected. Are you going to be all right with that?"

I felt a wide grin split my face and quickly tried to regain a nonchalant expression. "To be honest, I couldn't think of anything I'd rather do more. Sir."

He stood. "Perfect. I'll send a packet over to your department with information on how to get the paperwork started. They'll need your parents' signatures." He held out his hand, and I shook it firmly. "Ms. Gupta, this will be a difficult competition. I wish you the best of luck."

"Thank you. Thank you so much." I turned to go, and then a lingering question made me stop. "Sir, if you don't mind me asking. I thought there was no more money for things like this. After Mars, we were done with sending humans to space. I know NASA has, like, the smallest budget in its history."

Mr. Finley's pleasant expression changed subtly, but I couldn't read why. "This is coming through different channels than our typical funding. It's just how the government works. There's always money; it's just a matter of funneling it in the right direction."

I smiled. That sounded like something my dad would say. "Of course."

○ ● ◐

Like most couples, my parents had trouble conceiving. Unlike most people, though, they had the means to work around nature. When my mother, the geneticist, couldn't get pregnant on her own, she turned to science. Genetic engineering used to be a moral gray area, but now that infertility was becoming a worldwide epidemic, and in vitro was performed almost as a matter of course, the laws had gone lax. Geneering was safe and effective, and if you were already paying a hefty price tag to have a baby—maybe the only one you'd ever have—might as well make sure it's the best little embryo it could be.

I was among the first major wave of "designer babies"— along with the standard screening for genetic defects, my genes were specifically chosen for traits of athleticism and intelligence. You still couldn't screen for cosmetic markers, but anything that related to fitness of the embryo was allowed. So choosing a blue-eyed baby was out, but making sure she could outrun all the other kids on the track was practically a requirement. They'd gone through my DNA with a fine-tooth comb, weeding out any weak links. No genetic illnesses, no predispositions or structural anomalies. Maybe not the most beautiful, but strong and smart and healthy.

It had its perks: better than average hearing, eyesight, endurance. I'd probably live longer than my parents' generation. And I still had my dad's medium-brown skin and my mom's frizzy black hair.

But my genes were expensive. I was an investment. By

middle school, I spoke more languages than either of my parents. I was first-chair violin in orchestra and was the go-to piano accompanist for all the solo performances at my school, instrumental and choral. I was on track team, chess club, National Honor Society. My parents didn't just expect perfect; they had *paid* for it.

It used to bug me, their level of expectation. But not anymore. I wanted the same thing they did: to be the best.

Being the youngest person in space, even with all the danger involved, was exactly the kind of thing they expected from all my years of lessons and classes and tutors.

Unfortunately, my mom and I didn't agree. "Cassandra Harita Gupta. You only learned to drive last year. So now you think you're qualified to pilot a spacecraft?"

I steeled myself for the debate of my life.

My living room turned into a courtroom. Papa took my side. Mama was against. My uncle relaxed on the couch with a beer, a neutral spectator, watching like this was a game of cricket.

Dadi—she was the key. She'd lived with us ever since my grandfather had died when I was six, being first-generation Indian American and still *just* traditional enough to expect to live with us until she died.

Truth be told, she hadn't much liked it when my dad married my nonIndian mom. But since her other son wasn't about to get married and settle down anytime soon—and, in fact, also seemed content to live with us for the rest of his natural life—they were kind of forced to get along. Now they got along so well, they tended to take the same side of any family argument.

Which didn't bode well for me.

Dadi, small and round and wrinkled but as imposing as a monument even in her pajamas, sat with perfectly upright posture in the center of the couch. Undecided. Unreadable.

No way was I going to Houston without Dadi's okay.

"My car drives itself," I muttered carefully under the range of human hearing.

"This is your daughter's dream." My father spoke over my head. He was still wearing his work clothes, the standard government-civilian uniform of a striped dress shirt, tie, and gray pants. I was sitting in a kitchen chair in the middle of the room, holding the permission forms in my lap. "She has a chance to do something great."

I was counting on my father. He'd turned away from his parents' expectations to follow *his* dream. It was how he met my mom: in college, two nerds with big dreams. He'd forged his own path, just like I wanted to do.

I only wished my mom could see how similar we were.

"Something dangerous, you mean." Mama's crown of frizzy graying hair bounced as she shook her head, lines of worry creasing her eyes.

"Aw, let her go," said my uncle Gauresh. My dad's younger brother had moved in with us shortly after Dadi. He was supposed to live with us only temporarily, but he never seemed terribly worried about either getting a job or his own place. The only time I'd seen him wear something other than jeans and flannel shirts was at my grandfather's funeral. But since he helped out around the house, he had Dadi's protection. Her word was as good as law around here. "You said it was a competition. Maybe she won't even make it."

I shot him a wounded look. "Thanks for that."

He shrugged and gave me a lopsided grin. "Just trying to help, beti."

"Enough of this," Dadi said, standing. "Old people need to sleep."

Dadi crossed the room and laid a sympathetic hand on Mama's arm. "Your daughter works very hard. Give her a chance. She deserves it."

Whoa. The tide was turning unexpectedly in my favor.

Mama sighed and surveyed the room. "I'm outnumbered." Her eyes fell on me and hovered there. "Okay, fine. I know you'll just hold it against me the rest of your life if I say no. Get me a pen."

I grinned and threw my arms around her shoulders. I felt her heavy sigh, what it cost her to say yes.

She returned my embrace, reluctance radiating from her body. "Quick, before I change my mind."

The loud clicking of my suitcase wheels over the concourse floor went silent as I yanked my bag upright. Reluctantly I turned to greet my entourage of two. "We have to say good-bye here. You guys can't come through security without a ticket."

My mother was all wrinkles—her brow, her frown lines, her

wringing, nervous hands. Dadi looked solemn and regal and utterly unperturbed by the fact that she'd only woken up about twenty minutes ago. Gauresh couldn't be bothered to get out of bed before sunrise, and my father had to be at work.

Neither of them said anything. I shifted my weight, anxious to get through this part, impatient to be on the plane even though we'd arrived with plenty of time to spare. Part of me was worried they'd take it all back, change their minds. "Well, good-bye, I guess."

My mom crushed me to her chest before I even finished getting the words out. "Be careful," she said, her voice quaking, and seemingly unable to get out more than two words at a time. She held me at arm's length, eyes watering freely. "Be good. Try hard. Be safe. Make—try to make some friends, huh?"

She wiped at my cheek with her thumb as though I was the one crying. I was surprised to feel wetness there. "It's not summer camp, Mom."

"I know, I know. But you can't go through life alone. One friend. That is all I ask. Okay?" She smiled through her tears. "And I'll see you in a few months."

I was about to tell her this was about space travel, achieving my dreams, not about making friends. And that I wouldn't be home anytime soon, unless I failed.

But I didn't. I wrapped my arms tight around her, closed my eyes, and counted to three. I told myself these were the last seconds of my old life. Tried to enjoy them. "It's okay, Mom. I just want to do something important with my life."

Then Dadi took my arms in her fierce grip and looked deep into my eyes. "You are like your father," she said. "You go after what you want, no matter what anyone else tells you. It is hard for parents to accept. But for good or ill, you will make your own destiny." She pulled me into an embrace. "Good luck," she said, and kissed both my cheeks.

I inhaled deeply, holding the air in my lungs, and imprinted this moment in my memory. Her words felt prophetic. The universe seemed open and waiting for me, and I was ready to meet it.

TWO

ONE DELAYED FLIGHT, two layovers, three Beethoven sonatas, and five days of exhaustive medical-clearance tests later, I found myself sitting in a chilly NASA auditorium in Houston.

It was August first—my eighteenth birthday.

I'd left the hotel an hour early so I'd be able to sit in the front row and maybe eavesdrop a little. The first person I noticed was the man onstage. He looked older but no less intimidating than the pictures of him in my textbooks. His closely shaved hair was mostly gray now, but it was him, incredibly real and breathing in front of me: Charles Pierce, the first man on Mars. I actually gasped out loud, then covered my mouth, embarrassed.

He stood in a gray flight suit beside a woman in a pink pant-suit with teased blond hair. The two hadn't said a word above a whisper, and not even my excellent hearing caught anything interesting.

A handful of other candidates arrived shortly after me, each taking seats spaced far from one another. I caught a pair of Desi boys sitting together. A hijabi girl with a deep-purple headscarf and the most precise eyeliner I'd ever seen. A few stereotypical muscle-bound jock types. A room full of sharp eyes and strong bodies and ambitious, hungry faces.

A blond girl with a low ponytail, wearing white jeans and a white blouse, stared openly at the other candidates as though they were test subjects she was observing. A white guy who looked like he'd just walked off his father's yacht was trying to flirt with the blond girl, and she was utterly ignoring his existence.

I was glad to be left alone, even though I was bursting to say it out loud, just to share it with someone else: *that's Charles Pierce!*

So far, I was unimpressed with my competition. Even if they were probably all valedictorians and had skills that rivaled mine, most of these people wouldn't have my drive, my connection with NASA. They couldn't. I'd guess there were some strong candidates—maybe a handful who appeared intelligent, who sized me up like I was doing to them, and there were quite a few impressive physical specimens. But the rest seemed average, watching vids on their cells and texting like they were in class. No different from my spoiled rich prep-school classmates back home. I was familiar with that type: they had the ego, but not the skills to match.

Suddenly a kid dropped into the chair beside me, making me jump. It was a Latino guy with a head of black curls. He was wearing a plaid shirt like the ones Uncle Gauresh liked, unbuttoned and loose over a cartoon character T-shirt. He dumped his bag on the floor, the sound echoing loud enough in the quiet hall to make me cringe.

"Howdy." He stuck out his hand. "Emilio Esteban. You can call me either one, I like 'em both."

Nobody else was talking, at least not above a whisper. After a second of hesitation, I shook his hand. I didn't want to seem like the cold blonde in white sitting three rows back; that was a fast way to make enemies. From what I could tell, she'd shut down the yacht boy's advances, and he had moved on to easier prey.

My mother's voice chided me in my memory. *One friend. Just one.*

"Cassie," I said.

"Cassie . . . ?" he prompted.

"Gupta."

"Nice to meet you, Cassie Gupta. You on board with all this crazy space shit?"

I inhaled deeply to give myself time to find patience. "Yes."

"Cool. Me too."

The door in the far back corner of the room opened and a few more boring-looking kids filed in. Skinny white kid with tattoos on his arms, Asian girl with a pixie cut, tall black guy wearing glasses that displayed a flickering cell phone interface. A couple more brown-skinned girls filtered in. One of them smiled at me; I only nodded back.

I quickly counted them up. Sixty-two, counting the last girl taking a seat to my right. A sideways glance told me she was tall and muscular, with long black hair and an intimidating beauty. Possibly Japanese.

Sixty-two people I had to beat.

And then the door opened one last time. Tall guy. Dark-blond hair. Dressed like he was going to church, in khaki pants and a crisp button-down shirt with a tie. An actual *tie*.

A spark of recognition—I *knew* that guy. Luka something. The Georgian ambassador's son, who'd visited Marshall that one day. I hadn't paid much attention to him at the time, but now he was *right there*.

Then it hit me. What had the ambassador said? How his son would help America return to the stars. This must've been why they were visiting my center at Marshall.

Oh, all the gods in heaven. I was going to have to compete against the son of a UN ambassador.

Luka took a seat in the far left corner. Onstage, the woman cleared her throat. She didn't need a microphone; the room was full of rapt silence. Her bracelets and earrings shimmered as she spoke. "Looks like we're all here, so I'll go ahead and introduce myself. I'm Madelyn Krieger, the representative for the Society of Extrasolar Exploration, NASA's partner for this project. You may recognize Colonel Pierce to my left, who was the first and so far only man to touch foot on Martian soil and return safely to Earth. We are very honored to have him head up our selection committee. You'll be seeing both of us from time to time, and I for one am looking forward to getting to know each and every one of you special people."

I'd sat through some cheesy school presentations in my time, but this was almost embarrassing. She smiled wide, her teeth as white and shiny as Miss America's. "You all know, to an extent, why you're here. You should have some understanding of the dangers you'll face should you be chosen. But I hope that you are here because you all share the belief that we at SEE and NASA both hold deeply: that exploration beyond our home planet is vital and necessary to the continuing achievements of mankind."

She paused, looking into each of our faces. Were her eyes really misting, or was that a trick of the light? "You are also here because we believe there is something special about you. Some potential that we are eager to tap. When the space program was in its infancy, our very first astronauts were selected from a narrow pool of test pilots who were chosen mainly for their ability to operate under incredible stress and for their willingness to risk blowing themselves up."

That brought a few chuckles, but not from me. People had died to advance human space travel. I didn't think that was funny.

Neither, apparently, did Colonel Pierce. His gaze was steely.

But Ms. Krieger smiled, indulging the laughter. "But this

new team will require a different set of skills. NASA hasn't opened the doors to new astronauts since the first Mars landing in 2033. But with our partnership, new doors have been opened. This is an unprecedented opportunity, and I surely hope you understand the dedication it will require."

I found myself nodding and leaning forward, getting a little caught up in Ms. Krieger's emotions. The colonel, on the other hand, hadn't moved a muscle.

"You may be wondering why you're here—" she began.

"Not really," muttered Emilio beside me.

"—or why the average age of the contestants in this room is a mere twenty-one. I assume I don't have to tell all of you that you're the best and brightest of your generation. Or that space is very large, and modern space travel takes a very long time. With what we hope to do, we will have need of your youth, your physical fitness, your determination. NASA and its international partners have recruited you from all over the world: JAXA in Japan, ISRO of India, ISA of Israel, CSA of Canada, and ESA, encompassing twenty-two European countries—just to name a few! We have representatives from over fifteen countries, including such faraway locales as Mongolia and Qatar. I feel safe to say that I am looking at the best that Earth has to offer. I'm proud to be able to call you astronaut candidates.

"Technically, it takes two years to earn the title of astronaut. But these are special circumstances. I think a little leeway is allowed." That earned a flick of an eyebrow from Colonel Pierce, but Ms. Krieger continued unabated. "You may have noticed there are more than sixty candidates in this room. At the end of the selection, only the top two ranking candidates will go on to train with the rest of the crew. One crew member, and one alternate. The selection process will be short and intense, and unfortunately many of you may be flying home before the end of the week. There will be two phases to your training. At the end of Phase Two, we will take the top two candidates on to Phase Three, where they will train with the rest of the crew in preparation for the mission. Colonel Pierce?"

Pierce took a step forward, thick arms locked behind his back. "If you make it past the first phase, you'll be dealing directly with me. I expect you to call me Colonel to my face and Jackass behind my back. Don't let me catch you getting those two confused." There were a few laughs. I didn't dare join them.

Colonel Pierce glared and the laughter choked off. "I'm your reward for getting through the next few weeks, so if you don't think you want that, save yourself the trouble and go on home now. You may have noticed the doors you entered on your way here were painted red. If you choose to drop out at any point, it's as easy as walking out the big red door. I wouldn't blame you. Hell, the fact that most of you are sitting here now and not a one of you is older than twenty-five is already a miracle. You're the strongest, smartest young people NASA could find this side of the sun, but don't let that go to your heads. You'll have to get a hell of a lot stronger and braver to be the kind of person we need. Got it?"

There were murmurs of "Yes, sir." Emilio shouted it so loud my right ear rang.

The colonel amped up his glare. "Let me just tell you now. Everything you see, hear, and do from this point forward is confidential. The only people who know more than you hold top-secret security clearance. No one outside these walls should hear anything about this competition beyond what you had for breakfast, and I'd be vague on the details of the syrup selection if I were you. If you can handle that, you can hand over your electronic gadgets on the way to your rooms. Absolutely nothing with recording capability will be allowed.

"You have four instructors who will also serve as your resident advisers: Dominic Bolshakov, Michele Jeong, Logan Shaw, and Dr. Harper Copeland. They'll brief you on the rules, so make sure you stick to them. Testing begins tomorrow bright and early, outside on the track."

I was surprised to recognize the names. They were all astronauts. A few years past their prime, maybe, but experienced *astronauts*.

I nodded, heart thumping, fingernails digging into the scratchy fabric of my seat. *I can do this.*

His voice changed tone subtly. He spoke slower. "This isn't a game, kids. We're going to push some of you to the breaking point. But it's not for shits and grins. Everything we do here has a purpose, and our end game is of monumental importance. Just remember that."

Next to me, Emilio's hand shot up, uninvited.

"Yes?" Colonel Pierce said in an arch tone that made it clear he hadn't asked for questions.

Emilio stood up, back straight, suddenly composed. "Just so I'm clear—what's the purpose of this mission?"

I instinctively leaned away from him. Didn't want my face to be associated with the first kid they kicked out.

"I mean, maybe I'm the only one who doesn't know, but I think it's only fair. Are we going back to Mars?"

Hadn't anyone told this kid what "top secret" meant? Did he think all that paperwork he filled out was for fun?

Colonel Pierce's mouth became a tight, bloodless crease, but Emilio continued. "Or farther, beyond the solar system? Is that why you need someone young?"

"You'll be informed of the details of the mission before launch," Ms. Krieger said, forcing an award-winning smile. "If you get that far, of course. Anyone else have questions?"

Thankfully, no one else raised a hand.

Colonel Pierce looked at Emilio like he knew what the future held for him. "Good. Then I suggest you get to your rooms and settle in. Some of you may not have much time to enjoy them."

I hung back as the sixty-three (including the Georgian ambassador's son) other kids rushed toward the room assignment list posted on the doors. None of us knew anyone else here—who cared what room you were in? Like Ms. Krieger said, I wasn't worried about having to deal with roommates for long.

When I was able to get close enough to the form to read

without being jabbed by elbows, I found my name under Room 4, along with:

Hanna Schulz

Mitsuko Pinuelas

Giselle Ojeda

I followed the crowd down the hall to the dorm wing. Room 4 was marked with a black plastic sign and already had one occupant: the blonde in all white, who was already in the middle of unpacking her suitcase of folded clothes onto her bed. We both did a polite nod.

As soon as I put my bag down on the bed farthest from the blonde, the door opened again. It was the tall Japanese girl who'd sat beside me in the auditorium, smiling breezily in a sleeveless black tank and shorts, her legs tan and long.

I could hear some laughter and shouting from the hall before the door closed. They were acting like this was spring break. I was one of the youngest candidates, but definitely one of the more mature ones.

The new girl raised her eyebrows. She must have been a few years older than either of us, maybe even too old to be geneered, and had way better makeup-applying skills than I'd ever hope to acquire. "What's with the faces? Aren't you psyched to be here? Look around! We're at JSC! We're going to space!"

"*One* of us is going to space," the blond girl corrected. There was a lilt to her voice, some kind of accent so subtle it could've been Canadian or someplace far north. "One. I'm not about to celebrate before there's anything worth celebrating."

That didn't deter the other girl. She rolled her eyes like she thought she was dealing with children and smiled. "I'm Mitsuko. Or are we not introducing ourselves in this room?"

"My name is Hanna," the blonde said. "I'm from Potsdam. I took a year off from my studies at Uni Heidelberg to be in this program." German—that was the source of her accent.

And she'd taken off a whole *year*? Well, that was mighty presumptuous of her.

They turned to me.

"Cassie," I said.

"That wasn't so hard, was it?" Mitsuko said. "So now we're just missing Giselle."

"Mitsuko Pinuelas?" Hanna asked.

"That's right." A lock of shiny black hair fell across Mitsuko's face. She reached up to tuck it behind her ear, and I noticed a telltale ring on her left hand.

Hanna didn't miss it, either. "Really? You're married?" Hanna asked, her nose wrinkling a little.

"Hence the last name." She laughed but was clearly getting annoyed.

"How old are you?"

Mitsuko gave her a long look before answering, eyebrows raised. "Twenty-three. You got a problem with that?"

Hanna shrugged, but her point was clear even to me.

Mitsuko shot her a patronizing glance. "Honey. I'm far from the oldest person here. And I'm multilingual, I have a pilot's license, and I'm scuba certified. So I've had a bit more time to polish my skills."

I flinched inwardly and kept my hands busy with unpacking, far slower than necessary. I didn't want to get in the middle of this. Five seconds into the first day and already egos were clashing.

"That's not what I meant. I'm sure most of us are in Mensa," Hanna shot back, the German accent coming on a little strong. "But most of us don't have a husband at home. You *did* leave him at home?"

"Back in San Antonio," Mitsuko quipped, setting her stuff down on the bed beside Hanna. "Why, does it surprise you that I'm allowed to be here all by myself?"

"Well, you're older than us. You have a family. I'm willing to bet that neither of those things are going to work in your favor."

Mitsuko smiled, showing perfect white teeth, and bopped Hanna under the chin as if she were a toddler. Hanna flinched away. "It's sweet of you to be concerned, but I'm not worried about my chances."

This was getting a little much. I tried to deflect Mitsuko's attention. "So you live in San Antonio?"

Mitsuko turned as if noticing me for the first time, and smiled as though nothing unpleasant had just happened. "Just for now. It's where my husband's from. I just graduated from the University of Tokyo and was looking for a job. I was actually trying to get a job here, at Johnson." She laughed. "Worked out a little differently than expected."

I whistled, legitimately impressed. "So who recruited you?"

"One of my old professors had some contacts here, put in a good word for me."

At that moment the door opened and in walked a girl with long chestnut hair, blond highlights, and golden-brown skin—much of which I could see, as her shorts were very short.

Giselle.

She looked as young as me, but that could have been because she was wearing huge bug-eye sunglasses and carrying a pink leopard-print bag. She had the slight, muscular physique of a gymnast, or maybe a dancer. She surveyed the occupants of her room with a sour look on her face and said nothing.

I'd followed the suggested packing list I'd been given: four to five casual outfits, one formal outfit, exercise clothes, one pair of everyday shoes, and my running shoes. It didn't take long to unpack. While I transferred everything from my suitcase to the footlocker, I mentally crossed my roommates off the list. *First Giselle. Then Mitsuko. Hanna might stick around awhile.*

The door didn't even have a chance to close. Right on Giselle's heels came a tall, lithe black woman in a blue JSC polo, with close-cropped hair. I immediately felt like standing up a little straighter. Maybe even saluting.

"All right, ladies," said the woman. "I'm Dr. Copeland, your RA and medical instructor. Despite the title, this isn't your college dorm, and I don't want to hear about it if your roommates snip their toenails too loud or leave their dirty underwear on the floor. It probably won't be long until you can have the room to yourself, so just suck it up until then."

I'd certainly never heard a doctor talk like that. I already kind of liked her.

She opened up a bag and started handing out tablets, starting with mine. The gray device was heavy and clunky, a little scratched up, possibly older than I was. Her words were crisp, efficient, matter-of-fact, like she was checking items off a mental to-do list. "These are preloaded with all of the textbooks you'll need for the classroom portion of training. There's no wireless here, so don't bother trying. Leave your dirty laundry in the laundry bag with your name on it outside your door, and it'll be washed and returned the next day. The RA office is down the hall. There's four of us who double as your instructors, and we take turns with office hours. You're on your own after nine thirty, so try not to kill any of the other candidates in their sleep."

Hanna raised an eyebrow, like she hadn't thought of that yet.

Copeland noticed the look and closed her eyes for a moment, like we were giving her a headache. "You'll each get time to send emails to your loved ones. Outside communication will be monitored. No live calls. Possession of a cell phone or any recording equipment is grounds for immediate expulsion from the program. Understood?"

We nodded.

"Stay inside the facility at all times. That means the red door is off-limits unless you want to go home. The door leading off the cafeteria will be unlocked, though, if you'd like to run on the track. Otherwise, I don't care if you bring food or boys or bazookas into your room, as long as you aren't selling government secrets. See you in class." She gave us a brisk nod, met each of our eyes, and left, letting the door fall shut behind her.

"She's a peach," Mitsuko said cheerfully into the silence, plopping onto her bed and crossing her legs.

Giselle dropped her bag in the middle of the floor and collapsed backward on her bed—she'd chosen the one next to mine. Luckily a nightstand separated our beds, so she wasn't too close.

I flashed back to space camp, age twelve, sharing a room for the first time with dozens of other kids, both boys and girls. My bunkmates had formed a clique almost instantly and decided it would be funny to pretend I didn't exist for the entire week.

I told myself that this time, I wouldn't care. I wasn't here to make friends.

Sorry, Mom.

I'd only brought a carry-on full of clothes and a few essential extras, so unpacking didn't take long. We'd been told not to bring anything electronic, so it had been pretty hard to figure out what I *could* bring. My cell was basically everything to me besides food and shelter, and now it was locked up in some government box for the foreseeable future.

My head buzzed with electronic emptiness.

Back home, I'd found an old paperback in my mom's closet. It smelled weird and had yellow, crinkly pages, but at the last minute I'd stuck it in my bag. It was better than reading nothing at all. I put the book on the nightstand for later.

"Wow, look at this bathroom," Mitsuko said. She'd pushed open a door opposite my bed.

Hanna and Giselle came over to see.

"It's smaller than my closet," Hanna said, which sounded kind of bitchy, but when I got up to join them I had to admit that yeah, my closet at home was bigger than that, too.

One shower. One sink. One toilet. For four girls, for two months—or however long we lasted.

THREE

I GAVE UP trying to sleep at five thirty and slipped out of bed and into the bathroom. When I came out, freshly showered and dressed for running, the room lights were on and everyone except Mitsuko was awake.

Giselle pushed past me, towel in hand, into the bathroom. She shut the door and the shower started up. Hanna was already dressed in a tracksuit, hair in a ponytail.

"Aren't you going to shower?" I asked, not really bothering to keep my voice quiet. Mitsuko didn't stir from sleep.

Hanna, on the other side of the room, applied sunscreen in front of her mirror and looked at me. "They told us we'd be running first thing. No point in showering now, when all the hot water will be gone anyway. I don't care what anyone here thinks of how I look."

I shrugged a shoulder and went over to the wall mirror to twist my wet hair into a thick, tight knot, then spread sunscreen across my face.

A few minutes later, Giselle emerged from the bathroom in a cloud of steam, her hair hanging in dripping strings around her bare shoulders. Hanna slipped in after her and was back out within five minutes. Efficient.

Just as the three of us were about to walk out the door, Mitsuko rolled out of bed, fully dressed. After a grand total of thirty seconds in the bathroom, she stuffed her feet into tennis shoes and turned off the lights behind us.

"Beautiful morning, ladies!" she said as she caught up to us in the hall, gathering her long black hair into a high ponytail.

"Nice breath," Giselle said, the first words I'd heard from her. "Ever heard of a toothbrush?"

Mitsuko just grinned.

There had been a daily schedule loaded onto our tablets. Breakfast was at seven every day. First class today was at eleven. Lunch at one. Classes the rest of the day with each of our four instructors.

The suspicious amount of time between breakfast and class had me running mental scenarios. *Something* was going to fill that time. And I suspected it was going to be something big— something to weed out the unworthy ones.

We were on the early side, but soon kids poured out of doors on both sides of the hall, joining the throng on the way to breakfast. We passed the set of double doors we'd entered through on our first day, the ones painted red like a giant stop sign. It was almost eerie to look at it, as if I were breaking a rule by noticing its existence.

The exit.

We entered the cafeteria with most of the other candidates. A line formed for the buffet: piles of every kind of breakfast food imaginable, and some things I couldn't even identify.

I took a plate of eggs, a waffle, and an apple, and picked up a bottle of water. Somehow, by default I guess, I ended up sitting with Giselle, Hanna, and Mitsuko.

"Good, the gang's all here," Mitsuko said, leaning in over her plate of eggs and cantaloupe. "We should discuss our strategy."

"It's not a team effort," Hanna said.

"Not yet, it isn't. But if we work together, we might be able to outlast some of these yokels."

Before anyone could reply, a body slid into the empty seat between me and Giselle. "Good morning, beautiful ladies," a male voice said.

I snuck a look at him from the corner of my eye and groaned inwardly. That preppy trust-find type who had been bothering Hanna yesterday.

"So what do you think they'll have us do today?" he asked, settling in. He must have already eaten, because he didn't have a plate.

"I'm sorry, who are you?" Mitsuko asked, her voice suddenly unfriendly.

I decided I wanted her to stick around a little longer.

The guy's gaze passed right over Mitsuko and lingered on Hanna like she might introduce him, but she didn't look up from her toast.

Changing tactics, he turned on the charm like nothing had happened. "Landon Blake," he said. "I would have thought you'd heard of me."

"No," I said quickly. "The only guy here I know is Luka Kereselidze. His dad is an ambassador for the UN. You know him? He's sitting right over there." I nodded over to where Luka sat, alone. He looked kind of forlorn, but like he was used to it. I felt a little bad for him, actually. The fact that I was sitting at this table with four other people was a temporary fluke. Normally I was the lone wolf in the lunchroom.

I took a small amount of guilty pleasure seeing Landon's smug expression fall just a little. Once he realized he wasn't recognized or welcome, he slid out of his chair with a sour look and wandered to find a new group to bother.

"Did you guys get some weird brain scan thing?" Giselle asked. "In all those medical tests?"

"An EEG? Yeah, I think I remember getting one of those, somewhere between the eye tests, the blood draw, and the pee test," Mitsuko said.

"That was weird," I agreed quietly.

"Yeah, wasn't expecting all those electrodes." Giselle popped a chunk of biscuit into her mouth. "Just wondering."

"Do you think it'll be a race?" Mitsuko asked.

"Yes," Giselle said firmly. "I bet they'll cut everyone but the top ten. Or maybe even the top five. That'll get the pool down quick."

"They won't cut it short so fast," Mitsuko said, sounding far more reasonable. "There are people with a lot of different talents here. It depends on what they're looking for. This isn't the Olympics."

I flinched as a shrill whistle broke into the quiet din of small talk. Colonel Pierce marched into the room, flanked by two women holding stopwatches.

"All right, campers! Welcome to your first day of training." Colonel Pierce's voice bounced off the walls. "Breakfast's over. Everyone outside, now!"

There was an orderly stampede to the doors. Everyone left their plates on the tables.

We followed the colonel to a quarter-mile track. A barbed-wire fence, maybe fifteen feet tall, lined the perimeter. Empty yellow prairie grass and scattered cacti stretched for a long, long way.

It was August, the sun was barely in the sky, and already it was in the eighties. Swarms of gnats flitted against my ears and eyes and ankles. Gross but familiar. I'd run plenty of miles in Alabama summers, which I hoped gave me an edge. The humidity was so thick we might as well have been swimming. A few wisps of hair stuck to my forehead, my neck. And we hadn't even started running yet.

Colonel Pierce blew his whistle again, and the whisper of conversation hushed until the only sound was the buzzing insects. I had to constantly wave my hand in front of my eyes to keep them at bay. God, they started early.

"My assistant's handing out some numbers. It's random, so don't go fighting about which one you get."

Pierce and his assistant moved through the crowd, handing out numbers. Mine was eighteen.

"If you hear your number called, you come over and sit on the grass. Everyone else, keep going till we say stop. We'll be making cuts as we see fit. There is no grievance policy. If we say you're out, you're out."

Some guy up front raised his hand. "Sir, but—we just ate."

I had to stifle a laugh. Had he even been here yesterday? Had he thought a man who expected us to call him jackass would give us time to digest our breakfast before sending us out into the heat to run? This was a *competition*.

The colonel's face contorted into something between a grin and a grimace. "I didn't fail to notice that, Number Fifty-Three. Hopefully you all had the foresight to eat light this morning. Believe me, puking in your space suit is neither fun nor pretty. You're lucky in that all that will happen to you here on Earth is a free ride home."

I tried to take deep, calming breaths. I felt the weight in my stomach of the few bites of breakfast I'd been able to eat—light, but noticeable. The water I'd drunk was the worst part. I could feel it sloshing around.

"You get five minutes to warm up. Starting—" Colonel Pierce clicked his own stopwatch. "Now!"

The group scattered, each person trying to make enough space for themselves. I found a bubble of open grass for myself and did a few lunges, heart already pounding from sheer adrenaline. This air was like breathing soup. I filled my lungs from my diaphragm, trying to prepare them for what they'd have to do. The good thing about the heat was my leg muscles were already pretty warm.

"And that's five. Everyone line up on the track. Spread yourselves out some."

I jogged to the track, relieved when the liquid in my stomach stayed put. I situated myself near the back of the pack. The bodies in front of me would give me an edge in wind resistance, and the inside edge was a shorter circumference than the outside.

The others all wanted to be first, to have their numbers easily visible. But that wasn't important at the beginning of the race; it was only important at the *end*.

I looked around me and saw Hanna had the same idea—she was right behind me. Mitsuko was somewhere in front and to my right. Giselle was nowhere to be seen.

"Hey, Cass!"

The boy who'd sat next to me in the auditorium came up behind me. "Emilio Esteban," I said. "The boy with two names."

He grinned. "You remembered!"

I jumped around a little, shifted my weight on the balls of my feet. "Good luck." It seemed like a nice thing to say to end the conversation. Sort of like "have a nice day."

"Don't need luck. But same to you!"

Another shrill whistle to quiet us down. Colonel Pierce's voice came flying over our heads.

"This is not a race," he called out. "On the next whistle you will start to run. You will keep running until you hear a second whistle. Feel free to stop before that time. We don't want any heatstroke cases today. But we also don't want any quitters on our team, so keep that in mind. Ready!"

I sucked in wind, my nerves jumpy.

The whistle blew. It took a few seconds for the front half of the pack to get going enough for me to start up, but by then I was more than ready. For the first lap we were all jogging the same leisurely pace, staying together in one entity, like a school of fish swimming in slow circles. It was hardly an effort, barely more than speed-walking. After the first two miles, the wheat began to separate from the chaff.

I stayed about in the middle, letting the slower ones fall behind me, not trying to advance. Endurance was the name of this game.

Five miles in and I was feeling good. Hanna was now nearly beside me, and though she hung back I didn't think it was due to weakness. We were in the front third now, our feet pounding the cushioned pavement in a rhythm that made it easy to keep going.

Humans really are herd animals. I almost always ran alone, but it was so much easier to keep going when you were surrounded by other people.

Sweat ran into my eyes and down my back, and the air began to feel like water in my lungs, heavy and slow. But the rhythmic pounding, pounding of many feet, was like the beating of a giant heart that never stopped. It propelled me forward.

I heard coughing somewhere behind me but didn't look back. I wiped the sweat from my eyes and slowly let go of my thoughts, letting consciousness fade from my body, which was just a tiny segment of this beating heart muscle to which I belonged.

Rounding the corner to the thirty-second lap, people began to fall out. It was bound to happen. I'd seen vomit on the track the last few rounds.

I was just starting to feel fatigue. I tried not to look at the people bent over on the grass, heaving, gasping like stranded fish. The failures who couldn't hack it. It would be too easy to stumble and give up. Too easy to become one of them.

I lost track of the laps after that. Round and round we went. My cheeks were on fire, my quadriceps burning, my feet hot in shoes of cement. The group thinned out and I lost the rhythm of the beating heart. Sweat ran down my face like water, unable to evaporate in the humidity, unable to cool my body even a degree. My tongue grated against my teeth, dry and thick as wool. Everyone I passed was floundering.

Each time I rounded the corner, I glanced furtively at the colonel and the two women staring at their stopwatches, hoping that this would be the last, that someone would look up and realize they'd forgotten to tell us to stop.

My lungs ached.

How long were we supposed to keep going? I couldn't keep this up forever. How long had it already been? My inner clock had become unreliable. The sun was higher than when we'd started, its face scorching the dry earth. Despite the sunscreen, my skin felt like a raw egg on a hot skillet, charring beneath the heat.

Until now, everyone who had fallen out had done so voluntarily. Now that we were so far apart from one another, our numbers were visible, and we began to hear them called out.

"Number five!"

I'd passed number five three times already. He was not even jogging anymore, but walking with a little bit of a jump in between steps.

So we couldn't just stay in the game. We had to keep up.

A sharp ache grew in my stomach, like a little knot of pain rocking back and forth. Jolting around inside me.

This wasn't just a physical test; it was a psychological one. Some lesson about the unknown quantity of time passage in space, the monotony of it, how it can fracture people's minds.

I'd run miles and miles before. But I always knew when I got to stop. I was in control of it. Not knowing when it would end was brutal.

That must be the point.

I began to miss breaths. My stride shortened. No, no no no.

What the hell was wrong with me? I'd run this long dozens of times. Hadn't I?

"Number thirty-seven! Number fourteen! Number twenty-two!" Nearly everyone behind me went away.

I was next.

Someone passed me. I looked up and blinked away sweat, my exhales as loud as my footfalls.

It was Hanna. Our eyes met as she passed.

The fair skin on her cheeks flamed red. Her blond ponytail was plastered to her neck and she limped slightly on her left side. She was struggling just as much as I was. Yet she was passing me.

Her eyes narrowed. She held my gaze a second longer than was comfortable. And I knew suddenly what she was saying. *I dare you to keep up.*

I felt my stride lengthen until we were evenly matched. My lungs protested, but as long as we were *both* last, we were both safe.

I hoped.

Silently egging each other on, we caught up to the runners ahead of us. The group was a fraction of what it had been. Emilio was ahead of me, black curls matted against his forehead but huffing along in a comfortable and strong rhythm, like he'd been born running.

That should've been me.

Luka was leading the pack. He was pouring sweat like the rest of us, but his rhythm was solid, his breathing steady, his form still perfect. His face showed no sign of stress. What the hell was this guy, a robot?

We jogged together so long I felt that this would simply be my life from now on. Jogging, heat pouring from our combined bodies, sweat staining the red track until an asteroid destroyed the earth and we all dissolved into atoms.

Was that a whistle I just heard?

"That's it! Catch your breath," Colonel Pierce called.

My first thoughts were incoherent strings of thanks to all the merciful gods who'd kept me alive. My second thought was that I was going to die.

My body screamed and seized. Lungs wheezing and legs trembling. Streaks of pain arced up my legs. Brain fuzzy. But I forced myself to walk and not stop. My heart was pounding so fiercely that if I stopped, it might just gallop right out of my chest and keep on going without me.

Groans of relief surrounded me, and as soon as the gray faded from my vision I was able to see who else was left. Hanna was bent double with hands on her knees, grimacing and covered in sweat. Mitsuko stood on the track, stretching, graceful as a gazelle. Emilio broke out into a huge grin and began moving through the crowd to high-five everyone who could raise their arm. Luka smiled as Emilio slapped his hand.

The girl in the hijab was still there, too—she'd managed to keep pace even with her head and arms covered. Holy hell. Now that demanded respect.

I caught her eye, gave her a nod, mouthed "wow" because I didn't have breath for words. She jerked her chin up in acknowledgment, like she'd expected to be underestimated. Expected to exceed our expectations.

Emilio jogged over to me, huffing but somehow still animated.

"Guys. That was awesome. We did it!"

I couldn't talk. All I could do was nod breathlessly, sucking wind like I was drowning.

Mitsuko caught my wrist with both her hands and leaned her forehead on my shoulder, grinning with relief. I couldn't help but smile, too.

We'd made it.

We walked a victory lap together to recover and then collapsed as one on the finish line, gasping and retching and rubbing our calves and yet unable to stop grinning. I looked over to find Hanna sitting on the track with us, bent over and heaving up a liquid version of her breakfast. Well, at least she managed to hold it down until the whistle.

Water had been left out for us in ice-filled coolers. As soon as I could breathe normally I chugged all the water in my bottle and lay flat on my back in the dry grass, feeling my heart knock against my ribs with less and less force.

Colonel Pierce had been conversing with his two attendants, comparing notes. Now he looked over at us pathetic lumps on the ground. "Everyone still on the track—congratulations, you're in. When you're ready, you twenty-five can go inside and cool off. Everyone else, we'll escort you to your rooms to pack your things."

I climbed to my feet gingerly—every individual muscle and tendon in my legs groaning at once—and a sudden white haze came over my vision. The world evaporated away from my eyes, and some small part in the back of my consciousness realized *I no longer had any idea which way was up.*

Hands reached out and grabbed me at the elbow, kept me up. Gradually the colors of the world bubbled back through the haze. I swayed, unsteady, but the dizziness was draining away.

"That was weird," I mumbled, confused. Time seemed to stand still. My eyes moved slowly up the arm that was keeping me vertical.

Luka was looking down at me—he was taller up close—with a look of concerned bemusement.

His hands were wrapped around my upper arm. He'd caught me. I'd basically fallen into him.

Emilio bounded up beside me, hands closing around my other elbow. "Whoa, Lola, you okay? Come on, let's get you back into the air-conditioning."

My brain was running slow. I could've sworn Emilio had just called me "Lola." I looked back to Luka, but he was already gone.

The losers glared at us as they went inside. Limping back into the building, my entire body was in agony. Everything was sticking to me—my skin feeling like I'd rubbed it raw with hot sandpaper, throat dry as wood shavings no matter how much I drank. I collapsed into a chair, put my forehead against the cool slate table, and closed my eyes. The dizziness was still there, tossing me around like gentle, insistent waves.

After a while I realized Giselle had been among the ones who had thrown up and been tossed out early. I didn't see her leave. Landon, whom we all were supposed to recognize, was gone, too.

I thought we'd go straight back to our rooms, but Colonel Pierce and Ms. Krieger came to us first. Today she was dressed casually, white polo tucked into khaki pants, but her hair was still blow-dried Texas high.

"Congratulations," Ms. Krieger said. "You made the first cut! I'm sure you'll all be very relieved to know that you passed the hardest physical test we plan to give you. The rest will be academic and psychological, and those tests, for some people, will be much harder. Good luck on the rest of your week!"

The colonel spoke. "We've ranked you based on your times on the track. These rankings will be posted here in the cafeteria and will change depending on your performance throughout the rest of the selection."

We were dismissed. Most headed back to their rooms, though a few stayed in the cafeteria to load up on some more food. Personally, I didn't want to see food again for a week. I wanted a shower and a nap, preferably at the same time.

Emilio and some of his friends whooped down the hallway, jumping and waving their sweat-soaked shirts around over their heads like victory flags.

"How are they able to do that?" I complained. My muscles were barely working.

"Oh God," Mitsuko groaned, clamping a hand over my and Hanna's shoulders to support herself. "I feel like all my bones are made of shrapnel."

Hanna pried Mitsuko's hand off her shoulder, where it left a white handprint on her flushed skin. "Yeah? Well, my skin feels like it's been baked, so let's ease up on the touchy feely."

Our room felt slightly bigger without Giselle and her luggage. I was about to fall headfirst on my bed when Mitsuko called out, "Don't!"

I only had enough energy to raise my eyebrows.

"You're disgusting. No offense. But who wants to sleep in dirty sheets?" She fell backward onto Giselle's bed with a soft thump and raised an upside-down eyebrow like a question mark. "She won't be using it again."

FOUR

THEY GAVE US a half hour to recuperate, most of which I spent waiting for my turn in the bathroom. Our first class was at eleven, which meant we'd circled that track for at least three hours.

Showered, sore, and limping, I hobbled to class with my roommates, fuzzy-brained but ready for whatever else they might throw at me.

With only twenty-five of us still in the competition, we were all in class together. As I opened the door, my eyes swept over the remaining candidates. Before the race, a little under half of the contestants had been girls, and that ratio seemed to hold up afterward.

Emilio was already there, busy talking to a group of guys—

that kid made friends faster than the speed of light—so I took a seat near the door with Mitsuko and Hanna. We were quiet, too tired to talk, which was fine by me.

No windows in the cinder-block walls, no decoration, only a desk and a digital display board at the head of the room.

Emilio, laughing, turned around and saw me. "Hey, Lola! What are you doing all the way over there?" He patted the empty desk beside him. "Come sit next to me so I can cheat off you." The boys around him were smiling, too. Everyone was still basking in the glow of making the first cut.

I smiled tentatively, feeling an unfamiliar sense of cama-raderie instead of typical annoyance that came from social interaction. I'd never had an invitation to sit next to someone before, so I slid out of my chair and into the one beside him. Mitsuko gave me a raised eyebrow, interest piqued. But Hanna didn't seem to notice or care.

"You don't even know my name, do you?"

"Of course I know your name, Cassandra Gupta. I remember everything." He tapped his temple. "Perfect memory. But I've decided you look more like a Lola. No offense?"

"Nicknames are kind of Esteban's *thing*," said a smiling boy behind Emilio.

I was warming to Emilio. He'd apparently had enough chops to make it through that grueling run and he still managed to have a smile on his face afterward. And I'd never had anyone in my last eleven years of private school be as nice to me as he had been in the past twenty-four hours. "Nah. I like it."

"Cool." He winked. "Have you met Antony?"

The other guy had an open, friendly face and curly brown hair. He put out his hand for me to shake. "It's actually Antonio— most people call me Anton, present company excluded. I had the good fortune to end up Esteban's roommate."

I smiled politely. "Good luck with that." He laughed.

"Antony's from Brazil," Emilio said proudly. "So he speaks even better Spanish than me. Which, to be fair, isn't too hard as I have, like, preschool-level Spanish."

"We speak Portuguese in Brazil," Anton said with a teasing grin, elbowing him. *"Hombre."*

Emilio laughed, taking the hit to his ego without flinching. "I knew that."

Just then, the guy sitting in front of Emilio turned in his chair, and I realized with a start that it was Luka. Clean, with his blond hair still a little wet from the shower, combed neatly just as it had been when I first met him.

Did he expect me to greet him because we'd met before? Awkwardly I opened and closed my mouth without making any sound. Luka cocked his head a little at me, his expression curious like a bird's.

Just in time, a man in a blue polo came through the door. "Good morning, candidates," he said with a genuine smile. Laugh lines crinkled around his bright, intelligent eyes. Rusty-red hair fell over his brow, and though he looked youthful, his skin looked prematurely aged from the sun. I'd guess mid-forties. "Welcome to your first class. I'm Logan Shaw, former

NASA astronaut and mission specialist with ten days logged in space. I have degrees in aerospace and mechanical engineering, as well as astrophysics, so that's mostly what we're going to talk about in here. Since this is your first class, and you will be spending pretty much all your time together, why don't we start by learning each other's names?"

Everyone went around the room introducing themselves. The boys I'd noticed earlier were Deepak and Samir. The hijabi girl was Nasrin; the girl with the pixie cut was Katrina. There was a Boris, Mahdi, Pratima, Kendra, Sarnai, Marisol, and Giorgia. Names and people from all over the globe.

Shaw said, "Who knows the closest star to the sun?"

Everyone raised their hands. I smiled as he looked over at me and nodded. "Proxima Centauri," I answered. Really, *this* was where we were starting? With the basics?

"Of course," Shaw said. "And it is how far from Earth?"

"Approximately four light-years," Anton said.

"Right again. So here's a thought experiment for you. Say we want to get to the Alpha Centauri system. How would we do that?"

"Nuclear pulse propulsion," Deepak said. "It's been in theory since the first moon landing."

Shaw nodded thoughtfully. "We could do that, if we had the inclination. But four light-years? Even with nuclear propulsion systems currently in design, that would take us . . ."

"Over three hundred years," said Katrina.

"Problematic," Shaw said with a smile. "Any other ideas?"

"Ion engines," I said. "They generate smaller levels of thrust, but they can last for hundreds of years and accelerate almost indefinitely."

"Good," Shaw said, nodding. "A primitive version worked for the *Deep Space 1* mission at the turn of the century. What else?"

The room was quiet, and then Emilio spoke. "What else is there? Short of breaking the laws that hold the universe together."

"There's antimatter catalyzation," said Mitsuko.

"That never got out of its infancy," Emilio argued. "Nobody wants to pay for it to be studied nowadays."

Hanna joined in. "Even if we had technology like that, you're still talking about a star so far away that *light itself* takes four years to reach it. What's the point? Without faster-than-light travel, it's impossible to get to another solar system within a human life span. And *with* FTL travel, if we ever circumvent the known laws of physics, you're still asking an astronaut to leave Earth as they know it, maybe forever."

She had a point. A depressing one.

The way Shaw watched the discussion, arms crossed and leaning against the desk with an amused look on his face, made me suspicious. I cut in. "Just because we don't know about it yet doesn't mean it doesn't exist."

Shaw smiled. "How right you are. Who here has heard of something called an Alcubierre drive?"

My heart skipped a beat. I raised my hand. Maybe half the

other kids did the same, including Hanna. "It's not a real thing," Hanna said.

"It's theoretical, true. For those who aren't aware, an Alcubierre drive is a speculative engine that works off the principle of theory of relativity. Instead of breaking the laws of physics, it would only . . . bend them. This technology would allow a spaceship to contract and expand space-time in a small bubble around itself, allowing humans to approach relative speed of light, without the time loss of conventional faster-than-light theories. No one has ever built a full-scale model with conclusive, positive results. Until now."

The room fell so quiet I wondered if I'd lost my hearing.

"Sir . . . are you saying that humans have developed faster-than-light travel?" Anton asked, a hush in his voice.

Shaw's face was enigmatic. "No, I'm not saying that. But let's labor under the presumption that we *have*, and discuss the possible ramifications of this technology. How would it work? How fast could it travel? What are the risks?"

The discussion continued for two more hours, leaping way beyond me, delving deeper into theoretical aerospace engineering and astrophysics than I'd ever learned about either in school or on my own. I perched on the edge of my seat, watching words fly like Ping-Pong balls, volleying whenever I could, soaking up as much knowledge as my mind could retain.

By the end, I felt dizzy. Shaw had effectively just told us that humanity had made the most significant space travel breakthrough in its history, and it hadn't been made public. Why?

Because it hadn't been tested? Because it was dangerous?

We broke for lunch, heading to the cafeteria en masse. I silently made myself an avocado and hummus sandwich and sat at an empty table, mind still reeling from class, wanting time alone to think.

"Hey."

I jumped. Hanna was leaning over the seat next to me. "Hey," I answered, wary.

"What'd you think of class?" She was looking at me in that scientific way, unsmilingly curious, trying to examine my face for clues like I was a new species she didn't understand.

I hadn't gotten a good feel for Hanna yet. Unsure what she was looking for, I kept my answers curt. "Kind of out there, isn't it? The Alcubierre drive stuff?"

"Yeah, wild." She didn't seem too interested in discussing it.

"I've never had a class like that. But at least they aren't grading us."

Hanna nodded slowly. Then she said, "You realize they are watching us all the time."

I stopped chewing. "What?"

"There's no grades because they don't care how well you can regurgitate answers from the book. We're in a controlled experiment. There are cameras in the halls and the classrooms. Maybe even in here." She looked up and over her shoulder, leisurely, like one might expect from someone saying such paranoid things. "Haven't you noticed? There are no windows, no natural daylight. No calendars to mark the days. The only clocks are the digital alarms in our rooms. We have no access to outside information, only what they tell us. The only entertainment is what we find for ourselves. We may be allowed to go outside—for now. But really? This is a simulation of a spaceship environment."

The facts were there, but I wasn't convinced it was all a conspiracy. "Maybe so. It doesn't bother me as long as nobody's watching me in the bathroom."

Hanna finally decided to sit. Her tray held an apple and a turkey club. "Maybe try looking at the leaderboard over there, and see how you feel then."

Somehow in the post-marathon haze I had forgotten. Our rankings were posted on the wall above the buffet table, as big as a basketball scoreboard.

Luka Kereselidze was first. Emilio, near the top at number seven. Mitsuko even higher at number five. I had to scan and scan to find my name: near the bottom, with Hanna.

Twenty-two. I ranked twenty-two out of twenty-five, and Hanna's name was above mine.

I wanted to open up the floor and crawl underneath the linoleum.

Hanna was watching me, gauging my reaction. "We can help each other."

Mitsuko had said the exact same thing this morning, but Hanna had shut her down. I leveled my gaze at her. "Why?"

"Because we're better than they are."

Not according to the board. I took a long, deep breath through my nose. Looked away from her. She was either nuts or a secret genius, maybe a little of both.

She kept trying. "It's the first day. The only thing we're being judged on right now is our performance in the race. If we help each other, we can get into those top two slots."

I wasn't sure I could trust her, but curiosity won out. "Help each other how?"

She scooted her chair closer. "Soon, they're going to start tightening the screws. Increase discomfort. Increase stress. Whatever they can do to impair our ability to think rationally and work together. They want to know how we will react in close quarters with people we don't like, in situations we can't control. If we're prepared—if we show that we have healthy methods for conflict resolution—we'll stand out." She dropped her voice low. "I'll look out for you if you do the same for me."

Honestly, I doubted Hanna could handle any additional pressure. Just because she knew what was coming didn't mean she could handle it. That girl was already wound *tight*.

A hand clapped my shoulder from behind, and Mitsuko's face descended between Hanna and me. Her voice was a stage whisper; her lips were painted shimmery coral pink and were too close to my ear. "Good idea. I'm in. Three musketeers! Woohoo!"

Michele Jeong, a fortysomething Korean American retired navy pilot with razor-sharp intelligence behind her black glasses and gray highlights in her short black hair, spent two hours leading us in troubleshooting scenarios of various problems with life support systems.

A half hour break, then two hours with a professor named Dominic Bolshakov, who was in impressive shape for a man in his late fifties, with ropy forearms, short gray hair, and age spots on his roughened hands. He taught us celestial navigation, how to calculate trajectories with nothing but our brains and the stars, and then ran us through flight simulators on our tablets.

The evening class turned out to be taught by Copeland. She wore the same blue polo and khakis as all the other instructors, but for class she'd put on makeup and big silver earrings.

Mitsuko spotted me as soon as I came in and patted the desk behind her, inviting me to sit. Wearily, I slipped into it. As she smiled and asked me how I was holding up so far, I felt, for the first time, like maybe I wasn't alone. Like maybe I'd finally found a place where I belonged.

But I couldn't afford to think like that. These people were my competition, not my friends.

Copeland's opening line was ominous. "So you kids want to go to space?"

She then proceeded to describe all the ways in which previous space missions had proven fatal. I knew about them—I'd be stupid not to know—but even still, hearing exactly how the doomed crew of *Columbia* died from being flung violently around the inside of their damaged shuttle as it spun out of control sobered me. They were so close to home, but never made it.

"The damage to the shuttle was only about the size of a dinner plate, and went unnoticed upon takeoff. But it was a fatal injury to the shuttle. At least one crew member was still alive and pushing buttons for up to thirty seconds after the first alarm sounded, but at that point, there was nothing anyone could do."

Then we heard all about the second attempt to land a man on Mars—the Chinese three-person crew that launched on a two-year mission and lost contact within three months. "We still don't know what happened to them," Copeland said. "If the Chinese found anything in their investigation, they didn't share it with us."

After her lecture—during which no one said a word—she finally began outlining the ways we could maybe keep ourselves from dying. She explained the mechanisms in space suits, the new self-healing semi-gel insulation that allowed material to be so thin that it didn't compromise mobility but kept us safe from radiation and even small tears in the fabric. She drew schematics of the current life support systems and told us to memorize them. We went over the basics of CPR and how to recognize the early signs of hypoxia. Then we were tested on them, verbally, until the end of class.

When I was twelve, right after I'd come home from space camp, I'd tried strapping myself to a tree branch to see if I could sleep like astronauts did. My dad found me hanging upside down from a few of his nicest belts, and told me that those methods worked better in weightlessness. I knew people had died in space, even recently. I also knew that we never would have gotten anywhere if we didn't keep trying. I was willing to take the risk.

Most kids looked pale when we left. Me, I was prepared for discomfort. For risk. For no privacy. For claustrophobia. Whatever test or danger they could throw at me, I'd read about it and I'd probably practiced it.

"Wow," Mitsuko said as we left, walking down the main hall to our next class. "That's—wow. I'm going to have bad dreams."

"Would you rather die from heart disease in your sixties after your uneventful life, having accomplished nothing worthy of history, or on your way to some distant planet that no human has ever seen before?"

Mitsuko's dark eyes searched me appraisingly. She raised her eyebrows, nodded. "Point taken."

Nothing was going to scare me away.

After class, Mitsuko headed back to our room, but I lingered in the hall. The last item on my schedule said "psychological interview." It must have been near eleven at night, though I hadn't seen a clock since before lunch. My eyelids stuck to my eyeballs, my brain was struggling to hold on to every detail of the lecture I'd just heard, and muscles that I didn't even know existed in my body ached.

They'd designed it this way, of course. Scheduled the interview late, so that I'd be tired and maybe more likely to break my composure or say too much by accident.

Alone, I found my way down the hall perpendicular to our classrooms, full of unmarked doors. Not till the very end of the hall did I find the room number matching my schedule. Did they put this place as far away from the classrooms and dorms as possible on purpose? I could hear no other sounds, no people anywhere, and wondered if all the rooms I'd passed were simply empty.

The door was ajar, the light on inside, so I hesitantly walked in to find a room smaller than my dorm. There were two chairs facing each other.

A man sat in one of the chairs: maybe late twenties, tan skin, glossy black hair. Black silk vest over a deep-purple collared shirt, black square glasses, a five-days'-post-shave beard. He smiled and stood when I entered, shaking my hand.

He was a shrink, and everything I said would be dissected and scrutinized. I had to proceed with caution.

"Hello, Cassandra," the shrink said as he sat back down. Then, almost as thoughtfully, added, "Cassandra. That was the name of a Greek prophet cursed to always speak the truth and never be believed. Such a fascinating story." He smiled. What was he trying to do? Connect with me? I considered telling him the reason the prophet Cassandra was cursed by Apollo was because she refused to sleep with him—but I figured telling him his favorite Greek myth was problematic wasn't going to do me any favors. "My name is Felix. Please, have a seat."

The chair was metal and cold and dug into my thighs. It didn't have arms, and I had nowhere comfortable to put my hands. So I crossed my arms over my chest, realized that it probably made me look standoffish, and decided I didn't really care.

"So, Cassandra. How have you been adjusting to life in the program?"

"It's fine," I said. "About what I expected."

That smile stayed fixed on his features, already beginning to annoy me. "Some of the candidates have trouble, you understand—with our rigorous standards. Bit of a shock to the system. These interviews are just a way to gauge your state of mind, make sure you're coping well with the demands of the program. Especially with you being our youngest candidate. How are you feeling after your first day? Not unduly stressed? No interpersonal conflicts thus far?"

I bristled internally—why did he feel the need to bring up my age?—but knew it was in my best interest to play ball. "No more than anyone else. We all just met and we're from different countries. There're some cultural differences, maybe, but everyone is still on their best behavior. Probably why we're getting along."

"Good, good. Glad to hear it." He made a tiny notation in his files and looked back up at me over his glasses. "Now that may change in the future. This program will put all of you under a good deal of stress. It's important that you are able to continue working amicably with your fellow candidates. Do you foresee yourself having problems in that area?"

My muscles clenched reflexively, and I sat up a little straighter. Did he think I was antisocial? How much, exactly, did he know about me? "I'm getting along with everyone fine. And aside from the run this morning, I've been enjoying myself so far."

"That's good to hear. You go to a private high school, correct?"

I nodded.

"How did you fit in there? Have a lot of friends?"

How to answer that? "I'm in a lot of extracurricular activities."

"Do you have trouble making friends?"

"I . . . wouldn't say that. I mean, it's a small school; there are a lot of cliques. It can be hard to break in. People tend to stick with . . ." What was I doing? I could have just lied and told him sure, I had loads of friends, I was perfectly well adjusted.

Redirect. "It's not like that here, though. Everyone seems to mix pretty easily. You guys collected a diverse pool of candidates. It's kind of nice, actually, not to stick out because of how I look, for once." I adjusted my posture, well aware of what Felix would write in his chart about body language, trying to portray ease and confidence. "I prefer to stand out for my merits and achievements. That's the only challenge I have being here. I *want* to stand out. But here, it's actually hard to do."

He nodded slowly, eyes still on my face, and I wondered if I'd passed the test or fallen for the bait. He wrote a little more and looked at me thoughtfully. "If you are selected, you'd be a pioneer in more ways than one. Not only would you be the youngest astronaut ever, but also an Indian American. I'm sure you must be familiar with Kalpana Chawla?"

"Of course. The first Indian woman in space. I had a poster of her in my room when I was little. But I'm only half-Indian."

His gaze grew steely, the friendly expression going cold. I braced myself.

"Was your desire to become an astronaut influenced by women such as Kalpana? Did what happened to her—the fact that she died in the *Columbia* explosion in 2003—ever temper your desire?"

Was he trying to get a rise out of me, or was he genuinely asking if I was afraid to die in space? I shifted, consciously unclasping my arms and holding my hands in my lap. "I know space is dangerous. Maybe even more than most of the others here. But Kalpana knew it, too, and she was willing to take the risk."

"But still," Felix pressed, wearing that infuriatingly calm smile. "It must affect you."

What was this guy trying to prove? Was he being obstinate on purpose? Frustrated, I lost a little of my composure. "Affect me how? You mean, does it scare me that a woman who looked a little like me died in space?" I started ticking off names on my fingers. "Kalpana Chawla, Sally Ride, Christa McAuliffe, Sunita Williams. All of those women mean something to me. I mean, they each had to pave their own way. Even when it was dangerous and scary and difficult, they did it anyway. It's because of them that I can be here right now, because they fought to be taken seriously and treated equally. Some of them sacrificed their lives. Yes, Kalpana means something to me. But I am my own person, and I want to make my own legacy. If I was afraid when they were brave, I'm not honoring their memories, am I?" I was talking too fast, getting emotional, but my words came out like I was running downhill. "I'm not afraid. They did it. So can I."

I clamped my mouth shut, suddenly aware of how fast my heart was beating. *Calm down.*

Felix had dropped that unreadable smile. He waited a moment to make sure I had finished. "It's that simple, then?"

"It is to me."

Felix scribbled something in his notes, and I mentally kicked myself. He was purposefully trying to push my buttons, to see how I'd react. And I'd certainly *reacted*.

But from what I could tell behind his beard and glasses, Felix looked relatively pleased.

For the next forty-five minutes, he grilled me about my high school performance, asked me about my friends, my classes, my extracurricular activities, my home life. Quick, like he was reading from a list. I lobbied answers back at him just as quickly, hoping to get through whatever personality worksheet he was apparently reading from. Then came a long pause while he studied his clipboard and looked back up. And I sensed the tenor of the conversation had shifted.

He studied me for a moment, his half smile and intense, unblinking gaze making me nervous. When he spoke again, his voice had a distinctly different tone than before. Lower, slower. "It's very important to you to be the best, isn't it? You have been, after all, consistently at the top of your class. And yet you had trouble naming even one long-term friendly relationship. Would you say that you often sacrifice interpersonal relationships for success?"

My breathing became constrained, from anger or trying to reign in my offense. I'd relaxed, thinking we were nearly finished, and he'd caught me off guard. "I don't mold my identity to make others more comfortable. I'm just myself. I make goals and I go after them. If that puts people off, that's on them, not me."

He'd done it all deliberately, of course. All that poking around, trying to find soft spots. But I thought I'd handled it as well as could be expected.

When he finally let me go, I felt like a zapped battery. Like a sediment of buried emotions had been stirred up, making me doubt my own mind. And the back of my shirt was damp with sweat despite the heavily air-conditioned room.

I didn't see anyone in the halls. Back in our room, Hanna was in bed, reading with a lamp on.

"Where's Mitsuko?" I asked, stripping out of my day clothes. I'd never been modest, and Hanna wasn't looking at me anyway. I didn't care about anything but getting to sleep as soon as possible.

"Sending a message to her husband."

I pulled a nightshirt over my head and went to the bathroom to brush my teeth. "I cannot believe she is married."

Hanna put down her book. "It was a stupid thing to do."

"What, getting married?" I poked out my head and asked around my toothbrush.

"If she wanted to go to space? Yes."

"Why?"

Hanna cocked her head at me. "You always ask a lot of questions. Are you really so unintelligent that you need everything spelled out for you?"

I spat into the tiny sink, got into bed, and turned off the bedside lamp, so the only light in the room encircled Hanna's pale head. "I'm a scientist; I'm naturally curious."

Was that a smile on Hanna's face? Oh, nope, not anymore. "No matter how smart someone is, no matter how qualified, if it comes down to two people with equal qualifications, they will lean toward choosing the candidate with less baggage tethering them to Earth. You and me? Nothing here is holding us back. I think we have that in common."

I turned to look at her with one open eye. Something had changed in the air between us. Maybe that was what made me ask. "The other astronauts on the crew are probably married, at least some of them. Maybe even have kids. And it's not like we're orphans; we have families, too. Your parents don't care that you're here?"

To my surprise, she actually answered. "Oh, they care. One of my moms has wanted this for me forever. The other—she loves me but she doesn't support me. She didn't want me to come here." Hanna picked her book back up. "Luckily it wasn't up to her."

It hadn't been my mother's choice, either. The only difference between me and Hanna was that Hanna hadn't needed her parents' permission.

"Two moms," I said, fighting a yawn. "I had a hard enough time getting my *one* to let me go."

"People who aren't one hundred percent for you are against you," Hanna said, eyes on her book. "It took me a long time to understand that."

Hanna was clearly finished talking to me. I was relieved. One could take only so much concentrated Hanna at a time.

FIVE

MY TIME SLOT to write to my parents was after breakfast the next morning. Jeong pointed to an old computer that was slower than my grandmother and was apparently capable of handling nothing but a simplistic email program. I was brief and positive, knowing in all likelihood NASA was reading our messages. In all the paperwork we had to sign, there had been no promise of privacy.

Heading into my next class, it was clear that the camaraderie born out of yesterday's selection hadn't lasted long. The rankings now clearly posted, people remembered this was a competition. They spoke over one another, argued until Copeland actually had to tell people to get back in their seats. I participated without succumbing to the temptation of name-calling, but I was in the minority.

By the time lunch came around again, my name had jumped three spots, and Hanna's had jumped four. I tried not to let it bother me. It was still early, still anyone's game.

After lunch, I was sitting at a desk, waiting for our next class to start, trying to comprehend an unusual schematic drawn on the digital display board when Mitsuko came in, laughing with Nasrin, who today wore a gray silk hijab, and Katrina, who looked like a willowy ballerina in a black wrap-top and gauzy pink skirt. It made me consider my own outfit for the first time that day: khakis and a navy blue polo shirt—basically, my school uniform.

It hit me with the reminder that I was the youngest person here. The kid who was still in high school. Who must look so incredibly childish compared to these sophisticated and lovely girls, who undoubtedly went to prestigious universities, maybe even lived in their own apartments, who'd already figured out who they were and were utterly confident in themselves.

So much for "three musketeers!" I guess she'd found a group of girls who were more her style.

But when she saw me, she split off and sat by me. She leaned in, raven hair falling over her shoulders, and I caught a whiff of her flowery perfume. "Those girls have the best gossip. Did you know there's some kind of a foreign politico here? And he's effing *leading* the board?"

"I know," I said. "I kind of met him a few months ago."

Her eyes bugged out. "You *kind of* met him. So he's not

a NASA plant designed to test us? *Shit!*" I laughed, but she continued unabated. "I knew I picked the right girl to sit by. Seriously, I've gone down two spots since yesterday, and has that kid's name even moved from number one? No. How is that fair? How is that *human*?"

I scanned the room to make sure Luka hadn't arrived yet, and shrugged. "Maybe we should kill him."

"Now what did I tell you kids about plotting to kill the competition?" Copeland's voice announced her presence in the doorway.

"Not when you're within earshot," Mitsuko chirped without missing a beat.

Copeland shook her head, amused. She took her place at the head of the room as the remaining candidates, including the guy we'd just been plotting to murder, filtered in. Mitsuko had to stifle her giggle behind her hand. Luka sat across from her, blissfully unaware.

Dr. Copeland gestured to the board. "I want everyone to study this diagram, if you haven't been already. What do you theorize this image to depict?"

I'd seen that diagram before. Somewhere in the files on my tablet. I'd tried to memorize it with bleary eyes before bed, but I didn't remember if there had been any explanation of its purpose.

"Some kind of shipping container for high-tech payload?" asked Anton.

"Energy reserves," said another.

"Engine coolant!"

"A space refrigerator," said Katrina. Her friends laughed.

Copeland zeroed in on the girl. "What's your name again?"

"Katrina. Everyone calls me Trina."

"Trina. Okay. Explain to me what in this diagram makes you say that."

I expected the girl to wilt under the pressure of that terrifying stare, but her face went solidly blank and she stood up to answer. I knew that expression intimately: it was the face of a person who knew precisely what she was talking about. "Tubes one to four appear designed to input gaseous or viscous fluid. They seem highly insulated and have a diameter of at least five centimeters, so most likely the latter. The container is roughly rectangular, at least six feet long and two feet at its narrowest, with several inches' worth of insulation. Typically that kind of insulation is designed for keeping things cool rather than keeping them hot, but you can't tell from the schematics, so I took a leap there. Going by the rule of Occam's razor, the simplest solution is most often correct. Thus, space refrigerator."

She sat down. One of the boys whistled low, impressed.

Copeland arched an eyebrow. "Why would anyone need a refrigerator in space? Might as well take a cooler to Antarctica."

Trina shook her head, like that was all she had. The class waited silently for Copeland to give us the answer, but she appeared to be waiting for one of us to speak.

"You wouldn't," I finally blurted out. "Astronaut food is

freeze-dried and nonperishable. No need for a cooling system. Unless there is a specific type of payload this mission requires to be kept cold, I would almost say it looks like it's meant for human use."

I could feel Trina glare daggers at me. But Copeland's gaze was thoughtful, and it encouraged me. I stood up and went to the diagram. "This? On the door? It's just a square here, but it could be a small window. Also, here. These wires loose on the inside of the container. What else would you need loose wires for inside a container? Maybe for measuring vital signs?"

I looked up at Copeland, at a loss. "Am I even close?"

"Sit down."

I retreated to my chair, heart pounding, wondering if I'd just made a fool out of myself.

"This," Copeland said, pointing at the compartment with her pen, "is experimental technology, and a major part of why you all are here. As Cassandra correctly theorized, it is meant for human use. On long-range interstellar missions, the amount of water, oxygen, food, and waste disposal necessary for maintaining human life is a significant weight that the rockets must propel out of Earth's gravitational pull. It slows down travel time, which then increases the need for even more oxygen, food, and fuel. You see where I'm going with this?"

Kendra, in her British accent, gave voice to what I was thinking but was afraid to say. "A cryogenic container."

Copeland nodded. "This is what has made interstellar travel more than just the gleam in a science fiction writer's eye. This is something our scientists have worked on for years, and it's just now within our grasp. Crewed spacecraft can travel faster and lighter and farther than ever before."

"Assuming it works," Mitsuko whispered.

We all had the same looks on our faces—like someone had sucked out our ability to have any other emotion but skepticism.

"So . . . whoever goes on this mission will be turned into a human Popsicle," said Mahdi.

"The Human Hibernation Module has been judged to be safe and effective in multiple tests. You're looking at the Lexus of space travel."

"So if all we have to do is sleep, why are they making us run freakin' marathons?" asked a massively tall, muscular guy who could barely fit in his desk.

"Because being in zero gravity isn't exactly good for you. You're built to live under Earth's gravity, and things go all wonky with your wiring without it. The better shape you're in when you leave, the better off you'll be," Mahdi responded.

Copeland waved him off and went back to the digital display board. "That's enough theoretical questions for now. Memorize how it works. Because if this malfunctions when you're out of Earth's atmosphere, either you or one of your crewmates will die of dehydration or choke to death on cryogel. And seeing as I will *be* a member of this crew, I have a vested interest in your ability to repair it. Expect no mercy on the exam."

"Ma'am? What about the ninety-nine percent of us who don't make it on the crew? We're supposed to memorize something that I assume is classified, or at least privileged technology, and then just . . . go home with this knowledge?" asked Kendra, her posh British accent making her seem at least 25 percent more intelligent than the rest of us.

Dr. Copeland gave a rare, closed smile. "How kind of you to look out for SEE's patents like that. But don't worry. This device has limited usage beyond the scope of this mission, and requires a key piece of technology in order to function correctly, which you will *not* learn anything about unless you need to know about it. Feel better?"

As we walked out the door, Copeland kept me back briefly to say, "I told them it was useless to put a window in the hibernation unit when the person inside isn't going to be using it, but some bioengineer thought it was important." She smiled and nodded me off.

In the hall, Mitsuko leaned into me and whispered, "Ten points to Gryffindor."

"How old are you?" I asked. "My *grandma* read Harry Potter."

"And?"

By dinner, my name had jumped up to eleven.

Emilio led his two remaining roommates—Anton, and a wiry kid named Hector with eyebrows like bristled test tube brushes—over to my table, and they actually congratulated me on my jump. Nearly ten spots. Emilio was now my closest competition. I didn't understand him; how he could be so friendly and so without jealousy. Once I surpassed him in the rankings, would he turn around and murder me in my sleep? He didn't seem the type, but I had to be wary.

Eleven was a long way from one, and Luka was still holding strong in the top slot. His ranking hadn't budged. I had to do better.

Emilio's friends were a lot like him; they smiled easily and already had a backlog of inside jokes, as if they'd been friends for years. Emilio was telling an arm-flailing story—something about his girlfriend breaking up with him before he left because "space is just too much of a long-distance relationship!"

Hanna, the gold-medal winner in Ignoring Boys, put on a good performance, but even she succumbed to occasional laughter. Mitsuko flirted her little married heart out with Hector, who blushed all over himself.

I didn't take any of it seriously. I'd seen it enough in the hallways at school to know some people flirted recreationally.

I took a page out of Hanna's book and sat out most of the conversation. Instead, I took in the faces around the cafeteria, marking who was still here and what state they seemed to be in.

Luka I picked out easily enough. He was sitting at a table alone, reading. One or two people tried to engage him in conversation, but he barely looked up from the pages, and they eventually gave up.

It was then that I noticed the way the others in the room were looking back at me. Not steadily, not all at once. But there was a definite vibe in the room of being watched. And not kindly, either.

And I realized about half the top ten list was seated around me.

Were people actually *glaring daggers* at us? Were they so petty?

Nobody else at my table seemed to notice. Even Hanna was more absorbed in studying her tablet than what was going on around us.

Mitsuko rose out of her chair to get another plate of dessert for the table. On her way back, someone at a neighboring table—I couldn't see exactly who—subtly, almost by accident, positioned their foot in Mitsuko's path.

She didn't see it. I knew what was about to happen a millisecond before it did.

Mitsuko fell forward, the plate hitting the linoleum with a crash that silenced the entire cafeteria. Chocolate frosting from the slices of cake she'd been carrying splattered like mud.

Emilio was first on his feet. "Suko! You okay?"

She was already picking herself up, grimacing and rubbing one of her wrists. "Fine." She allowed Emilio to help her to her feet.

There was chocolate smeared across her designer jeans. She looked down at herself and swore.

Low snickers from the offending table marred the silence. Everyone was looking our way now.

I felt a familiar, forgotten rage warm my chest.

"Somebody's feeling threatened," Emilio said, his voice unusually serious. Then to Mitsuko, "You sure you're okay?"

She turned on those who were making a poor effort at

masking their laughter. "You could have broken my arm!" There was fury in her voice. A break—even a bad sprain—and she'd likely be out of the competition.

"I seem to remember any violence against other competitors being grounds for immediate expulsion," Hanna said crisply. "So was it worth it, really? Did you get the laugh you wanted? Because you'll likely be gone by morning."

Now the kids around the table put on innocent faces. "It was an accident!"

"I'm sure," Mitsuko spat, still rubbing at her arm, her eyes burning into each of them in turn, trying to decipher who was the responsible party.

"Not worth it, Suko," Anton said quietly.

"Just let me glare at them a second." Mitsuko sat back down and swore again, dabbing at her clothes with a wad of napkins.

I'd frozen, my muscles locking me in my seat. I'd never known what to do when things like this had happened to me. I'd just stewed in my embarrassment and anger, the laughter at my expense feeling like a literal hot brand of humiliation. And I'd never said a word.

But then, I'd never had backup, either.

It had been foolish of me to think bullies couldn't follow me here. The space program had never been immune to jerks, racists, or misogynists. Even the smartest, most talented people could still be horrible human beings.

I struggled to keep my voice even. "It was bound to happen to somebody."

"Don't worry about it," Anton said, his voice bitter. "Those kinds of people aren't going to make it."

My pulse was still drumming thick in my ears. "I thought Mitsuko was about to deck that guy."

"I *was*," Mitsuko said. "Damn it, these are my favorite jeans! If they're mad I'm ahead of them in the rankings, that's their problem, not mine."

"Yeah, I mean, it's not like you guys want to kill me for my rank, do you?" Emilio asked, breaking the tension. "Guys?"

Relieved, laughter bubbled out of me. I started to relax, but then I found myself locking gazes with Luka, a few tables over. I realized with a start that he'd been watching the whole time, entirely still, waiting to see what would happen. His book was closed on the table, his body still poised as though he'd been about to stand. To intervene? To get out of the way before things got ugly?

Slowly, almost deliberately, he picked up his book. But now I doubted if he'd ever been reading it at all.

SIX

THE NEXT MORNING there was no breakfast in the cafeteria.

I'd woken up before sunrise to run a few miles while it was cool and there was just enough predawn light to see. I metaphorically pounded yesterday's stress into the dirt underneath my tennis shoes. I'd been looking for some alone time, but Luka was already there. He ignored me for the most part, and we ran on opposite ends of the track, both of us sort of agreeing not to pass the other. Just the two of us locked in our separate orbits, thoughts, and solitary tempos. It made me wonder what was going on in that silent, square head of his that required the help of a predawn jog. Maybe Wonder Boy had issues that nobody knew about.

I came inside just as the sky was changing from navy to a

dull, sleepy lavender, wiping the sweat off my face with the edge of my shirt.

A handful of sleepy-eyed, PJ-clad candidates filtered into the cafeteria and each gazed upon the empty buffet with the kind of blank stare usually reserved for zombies.

"Did I miss breakfast?" I whispered to Mitsuko, not wanting to disturb the unsettling fog of confusion we'd waded into.

"No," she said, equally dazed. "We should have two more hours before they clear out everything for lunch."

There was nothing. The buffet trays were closed. The coolers that usually held drinks and fruit were empty.

I shivered as the air-conditioning hit my sweaty skin.

"It's starting," Hanna said very quietly. "They're tightening the screws. Trying to see how we'll react."

"Well," Mitsuko said, crossing her arms over her pajama shirt. "How *are* we going to react?"

None of us moved. A few peopled ambled out of the cafeteria, grumbling.

Mitsuko stopped one person who was leaving and asked, "Where are you going?"

"The RA office. Somebody screwed up royally."

Emilio sidled up to us, silent as a ninja. "Just been there," he said. His face lacked any of its usual humor. "Door's locked. Nobody home."

"Great," Mitsuko said. "I'm starving, and they want to play games." She gave a high, sharp whistle, and a handful of candidates turned to look at her. "Okay, people—listen up. Looks like we're not getting breakfast today. Whichever RA is teaching the first class today will sort this out. Let's not forget ourselves here."

A couple of the guys seemed unimpressed. One of them, a human tank named Cliff, rolled his eyes. "We're not inmates. I'm hungry, and I'm going to get something to eat." He jumped up over the buffet and into the kitchen. A few of his friends followed. They began rifling through drawers.

"Hey!" Mitsuko shouted, taking a few steps toward the kitchen. "You want to get kicked out of the program?"

They ignored her. The remaining candidates seemed torn between following Cliff and listening to Mitsuko. A few more kids, including Trina from my earlier class, jumped the bar and joined the kitchen pilfering.

"This is so wrong," I said, slinking back against the wall near the door.

"If they want to get kicked out, fine," Hanna said, sniffing. "More room for us."

"Unless that's what NASA wants," Emilio said darkly. "For us to take initiative and solve our own problems."

That made us all stare.

"Kid has a point," Mitsuko said, hesitant.

"No," Hanna said flatly. "Not like this."

"Yeah, I don't think this is the kind of problem-solving they want," I said as we all winced at the clanging of a huge metal bowl falling to the floor. Cliff's followers were getting rowdy with frustrated hunger, apparently not finding anything edible.

And now that they'd had a touch of rebellious freedom, they were running with it. "Ugh. I can't watch this anymore."

"Yeah," Hanna agreed. "Let's get out of here before they turn on each other."

Emilio and Mitsuko followed us out into the hall.

"I mean, I know they all have genius IQs, but how stupid do you have to be?" Mitsuko grumbled. "Acting like animals. Honestly."

"Some people can't handle discomfort," Emilio said. "Even for a few minutes."

"Then they don't need to go to space," I said.

Hanna nodded firmly. "Agreed."

I flung open the door to our room and marched inside, my stomach grumbling. Hanna went straight to the bathroom, and a few minutes later I heard the shower turn on. *Nice*, I thought. *I'm covered in sweat, but she doesn't even ask if I want to go first.*

Mitsuko knelt by her footlocker while I sat on the edge of my bed to take off my shoes.

Emilio plopped down on his back on Giselle's old bed. "So this is what a girls' room looks like. Not bad." He laced his fingers behind his head and surveyed the room approvingly.

"You've never been in a girl's room before?" I made a derisive snort.

He made an attempt at earnest puppy-dog eyes and traced his index finger over his chest. "Cross my heart."

"I don't even believe that a little bit. What about all those girlfriends you were talking about last night?"

He sighed. "You caught me, Lola. I am a geek of the highest caliber. It may surprise and sadden you to hear that back in Denver, I was not considered the ladies' man I am here."

I rolled my eyes, not able to keep from laughing. "I'm sorry, I didn't mean to laugh so loud. And Denver, really? You don't look like a mountains-and-snow guy to me."

Emilio sat up and spun around, his cheeks flushed red. "What, just cuz I'm kinda Mexican? You should see me snow-board. I haven't even told you my last name. I could be Polish, for all you know."

"I thought Esteban was your last name," Mitsuko said from the foot of her bed.

He shook his head with a mischievous gleam in his eyes.

"So, what? Your name is Emilio Esteban Kowalski?"

He grinned. "No, actually it's Campbell. Took my stepdad's name. Looks can be deceiving, Lola, that's all I'm saying." He propped his chin in his hand. "Anyway, where are you guys from? I grew up in Denver and California."

"San Antonio by way of San Francisco," Mitsuko chirped. "But I went to school in Japan. That's where I met Michael, actually. He was stationed there at the same time."

I shook my head, kicking my shoes under the bed. I hated telling people I was from Alabama. My background was so *boring* compared to everyone else here, their lives so cosmopolitan. "My dad works at Marshall."

"Where's that?"

"You're smart. You'll figure it out."

Emilio groaned and fell back onto the bed. "Man, I miss my phone. I keep getting the urge to Google stuff."

Mitsuko looked at him askance. "You seriously don't know where Marshall Space Flight Center is? What kind of wannabe astronaut are you?"

"Here I am, starving to death, and you're being mean to me." He held his hands to his stomach. "I feel like I'm dying. I mean, not just regular dying. I mean like how a star dies, imploding in on itself until it tears a hole in space-time and starts consuming light itself. *That's* how hungry I am."

Mitsuko tossed her hair over her shoulder and stood up. "You ate, like, three cheesesteaks last night. How are you starving?"

"I'm a growing boy!"

Mitsuko came over and dropped something small on Emilio's stomach. He grunted and popped up.

"What is this thing?" he asked, holding up a shiny rectangular object.

Mitsuko smiled and handed me one, too. It was a peanut butter granola bar in a foil wrapper. "Breakfast, my darlings. You're welcome."

I felt a deep, overwhelming surge of affection for Mitsuko just then. It was either affection, or maybe stomach acid. "Thanks, Mom."

"Dude, Suko, you're awesome. *Muchas gracias.*" Emilio tore into the foil wrapping, took a bite, and spoke with his mouth full. "I knew I made the right choice hanging out with you guys."

Mitsuko sat next to me and we unwrapped our breakfast

together. "I always like to be prepared," she said. "I'm sure this is temporary. NASA has no vested interest in starving us to death."

"I wouldn't be too sure," Emilio said. "Those guys have some secrets."

"What do you mean?" I asked a little too quickly. "What do you know?"

"Nothing," he said. "That's precisely the point. Didn't you wonder at all how the government is getting the money to fund this thing? And why, for God's sake, they're recruiting from high schools? Lola, you're, like, what? Eighteen?"

I felt a sting. "Barely, yeah."

He swung his arms for emphasis. Granola bits flew. "See? Who does that? There's gotta be a reason, that's all I'm saying. Not that I'm not grateful for the opportunity, obviously." He directed that last bit, loudly, to an empty corner of the ceiling. "Just in case you all are listening. I AM VERY GRATEFUL TO NASA."

Mitsuko laughed and chucked a pillow at his head, but I didn't smile. The chill on my skin wasn't from the air-conditioning anymore. "No, you're right. It's all off. Since the beginning. I mean, I'd never heard about this mission, and out of the blue, my boss just up and asks me if I want to go. I didn't apply or anything."

I was surprised by their sudden, rapt attention.

"Me too," Emilio said quietly. "I was working in a lab in Denver when I got an invite."

"Working for NASA?" I asked.

"Indirectly, yeah."

"Same with me," Mitsuko said. "Robotics testing facility in Austin."

"Weird," I said. "I was an intern. I never did anything important. And I'd started only a few months ago."

"That *is* weird," Mitsuko agreed, her eyebrows creasing in worry. But they smoothed out again quickly, almost as if she forced it away. "Well, hey, God's supposed to work in mysterious ways."

"You think God's responsible?" Emilio asked, shaking his head. "It's not God, Suko, it's the government. We all got picked, somehow. And that's great and all. But why us?"

This conversation had grown way too serious for me all of a sudden. But some switch had been tripped in my mind, and I couldn't stop it now. "You guys . . . you don't happen to be geneered?"

Mitsuko nodded. "Yeah, actually. You too?"

But Emilio was shaking his head. "Not me. Conceived naturally, baby."

"There goes my hypothesis," I sighed, sitting back against the wall.

"What, you think they're picking kids with enhanced DNA? Okay, that'd be a good reason for all the under-twenty-five-year-olds. But geneering is a lot more common these days. So maybe it's just a coincidence," Mitsuko said.

"Yeah. Like I said, just a thought."

Emilio leaned across the space between the beds and patted me on the back. "Good idea, though."

The sound of running water in the bathroom had stopped.

"Emilio, if you're still here, get out!" Hanna's voice, muffled yet somehow still shrill, came through the bathroom door.

Emilio's face shifted into his usual mischievous smile. "Oh, it's okay, you can come out in a towel. I won't be offended."

"LEAVE!"

Emilio looked to us, eyebrows raised. Mitsuko jerked her thumb in the direction of the door and I shrugged.

He left and closed the door behind him. Almost immediately, he poked his head back in and mimicked a high-pitched girly voice. "Okay, he's gone, you can come out now!"

A pillow flew toward his head but hit a closed door. Hanna darted out of the bathroom in a towel, tapped the door shut, and locked it, just to be sure.

Shaw apologized for the breakfast mix-up, promised it wouldn't happen again, and started us talking about ways we could circumvent conventional logic about faster-than-light travel. We started out fairly routine, but as he kept encouraging more outside-the-box thinking, the ideas flying around the room became more absurd. Using nuclear explosions and antimatter to distort space-time. Somehow creating micro black holes inside a reactor to power engines. It was wild but fun, and diverting enough that the two hours flew by.

Stomach growling with a vengeance now, I headed cautiously toward the cafeteria. It was as if the hiccup this morning hadn't even happened. Food had magically reappeared in even greater quantities than usual. I got in line and loaded my plate with chickpea salad and tropical fruit.

Emilio was waving me over to his table frantically, where Hector, Anton, and Hanna were already sitting. But I looked past them.

I craned my neck over the sea of talking heads to the leaderboards. And blinked.

There were no longer twenty-five candidates.

Cliff and his cafeteria followers from this morning, including Trina and a few others, had been eliminated.

Gone, just like that. As if they'd never existed.

My name had moved up to tenth place.

I sat down with a white-hot glow in my chest and reveled in it. Smug superiority. Triumph. *Victory.*

Emilio had stacked three sloppy joes on his plate along with fistfuls of fries and some Mediterranean roasted vegetables. "Hey, 'Ola," he said, showing a mouth full of ground beef. "Oh my God, I forgot how good food tastes."

I'd broken into the top ten. Mitsuko's name was right above mine. Hanna, though, was above both of us, at number seven. Emilio, number eight.

Luka the Boy Wonder was still number one. Numbers two through five were a grab bag of kids: Kendra, the British engineering student and triathlete; Rachel, a white valedictorian and volleyball player not much older than me; and Boris, the

Russian kid built like an ox. The only other Indian girl left, Pratima, was number five, and Nasrin number six.

I turned back around. "I guess they frown on rulebreakers after all."

Everyone else was relaxed and smiling, having survived the latest round. But inside I was quietly smoldering. All of my "friends" were ranked higher than me. Hanna, Emilio, Mitsuko, me.

Every name above mine made my skin feel hot and antsy, as if everyone knew I wasn't good enough. Why was I last? What were they doing that I wasn't? What invisible rubric were they using to grade our performance?

"I'm going to the gym tonight," I announced.

Emilio's eyebrows perked up. "Hey, I'll join you. I have to go get my head shrunk first, but I can meet you there."

I hadn't exactly asked for volunteers, but of any of them, I minded Emilio's company least. He might even be helpful as a spotter.

Hanna shook her head. "I don't do weights. It's mostly guys in there."

"So?" I asked. "You lose muscle tone and bone density in space. Especially women. We need to be as prepared as possible."

She shrugged and didn't look at me.

"Just you and me, then, Lola," Emilio said, raising his arm to wipe sloppy joe from his chin. I grimaced and shoved a napkin into his chest.

◑ ● ◐

After Copeland's class, where she tested us verbally about the cryogenic capsule blueprint and made us brainstorm all the ways it could fail—and outline plans to prevent those failures— I stopped by my room to change. Emilio told me he planned to be finished with Felix around nine thirty, so I had a little time to kill.

Nasrin, Pratima, and Kendra were chatting outside one of the rooms, clustered tight together but not trying to keep their voices down. I slowed my pace out of curiosity.

"—bring in contestants from all over the world. The best and the brightest. But who's always leading the board?" Pratima was saying. "The blond, blue-eyed white guy."

"He's supposed to be the son of a foreign diplomat. Maybe his dad bought him a few favors," Nasrin said.

Kendra had her arms crossed over her chest. "Either way, I don't like it."

The thought made me bristle as I passed by, unable to stay and hear the rest of their conversation without being obvious. I had come here expecting a fair shake, an honest competition. But if it was useless from the start because they'd already picked their chosen one, then what was the point? I flashed back to meeting Luka at Marshall. He'd been there talking to my boss. Why? What had they really been doing? Had Mr. Finley given him a recommendation, too?

Maybe I was naïve. The space program definitely did not have an unblemished record when it came to equal rights; I knew that. But I'd thought—hoped—it wasn't like that anymore.

Maybe Luka's being here was political in some way, some kind of favor. But they wouldn't go through this whole charade, spend all this money recruiting, training, and ranking us if they'd already chosen their candidate. Maybe Luka did have an unfair advantage. Either way, my goal was unchanged. I'd just have to make it obvious to everyone that I was the best.

When I got in the room, Mitsuko was lounging on her bed reading something from her NASA-issued tablet. "You've got mail." She jerked her head toward my pillow, where a thin envelope was resting.

It was a single sheet of paper, folded twice and sealed. I tore it open, to immediate disappointment. Only two lines of text. The emptiness of the rest of the page made my heart sink.

It was an email message from my mother, printed and delivered by the staff. Our email was outgoing only, so all messages came to us on paper after approval by the censors or whoever.

I read those two lines four times and sank onto the edge of my bed.

"What's it say?" Mitsuko asked. She laid her tablet on the pillow and perched up on her elbows.

I'd already memorized it. "'Our dear Cassie. Your father and I are so very proud of you. I hope you are eating well and making friends. Best of luck. Love, Mom, Dad, Uncle Gauresh, and Dadi.'"

Mitsuko made a derisive snort. "Are your parents robots?"

"That's just how they talk. They're scientists." But inside, I was thinking, *That's it? Papa didn't even bother to write me himself?* I mean, he wasn't good at the face-to-face stuff, but usually he spoke pretty well through a computer. There wasn't a single personal touch, despite it being from my mom.

"No big. They probably censor out a lot of stuff. For whatever reason."

"Yeah. Maybe."

I stuffed the paper under my pillow and bent down to unlace my shoes. "Haven't you gotten any mail?"

"Sure. Michael's sent me a few little notes here and there. Nothing much. 'Love you, baby, don't do anybody I wouldn't do' is pretty much the gist of it. But that's just him. Not a shred of outside news."

"Seriously." No phones, no internet. It was like living in a cave in the Dark Ages. "It's kind of making me a little crazy, not knowing what's going on out there."

Mitsuko's eyes went suddenly wide and she shook her head fiercely. I clapped a hand over my mouth.

Rule number one: You *never* say the c-word when you're trying to get permission to be launched into space in a tiny metal tube with a handful of other humans and billions of dollars' worth of technology.

If they really were listening—and I was paranoid enough not to rule out that possibility . . .

"But on the other hand, I have plenty to keep me busy here," I said quickly. "And it's easier to focus without all the distractions and technology."

"Yeah, I totally know what you mean," Mitsuko said, projecting her voice unusually loud. She smiled and winked. "So, anyway," she began in her normal voice, coming over to sit opposite me on the unoccupied bed. "I hear you're working out with Emilio tonight."

"Yeah, in a little while. Want to come?"

She shook her head, her hair falling in glossy black sheets over her shoulder. "No. I just thought we could gossip about that for a while."

I rolled my eyes and started to change into workout clothes. "What's to gossip about?"

"You. A cute boy with a penchant for flirting. Alone in a room. Sweating. Grunting. You see where I'm going?"

"We won't be alone, Suko. It's a public place." I pulled a fresh shirt over my head and secured my hair with an elastic. "And unlike some people, this is not just a giant dating pool for me. Stop being ridiculous."

She scooted closer. "It isn't ridiculous. Look, they're sending one of us into space for a long time. Maybe even two of us. Surely you've read studies about the astronauts who lived in the space station, all the tensions that came up about the first few tries. There are going to be mixed-gender groups locked away together for a long, long time. NASA might be looking for people who are okay with being . . . you know, confined in a small space with people they're attracted to."

I stopped and stared at her. "You're serious."

"Deadly. Look, they've done studies. Mixed-gender groups

worked best. Bonded-pair groups worked even better. Remember, we talked about it in Copeland's class the other day. It's just human nature."

"So you're saying I should sleep with Emilio." I didn't hide the derision in my voice.

"Maybe not *now*. But if it was just you and him for the next five years . . ."

I had to resist putting my hands over my ears. "I am *not* listening to this. Emilio's just a boy. I'm not attracted to him. He's like . . . like my little brother or something."

"Cassie, he's nineteen," Mitsuko said gently.

I gave her a look. "He doesn't act like it."

She scooted closer to me, her eyebrows knitting. "Cass, have you never had a boyfriend before?"

Mitsuko had such a big-sister vibe, such an earnest, caring face, that I was tempted to confide in her. That I wasn't interested in him because I'd never been interested in *anybody*. And I didn't foresee that changing.

This is a competition. She is playing you.

I bent down to tie my shoes to escape, trying to ignore the burning in my cheeks. "All the boys at my school are idiots."

Her hand wave was impatient, like swatting away a fly. "Goes without saying. But look, you're a grown-up now, and this is a grown-up situation. I'm just trying to prepare you."

Just tell her. Shut this conversation down. But I didn't want to make a spectacle out of myself. Make this a topic of conversation. It wasn't her business.

I stood upright again and glared at her. "Thanks, but I'm fine. They probably won't pick two of us anyway, and all the rest of the crew are old. So it's not even an issue." I turned the focus around on her. "Why aren't you worried about being locked together with Emilio, or any of the other guys you were flirting with at dinner? What about your husband?"

"Michael and I had a talk before I came." She looked away for a minute, and then her gaze was steely. "He understands that if I make it to space, well . . . I do what I have to do."

"What happens in orbit, stays in orbit?" I snorted and moved toward the door.

"More or less. Cass, wait." She stood and caught my elbow. "I didn't mean to embarrass you. I just thought . . . you're so young. I just wanted to help."

I softened somewhat. She really seemed sincere. "Thanks, I guess."

She reached over and gave me a hug. When she pulled away there was a sly smile on her face. "You know there's some Indian guys here."

"Yeah, I did notice that," I said. "Not interested. Excuse me, I have a competition to go train for."

She cocked her head. Tapped her pursed bottom lip with one manicured finger, as if considering. "Cass, have you ever thought that you might be, like, asexual?"

I didn't look at her. My hand froze on the doorknob; my entire body was a bated breath. "Yeah," I said, having waited too long to respond, the words flying out of me in a rush that was half panic, half relief. "I think I am, actually."

"Oh," Suko said. My eyes darted to her. She'd gone still a moment, her lips still forming the circle of her response. Then her face brightened. "That's cool! I'm bi."

"Cool?" I sat down on the edge of the bed, my knees gone mysteriously weak.

"Yeah." She was smiling, excited, like we'd just discovered we had the same favorite book. When I didn't match her enthusiasm, she backed off. "Sorry, I—some people still don't know that asexuality is even a thing. I just thought . . . I thought you might . . . For real, I wouldn't have said anything if—"

"It's fine," I said. Mitsuko never got flustered like this. "I've just never really said it out loud before."

"Oh, hon." She sat down beside me on the bed. "You're like a little kitten. I just want to adopt you."

"So you'll stop badgering me about guys now, right?"

She smiled. "I *guess.*" She paused, squinting at me. "Are you mad?"

I gave her a smile back, relief swimming amid the remnants of my fears. "Nope. I just . . . don't talk about it. People hear something like that, for some reason they try to convince you that you're not. And it's not something I really . . ." *Know for sure,* I finished silently. "It's just private."

"Oh, be*lieve* me, I get it. But thanks for sharing that with me. Even though I did kind of drag it out of you. I won't spread it around, I promise." She bumped my shoulder with hers. "And I don't care if people know about me—Emilio already does—it's just that some guys think being bi is an excuse to be disgusting to me."

"Yeah, of course." I untangled my fingers, which had wrapped themselves into a bloodless knot. This conversation had changed course pretty dramatically. But it actually felt anticlimactic, to have this secret thing I'd thought about myself out in the open now. "So . . . you're bi and married?"

Her voice went a little tight and she raised an eyebrow at me. "I can be both at the same time, you know."

"Of course, yeah. I didn't know. I don't think I know anybody who's bi."

Her smile came back. "Now you do."

"Pretty sure my uncle's gay, though."

She burst into surprised laughter. "Now are we gonna name all the people we know who aren't straight?"

"He thinks he's all sly about it. He's really not. My grandma's, like, eighty, and she totally knows. But he just keeps sneaking around for no reason. It's not like we care."

Her laughter calmed, eyes still sparkling but her expression becoming solemn. "You know it's fine, right?"

We weren't talking about my uncle anymore.

"Yeah." It was more sigh than sound.

"Totally normal. Hell, it's probably an advantage. Everyone here is *ripped*. It's super distracting."

"Anything to win," I said, and she dissolved into laughter.

Now all I could see was Emilio standing in front of me, shirt off, teaching me the best way to do lateral pull-downs as I wondered what it might be like to kiss him. *Thanks a lot, Suko.*

Not that I *wanted* to kiss him. It was purely scientific curiosity. I didn't feel anything when I looked at Emilio. I didn't especially like the idea of kissing anyone at all. But should I? What if he was the last man on Earth—or, more accurately, in space. What if we managed to both get in? They said they'd pick two, after all. It wasn't impossible. What if this was as close to someone as I'd ever feel? I was pretty sure other people weren't lukewarm—at *best*—about kissing people they liked.

Could my feelings change over time? I mean, I liked Emilio well enough. I enjoyed his company more than most. But I'd never once, not till this moment, considered even the possibility of anything physical. The very thought made me uncomfortable.

I shut my eyes as if I could force the image from my retinas. She'd definitely done this to me on purpose. Was this what it was like for everyone else, all the time? Were other people thinking of *me* like this?

"Come on, three more reps," Emilio said. He leaned his arms on his knees, his face near mine, sweat beading on his forehead.

It was like Mitsuko had adjusted my focus, sharpening details that had always been background noise to me before.

"Concentrate," he said.

Eyes still closed, I focused solely on the feel of my muscles working. After a few more reps, I was sweating and my mind was clear again.

We could just be friends; there didn't need to be anything more.

"I need a break. Let me spot you for a while," I said.

Emilio didn't really need me to spot him on the bench press, so I leaned against the wall and kept an eye on him. We weren't alone in the weight room tonight; there had been five other guys in here when we'd arrived, though now it was down to three.

What would it be like to be stuck in a spaceship with only one other person my age? I'd never thought about guys much before, except in an abstract way. They had been distractions at best, annoyances at worst. Like: Okay, yes, I knew that I wasn't gay. But that's about as specific as it ever got.

The thing was, I could look at Emilio, notice all these things about him that should be attractive, that were aesthetically pleasing, but it didn't make me *feel* anything except slightly creeped out at myself for noticing.

I didn't date—that had been my choice, even if I did make jokes about my grandmother arranging a marriage for me out of convenience. I'd just never been interested in anyone enough to take time away from studying. My goals were more important than anything. Still were.

Mitsuko was right. I was eighteen and I'd only been kissed once, kind of accidentally, by a guy from orchestra who was tipsy after our Christmas concert sophomore year. He had apologized all over himself and then fallen asleep in the storage room, and I had avoided him ever since.

I'd spent eighteen years doing nothing but trying to become an astronaut. Was I suddenly going to find myself attracted to someone to the point of distraction? This might be something I needed to get a handle on.

"Lola? Cas! Little help?!"

"Whoa, sorry!" I snapped out of it, leaned forward quickly, and snatched the bar from Emilio's sweaty palms. Emilio lay on his back, gasping, with splotches of red in his cheeks. "What's with you tonight? You're totally spacey. Pun intended."

"Sorry," I said again. "It's just . . ." It's what? I blurted out the first thing I could think of. "I got a letter from my parents today. And they hardly wrote anything at all. It was, like, two sentences."

Emilio rolled up, swung around so he was straddling the bench, and faced me. To my surprise, he looked genuinely upset. "Damn, I'm sorry. I forgot you still live with your parents. Of course you'd be homesick."

Homesick? No. That didn't seem right. "It's not that," I said.

But he kept on. "It sucks not being able to talk to your family. When I first moved out, my mom would call me just about every night after I got home from work. I got a letter from my sister the other day, and it was like a mile long."

"That's just it. They barely wrote at all. I feel like . . ." My eyes suddenly got hot and an alarm went off inside my head. *Abort abort abort!* ". . . Like they barely notice I'm gone."

Emilio just looked at me with a mix of pity and empathy. "Hey, I'm sure they do. I'm sure they miss you."

"Yeah? How? You don't know them."

"Because they're your parents, and it's the law."

"Yeah. I guess you're right." This was just a tactic of theirs, I told myself. They were testing me. That's all it was.

"You want to go beat up some punching bags?"

I smiled. "Can we, please?"

SEVEN

THE NEXT TIME I saw the shrink, he asked about my parents.

If I didn't think NASA had bugged the whole installation before, I definitely did now.

He led off with the same old innocuous stuff. How did I like class, how were things going with my roommates, was I making friends? Then he went straight for the heart. "How do you think your parents feel now that you're here?"

I'd been turning this question over in my head every night since the ridiculously short letter, so I was prepared. "I'm not sure. I'm not there with them right now, am I?"

"No, but I'm interested in hearing your estimation. You've had a letter from them, I believe?"

"Yes." I exhaled through my teeth.

"Elaborate, if you don't mind."

"It was short. They wished me well." I wasn't about to share my fears with him.

Felix's bespectacled eyes bore into me. "So they haven't been in close contact with you."

"How could they? With all the security around here, I'm glad I got a letter at all."

"And you're okay with that? With not speaking to your family for a long time? Are you not close with your parents?" He seemed to sense the truth beneath the lie.

I unfisted my hands. These rapid-fire questions were trying to stress me, throw me off. Had to keep up the volley. "Of course I am. We don't have to talk every day to be close."

"But this is your first time being so long away from home."

"No, it isn't, actually. I've been to camp before." Though I was ready for it, he didn't ask another question right away. He waited expectantly, and the longer it went on, the more the silence became unnerving. "They have their own lives. My parents are both scientists. They have their work to keep them busy."

He held back a smile. I knew instantly that I'd slipped up and showed him the weakness he had been probing for.

"How does that make you feel?"

"About the same as I feel about being half Indian," I shot back. I was still kind of mad at him for deliberately baiting me about Kalpana Chawla. "They've always been like that—it's a fact of my life. It's not something I think about. You wouldn't ask a dolphin how he likes living in the ocean. He doesn't know any different. He just does."

Felix nodded slowly and scribbled on his notepad. Pen and paper—who still did that, anyway? "Do you miss being at home?"

The question caught me off guard. "No."

"Not at all?"

"I love my parents—and my grandma and Uncle Gauresh—but being here is the best experience of my life. Everybody leaves their parents at some point. This time next year I'd probably be leaving for college."

"I'm glad you're adapting so well, Cassandra. It shows a great amount of emotional maturity on your part. I just have one more question, and then you can get some sleep. Do you think your parents love you?"

I startled, then glared. "Of course they do."

He looked at me, infuriatingly calm. "Let me rephrase it, then. Do you feel that your parents miss you?"

"Without a doubt."

"And you miss them?"

I nodded, unwilling to say it aloud.

"If you were to go for months or even years without speaking to your loved ones, would you find that troublesome?"

I held my head up, my expression confident. "I can handle it. Don't you worry about that."

He smiled that serene smile of his, and jotted it down in his pad.

◐ ● ◐

"How did—" Mitsuko started.

Walking through our dorm door, I breezed by her so fast her hair moved. I flopped straight onto my bed, face buried in the comforter. "He said I'm an object for my parents to see their own reflections," I mumbled.

"What was that?"

I rolled over. By the look on her face, she'd heard me clearly enough. "I said, I'm not an object. And my parents aren't vain."

"Maybe not. And it doesn't mean your parents don't love you."

"I know that!"

"But they did send you off on this dangerous, experimental mission where they can't have any contact with you."

I sat up. "Because it's my dream. Because they think I'm old enough to make my own decisions. They let me come here because it's what I wanted. He's trying to mess with me, to throw me off. It's rotten."

She was silent, chewing her bottom lip.

I groaned into my pillow. "Don't look at me like that. I'm just exhausted. I'll be fine."

Mitsuko came over and hugged me. It felt so good I had to tamp down the urge to cry.

The rest of the week went by without another incident. I went to class. Took tests. Ate meals with my group. It was strange how quickly I adapted to having a social circle. Expecting people to greet me when they saw me, save me a seat next to them, ask me about my day—even though we moved through all of our days as a whole.

But even my friends I had to keep at arm's length. My brain churned constantly, calculating how to beat everyone else. What were their weaknesses? How could I show off my strengths?

I didn't hear from my parents again. But after my session with Felix, I was fairly certain they were holding my mail on purpose, to test me. I put it in the back of my mind.

The names on the leaderboard shifted negligibly. Our names rose and fell like an irregular heartbeat. Hanna broke briefly into the top five. Mitsuko was ranked number two for an entire day. Emilio held steady in the middle of the pack, but our ranks seemed tied together: if I rose, so did he, so that I never surpassed him.

Even if the ranks didn't seem to last, or matter, I was obsessed with every minute change.

I was beginning to think this was just another game they were playing.

I answered every question in class that I even thought I knew the answer to. I memorized diagrams from our tablets. I ran every morning, lifted weights in the afternoons, and slept like the dead every night.

I forgot an outside world existed.

My brain was fried. Even without tests, classes were exhausting. I didn't have access to my usual methods of stress relief—no internet, no books that weren't textbooks, and definitely no piano. I'd reread the one book I'd brought enough times to be sick of it. I hadn't heard music in so long, aside from Emilio's occasional off-key whistling.

I had no idea what day it was.

So after breakfast, when I headed down the hall toward class, Mitsuko tugged on my arm. "Earth to Cass! Where are you going?"

I turned bleary eyes on her. "What?"

"It's Saturday."

Hanna and Mitsuko were both staring at me quizzically.

I shook myself out of my fog. Weekends were supposed to be downtime, but there was nothing to do except exercise or study. I followed my roommates out to the track, where a few other candidates had decided to spend their day in the sunshine.

Emilio met us in the hall, eyes alight with some juicy bit of gossip that burst out of him before even a hello. "A guy in my room dropped out today."

Now I was fully awake. "What? Who? This morning?"

Emilio nodded. "You know Roman? Number seventeen?"

I knew his number better than his name, but nodded.

"He'd been moaning and groaning for days about being bored. He was missing out on college football or some shit. Can't really sympathize, but whatever. We got up this morning and his bed was made and he was just gone. Apparently he went to the RA office last night and checked out, like a damn hotel, just like that. Without saying a word to anybody."

I had an image of Luka, sitting alone at his table at every meal.

Mitsuko clucked her tongue. "Sad."

"No, it isn't," Hanna said. "Anybody who doesn't want to be here needs to go home. If they can't handle it, they shouldn't be here."

"I don't disagree," Mitsuko said. "But dropping out because you're bored? I mean, come on."

"After what we had to go through to stay here?" I asked, incredulous. "That marathon? He basically threw away the chance of a lifetime—of *multiple lifetimes*—in exchange for getting to watch TV. It's disgusting. I'm with Hanna; I'm glad he dropped out."

"No skin off my nose," Emilio agreed. "To each their own. But listen. I overheard some of the profs talking when they didn't think I could hear—I have excellent hearing, by the way—and apparently it's not just Roman. Some kids are complaining to the shrinks about being burned out. I guess some of them—the profs, I mean—are getting concerned."

"That's ridiculous," I said with a snort. "What did they expect? This isn't Disney World. There's no television in space."

"Stress can make people batty," Mitsuko said. "But there's a fine line between training for stressful conditions and running off your potential candidates—most of whom have never had to deal with being deprived of entertainment for longer than it takes for them to sleep."

"So kids these days are just too spoiled for something as rigorous as astronaut training, is that what you're saying?" Hanna made a disgusted face. "I beg to differ."

"Maybe some are. And that's what they get for picking young people for a mission like this." Mitsuko shrugged and leaned in close. "So that's just one more thing we have that makes us better than them."

EIGHT

SHAW HAD AN announcement for us at the end of class on Monday.

"Congratulations on the end of your second week as candidates," he said, smiling through his beard. He looked worn out and wrinkled around the edges, but his smile was genuine. "Phase Two of your training starts tomorrow. Somebody is going to come collect you immediately after breakfast every morning for a little outside-the-classroom training."

"The Vomit Comet?" asked Sarnai, number fifteen, a ruddy-cheeked girl from Mongolia.

Shaw only smiled. "I'm not sure. They don't tell me any more than they tell you. But this is probably our last class, at least for this week. Whoever comes to get you will hand out your new schedules. Good luck, and Godspeed."

Shaw stood beside the door as we left. I stopped, and he smiled and held out his hand. I shook it. Emilio did, too, but went a step further and embraced him.

"Keep up the good work," Shaw said, and then his eyes shifted over, as if he meant that for me, too.

"That's wild," Emilio said as we walked together to the cafeteria. "No more class. We're really about to get out there and do actual astronaut stuff."

"Yeah," I said, but I was hardly listening. Blood was rushing loud in my ears. I had only myself to blame for my poor ranking. Before, I had *always* been number one. I wasn't working hard enough. The weekend had been a prime studying opportunity, and now I'd wasted it relaxing outside with my friends.

Time to cut out distractions.

Mitsuko appeared on my other side. "Did you hear?"

I let Emilio and Mitsuko talk to each other across me. Suddenly I felt like Hanna, and I realized: she'd been pulling away from us for days. Maybe this whole time. She'd been distant, and I hadn't understood that she had obviously come here with more resolve than I had.

Making friends, making allies—it was a waste of time. Her rank proved it.

But then, Emilio was higher than all of us, and it seemed like he was friends with every single person here. He knew everyone's first name, not just their rank, and he waved to everyone we passed in the halls.

Two completely opposite strategies.

Which was the correct path?

Someone tapped on the side of my head. "Earth to Cass. Are you going to actually pick something for lunch or just stare at it?" It was Mitsuko.

I snapped back to life and realized that we had made it to the cafeteria and I was holding up the buffet line. I threw some sandwiches on my plate and slopped some kind of side dish next to them and quickly caught up with Mitsuko.

Our usual table was taken, so we sat with three candidates who were lower ranked than us.

Emilio looked at me strangely. "You gonna eat those?"

"You're already poaching my food? You haven't even eaten yours yet."

He looked confused. "No, I mean—I thought you were veggie, that's all."

I looked down at the sandwiches. *Ham.* I groaned and plunked them onto Emilio's plate before heading back over to the buffet.

Earth to Cass. Wake up, Cass.

Six thirty in the morning. All of us candidates—the eighteen that were left—stood around an Olympic-size swimming pool. Waiting.

We were all wearing the black, skintight Space Activity Suits, or SASs, that we'd studied in class. I'd had to strip down to nothing in the bathroom, and it took me about twenty minutes and, eventually, the help of two aides to squeeze myself into the thing. They were like wet suits, except the material was different: it was at least half an inch thick, and incredibly flexible, with a minuscule honeycomb pattern only barely visible in the shifting light. It was constrictive, necessarily so in order to maintain pressurization in a vacuum.

I examined my hands: the material there was fantastic. Thinner, but just as strong, with whorls that mimicked my own natural fingerprints. I ran my fingertips up and down my arms, expecting to feel nothing but the distant plasticky sensation I was used to from wearing gloves in biology lab. But it wasn't like that at all. The rubber ridges on the suit's fingertips translated sensation to my skin.

"This is wicked cool," Emilio whispered in my ear, his voice full of reverence. I had to agree.

No one dared speak louder than a whisper. Nervous anticipation seemed to put people deep into their own heads.

A loud, metallic echo made every head turn, but it was only a door opening. The colonel and Ms. Krieger marched in with a few techs in blue flight suits. Behind them trailed two people in scuba gear.

"Welcome to the Neutral Buoyancy Lab," Ms. Krieger said as the last click of her heels on the cement echoed around us. The safety divers slipped into the pool wordlessly, shattering the calm surface and sending ripples licking at the pool's edge. "Today will be your first simulated experience of weightlessness. Though there are no planned space walks for this mission, you need to be prepared for anything. I assume most of you have been in a pool before. This is more of an introduction to the new generation of space suit technology and orienting yourself in four dimensions." She paused. "You were given a series of tasks to memorize last night. Today you will complete those tasks, as well as a few that are unfamiliar to you, in our underwater sim lab. You will be ranked by the times it takes you to finish and accuracy of tasks completed."

We all peered down into the water. I saw something under the shimmering surface. Something very large and white, sitting at the bottom of the pool. Fifteen, maybe twenty feet under.

"You'll each be tested individually. Do I have any volunteers to go first?"

My hand shot up before my brain even realized what was happening. Luka's arm was a millisecond too late.

Ms. Krieger focused on me, followed by everyone else. My heart was suddenly banging the inside of my rib cage. "Good. Come here, and we'll get you suited up."

I stepped forward. I felt Luka's side-eye as I passed him, and hid the smug smile that I felt. *Ha! Finally, something you didn't win.*

Colonel Pierce went to a rack on the wall and came back with a large helmet for me. One of the techs slipped straps over my shoulders, and then I felt the weight of an air tank on my back. I methodically repeated the pattern of tasks I'd memorized last night, mouthing the instructions from the text.

The colonel looked me dead in the eye. I'd never stood so

close to him. He was taller up close. I could see the crinkles around his eyes and the white scruff of a day-old beard, and smell his faintly old-man smell . . . and the air of a man who had seen Earth as nothing more than a distant pale dot in an alien sky. "If you breathe normally, you have an hour and a half of nitrox, but it shouldn't take that long," he said. "Check this gauge to see how much is left. Come back when you have ten minutes left, finished or not. I know how you overachievers are. Just remember, if you drown, you're not going into space."

I smiled, feeling both cocky and nervous. "Duly noted."

The colonel huffed and slid the helmet over my head, and suddenly everything went very quiet and fish-tank-like. There were a few minutes of tugging as they adjusted everything. After a second, I heard the whoosh of the air pump kick in, and my helmet filled with the metallic smell of room-temperature nitrox.

The colonel tapped his wrist, reminding me of the time limit. Then I was helped down the ladder and into the water.

I expected it to be cold. But of course, I felt nothing. This suit was insulated for *space*. Maybe now I knew what a molting snake felt like, covered in a layer of skin that was no longer really part of myself.

As soon as I reached the objective, I was over the novelty of it and completely focused. Now I could see that the strange white object was like a massive, elongated igloo, with a tunnel opening at opposite ends of the sphere. The weight on my back was only enough to keep me underwater, not bear me to the floor, so I pushed off the wall with my toes and swam into the entrance of the tunnel.

It was a tight fit inside, and darker than I'd imagined. Unbelievably eerie, to float in a world of silence and darkness, closed in all around. Dim lights and buttons glowed, interspersed in the arch above my head. My elbows hit the walls. I could barely see. I had no flashlight.

Focus.

The tasks were simple, almost babyish. Turn four red knobs 180 degrees. I found them. That unlocked two yellow levers; pull the right first, then the left. I became a robot, methodical and mindless. When I finished the tasks in the mouth of the igloo, I floated down farther into the dome. The space opened up wide.

Here it became more complicated. My sense of up and down was obliterated. They'd purposely mirrored the floor beneath me so I instantly became disoriented. Lights above my head, or beneath my feet? Which was real? *No,* I thought. *Don't look down. Don't think, just do.*

Now everything was a puzzle. They hadn't prepared us for this section. What combination of colored buttons would open the smooth metal door that led to the next set of tests? I hit them in rainbow order, then reverse, then alphabetically—and it opened. Next.

They were simple patterns, but they required a clear head and a logical progression of thought. They were probably counting on disorientation and fear to delay us. But I'd pushed the fear away until it was nothing more than fog pressing against a glass door, too weak to get inside.

I'd been scuba diving more than once on family vacations to the Gulf; there were divers in the water in case I had a problem; there was nothing to be afraid of. I just needed to stay calm and concentrate.

I finished the last puzzle, releasing the door that led to freedom. A rush of pleasure warmed me. I'd done it perfectly. And according to the oxygen readout, in plenty of time.

I swam out the other end of the igloo and surfaced near the wall. Two assistants helped lug me up; the tank on my back was a lot heavier than I remembered it being.

They took off my helmet and it was as though I was suddenly alive again, as if I'd waken abruptly from a dream, and sights and sounds were too bright and loud to handle. I blinked stupidly a few times.

Emilio caught my eye and gave me a half grin. Other candidates watched me anxiously. Luka had apparently volunteered as the next one up. He stood beside the pool, looking down at the sphere, and didn't acknowledge me as I passed.

Water slopped from my suit onto the cement floor as I readjusted to the feeling of sound waves hitting my eardrums again.

"Not bad to lead us off," Ms. Krieger said, looking at a stopwatch. "Fifteen minutes."

That was all? It'd felt like an hour.

One of the assistants led me off to get changed back into

normal clothes. The woman had to literally peel the suit off me.

As soon as it was gone I felt like a turtle with its shell missing, cold and vulnerable and my body too light. It wasn't until I put my clothes back on that I realized my heart rate was back to normal. And it was a letdown. Like the feeling you'd get after riding a roller coaster—all I wanted was the chance to do it again, to feel that exhilaration.

The assistant let me go back and sit with the other candidates who were waiting for their turn. "As long as you don't talk about the test."

"Of course not."

I sat down next to Emilio, who nodded at me and tried to smile, but didn't talk. His knee was bouncing like he'd just ingested a gallon of sugar water. Hanna was on the far side of him. She stared straight ahead, still as stone.

There was a brief intermission while the divers in the water reset the simulation. I watched Luka surreptitiously, already suited up with everything but his helmet. He sat alone at the other end of the bench, elbows on knees, hands clasped together. His eyes watched the water intently. A muscle in his jaw jumped.

Was he nervous?

When the divers signaled the okay, the colonel helped Luka fit his helmet over his face and Luka slipped into the water with barely a ripple. I counted the minutes.

"Twelve minutes, seven seconds," Colonel Pierce announced as Luka's head broke the surface again.

Damn that guy.

The next two were slower, but Mitsuko nearly beat me, coming within two seconds of my time. When she came back from changing clothes, she whispered to me, "Just luck. My head was spinning in that dome so bad I actually swam into the floor twice."

Emilio did slightly worse, and so did the next few after him. They were averaging about twenty minutes. I was trying hard to hide the grin that was fighting its way out. *This is the beginning of my rise to first place.*

Hanna's turn. She looked pale and sick as the colonel slipped the helmet over her head, and then I couldn't see her face anymore. She climbed down the ladder, slipped beneath the surface of the water, and was gone.

And she was gone a long time. Twenty, maybe thirty minutes.

"Something's wrong," Emilio whispered to me.

"No way," I mouthed. But I was worried. I nudged Mitsuko. She shook her head and shrugged, apparently not concerned.

Maybe ten more minutes went by, until she was officially in last place. The colonel and Ms. Krieger whispered to each other. Pierce looked at a small device in his hands that I realized must've been a remote sensor—maybe checking her air levels, her vitals, maybe even a video feed. I caught the words "almost out" and didn't know if that meant she was almost finished, or about to run out of nitrox. His grave demeanor indicated the latter.

Finally, the colonel nodded at the two safety divers in scuba suits who hung on to the pool wall. "Go get her."

The divers slipped beneath the water, two black, wavering forms beneath the blue. Emilio stood and moved to the edge of the pool, and I followed as if drawn by a magnet.

Nothing bad had happened. Not to Hanna. She was a machine. This was so simple! Hanna wouldn't have screwed it up. She couldn't.

Suddenly I realized I was holding Emilio's hand. I don't know who reached out first. Mitsuko grabbed my other hand and clutched it tight. We were like a chain, holding on to one another as if hope could make Hanna be okay. Even Luka, though stone-faced as usual, was peering over the edge of the pool with the rest of us, a line of concern etched in his brow.

It seemed like forever before the shimmering black shapes came back into view. I peered hard into the water, trying to count them.

Somehow I felt it—all three of our bodies releasing a breath as Hanna surfaced, braced by the two divers on either side.

The colonel helped pull her over the side of the pool, and with his help, Hanna ripped her helmet off. She collapsed on the concrete in a puddle of water, gasping.

"What happened?" Colonel Pierce demanded.

Hanna just shook her head, her breath coming in wheezes.

"Get her up," the colonel said to the two assistants. "Walk her to the clinic. Next volunteer!"

The assistants picked Hanna up by her arms and half led, half dragged her away. Her watering blue eyes flitted toward me for a millisecond, and then she dropped her head and looked away. It was enough time for me to see the dejection in her face and the bloodless pale of her lips.

In the quiet after the door shut behind them, I realized awkwardly that I was still holding Emilio's hand, and let go. He didn't seem to notice. His face was still filled with concern, eyes watching the door where Hanna had gone.

When the last candidate came up for air, I was ranked third in the times. Luka and the Russian guy Boris had beaten me.

We were sent back to our rooms. No evening classes. Instead, we were doing psych evals. Mitsuko had hers right after lunch, so I was alone in my room when Emilio knocked.

"Hey," he said, and for some reason he hugged me when I opened the door. He pulled away, hands still holding my elbows. "Let's go see Hanna."

"I think this is it," he said, rounding the corner and pushing through an unmarked door. The door swung behind us and softly clicked shut, and I felt the air rush out of the room.

A girl sat alone on a narrow hospital bed. One who looked nothing like the Hanna I knew.

She wore white scrubs—probably the nurses' spare—that hung like a tent from her narrow frame. Her blond hair was wet at the ends, scraggly, hanging on both sides of her face in limp, loose waves. Her skin was nearly the color of the scrubs. The only color was in the red rims around her eyes and the blue tint of the veins beneath her skin. She sat hunched over. She didn't move a muscle, even when we came in.

I didn't know what to do. She looked ghostly and somehow dangerous, like a wounded predator.

Emilio left my side and approached the bed. "Hey. How are you?"

He sat beside her. Hanna shifted a little but otherwise didn't move.

"What's the matter?" I asked, coming closer. I might have guessed what the matter was, but a screwup on a test shouldn't have freaked her out this bad. There must be something else. I tried putting a hand on her shoulder and she flinched away from me.

"We were really worried about you," Emilio said, his voice mingling both sincerity and annoyance.

Hanna's face became an ugly expression of disgust, intense as a solar flare. Then it was gone.

Emilio stood up, his voice angry. "Hey, don't take your anger at yourself out on us. We're your friends. We just wanted to make sure you were okay."

Hanna scoffed. "We're not friends. We're competitors. And I just *lost*, okay? I don't need you coming in here to gloat. It's kind of humiliating. So just get away from me."

I stepped away. We weren't friends? Fine. Anyone who could reject a friendship like Emilio's—sincere and freely given—was certainly not worth mine.

Emilio apparently didn't feel that way. "Shut up," he said. "I don't deserve that, and neither does Cassie. We've never been anything but supportive to you. So what, you flub one test. You burn your bridges so you can wallow in self-loathing? That's really how you're choosing to deal with this?"

"Who cares about your score?" I said, trying halfheartedly to follow Emilio's lead. "You finished it, didn't you?" Awkwardly, I reached out but then changed my mind, my hand hovering in midair before retreating behind my back.

She shot me a withering stare and then snapped at Emilio. "Don't you get it? I'm out. That test was not about solving puzzles or pushing buttons, it was to see how we react under pressure. And I just showed them how completely, utterly shitty I am at it. I panicked. I couldn't even find my way out of that damn igloo. There's no way they're going to put me in a rocket after this."

"Are they kicking you out?" I asked quietly.

She shrugged and looked away, her anger suddenly gone, leaving her almost visibly deflated. "No one has told me anything. But what does it matter? I might as well go home. I'll definitely be in the bottom now, anyway."

"Do you want to stay?" Emilio's voice had gone quiet and low. I hadn't realized how deep his serious voice was.

Hanna stared at the tile a long time. I was about to grab Emilio and get the hell out of there when she finally answered, her voice a ghost. "Yeah."

Emilio crossed his arms. "Then act like it."

He turned around and left the room.

I hurried to catch up with Emilio out in the hall. "Why do you even bother with her?"

He didn't look at me. In fact, he seemed deflated, his hands limp at his sides, all the fire from a second ago extinguished. He stopped walking and stared at me until I shifted uncomfortably. "Why do I bother with her? Why do I bother with you, Cass? Or anyone here?"

It was like whiplash. I went stiff, my heart leaping into my throat.

Emilio's brown eyes continued to evaluate me, and I didn't like the person he was seeing. He spoke like I'd never heard him speak before. "Do you ever think about what other people are going through? You and Hanna, you're like the same person. Not a lot of differences there. Same ruthless, win-all-or-die-trying attitude. Except she just found out something about herself that might mean the end of her dream. Forever. Maybe try some empathy."

I was stunned, silenced, embarrassed. "You didn't exactly mince your words back there."

"Sometimes it's necessary."

"Well, why is it your job to motivate her? Why do you care if she leaves?"

A muscle in his jaw jumped, as if there were words he was biting back. His eyes shot down the hall and returned to me. "Maybe, Cass, you should ask yourself why you *don't* care."

And he walked away.

NINE

I MET MITSUKO in the hall after her psych eval and filled her in on Hanna.

She scoffed. "If she's not getting kicked out, I hope she leaves."

"Why?" I was still reeling from Emilio's words. *Ask yourself why you* don't *care*. That kept running circles around my head. He'd made me feel like a terrible human being, absent of empathy.

No, I corrected myself; *he* hadn't made me feel that way. My *actions* had.

"'If they can't handle it, they shouldn't be here,'" she quoted in a mimicry of Hanna's voice. "Remember? And it seems like someone can't handle it." We headed to our room to change into running clothes.

She didn't get to finish whatever admonishment she was preparing, because Hanna was standing in the middle of our room.

"Pissed off at me?" Hanna asked. She was back in her own clothes: jeans, a vaguely pink tank top and cotton jacket, her face scrubbed clean of makeup. She looked smaller than normal, like a child playing dress-up.

"Only returning the favor." Mitsuko breezed past Hanna to plop herself down on her bed. "Are you here to say good-bye?"

"No." Hanna crossed her arms over her chest. She'd pulled her hair back into a low ponytail and her face was impassive. "I'm going to go talk to them now. I was just changing."

"Well, good-bye," Mitsuko said. She went into the bathroom and closed the door. Hard.

Hanna stared at the door for a few seconds. Her fists balled up and then relaxed. Her eyes fell on me.

I didn't have any clue what to say. So I shrugged.

Without a word, Hanna walked past me and out the door.

"Hey, hotties!"

Emilio slipped out of the classroom door at precisely the moment Mitsuko and I walked by, on our way back from the track. He wriggled his way around a handful of other classmates and butted in between us.

He put his arms around each of our shoulders and I cringed away. "Sweaty," I said by way of explanation. "We've been running."

"Oh, is that why you're wearing running shoes? Funny how I didn't notice." He jerked his head toward Mitsuko. "Is she all caught up on the gossip?"

"I am," Mitsuko said haughtily. Emilio still had his arm around her. Funny—*she* never seemed to get sweaty. Why couldn't my parents, when picking the genetic traits they wanted in their future daughter, have thought, "Oh, and let's have her sweat slightly less than normal, too"? But no.

And now I was thinking about my parents again. I mentally shoved those thoughts away.

"Hey, Cass? You coming?" Mitsuko and Emilio were poised at the door to the cafeteria, waiting.

"Uh, no. I need to go take a shower real quick, I think. But I'll meet you later."

Mitsuko shrugged and they headed in to dinner.

Once alone in the hall, I surreptitiously tried to figure out if I smelled as bad as I looked. Mitsuko popped her head back out and I jumped.

"Sorry." She looked like she knew what I had been doing and was trying to keep from laughing about it. "But I thought you would want to see the leaderboard, like, immediately."

My heart leaped. I followed her through the door into the cafeteria and craned my neck above the buffet line. And I stared.

Cassandra Gupta. *Number four.*

Luka was still ahead of me. But *four*. From *ten*.

"And that's not all," Mitsuko said drily.

My eyes slid down the boards, noting Mitsuko's name now resting comfortably at nine.

And Hanna, at rock bottom.

Oh man. *I hope she did go home. If she sees this, we'll have to have her committed.*

Some names had disappeared completely. So if Hanna was still there, that meant they thought she actually had a chance. Guess Emilio was right—it wasn't time to discount Hanna just yet.

I stood there in shock, drinking in the pleasure at seeing my name so high, until I felt a tug on my sleeve.

"Lola, just come eat with us. You don't smell that bad."

I smacked his shoulder pretty hard, but he only rubbed it and grinned. "Fine," I said, getting in the buffet line with them. "I was really just trying to be polite, but whatever."

After dinner, Hanna was coming out of the door to our room just as Mitsuko reached for the doorknob. All three of us froze.

Mitsuko broke the standoff by walking right past Hanna and slamming the door. I stayed.

Hanna turned her eyes to me as if dreading my reaction. "Do you hate me now, too?" She sounded tired.

"No," I said automatically. Emilio's words still bounced around my ears like echoes. "Not your biggest fan at the moment, but I don't hate you."

The corner of Hanna's mouth twitched downward. She'd never looked so unlike herself.

"What'd they say?" I asked. "The NASA people."

She shrugged. "I'm not kicked out. Not that it matters. I know I'm in the bottom now."

I couldn't seem to find the anger I'd had earlier. She just looked so defeated. "Some people have already gone home over this. If they didn't think you could make it, you'd be gone, too. You still have a shot. You have to fight for it."

"Yeah." She didn't seem convinced.

"I'm not sure why Suko was so mad. When you were in the pool for so long, we were all really worried about you. That was probably . . ." My hand, unsure of what to do with itself, found the edge of the door frame. "Probably really scary."

The whites of her eyes were almost pale blue; they seemed to swallow her irises. Her throat worked, up and down.

This awkward encounter stretched on a little too long. "Well, I'm glad you are okay and all." I moved to pass her.

"Hey, Cassie." She caught my wrist. "Thanks."

TEN

IN THE MORNING, we were down to ten.

It didn't make sense, the way they made the cuts. Hanna had been ranked at the bottom, and she was still here, eating cornflakes at a table by herself, chewing mechanically and staring into space. Marisol, who had done fine yesterday, was gone.

From our viewpoint, they seemed to have cut at random, not based on yesterday's test.

Luka was number one. Kendra was number two. I was number three. After that, it was Mitsuko, Emilio, Anton, Giorgia, Pratima, Boris, and finally Hanna, at the bottom. But they weren't finished with surprises yet—they were only getting started.

After breakfast, we were loaded onto a bus and driven out to an airstrip. Turned out we were going to ride the Vomit Comet after all.

I'd spent the night trying to do what Emilio had said: imagining switching places with Hanna. Imagining having some fatal flaw that threatened everything I'd ever wanted.

The feeling was not a good one.

After a night of claustrophobic nightmares, I made a little pact with myself: be kinder to Hanna.

Seated behind her on the bus, I watched the back of her blond head and wondered what was going on in there. She was still here—she hadn't given up. She must know that staying meant facing her fears again and again, and maybe all for naught.

I had to respect that. And I wanted to be more like Emilio, who had a passion for life and who had genuine affection for just about everyone.

As we were getting strapped in to the specially outfitted little plane, I gave silent thanks to whatever it was that made me eat nothing but hash browns and apple juice that morning. The forty-minute parabolic flight alternating between free fall and double-g resulted in three of the ten candidates losing their breakfasts. Egg, ham, bacon, and—worst of all—cereal and globs of sour stomach-acid milk occasionally escaped the puke bags and floated into the cabin.

For the forty seconds or so that we were weightless, we were like kids on a playground, chasing one another around the padded open cabin of the plane, laughing and joyful. For forty seconds at a time, we weren't competitors, but a bunch of kids fulfilling a dream.

Hanna looked a little green, but she managed to keep her

stomach contents to herself. She hadn't spoken to any of us since the night before. Hanna had separated from our group in a clean break, like an amputation.

I didn't feel nauseous until the very last parabola, but by then I was having too much fun to worry about it. I didn't think it was due to the motion sickness, but seeing other people vomit for a couple of hours eventually got to me.

Now that we were back on Earth, my nausea had faded, replaced instead by an electric energy that made sitting still incredibly difficult. I had felt zero-g. I'd seen my braid floating over my shoulder as if by magic. I'd somersaulted in midair. I'd zoomed around inside the padded cabin as easily as a fish swims through water. It was an unbelievable feeling. I felt *alive*. And I wanted more.

The euphoria lasted all the way until we got off the bus and headed back into the squat metal compound that was home. I had some lingering vertigo, a watery-legged feeling like you'd get coming back onto solid ground after spending hours at sea, so I plopped onto my bed to rest while Mitsuko took over the bathroom and turned on the shower. Hanna must've gone on to lunch without us; at least, I hadn't seen her since getting off the bus.

I got about two minutes of shut-eye before a knock came at the door. It was a woman, blond hair pulled back into a sleek businesslike bun, wearing a blue flight suit and a stony expression, which immediately made my heart skip a beat. "Cassandra Gupta," she said. It wasn't a question. "Please follow me."

Numb, and still a little wobbly, I followed her out and down the hall, hesitating only briefly to glance at the bathroom door. Mitsuko would wonder where I was when she emerged from the shower and the room was empty.

But her robotic pace didn't slow, so I jogged to catch up.

She led me out a door I'd never seen used before and into the hot afternoon sunlight. I shaded my eyes and blinked. There was a black van parked on the curb with the side door open.

"Get in," she said.

This was off script. I didn't know who this woman was. But she was wearing a flight suit with the JSC logo, and I wasn't in any position to question orders. I slid inside.

"Give me your left hand." She slapped something like a plastic medical bracelet around my wrist, sealed it like a handcuff, and closed the door.

The inside of the van was air-conditioned and smelled like leather seats. There was a dark partition behind the driver, so all I saw was a shadowy figure in the seat in front of me. The outside windows were tinted, too, so dark they might have been curtains. Pretty sure that wasn't legal.

I twisted the bracelet around and around my wrist, but there were no clues as to its purpose, no words or identifying marks. It was light as plastic, but stronger. Some kind of material I'd never seen before. It was translucent gray, with what appeared to be a tiny gold microchip embedded in the plastic. I couldn't slip it off if I tried, and I had a feeling that scissors wouldn't do me any good.

They hadn't told me to pack my things. That was the good thing.

Why had I been tagged? And how long was I supposed to wait in this van before someone told me what the hell this was all about?

Apparently not long. The door slid open again, this time revealing Luka—looking as perplexed as I felt. I slid over to accommodate him, and the door was closed again. And we were moving.

"What's going on?" I whispered, hurriedly clicking my seat belt into place.

He just shook his head, lips pressed tight together, and buckled up.

The driver kept going. With the windows tinted, I couldn't tell trees from streetlights, couldn't even hear if we passed other cars. I could hardly tell if the sun was still shining.

"Can you see anything?" I asked.

Luka shook his head, but continued to watch the windows.

"Theories?" I muttered. "I'll take anything but silence."

"Another test," Luka said. "It seems we've been paired together."

He had on a bracelet, too. We'd compared ours, and they seemed identical: thin, gray, nondescript but for the gold chip.

Just when I was beginning to get drowsy from the constant drone of the engine, we seemed to slow.

"How long do you think it's been?" Luka asked quietly.

"Going by my stomach, not much more than two hours," I said.

He gave me a quizzical look.

"If it was lunchtime, I'd be hungry."

"Is that an accurate way to tell time?"

"In the absence of anything else? I'd say yeah. My biological hunger clock is pretty consistent."

The van eventually came to a stop. We waited only a heartbeat or two before the door flew open, the muted sunshine hurting my eyes.

"Out," barked the stone-faced woman. Luka and I tumbled out into the humidity. The woman shoved a pack in my arms, closed the door, got back into the van, and peeled out down a dirt road.

The two of us stood, dumbfounded, in the middle of nowhere. A chorus of cicadas and frogs filled the air, as thick as the humidity, but there was a heavy quiet underneath the noise—a blanket of silence that meant we were far from any cars, roads, or civilization. The sun was on its way toward full strength, but I was already sweating, my hair and shirt sticking to my skin.

"What'd she give you?" Luka asked, redirecting my focus.

I looked down at the backpack. It was bright orange, and not nearly as heavy as I felt like it should be. I was pretty sure now what kind of test this was going to be.

Together, we knelt on the dry ruts of the dirt road and emptied the bag. Contents: two solar blankets, a length of rope, compass, iodine tablets, a serrated knife, a first-aid kit, flint and steel, two fishing hooks and line, one large metal canteen (empty), a can of bug spray, a flashlight, two MREs shrink-wrapped in foil (pasta and vegetable flavor), two packs of crackers with peanut butter, a narrow tube of SPF 45, and a flare gun with two shots.

There was also a three-by-five laminated orange index card. I read aloud: "'Your reentry capsule has veered off course and crash-landed outside of your intended landing zone. You recovered only your standard-issue wilderness survival kit from the capsule. It will take twenty-four hours for rescue workers to reach your location. In order to pass this trial, you must use the tools from your wilderness survival kit and make it to the rendezvous point in time to be rescued.'" I flipped the card over to see a crudely photocopied hiking map. "The rendezvous point is fifteen miles north of here."

We shared a long look.

Luka squared his jaw. "Then we'd better start walking."

We hiked in silence.

They must've dropped us in some kind of wildlife preserve, because it was pristine—for what looked like a swamp better suited to Louisiana. The dirt road we'd been dropped off on led away from the rendezvous point, so we had to hike through mushy underbrush pockmarked with mud that suctioned with every step.

After weeks of being stuck inside, seeing the outside world

only through a barbed-wire-topped fence, the fresh air was intoxicating. Even the heat and the mosquitoes and the rough terrain couldn't dampen my spirits at finally being somewhere *else*, being free.

There were no trails. Flowing water kept appearing beside us, sometimes in thin trickles, sometimes in frantic streams, and then disappearing again. We filled the canteen in the faster-moving water, which I hoped would be a little cleaner. The iodine tablets might kill bacteria and viruses, but it wasn't going to turn swampy river water into a clear spring.

According to the map, we were traveling alongside a wide river. I just hoped we wouldn't have to swim across it. One knife was not going to be helpful against an alligator.

"Watch out for snakes," I said over my shoulder, as Luka followed in my footsteps over a rotten log.

"Snakes?" Like he'd never heard of the word.

I rolled my eyes. "Yes. Down here in the south, we have snakes. Poisonous ones."

He didn't say anything. I sighed and stopped, causing him to nearly run into me. "Okay, look," I said. "Our first-aid kit isn't going to do any good for a snake bite. Do me a favor and watch where you step. And if you hear a weird rattling noise, let me know."

His eyes went wide. I could've laughed. Pampered son of a diplomat. The poor thing had probably never had to worry about venomous snakes in his life.

I hadn't dressed for the outdoors—I was still in the clothes I'd worn to jog in early that morning. Luka, too, was about as ill prepared in a thin white T-shirt and cargo shorts. Nothing to protect us from the elements.

He offered to carry the orange backpack. I told him we could switch off. It wasn't heavy.

I'd burned through any residual anger at our situation by the time the sun was hitting high noon. This was the best exercise I'd gotten in weeks, and it invigorated me. Fifteen miles in twenty-four hours wasn't even a strenuous pace. They'd paired me with Luka, which meant they wanted to know how I'd compare with him, the number-one guy. That meant it was between him and me.

This was my opportunity to stand out.

We took a little break near a fast-moving stream, taking turns sipping iodine-laced water from the backpack. "So what's the plan?" I asked, sticking Band-Aids to the blisters that were eating through my feet in at least six distinct places. Damn cotton socks. "Hike until dark, set up camp?"

"We'll need to eat before too long," he said. "Do you know how to start a fire?"

"Yeah, I can do that," I answered. "But you don't need fire to cook MREs. Which is good, because I don't know how we'd find anything dry enough to burn." Everything, including the air, felt soggy. "We have enough food for only one day, so we should try to make it last."

"Perhaps in the morning, we can fish," Luka said. Then he cocked his head to the side. "I'm sorry. I forgot you do not eat meat."

"I don't really want to waste time," I said. "I'd rather keep

137

going as long as we can." I didn't remember ever discussing vegetarianism with him. How did he know I didn't eat meat? Had he been paying closer attention to me than I'd realized? "And it's not like I have much choice. Tofu doesn't exactly grow on trees around here."

He was still looking at me curiously and here I was, squatting in the mud with sweat dripping down past my eyes, swatting away gnats with dirty fingers. What did he see that was so interesting?

"I'd eat meat if I had to," I said, knowing NASA was probably listening. "Like right now, if there's no better protein source around and I have to spend a full day hiking. It's more of a personal preference."

Luka's expression suddenly changed, entire body tensing, his gaze narrowing and shifting to something behind me.

"What is it?" I whispered, afraid to move. "Alligator?"

He shook his head and put a finger to his lips, then motioned for me to keep my head down. I crouched deeper into the reeds and slowly looked over my shoulder.

About a hundred yards up the river were two figures trudging north. I could make out an orange backpack on one of them. Snatches of conversation reached my ears, but nothing intelligible.

I turned back to Luka. "That's Anton and Kendra," I said quietly.

He nodded, staying low. "It seems we are still in competition."

I gritted my teeth. "And they're ahead of us."

◗ ● ◖

Knowing the others were out there, too, and that they were likely headed for the same place, lit a fire under Luka and me. This was another race.

We veered off from the river, neither of us wanting to get into any sort of confrontation with Anton and Kendra. Not that I was afraid of them—but it seemed safer to keep our distance. Just in case.

By the time the shadows grew dark under the mossy canopy and the breeze off the water grew cool, my energy was burned out.

I was hungry. I was cranky. I was covered in itchy mosquito bites despite a liberal application of bug spray. I was splattered, neck to shins, in dried mud. But Luka was the one who wanted to stop.

"I think we should set up camp for the night," he said. I'd been carrying the backpack for a few hours, and Luka was taking point, helpfully clearing the path of spider webs for me.

"Already?" I stopped, looking up to gauge the position of the sun through the bare limbs of gangly trees, just a low red disc sinking into the horizon.

"We made good time today. We should get some rest and eat before it gets too dark." His cheeks were sunburned despite the sunscreen, sweat dripping down his temples, and for once he didn't look like he was having the easiest time of it.

"We have a flashlight. It's cooler to travel at night."

"They already know we can hike fifteen miles in a day. I doubt they are testing us on our physical capability." I bristled at that, but he continued. "We will make it to the rendezvous point by tomorrow at noon."

But will we make it there before the others?

Luka waited for me to consider the options. Should I try to be the leader, tell him he was wrong? Or was it better to act the team player and give in to his suggestion? We'd been playing nice so far, but how long would that hold out? This exercise seemed designed to test our interactions under stress more than any actual wilderness survival skills.

I swallowed hard. The grimy aftertaste of iodinated swamp water coated the back of my tongue. The only reason I was able to tamp down my frustration was the little circle of plastic on my wrist.

Because I was willing to bet my grandmother that our every move, our every word, was being recorded.

What was more important: Getting to the rendezvous point first, or surviving this without biting each other's heads off?

Cooperation, I decided, was what this test was about.

"Okay, let's break for the evening," I said. "We can start fresh at sunup."

Making camp was problematic. By the time we found a suitable place—far enough from the water that I wasn't afraid of alligators, and dry enough for comfort—there was hardly any light left. And Luka had no idea what he was doing.

I had to show him how to prepare the MRE. "You pour the water in the bag up to this line, here, and it reacts with the chemical packets to generate heat. So then we slide the food into the sleeve, like this, see?" I demonstrated. "And then we lean it against a rock and wait twenty minutes or so."

I'd been camping only as recreation, not out of necessity, but at least I knew the basics. He seemed to sense this and followed my directions, like the smart guy he was.

Without any stakes, and only a rope and a knife, our options for shelter were limited. I'd wanted to find higher ground, but there was nothing there—it was all flat floodplain with just a few trees in clumps. "It's a warm night," I said. "We can sleep under the stars."

We settled on a nearby copse, checked the surroundings to ensure we wouldn't disturb any snakes, and cleared an area large enough for the two of us to sleep side by side with a good two or three feet between us. We had no bedrolls, so we'd have to rough it with the solar blankets.

But by this point, I was ready to be unconscious for a very long time, and I didn't care about the specifics. I had a guy I trusted—as much as I trusted anyone—next to me, a blanket to keep most of the bugs off me, and a pretty nice view of the sky framed by tree branches.

And then it started to rain.

I swatted at the first droplets that hit my face, thinking in my sleep that they were mosquitoes. And then they came again and again, so I buried my head under the crinkling solar blanket and groaned quietly.

It was the miserable sort of rain, where water was seeping

out of the air like the wringing of a damp sponge. Made my skin crawl.

Luka shuffled around beside me. "Do you want this?" Luka asked. He was holding the orange backpack.

It took me a minute to realize he was offering it to me as a pillow. "No, thanks." I didn't really like the idea of resting my head on a flare gun. And we couldn't take it out of the water-proof backpack, in case we needed it.

"At least the rain will help deter the mosquitoes." Then, "We could drape one of the blankets over this branch. To keep the rain off."

I wanted to groan, but didn't have the energy. "We probably should." It would suck to spend the next day soaked through.

Luka got up and arranged his blanket on a low-hanging branch to cover as much area over us as possible, a makeshift tent. He let me arrange myself how I wanted and then crawled back under the drape, only a little more sheltered from the rain than before.

I offered to share my own blanket for warmth, but he declined. "It's big enough," I said. "There's a cool wind coming off the water. You'll get cold."

In the dim light of the stars, his mouth twisted with indecision. Then he nodded.

I shifted the blanket to cover us both. There was barely an inch of open air between our bodies. The only way to avoid touching him was to lie completely still. Which was fine; my body protested any movement.

Even sheltered under the blanket with him, somehow, the

boy did not smell. We had been hiking in a swamp for half a day. I knew for a fact that I smelled. He, however, wafted only faintly of summer rain. The jerk.

Whatever crap may happen up there, among the stars that I couldn't currently see—no matter how cramped and uncomfortable, whatever awful things might befall a human away from Earth, space *had* to be a better experience than this. At least you could see the stars, unfiltered.

"What a fun night this is going to be," I muttered. I didn't have to speak very loud; he was *that* close. "They must do this on purpose, so we are extra motivated not to crash their expensive rocket ships."

Luka, on his back, turned his head toward me ever so slightly. Some tiny glint of light reflected off his pupils; the rest of his features were shrouded in indigo darkness. I felt his breath on my face.

He laughed—a loud, surprised sound. It was the first time I'd heard it. I felt myself smile.

"Yes. Are we not lucky to be here?" The smile was evident in his voice. Then his voice lowered to a serious pitch. "I find I don't hate it."

Despite the heat, despite everything, I shivered.

"Good night, Cassie." His voice was quiet, warm, happy, and right in my ear. His slight accent held a lilt of laughter, and it was as if the entire day of stress and frustration hadn't been that bad.

We were a good team. We could win this.

With warm food in my stomach, I was comfortable, even

with the rain and the slightly alarming proximity of a boy with good bone structure.

The rain gradually fell harder, tapping against the tarp and rattling it in the branches—but for the most part, we kept dry.

I fell asleep thinking maybe Luka wasn't so useless after all.

I crawled out of the lean-to before Luka woke, sore and stiff and completely devoid of the good feelings that had lulled me to sleep. The sky was still gray, but the insects had been up for hours. I'd scratched scabs into my arms overnight.

They must've bothered Luka, too, as he woke not long after.

"Here," I said, tossing him a packet of crackers as he came to sit beside me.

He rubbed at his eyes with the back of his hand. There was already stubble on his reddened cheeks and sleep was still heavy in his eyes. "Thank you. How long have you been awake?"

"Since dawn."

He blinked up at the deep-gray sky. "It's not dawn?"

"Nope."

"Hm. Perhaps we'll get more rain today."

We ate our meager breakfast slowly, trying to make it last, and shared the canteen between us. "You should put some of this on," I said, putting the SPF and insect repellant in his hand. "Your face is bright red. The clouds won't protect you completely, you know."

He took it, nodding.

Only an hour or two after breaking camp, the sky opened up on us.

"'Perhaps we'll get more rain today,'" I mimicked under my breath. "More like, What have we done to anger the rain gods?"

It was relentless, falling on us in sheets that made visibility poor and walking treacherous. We continued to trudge north, following the river to keep our fresh water close. But our progress slowed considerably.

It was too warm to worry about hypothermia, so even though my wet socks rubbed blisters into my heels, a little rain wouldn't kill us. As much as I may have wanted it to.

The rain swelled the river, forcing us to head farther and farther away to avoid its widening banks. The swamp was more water than land, and what was dry when we first encountered it could become the bottom of the riverbed in a matter of minutes. We took a quick break, checking the map and compass for our position, but without dry kindling or more MREs we couldn't eat. Raw fish was the last thing I wanted, so we drank lots of water and pushed on.

At some point I thought I might have seen the flash of an orange backpack deeper in the woods, but whoever it was never came closer.

"How are we doing?" I asked.

Luka was on point again, following the map and the compass. It took him a long time to find our position on the map, swiping water from his eyes often. "Should reach it within the hour." Suddenly he stopped short, made a noise that sounded like a curse in his native language.

"What?" I caught up with him.

"The rendezvous point is just there," he said, pointing.

And then I saw our problem.

The rain had swelled what was probably, on dry days, a shallow stream. Now, between us and our destination was an angry, turbulent creek, opaque with mud and clotted with debris. It was maybe twelve feet across, no telling how deep.

"Yeah, we aren't crossing that," I said.

"We could go around it?" Luka suggested.

"How long would that take?"

"I'm not sure. This is not on the map."

I took it out of his hands. He was right; only the main river, behind us, was outlined. Not the smaller tributaries. "Damn."

So this was our dilemma. Did we do the dangerous thing and try to ford a fast-moving body of water alone and without supplies? Did we wait here, hoping our "rescuers" would come and get us even though we were a quarter mile off from the rendezvous point? Or did we find another way around?

The problem wasn't so much *what* to do—it was what did *NASA* want us to do?

My default response to a problem was always to seek the most straightforward solution. Shortest distance from point A to point B lay across that creek.

"We should wait here," Luka said, just as I'd decided to go forward. "I don't think NASA would want us to endanger ourselves further. We are close enough to the rendezvous point.

They will come and get us."

"But we're so close. We could be the first ones there and win this thing. The others are probably right behind us. Do you want to be last, on top of everything? It's probably not that hard to cross. We can just find a few logs, make a bridge."

I started forward, but Luka grabbed my arm. "Cassie, no. It's dangerous."

I glared, and he dropped my arm like it was hot. "Going into space is dangerous. Are you going to stop me from doing that, too?"

His lips parted, as if he was going to speak but couldn't find anything to say. Then he closed his mouth into an unhappy line. "Fine, we will do it your way."

His accent was more pronounced when he was mad.

Just wait until we get back, I thought. *Once you're clean and dry and fed, you'll thank me.*

It wasn't hard to find a fallen tree or two. Problem was, I overestimated how strong they'd be. Most were little more than saplings, which were useless. The biggest ones were still wetland trees and had been soaked by rain for a day or more, rotting from the inside out. We found one that was only just starting to rot, and using mostly Luka's brute strength, plopped it across the creek.

It wasn't long enough.

"That's okay, we'll just get another," I said, having to talk a little louder because of the noise from the water. At least the rain had stopped.

Luka's eyes told me he wasn't too keen on this plan, but he did it anyway. The second log he tried to launch was immediately swept away and taken downstream.

"Cassie . . ." Luka's voice held a note of warning.

I snapped at him. "This will work, okay? We just have to do it right. Maybe you can anchor the log for me while I wade across?"

His jaw was set. "We've barely eaten. We've been hiking nonstop. Look at you—your hands are shaking. Even if we can make a way across, you don't have the strength to fight the current right now. This is not worth drowning for."

I wanted to shoot back that if this wasn't worth it, nothing was. But watching the log that Luka had struggled to lift get swept downstream like it was made of paper . . . maybe I didn't want to risk it.

"You rest. I'll find something to eat."

"No!" I wasn't going to let him do that to me. Make me look like the weak little girl who needed a man to feed her while I sat around because I was tired. I didn't want to waste time fishing, then cleaning, cooking, and eating—not when the end was literally in sight. But I didn't have any other ideas. "They're judging us both on our survival skills, not just you. I'll come with you."

We continued to follow the creek, hoping to find a shallow spot to cross, or at least a slower-moving section to cast a line. My thighs burned in protest, but I did my best to ignore them.

I'd taken to muttering curses under my breath with every

step. It seemed to help. But it also made me almost miss it when Luka whispered, "Look!"

Shoeprints in the wet mud ahead of us. Had to be fresh, or the rain would have washed them away.

"Should we follow?" he asked.

"I think it depends on if we're supposed to be enemies," I said. "Or are we supposed to be working with the other teams? You'd think they'd have told us." But then I had a thought. "If they found a way across, maybe we can, too."

And then I saw it. Whoever had come before us must've had the same idea, or better luck.

A giant log had been felled across the creek. Thin trickles of water streamed over the top, but the log held firm. A rope—very similar to the one in our own pack—had been tied to a living tree on our side of the creek, suspended over the log, and staked on the other side. A crude bridge.

"This must be how the others got across." I turned to him, tried to read his face. "Is this safe enough for you?"

He put a hesitant foot on the log, testing its strength, and tugged experimentally on the rope. "It seems sturdy enough." He didn't sound thrilled. "I'll go first. If it can hold my weight, it can hold yours."

"No," I said quickly. "If you slip, I might not be able to pull you back. Let me go first. Your weight might dislodge the thing and then I'd be stuck on this side."

A corner of his mouth smirked. "You worried I'd leave you behind?"

I quirked an eyebrow at him. "Should I be?"

He grinned, clasping the back of my neck in his strong hand in a friendly, and very Russian, gesture. "If I left you here, you would pay me back only tenfold when we got back, no?" He released me. "Go careful and slow. I will cover you."

I sucked in a breath, steadying myself. My hands still shook, but I gritted my teeth and took a first, balancing step onto the log. It sank an inch or two into the water, and a thin layer of creek streamed around my shoes. I held on to the taut rope with both hands and planned each footstep carefully.

I shot one last look at Luka. Far from joking now, his eyes were steely and focused on me, hands outstretched and ready to grab me if I fell.

"Wish me luck."

He nodded once, solemnly.

I took a breath. And then I took a tiny sideways step. And then another.

As I inched my way farther toward the center of the creek, the water grew more turbulent at my feet, the rope swaying dangerously. I dared not look anywhere but at my feet. *Just a little farther*, I thought. *Just far enough where I could swim the rest, if I had to.*

I was now so far away from either bank that neither side was within reach. No chickening out now. My only option was forward.

It seemed to take forever. The log dipped farther and farther beneath my weight, but it held firm and did not roll or budge.

The rope was strong enough to catch me once or twice when I nearly lost my footing. After what felt like an hour, I hopped gratefully onto solid ground on the other side.

"Okay?" Luka called.

"Yes!" I smiled and waved, flooded with relief and adrenaline. "It's sturdier than it looks. I'll spot you."

Luka ventured out on the rope-and-log bridge, following my technique of moving very, very slowly. He was taller than me by a few inches, and definitely heavier, but even though the log dipped low in the center, it didn't break.

He crossed the center of the river and was coming nearer and nearer to me. Almost home free, and we didn't even have to build the bridge ourselves.

Then I saw what was about to happen, and I still couldn't stop it.

Some debris in the creek passed over the log, right as Luka's foot came down on it. His foot slipped, he jerked off balance, and the rope, which had been tied securely to a sapling on the far side, couldn't hold his weight—the sapling tore loose, roots pulling easily from the wet earth. The rope that Luka was relying on for balance went slack, sending him flying forward into the creek.

And just like that, he was gone.

I dove for him, my torso hitting the edge of the bank hard, arms sinking into the water as far as I dared, trying to keep most of my body on land for leverage. The mud and debris in the water obscured almost everything, and for endless seconds he was lost to me.

Then his face broke the surface, just for an instant. He'd managed to fall forward, toward me and the bank, and had fought his way close enough for me to touch him. But the furious current pounded at him and he couldn't right himself. The water took him under again and again.

I grabbed for him blindly, one hand catching a handful of his shirt, the other hand wrapped around a sapling, anchoring me to the bank.

It wasn't enough to hold him. The water pulled his body from me, tearing the fabric out of my hand.

Not thinking, I let go of the sapling and used both hands this time. I plunged my arms into the creek until water soaked my chest, feeling blindly, scrabbling until I had enough purchase to pull him toward me.

I was flat on my stomach, holding him to the bank with force of will alone. With one hand keeping a death grip on the collar of his shirt, I grabbed for the sapling to use as leverage, twisted my body sideways, and wrenched him like a caught fish up out of the water and onto the bank beside me.

I lay on my side catching my breath as he turned and spat out rivulets of muddy river water. His head and arms were drenched with mud, his once-white shirt now brown and transparent, but he was coughing, which meant he was breathing, which meant he would live.

His coughing subsided and he rose to his knees. Only then, when I realized he was going to be okay, did I realize how fast my heart was ricocheting around my rib cage. My fingers were vibrating like someone had struck the bones with a tuning fork.

The entire musculature of my back, shoulders, and arms still screamed with the strain I hadn't even felt till now.

I put my hand on his back. I didn't know if he realized I was there, but I wanted to offer comfort—and also to reassure myself his chest was still moving. "I'm sorry," I said. He sat up and I let my hand fall to the ground. "I'm so sorry. I wasn't strong enough to—"

He stopped me by placing his hand over mine, both of them cold and slick and filthy. "It wasn't," he said, sucking air between words, "your fault."

"Are you gonna be okay?"

He nodded, held up a finger. When he'd caught his breath, he sat up and wiped water out of his eyes with the edge of his soaking-wet T-shirt. Then he took a long, unlabored breath, like a sigh of relief.

He was going to be okay.

We both went in for a hug at the same time, wrapped our arms around each other in a tight, quick embrace. "I'm so sorry," I said again, relishing the feel of his arms around me, strong and secure. His heartbeat was thundering, and I could feel it everywhere we touched. "Are you really okay?" I let go first, studying his face.

"I'll live." He ran a hand through his hair, shaking off drops of water and finger-combing it away from his eyes. "Do you realize what you did?"

"What?" There was a leaf plastered to my cheek; I swiped it off with my shoulder.

"You just. Saved. My life."

I shrugged. "Well . . . yeah."

"You could've died."

My eyes traveled back over to that dirty rushing water. Me dying hadn't been a consideration at the time. "I wasn't going to let that happen. To either of us."

He stared at me like I was an undiscovered species. "I . . ."

And then, a *thwack-thwack-thwack*ing of helicopter blades cracked the sky. We turned as one to see our salvation zoom over our heads.

The camo-green metal bird grew larger and lower in the sky, heading for the rendezvous point that we still hadn't reached.

We climbed to our feet and ran the last quarter mile, Luka seemingly reenergized, and me with nothing fueling my body except the relief that soon this would be over. We hustled across the open expanse of mud and reeds to an open field filled with red indicator smoke. Emilio and Hanna were boarding the helicopter.

We were the last on the chopper. Everyone else was already strapped in. All of them took in our soaking-wet selves with bewildered expressions, but we were too tired to explain.

Then we were in the air.

I couldn't even enjoy the views. As I caught my breath, I had the sinking feeling that Luka and I had come in dead last.

ELEVEN

THEY DIDN'T EVEN let us shower before hustling us down the halls to our evaluations. But in the waiting room, a young woman in cheery pink scrubs made sure we drank lots of bottled water while she took our vitals, and put salve on our burns and bites.

No one really talked. We all kind of eyed one another warily, trying to gauge how each person spent the night in the swamp. No one seemed unscathed. Kendra had welts on her face and arms. Emilio's messy dark curls were matted with dirt, and he looked more unlike his cheery self than I'd ever seen him. Hanna's cheeks and shoulders were an angry red, and she and Emilio weren't even looking at each other.

Mitsuko, a scabbed-over scratch on one cheek and usually immaculate hair filthy around her shoulders, caught my gaze and rolled her eyes—silently summing up her experience being partnered with Giorgia in the wilderness.

Luka and I were called last into Pierce's office, a plain, narrow cinder-block room with no windows and no personal effects.

There were no chairs. We stood side by side in front of his desk, which was piled with orderly stacks of papers and a laptop with the screen turned off.

"And group five," Colonel Pierce said, not looking up from his notes. I tried to peer over and see what was written on them. Probably the exact transcript of every word Luka and I had spoken since we got in that van, with readouts for our body temperature, heart rate, and other biometrics. But he was holding everything close to the vest, so instead I studied his expression, waiting for some hint as to what he was about to say.

His hard-lined face didn't soften. "You were our most promising pair. I have to say, Luka, I'm very disappointed."

I swallowed hard.

"We scored you as a team on a rubric consisting of a variety of criteria, including teamwork, creative problem solving, and wilderness survival skills, among others. Of the five teams, you two came in fourth. A distant fourth," he added disdainfully.

But we'd been the last to the rendezvous point. Luka had almost drowned. The question wasn't who did better than us, but who could have done *worse*?

"You're dismissed," Colonel Pierce said, already looking at another file.

I caught Luka's eye, questioning. He shook his head slightly. He didn't understand, either.

We split up—the first time we'd been apart in almost twenty-four hours. Hanna and Mitsuko had gone ahead of me to the cafeteria. Being alone in my room was almost as wonderful as the forty-five-minute-long shower I immediately took to wash every trace of the outdoors off me.

When I finally joined the others, it was almost sad to see how few of us were left. We were a motley bunch. So many empty chairs, empty tables; the remaining bodies filling them were hunched over their trays.

I searched the cafeteria for Luka but he wasn't here. Feeling strangely bereft, I took a seat between Mitsuko and Emilio. Everyone's plates, including mine, towered with food. Emilio had apparently taken an electric razor to his head, shaving the sides of his hair and leaving a lone strip in the center.

"I never want to do that again," I said. "I'd rather die in a fiery crash. So much simpler."

"Dear God, yes. Let me burn up on reentry rather than endure that BS again." Mitsuko looked a little better after a shower, her face scrubbed to poreless perfection—the wound on her face somehow making her look edgy but no less beautiful.

Emilio shrugged. "I didn't mind it so much, actually." He was more withdrawn than usual, but I chalked it up to exhaustion.

Anton joined our table. "So, are we talking about our rankings yet?" Anton asked.

"They didn't tell us we couldn't," I said.

We all waited for someone else to go first.

"Kendra and I came in first," Anton blurted with a grin.

"We were third. I think stupid Boris and Pratima came in second," Mitsuko said.

"Yeah, well, we were last." We all turned to Emilio, glumly stuffing forkfuls of spaghetti into his mouth.

"What happened, man?" Anton asked.

We waited until he swallowed. "I'd rather not talk about it."

Anton, however, was more than willing to tell us all about *his* experience. He called Kendra over, too, so they could lord their victory over us. Neither one of them had gotten a major win so far, so I didn't mind—I also didn't mind knowing how they did it.

Apparently Anton had basically grown up trekking through the rain forest, and Kendra was into mountain hiking. They couldn't have made a better team. I started to feel a little bit better about the whole situation. Luka and I were still the strongest overall competitors. The leaderboard hadn't changed, but maybe it just didn't reflect our new scores yet.

Luka finally came in just as we were leaving. I waved the others on without me and caught up with him near the door to the hall. "I looked for you," I said and then cringed inwardly. "You okay?"

He was clean and dry, but his face was a little drawn, a little distracted. "Yes. They wanted to check my lungs, to ensure they were clear. I should not suffer any ill effects from my dip in the creek. Thanks to you."

I waved that off. I didn't deserve praise; it'd been a reaction, a bare-minimum response. But now the air was weird between us, the gratitude in him making our relationship off balance. So I changed the topic to the one I'd want to know, if I'd been him. "Anton and Kendra came in first. Emilio and Hanna were last."

That piqued his interest. "Really? Even though they reached the rendezvous point ahead of us?"

"Yeah. That's the mystery. They won't talk about why, though."

It still nagged at me why we'd placed fourth. And he had a point: How could Hanna and Emilio have really done so much worse when they'd made it to the helicopter before us?

Luka focused his attention on the buffet. There was almost no one left in the cafeteria; only Kendra sitting along the back wall, sipping a drink and reading her tablet.

I wavered, shifting my weight. It felt like abandonment to walk away, to rejoin my friends and leave him to a cold dinner alone. He'd somehow begun to feel like one of mine—one of my allies, or friends, or at least someone on my team. And I knew how much it sucked to eat alone. "Hey, do you want—I mean, I already ate, but I can join you if you want? It's kind of lonely in here." And he didn't even have any roommates left, either, I realized.

He gave me a quizzical look. Probably wondering why I wanted to spend *more* time with him, when we'd just been stuck together for twenty-four hours. Probably wishing I'd leave him alone so he'd have a *break* from me. "I'm fine. I'm quite used to eating unaccompanied." A smile softened the words. "But thank you."

Needing to outrun the feeling of failure from our outdoor adventure, I headed to the track late that night, when I thought I'd get to be alone.

But Emilio was already pounding the tread when I got there, the dying sun sending our long shadows to chase each other as we ran out our stresses. He stayed behind me most of the way, until I slowed purposely and he caught up. We jogged together silently, breathing and foot strikes the only sounds we shared. I couldn't help but remember the first day, the long run they'd put us through where I thought I was going to fail. Everyone's sweat combining and evaporating off this track. Particles of ourselves mingling together, escaping into the atmosphere.

The only way I had gotten through it at all was because of everyone else running with me.

Endorphins and exhaustion finally dulled the edges of my emotions. I sat on the outer edge of the track where the grass had started to poke through, feeling the pebbles dig into my skin and the sweat drip down my back, and the amazing feeling of fresh air going in and out of my lungs.

Emilio jogged a few more laps alone, then came to sit beside me. We drank bottled water and watched through the fence as the sun melted red hot into the prairie grass.

After a while, Emilio spoke. "Something's been bugging me."

I turned toward him. He was leaning back on his hands, still watching the horizon. The deep orange light turned his skin to bronze. He could be good-looking, especially in moments like right now. Even his new haircut worked for him. I wondered what had made him do that—if it had something to do with what'd happened out there with Hanna. I wondered what it said about me that I hadn't thought to ask him until now.

And then I thought back to what Mitsuko had said. If I'd ever grow to look at people the way she did. If I'd ever grow to care about people the way Emilio did.

"What is it?" I asked when he was silent a long time.

"I feel like they're keeping a lot of information from us about this mission. I mean, obviously they are, they've said as much. But it's gotta be something major, right? This is so far beyond what I expected."

I leaned back on my hands, mirroring him, blades of grass shooting up between my fingers.

There weren't any walls here. We weren't wearing any wristbands. It felt safe to talk. "I've been feeling weird about it, too."

"Yeah?" He looked at me a second and trained his eyes back to the dying light. "Then I'm not nuts. I mean . . . I was even afraid to talk about this inside the building, in case they're listening. That isn't normal."

I laughed without much humor. "I was just thinking the same thing. Almost every astronaut ever was a trained military pilot, maybe the occasional scientist. And it took them two years to qualify for space. Why the fast track? Why are we so special?"

He sighed. "I really don't know, Cass. We've yet to even

touch any kind of technology that is involved in operating a rocket to space. They're focused more on our brain waves and psychology than us actually knowing how to work a spacecraft. We're not being *trained*, we're being studied."

I picked at a dry blade of grass. "There are going to be real astronauts on the mission, though. Maybe they're counting on that."

"Then what are we, an experiment?"

It gave me a little chill. *An experiment.* Hanna had said it and I had thought it. Now it was coming from his mouth, too.

I wasn't ready to contemplate this. "Not to change the subject, but—seriously, what happened with you and Hanna out there?"

"Cass . . ." I felt for a moment he might actually spill, but then he shook his head. "Sorry, buddy. That's something I've got to keep for myself." His lips pressed together.

My instinct was to let it go. But then I thought back to all the times Emilio had helped me—listened to me vent, given me advice. He didn't have to. He'd just shown up and been a friend, right from the start. And I hadn't even tried to be the friend he deserved in return.

I didn't want to be that kind of person anymore.

"I'm not trying to pry. You've just seemed really down ever since, and I don't like seeing you that way. Are you sure you don't want to talk about it? I could just listen, if you want."

I waited a long time for him to speak again, until the sunlight was gone and the stars twinkled through the indigo-velvet sky.

And then the exterior lights came on, bathing us in an artificial yellow glow.

Then he turned on his side, head propped in his hand, elbow buried in grass. "Yeah, okay," he finally said quietly. "Be nice to get off my chest, I guess. So. I've liked Hanna for a while. Out in the swamp, I took a chance and I kissed her. I mean, we were alone, and I kinda was getting a vibe from her . . . anyway, it was nice at first. We made out for a while, actually. Then, like a jackass, I go and tell her how cool it is that she likes me and how long I've wanted to do that." He groaned and collapsed to his back, rubbing his face with both hands. He kept his hands over his face, muffling his voice. "And she's like, whatever, dude, I was just bored and you were convenient. So that sucked. And then we just . . . argued. She took off for a few hours and left me alone, and I wasn't going to leave her, so yeah. She came back eventually, but we wasted a lot of time being stupid like that. The whole thing was about teamwork, and we showed we couldn't work together for even twenty-four hours."

He sighed heavily, his chest falling with a long, exasperated exhale. His hands fell to his sides, and he was quiet awhile. "You can imagine why I'm not super anxious to tell anyone."

My heart clenched up for him. Ugh, Hanna, why Emilio? He was like a puppy, and she just couldn't resist kicking him. "Hanna does what she wants, other people be damned." He didn't respond. "I'm sorry. It's just too bad you couldn't have been partnered up with someone nicer to make out with."

At least that got a laugh out of him, though it wasn't a

particularly happy one. "It doesn't matter. I don't think I'm going to be here much longer."

My head whipped around but he didn't flinch, didn't even meet my eyes. "What?"

"I'm not going into space. Not this time."

"Why not?" I demanded. "You're doing well in the tests. Everyone loves you. You've had a solid rank this entire time. You—you're great."

He shrugged. "I can't explain it. I'm not giving up just yet, but this place is too intense for me. I don't like what it's doing to me. What it does to . . . everyone."

I stared at his profile, willing him to unsay what he'd just said, and surprised that I wanted him to take it back. How long had he felt like this? "If you're saying this because of what happened with Hanna, it was just one test. Remember what you told her? One test isn't the end. If you want this, you shouldn't give up."

"That's the thing, Cass. I'm not sure anymore." His hands were unconsciously clenching in the dirt. "If I go, I go. I've made peace with it. The only thing is, I'd miss the people here. Anton and you and Mitsuko and . . ." He trailed off.

"Hanna?" I supplied, and then wished I hadn't.

He smiled tightly. "Anyway. Cass, I think you can go all the way. You do the right thing when it matters."

"Stop it," I said. He had obviously created a picture of me in his mind that wasn't true. "I'm not that person. You know that I've never had a friend like you?" My voice got a little too high and frantic, but I couldn't stop. "Before I got here, I thought a friend was someone you competed with on test scores and who kind of agreed with you on who were the stupid kids in class. I'd turn in my classmates for cheating if I thought it would help me. I had this huge complex about how great I was and nobody else was good enough and I—" I flashed back to my classmates, my coworkers. I'd snubbed all of them. No wonder I didn't have any friends. "You don't really know me."

Emilio shrugged it off. "Who isn't awful at least once in high school? You have the capacity to be better, though. You're already better. I haven't seen any of that stuff here. You're not as big and bad as you think you are. That's why I wanted to warn you. I don't want to throw you off your game when I leave."

He gazed skyward, his mind seeming to drift. "Look at all this sky. If it weren't for these lights, you could see Orion pretty well. If we could just jump this fence and hike into the prairie a few miles, I bet it'd be gorgeous." His eyes came back to earth, studying the slender, rustling shadows of prairie grass beyond the fence. "But we're still too close to the city. There's this amazing place back in Colorado. Out in the mountains. The sky is ink black and the stars just look like they're alive. You can't believe how many there are, trillions of stars that are above us all the time and you've never seen them before. That's where I want to go. That's why I came here."

My head tilted back. He was right. I could see Orion's belt and Venus and a waning gibbous, but not much else. "Me too."

"It's almost like a completely different sky. I'll take you out there sometime." For some reason, he seemed suddenly angry. His hand wrapped around a rock and pitched it like a baseball, lobbed it all the way to the fence with a tinkling rattle of metal. "Don't let this place get the better of you, Cass. If you have to get out, get the hell out. There are private companies that can take you into space if you really want to go. It's not worth becoming some . . . secret government weapon or something." Now I could tell he was kidding.

"Yeah, like I could ever afford a private jet to low-Earth orbit."

He grinned at me; his teeth shone for a second in the light, and then he was serious again. He stood, brushing dried grass from his shorts, and offered me his hand. "I'm gonna hit the hay. Are you coming?"

"In a few minutes."

I heard his tennis shoes crunching on the grass, and then I was alone with the sky.

"Good morning, and congratulations for making it this far," Felix said, altogether too cheerful for the hour. We were back on a classroom schedule, bright and early the next morning. But this was new—Felix had never come into the classroom before. "We have touched on the science of meditation and its effect on brain waves. Today we're going to put it into practice."

I fought the urge to roll my eyes, but then he caught my attention. "Let me show you what I mean. Any volunteers?"

Felix picked Emilio and gestured for him to sit in the chair in the front of the room. He fitted a few electrodes to one of the shaved sides of Emilio's scalp.

We sat quietly as Felix coaxed Emilio with soothing tones into a supposedly meditative state and watched the EEG scratch out a change. Emilio's eyelids closed and he looked normal, even bored.

"Now," Felix said, "Emilio is still conscious. Aren't you, Emilio?"

"Yep." His voice was calm but alert. He didn't sound like a zombie.

"But his neural oscillations are slightly different than ours are right now. At the moment all of you are probably in a beta state, alert and focused. Emilio's reading a higher output of alpha oscillations. Which means he's relaxed, but still able to react and respond to outside stimuli. Would you agree, Emilio?"

"Sure, boss."

"Thank you. You may go back to your seat." Felix peeled the electrodes off.

Emilio's eyes opened and he blinked. "Yeah, that didn't feel like much, doc." He moved back into his seat. "Honestly, felt like I was falling asleep."

"Exactly. What we want you to be able to do is enter a state between sleeping and waking. When you sleep, your muscles relax, your blood vessels relax, your body consumes less oxygen. Your digestive system slows down and you need fewer calories. This is the ideal state in an environment where every ounce of mass costs us in fuel. If we can reduce the need for oxygen and chemical energy, we can reduce the load that rocket engines will have to push out of Earth's gravitational pull and increase how long astronauts can survive on a deep-space mission." He cleared his throat, appearing a little uncomfortable. "But we do not want you to actually *sleep*. We want you to be able to maintain some awareness of the outside world. Someone needs to remain conscious on board should anything go wrong. We want to achieve a . . . *hibernation*, of sorts. There's a specific range of neural oscillations we're trying to achieve, and the person who is able to maintain that range without drugs will be a much more competitive candidate."

I shot a sideways glance at Luka.

"Who would like to go next?" Felix asked.

I didn't even raise my hand; I just stood up and sat in the chair next to Felix before anyone else could get there first.

Felix hooked me up and then talked me under, his voice low and soothing. "Picture a place where you feel most relaxed. A sky full of clouds. Hear waves crashing on a sandy beach, wind rustling through trees. Feel your muscles relax. Let go of your anxieties."

All this hippie nonsense was making me angry, not relaxed. It wasn't working. I could tell from Felix's frustrated little murmurs, which he probably thought I couldn't hear, that something should be happening by now.

I rifled through my mind, looking for some memory that made me happy. The first thing I could find was music. I buried myself in the memory of piano notes—the satisfying way the keys plinked under my fingers, the cool, smooth surface of the ivory, the music seamlessly streaming from my brain to my hands to the instrument and then filling the air like bubbles. Taking that indefinable magic from my imagination and making it a reality, a beautiful melody.

The world outside of my body—the tangy smell of Felix's aftershave, the feeling of the cold chair beneath my skin, and the sensation of everyone watching me—all faded like an old photograph. I was nothing but the blackness on the inside of my eyelids and the music inside my head.

He coaxed me out of it after a while, and it felt like I was slowly rising to the surface after being underwater for a very long time. When I opened my eyes, the lights felt too bright, and Felix looked perplexed as he removed the electrodes.

"What?" I pressed. He was looking at me like I'd grown a second head.

"You did it." He swiveled the EEG readout screen toward me and pointed. "Right here, this dip . . . you . . . you've balanced perfectly in semiconsciousness, right where we want you. And on the first try. What were you thinking about?"

"I was just . . ." I didn't exactly want to share my method with everyone. "Relaxing."

"Well, it worked. Good job."

Emilio's mouth was hanging open a little. He flashed me a little hidden thumbs-up without smiling, and I felt a twinge of guilt. Despite what he'd said on the track, I wondered if he'd already given up.

I got out of the chair and went back to my own. Kendra stared at me as I passed. Hanna ignored me.

Luka's expression was unreadable, almost angry, focused on the wall in front of him. We hadn't spoken since leaving Pierce's office, and it felt strange after how close we'd been during wilderness survival. I wondered if he blamed me for his first less-than-perfect placement. But wilderness survival hadn't seemed to affect his ratings at all; Luka was still number one.

Felix examined the readout a few minutes more before he remembered he was supposed to be teaching. "Marine mammals and some avians have evolved the ability to put one half of their brain to sleep while the other remains awake. This way, they do not drown or get eaten, because they are never fully unconscious. The brain is still sending and receiving signals from external stimuli even while the body is in a relaxed and motionless state. We've studied these phenomena for years, and I believe we now understand the type of neurotransmitter that is responsible. The astronauts chosen for this mission will be given this drug transdermally to induce this half hibernation."

He was animated, excited, carried away—but the looks on our faces stopped him, and his countenance changed. "I know how that must sound to you, but if you are uncomfortable with science that has not been fully proven to be safe, you know where the door is."

I sucked in a breath and held it.

They wouldn't need this technology if we were only going

to the moon, or even back to Mars. This was something *huge*. And I was so close.

Felix nodded slowly. "Let's continue. Hanna, would you come up here, please?"

Hanna did well. She maintained the right balance, stayed in control. Almost as long as I had. One by one, the entire class took their turns.

No one did better than me. Not even Luka. He struggled to relax. His brain waves rarely shifted out from beta. He was always alert, and that was his weakness.

No EEG the next day. Instead, we were told to meet at the training pool. Once there, we donned thin, short-sleeved wet suits, our shins and forearms exposed, and gathered like a team of divers a few feet from the water's edge.

I could tell Hanna was shaking just standing next to the pool.

The last time we were here, there were so many of us that I had had to be careful not to get shoved and fall into the water. Now the ten of us were spaced as far apart as asteroids in front of Colonel Pierce and a tall, elderly but athletic white guy in an expensive black suit. His face was plastered into an almost-smile, which was maybe supposed to be reassuring, but the expression was so wooden it was like looking at a marionette. His face was almost shiny in the watery light—like maybe he'd had a good amount of plastic surgery—which didn't help the whole puppet-face thing.

We stood in front of a large silver tube that looked suspiciously like a space-age coffin, propped upright. Except that coffins don't have tiny plexiglass windows in the lid.

I flashed back to class with Copeland, what seemed like weeks ago. The specs she'd shown us. It hadn't been theory. They had actually built this thing. They *actually* had the technology for human hibernation, which they intended to use. And they had, for whatever reason, kept it a secret.

I felt a thrill. That could only mean we were going somewhere far, far away.

"Welcome, candidates," said the marionette-faced man after giving us time to be properly in awe. His smile widened, exaggerating his already-prominent cheekbones, in obvious pride. "My name is Clayton Crane, founder and CEO of the Society for Extrasolar Exploration. I'm joining you today to observe this particular test, because the odd-looking thing before you is something my company built. We call it the Human Hibernation Module, or HHM. It is with this technology that we plan to boldly go farther than we've ever ventured into space." His face held a cheeky grin, and his eyes sparkled in electric excitement.

I found myself sharing a glance with Hanna. She looked a little terrified and a little angry beneath her otherwise stoic mask. This was not going to be easy for her. I looked around at Mitsuko and Emilio, but both were focused on the pair of men before us, Mitsuko's jaw set.

I steeled my will. Mr. Crane was here personally to observe; I had to be the best.

The colonel picked up where Crane left off. "The astronauts on this mission will enter the HHMs after exiting Earth's atmosphere and routing their course, upon which the ship will switch to autopilot for the duration of the flight. Each astronaut will wear a space suit with a specially fitted helmet allowing the computer to monitor their breathing, brain waves, and other vitals. The problem with the vital-sign monitor is that it can't take any action while the astronauts are in the HHM beyond its normal homeostatic capacity. Should there be an emergency, an alarm will sound. A human brain needs to be alert for that alarm, in a state from which it can be easily roused in order to take any lifesaving action that may be necessary. The rest of the crew will be in full hibernation, unconscious. The crew slot you all are attempting to fill will require you to remain in the lightest form of sedation with minimal drug influence, in order to maintain constant communication with the monitoring computer."

The pieces began to fall into place: why we had to learn to sleep with half our brain, like dolphins. Because we were the fail-safe.

"Today we're going to simulate the experience of being inside the HHM. In a real-world scenario, you would be fitted with heart-rate, oxygen-consumption, and brain-wave monitors, just to name a few, and an IV to provide you with nutrients, water, and other things necessary to life, as well as hormones to suppress any nonvital functions and a variety of waste-disposal systems. But today, your face mask will do little more than provide oxygen and protect your eyes. We're doing this today with only wet suits, so you can get the full experience of the cryogel. Don't worry; it's not going to hurt." The way he emphasized the word made me pretty sure he was lying. "The capsules will fill with gel that will help protect you from radiation and micro-meteoroids, and serve as a cushion in the case of any turbulence. Now, once we fit you inside, we'll shut the door and fill the tube. We'll start you off with five minutes, and if you can handle it, we'll go for fifteen minutes so you can get a good feel for the experience."

Emilio raised his hand. "Sir, how long can this thing sustain a human life in suspension?"

"The HHM can sustain human life with a minimum of function for many months, depending on the needs of the mission. We've had successful tests of up to a year and counting. Of course, there are drawbacks: loss of muscle function, visual acuity, mental and physical endurance, loss of microbiome and immune response. But these have all been shown to be tempo-rary." He waved away a hand as if dismissing all of these side effects we would potentially be exposed to. "We are not testing the HHM today. Rather, we are testing your ability to with-stand it. Whichever of you is chosen will not be sedated to the level of the other crew; a part of you will be aware at all times. Some can find it . . . troubling."

Aware. Of being kept alive in a test tube. Not eating. Not drinking. Not moving. For *months*.

I snuck a look at Hanna. This sounded like her hell on Earth. She must be freaking out, but her face was set like it was carved into Mount Rushmore. I waited for her to quit. She must know this was her weakness. But honestly, I had no idea who would be the first one to panic in that small drowning coffin.

Except that it wouldn't be me.

Anton went first. He climbed into the metal tube and the techs strapped a face mask flush against his skin so that it covered his nose and mouth. Then goggles. He looked like a swimmer who needed prescription lenses; the clear plastic encircled his eyes from eyebrow to cheekbone and made him look fish-eyed. The techs gave him something small, and he stuck them in his ears. The mask fogged up as he exhaled, and Anton gave us a thumbs-up.

They shut the door.

It made sense to me now why they included a window in the door to the HHM. Why they would risk a structural weakness in something meant to keep out the unfiltered radiation of burning stars in deep space. Without that window, you wouldn't know that there was anything alive inside the capsule. That window alerted someone to the helpless human life inside.

Not to mention the human life inside, alive and half awake.

From this far away, all I could see of Anton was a sliver of his goggles, of his head turning side to side as he watched the tube fill up with gel, a light blue tint distorting him as though he was underwater. Even as the gel covered his head, he seemed okay.

The colonel started his stopwatch. I counted the seconds.

The colonel's five-minute mark arrived seven seconds after

mine. "Okay, give him five more."

Anton made it the full fifteen without a problem. Apparently satisfied, they started to drain the gel. They wouldn't let him out until it was empty.

When the tech unlatched the door and opened it, Anton stood with his arms wrapped like vises around his torso, and he was shivering like my uncle's little dog in winter. The techs moved in to detach him from the oxygen, and then he practically fell out of the capsule.

One of the techs brought him a towel and quickly got the rest of the gel off him, pieces of the clear blue gel falling in semisolid lumps at his feet.

"It's okay," Anton said through chattering teeth as I moved closer to check on him. "The gel . . . it doesn't hurt. But when it's gone . . . it makes you . . . so cold . . ."

"In practice, the side effects of the gel won't be noticeable, as your skin will be covered with your suit and not exposed to the gel directly. It isn't harmful, however, and dissipates quickly." Mr. Crane's voice was detached and ultrareasonable as the techs led Anton away. "Best to know now, in practice, what it feels like, should there be any sort of malfunction."

I felt Mr. Crane's gaze fall on me and knew what was coming.

The colonel hardly waited a heartbeat. "Gupta, you're up."

TWELVE

I STEPPED INSIDE the tube.

It was actually more comfortable than it looked from the outside. The interior was lined with creamy high-density fabric, very high tech and plush, like expensive car upholstery. There was at least two feet of open space all around me, including above my head. I could only just see out of the window.

Techs strapped a mask around my head, and there was a moment of panic until I felt the oxygen kick in. I strapped the goggles over my eyes and fitted earplugs snug in their places. Secure in the fact that I could breathe, I lay back and got comfortable. This might turn out to be the easiest test yet.

The door closed with such a gentle, quiet click that I barely noticed it.

Then the gel started coming in, gurgling, thicker than water—a little like the consistency of pudding—and unnaturally blue. It slithered up my skin, a little lower than body temperature—like a warm pool. Not as comfortable as bathwater, not as bad as a cold shower. The gel reached my chest and my feet left the bottom of the capsule, my body less dense than whatever the gel was made of.

The moment when the gel reached my neck and inched up my chin, my heart rate doubled. The primitive parts of my brain didn't understand that I wasn't about to drown. *Hurry up*, I thought. The inching of the gel toward my nose was the worst part. It was simulated drowning. I had to fight the instinct to hold my breath and instead breathed deep and slow, drawing my belly button in toward my spine and back out again. *I can breathe. There is plenty of air.*

The gel enveloped my head, finally. And as strange as it was, as claustrophobic as it could have been, the fact that I had a sliver of window to see other human faces helped. The world outside the window was fish-eyed and tinted with the blue of the gel, but I knew there were people out there, watching me, looking out for me, judging my performance. It was both motivating and reassuring.

I felt like I was floating inside a water bed. I closed my eyes, drifting weightlessly inside the HHM. I tried not to think about the fact that I was suspended in gel inside a metal tube.

Despite my slow breathing, each passing second ratcheted up possible panic.

Like someone slowly turning up a dial, my heart rate increased.

Then, *Is there enough air? I can't get enough air. I—I can't get out.*

I found Felix's voice in my memory. *Relax your body, starting with your toes. Feel each muscle tense until you release it. Feel how easily you can breathe in. Breathe out.*

Thinking of Felix reminded me of yesterday, of the EEG. I'd combated that with music. I tried tapping into that well again.

My mind raced to find something to distract me and settled on Chopin, a nocturne I'd played last year at a recital. The rhythms came to me like an old friend, giving my brain something to do. Bit by bit I forgot the anxiety and felt the calm Chopin was famous for inducing. I drifted in the insulating gel, surrounded by softness, eyes closed and sounds muted.

I didn't even notice when the gel began to drain away, until I felt a semicircle on the crown of my head go very, very cold.

The gel drained as slowly as it had been pumped in, and every inch of skin that it left exposed was instantly chilled, as if I'd stepped from a sauna into arctic air still soaking wet. By the time the gel was gone, I was bouncing in place, teeth clacking together like key chains rattling, just barely keeping myself from banging the door open.

Finally the door released, and I stumbled out of the tube. I couldn't control my movements—my muscles jerked spasmodically. My legs quaked so much I had to reach out and grasp the edge of the HHM for balance.

A towel was draped over my shoulder. I grabbed it and held it with iron hands so no one could take it from me. My bones were ice. I was shivering so intensely I thought I'd fly into pieces. Deftly, the techs removed the oxygen mask, the goggles, and the earplugs, because I didn't have enough dexterity to do it on my own.

My eyes found Colonel Pierce. He held the stopwatch in his age-spotted hand and looked at me with an unreadable expression. Mr. Crane was not nearly as inscrutable; his face held a knowing smile, as though he'd bet on me and, against all odds, had won. Made me think that maybe he wasn't just there observing his new invention in action.

The female tech hurried me off through a side door before I could even hear my time.

Three female techs toweled me off in what looked like the women's locker room. When most of the remaining pearls of gel were gone, I began to feel a little more able to control my temperature, but my skin still tingled like I'd been doused in peppermint oil.

"What is this stuff?" I asked, but through my shivering teeth it was hard to understand me.

She wrapped a thermal blanket around me. "Hold on to this for a few minutes until you get your temp back to normal, then you can change into dry clothes."

I stopped her with an icy hand before she left. "How did I do?"

I must have looked pretty desperate, because she relented

when I suspected she wasn't supposed to. "You were in there twenty minutes. I tried to tell the colonel you were only supposed to be inside for fifteen, tops. But he said you were fine."

"I *was* fine," I said, a little in awe. I let go of her arm.

He'd pushed me further than Anton. Did that mean I'd done better? How did they measure our performance?

Or had he just been trying to break me?

I stood alone in the locker room, looking at myself in the mirror. My long black hair dangled wild and limp. My eyes were red and watering. I still shivered uncontrollably. I looked like a half-drowned rat.

But I'd done it.

I went back into the training pool just in time to see the door of the HHM closing on Hanna.

I slid onto the bench beside Anton, who was also dressed in fresh clothes. "Did I miss Luka?"

"Yeah," he whispered back. "They just now got him out. He did the full fifteen minutes just fine."

"Course he did." I watched the capsule, unable to see Hanna's face through the window, only noticing a glint of her blond hair. "I'm a little worried about her."

"Yeah?" He didn't seem to fully remember her incident last time we were here. "She still not good with close spaces?"

"I don't know what it is." My hands balled into fists on my knees. I found myself leaning forward, tense.

Hanna's sudden scream was muffled and terrifying. She

pounded on the door. I could see only flashes of her white skin and pale hair through the window, but it was clear that she was losing it.

I gritted my teeth, hands clenched around the edge of the bench. "He has to let her out," I muttered.

"That's it." Pierce slashed a hand across his throat at the tech. "Kill it. Get her out."

"Now, Colonel, the girl's barely begun. Give her a chance to prove herself," Crane said.

I gaped. Pierce stared back, surprised. The tech froze, halfway between obeying Pierce and obeying Crane.

Hanna stopped screaming. She was now pressed up against the back of the HHM, maybe trying to take control of herself. But it didn't last long. I could see the blue gel filling up to her neck, and that's when she broke, her face pressed up against the window in agony.

That part just before the gel had swallowed me whole—the brief terror that had filled me must be magnified a hundredfold for her.

I was on my feet before I knew what I was doing. "Let her out," I demanded. "You have to let her out!"

Pierce nodded tersely. "I agree. Do it."

The tech looked to Crane, who gave a little shake of his head.

"Let her out!" I ran to the capsule and stopped just short of pounding on it. "Turn it off. Reverse the stupid thing."

Hanna's face was submerged fully in gel. Blue and ghostly and silent now, her face was contorted in pain, eyes closed, as her hands slowly and fruitlessly slapped against the glass.

"Crane," Pierce said, his voice a hammer of authority. "You want to get sued?"

"She's perfectly safe," Crane said, his hands clasped behind his back. "She isn't in danger."

My breath was coming fast, chest heaving—as though I were the one inside the tube, the one whose mind told her she was drowning. "You said you'd let them out if they couldn't handle it." I pointed at the square window where we could see Hanna's panicked face. "She is obviously *not handling it*. There's no point prolonging this."

Crane turned his eyes on me, and I trembled but stood my ground. Not until that second did it catch up to me that I might be jeopardizing my rank for this.

"Go ahead," he said to the tech, coolly. "Take her out."

The tech reversed the gel pump, and slowly it started to empty inside the capsule. The pounding inside slowed and stopped. I looked inside, but all I saw was Hanna's hair hanging over her face, her entire body slumped over on the cramped floor of the HHM.

After what felt like an hour, the door released, and Hanna collapsed into me.

I caught her. Her ribs heaved against my hands as she shivered uncontrollably. My skin started to tingle where it came in contact with the remnants of the gel.

The techs quickly surrounded her, gently moving her away so they could remove her mask and goggles, vigorously toweling her. She was alive, conscious. The anger and panic in me faded.

Hanna sat on the ground, legs splayed, hunched over like she had no muscles at all.

"Hanna?"

She didn't look at me. Two of the techs helped her up and led her out to get changed. I followed. Once we were in the locker room, Hanna stood shivering and ghostly white under the harsh lights.

"Are you okay?" I asked.

Her eyes narrowed on me, glazed over with some mix of fury and defeat. The remnants of her panic stained her face: the whites of her eyes were red, watery. Her lips were grayish-purple from the cold, and I could see blue veins in her temples and hands. Her tone was venomous. "What do you think?"

I held her gaze. Felt the full weight of her rage focus on me. My hackles were still up from confronting Crane, but I fought the instinct to fire back at her. She wasn't angry at me. She was angry at herself. Maybe at Crane. We were alike in that.

"I hope you're happy," she spat. "I'm definitely out now."

No, I thought. *Weirdly, I'm not happy at all.*

"You're wrong," I said. "You were the only other one who did well on the EEG. This fear is just in your head. If you can overcome it, you might still have a chance."

"Really, Cass? You know everything, don't you?" A shaky breath, then, quietly: "There's no coming back from *that*." She turned her back to me, shutting me out.

I'd tried. There was nothing else I could do.

I left her with the techs.

◗ ● ◖

No amount of running made me feel better this time. I went to the gym and kicked around a punching bag for a while. It got the anger out of me, but not whatever dark emotion kept biting at my heels with sharp teeth.

I didn't want to be around anyone. I picked up dinner around four and took it back to my room to wait for this stupid day to end. I wished I had music—anything to distract me. I'd already read the one paperback I brought four times.

I didn't remember falling asleep, but I must have, because the next morning Mitsuko woke me with a pillow smack to the face. "Rise and shine, sunshine! Today is a beautiful new day." Through my bleary eyes I could see she was grinning. "Kendra just came from the cafeteria. We're down to nine."

Hanna.

"You slept through breakfast," she said.

I shot up. "Why didn't you wake me?!"

She stuck out a hip and planted her hand on it. "You were tossing and turning all night; I thought I should let you sleep." Then I noticed the plate of food on the nightstand: a bowl of steaming oatmeal, scrambled eggs, and toast. I turned back to give Mitsuko a sheepish apology.

She smiled. "You think I'd let you starve?"

Our instructors didn't give us much time to regroup. I had little chance to even think about Hanna. They hit us hard, all day long.

Jeong drilled us with engineering schematics and computer sims of in-flight emergencies. Dr. Copeland gave us pop quizzes on medical emergency scenarios. Even in Shaw's class our thoughtful discussions turned into relentless tests.

There were no computer simulations or theoretical schematics with Bolshakov; in his class, we had to build, disassemble, and repair electronics by hand, without instructions. And Bolshakov just watched, silent as a ghost, as we struggled to figure it out for ourselves. He'd give us a head start and then go to complete the repair himself—but by the time he'd finished, I was standing in front of him, holding my assembled piece while everyone else was still scrambling.

The change of expression on his face, from the smug assurance he was about to school us all, to shock and grudging respect—it gave me life. I could've forgone food and lived off that look for a week.

The relentless pace and my triumph in Bolshakov's class helped me forget about the day before, forget about Hanna and Mr. Crane and the whole thing.

At dinner I started eating without a word to anyone else at the table, my inner monologue a mantra of the facts I'd learned so far that day. It took me a minute to realize everyone was staring at me.

"Uh . . . Cassandra?" Anton tried to get my attention. "You may want to turn around."

His eyes were focused high, looking up at the leaderboard. I stopped midchew and whipped around in my seat.

Cassandra Gupta 2

I stared at it so long I forgot there was food in my mouth. When I swallowed, I coughed.

When I turned back, Emilio was smiling. Mitsuko looked a little aghast when she thought I wasn't looking, but then managed to give me a smile, too.

In those few seconds I had memorized the numbers. Luka, still strong and steady at number one. His only faults so far had been at the EEG and the wilderness survival, but that must not have been important enough to dock him points. Maybe I was coming close to overtaking him, for once. Or maybe those girls were right, and this competition was somehow politically motivated, giving Luka an invisible upper hand.

I'd have to show them my edge. Convince them that choosing anyone other than me was a mistake.

After me was Kendra, then Anton, with Mitsuko and Emilio lagging behind. Giorgia, Pratima, and Boris made up the last three slots.

Hanna's name being absent gave me a little stab of some murky emotion, which I ignored. But even seeing my name higher than it'd ever been before, I didn't feel the way I'd thought I would. Not satisfied—okay, maybe a little. But undeserving? Embarrassed?

I should not be feeling those things.

Emilio was overall great at everything and had an attitude to match. He was creative, energetic, never complained. He could be a little annoying sometimes, but he got along with everyone, and I'd already seen how valuable a skill that was.

He'd been more down than usual lately, but I was sure that was a temporary thing.

Anton could lift two of me over his head and went out of his way to help other people, to the point of absurdity. Kendra I didn't know so well, but she was whip-smart and more than capable. Mitsuko was a born leader, not afraid of anything or anyone. Me, I might've had better brain waves than everyone else, but just the day before I'd had a confrontation with the guy in charge.

If the EEG testing was so important that my success had me jumping over everyone else, why was Luka still number one and why was I still only in second place? I'd even stayed in the HHM longer, too.

I didn't understand this. I didn't understand anything at all.

That night, Hanna's bed was made and empty. There was no trace that she had ever been there at all.

THIRTEEN

WE HAD A couple more days of class at the same breakneck pace. I was pretty sure our instructors were intentionally ramping up the stress.

I was on my way back from breakfast with Mitsuko, mentally girding myself for another day of rapid-fire questions, when it happened.

Mitsuko hit the door first, hand trying the knob. It rattled uselessly in her palm. "Uh. Why the hell is our door locked?"

Nobody had keys. No one locked their doors.

I tried the one next to ours, which had been empty since the last cut. Nothing.

Mitsuko half groaned, half laughed. "Here we go again. What is it this time?"

All nine of us had been in the cafeteria for breakfast. As the others returned in ones and twos, they joined us in confusion. Every one of us was locked out of our rooms.

Once everyone recovered from their respective heart attacks, speculation abounded. Were we being moved, or were some of us going home? Was it another test? It had to be another test.

Ms. Krieger eventually came to get us. We followed her down the halls past the classrooms, far past any doors I'd ever had reason to enter, and through a set of double doors into a massive gymnasium, two stories tall and big enough for four basketball courts, though there were no hoops in sight. Sound seemed swallowed up in its vastness. Sunlight streamed onto the concrete floor from the high, narrow windows lining the far wall. I could see nothing but a thin strip of blue sky near the ceiling. I imagined that maybe they used this place to test drive Mars rovers or the moon buggy—set it all up with the proper environments, obstacle courses, the works—but right now it was repurposed for us.

Our fate, I surmised, had something to do with the large white pod in the middle of the room. It looked retro sci-fi, like all those digital renderings of future Mars habitats back when we thought we'd never get the money to do that. The dome was about twenty feet tall and not quite twice that around.

There was something like a submarine hatch at the end where we stood.

Ms. Krieger, the colonel, and Felix were there, along with a couple of techs in dark blue NASA flight suits.

Ms. Krieger spoke. "Welcome, everyone. This is the Simulated Living Habitat, based on actual models for use on Mars, albeit adapted for our use here. You'll be staying here for one week. Once inside, you may not leave without also leaving the program."

Nervous excitement fluttered in my chest.

"This is designed to simulate the actual experience you'd have living in cramped quarters with your crew members, only you'll have the luxury of gravity. You'll eat here, shower here, and use the toilet here for the next seven days. You'll be constantly monitored, given a variety of tests, and we will be in communication regularly via the radio."

Felix stepped forward, his expression carefully neutral. I could feel a tiny trickle of sweat drip down my sternum. "I don't have to explain to you that this is meant as a stressor. But it is a valid stress, and one that you will encounter if you are chosen for this mission. Tempers will flare. Nerves will fray. We expect some of that from everyone. But out of concern for your safety, any violence will be grounds for immediate expulsion from the program. We do expect you to work through any disagreements yourselves, peacefully, as you would have to do in space. You're all adults."

"If, at any time, you decide this isn't for you, simply hit the red button next to the hatch and it will open. You'll be on the next flight home." Colonel Pierce surveyed us coolly. "Anybody want to back out now?"

Nobody did.

The two men in navy flight suits were part of our "Mission Control." They spent the next half hour demonstrating how to use the shower, toilets, and emergency controls. We were each given a pack that included toiletries, underwear, and identical blue flight suits, and told we'd have no laundry service for the duration of our stay.

And suddenly—all too suddenly—they had crawled out of the hatch and were closing us in.

There was a rush to claim bunks. I didn't particularly care where I was, so I just slung my stuff onto the first free bed I saw. Emilio moved to claim the one beside mine, but Boris got to it first.

"What, you wanna sleep next to your girlfriend?" Boris grinned lewdly.

"Nah, I'm fine, dude." He went to the next bunk over.

Boris wasn't exactly my favorite person, but I didn't care. It was time to show what I was made of.

The bunks were all in a row, no partitions, no privacy. The beds were small and narrow, the mattresses and pillows equally thin. We each had one drawer under the bed and a narrow shelf next to the bed with a tiny lamp, to be shared between the bunks.

A shelf and a drawer, and the two-foot radius between my bed and the beds on either side of me. That was it for personal space.

Four guys. Five girls. One bathroom.

For a tense couple of minutes we all looked at one another,

wondering how we were going to change clothes in front of everyone.

Luka solved the problem for us by simply turning to face the wall, stripping to his boxers, and redressing in his navy flight suit without any attempt at modesty. The way he acted like he was the only one in the room, there wasn't even anything sexual about it.

It was one thing to change in front of other girls. I wasn't going to be topless in front of all these guys, especially Boris. I left my undershirt on and zipped my flight suit up over it.

Mitsuko plopped down beside me, forcing me to make room for her on the narrow bed. "Geez, I'm sitting on like half a butt cheek," I said.

"Oh, whine." Mitsuko pulled something silky and red from her shirtsleeve, wadded it up, and tossed it behind her to land on the bunk she'd claimed. Anton's eyes went wide, making Mitsuko and me laugh.

We had no tasks for the evening, so a few people wandered into the living quarters to check it out. Mitsuko, Emilio, and Anton hung out with me. It felt like a sleepover—at least how I imagined one might be, never having been invited to one. A mixed-gender sleepover, which was even more interesting. I allowed myself some small measure of enjoyment, listening to Mitsuko and Emilio trade jokes and barbs.

This wasn't going to last. The novelty of being here was still fresh—it felt a little silly, like camping in your own backyard and pretending you were in the wilderness.

This was a test to see how well we could get along with others in tight spaces. I was going to pass this one with flying colors.

The lights dimmed by half, the signal that we had five minutes left before simulated nighttime. The people on and around my bunk dissipated—too slowly. I wanted sleep. I needed time alone in my brain for a while.

I used to have problems sleeping, back before I started running. I guess because I was an only child, I never had to get used to noises and strange things going on when I was falling asleep. I got around it when I was older by exhausting myself physically. But today I hadn't been able to run.

When the lights went out completely and I was finally alone, I lay on my back and stared at the curved darkness over my head and realized I would not be able to sleep. For a while I listened to other kids in the room toss and turn on squeaky metal beds. A few bouts of snoring. A few whispers and giggles. The sounds tapered off to a steady white noise of sleep-breathing.

My eyes adjusted to the dull yellow safety lights in the floor, barely bright enough to do anything but keep you from tripping. I closed my eyes again and imagined I was flying through orbit at that very second, but that only made me feel more awake.

Mentally I went through each of the other candidates sleeping around me, invisible in the dark. I weighed them against myself with all the scientific impartiality I could muster. Could I do better than them? Yes, I thought. Most of them, yes.

Emilio? He had better social skills than I did. He was in

good shape. Mitsuko, too. But I had more drive. I was smarter, at least on paper. I had nothing holding me back to Earth like Mitsuko did, no sentimental attachment like I imagined Emilio would have; I had the ruthlessness and ability to think on my feet. Mitsuko had that, to a fault. Pratima was smart, capable, but prickly. Anton was athletic, sociable, not so good with tests. Kendra was smart, strong, and worked well with others, but didn't shine in the EEG. Boris was just a jerk.

Everyone had a weakness. Even Luka.

Luka had consistently performed at the top of the class and acted like he was bored most of the time. Could I do better than him? Physically—maybe not. Mentally, I thought we were evenly matched.

But time would have to tell how we might match up in other ways. Maybe he panicked under pressure. Maybe I was more creative. Sociability? I had made friends, and Luka spent so much of his time alone. But how much would that matter, in the end? There were just too many variables, and too many of them unknown at this point. Luka himself was entirely an unknown, a variable unto himself. He hadn't picked up the EEG skill quite so quickly, but I was willing to bet that was a temporary setback.

If I was making the decision—and if I was being honest— Luka seemed to be the right choice. But that didn't mean I was going to stop trying to beat him.

In the quiet, with no one watching me anymore, my thoughts focused on home. Somehow in the dark, it didn't hurt as much to imagine my family living their lives without me. What were they doing right now? Were they thinking about me? I could see Gauresh watching TV on the couch with his yappy little dog. Dadi tucked into the recliner, knitting. Papa reading his tablet, Mama on the phone with one of her sisters. That had been my every night at home. I'd usually be sitting beside Uncle, fighting over what to watch next, or sitting at the coffee table working on homework with his dog Saachi in my lap. It'd been oppressively, embarrassingly boring at the time. And I was happy to be here—I *was*. But I couldn't deny the twinge in my heart when I thought of home.

Dadi would pray for me: to Parvati for protection and Saraswati for the pursuit of knowledge and to Ganesh for luck and the removal of obstacles. Maybe she was praying for me right now.

That thought—of home, of Dadi telling me I would make my own destiny—finally helped me close my eyes.

And then the alarms screamed.

FOURTEEN

LEGS TANGLED IN the blanket, I tumbled out of bed, my hands and knees slamming into the floor with a sharp smack of pain.

Red lights flashed in the darkness. I saw faces, moving limbs—glimpses of the same panic that I felt—bathed in split-second blinks of red, like a living horror movie.

There was rushing, shouting. I yanked the sheets around until I was free, then I was up, unsteady on my feet, dizzy. No one seemed to know what they were doing. I stood still until I could block out some of the shrieking alarm and think.

The control panel in the kitchen. That was the only thing I could think of that might have some kind of switch to shut off the damn alarm. I made my way slowly down the bunks, feeling for the feet of the metal beds so I wouldn't break a toe or knock my freshly bruised knees.

Someone collided into me, banged my shoulder hard. It was Mitsuko, the whites of her eyes drenched with the bloodred light.

"The kitchen," I shouted near her ear, but I had no idea if she could hear me. I kept stumbling forward. I couldn't tell if she followed me or not.

A few of the beds I passed still had bodies in them, sleeping with pillows pressed over their heads. I rolled my eyes. *Don't worry, I'll fix it for you.*

Somehow I reached the control panel. I couldn't read any of the labels, so I just started flipping switches and hitting buttons without any expectation of success.

Suddenly there was another presence beside me, a large dark shape. I had to crane my neck to see his face, and in the flashing light, I realized with a start that it was Luka. He must have had the same thought I did. He didn't look at me, but scowled at the panel and punched a large red sphere at the top of it.

The sudden silence made me think I'd gone deaf.

There was a smattering outbreak of applause and half-hearted cheers. The sleepers grumbled and turned back over in their bunks.

I looked over at Luka, but my eyes were still adjusting to the darkness, and the details of his face were unreadable.

"Thanks," I said.

He nodded tersely.

"What was that?"

"*That,*" he said, "was the fire alarm."

The speaker right in front of my face crackled to life, making me jump. "Houston to SLH. Apologies for the false alarm. No action required on your end. Over."

Those bastards knew very well what they were doing. I had no doubt that alarm was meant expressly to make us lose sleep and put us on edge.

Luka hit the reply button. "Understood. Over."

He took his thumb off the button, and I could feel him looking at me in the dark. "False alarm," he repeated. "The first of many, I'm sure."

I smiled. "Maybe we should take shifts."

That earned me a little chuckle. "Great idea. You can get the next one."

Luka went back to bed. I certainly wasn't going to be able to get back to sleep, so I took a shower while I had the chance for privacy and went to explore the other half of the SLH. The SLH was one large dome, with the bunks separated by a thin wall from the living and working space. The kitchen and bathroom were side by side, near the entrance hatch. A control panel, with screens and readouts that were mostly blank, took up an entire wall beside the kitchen.

The living space consisted of chairs and tables, even a small gym that contained a few weights, a stationary bike, and a treadmill. A large screen took up a good part of one wall, but it wasn't a TV—at least not one that we could figure out. There were no books, no windows, no clocks. Nothing to help pass the time.

Seven days living in an isolation dome with eight people and nothing to do.

Challenge accepted.

The others woke in spurts after the lights came back on for morning. There were a few short squabbles over the bathroom, and a few grumbles about the alarm, but all the kids who were left knew by now that every action and every complaint was being observed, dissected, scrutinized. Everyone was intensely conscious of the fact that this SLH was something actually designed for use in space, and if someone couldn't handle living there, then they needed to give up now.

Food came in shrink-wrapped trays through a port in the wall three times a day. One plastic tray for each of us, identical except for special dietary concerns. I was impressed that mine was vegetarian.

This wasn't a vacation, however. Our hours were scheduled down to the minute. That day we were to fill out psychological evaluations, which consisted of essay questions and complex tests trying to ferret out any defect or propensity for falsehood. In the afternoon, the screen in the living quarters came to life—its purpose now apparent—and someone from Mission Control walked us through hypothetical emergency scenarios, quizzing us on what actions we would take.

We each had to spend two hours per day exercising, which was tricky, considering there were two machines and one set of weights for nine people. I solved the problem by finding a free patch of floor space and doing some yoga.

In the evenings, after dinner trays had been put back into the port in the wall and everyone had finished their paperwork, we were allotted an hour of free time. But there was precious little to do. Someone had found a deck of cards in the living space— maybe forgotten about, maybe left there on purpose. So people made up games using the only supplies we had: the paper from our psych evals.

Mitsuko tried to get me to play cards, but when she found I didn't know any card games, she huffed away and asked Kendra.

I was tapping my fingers on the table, daydreaming about playing piano, when I realized the music I was tapping along to wasn't coming from my own head.

Am I losing it? I quashed that thought before it could finish forming into words.

Of course not. There *was* music in here.

Slowly, keeping an eye on the others, I rose out of my chair and made my way around the living quarters, trying to figure out where the sound was coming from. It never got any louder than the quietest whisper, but I recognized it: Beethoven. The Moonlight Sonata. One of the most famous pieces of piano music in the world, and no one else heard it? In a room full of people with enhanced senses?

Unbelievable.

The music followed me all the way to bed, never getting louder, never closer. By lights-out I was beginning to think I might be in danger of losing my calm.

I lay in bed, sheet pulled up to my chin, and talked myself out of it. I closed my eyes and imagined I was sitting in the auditorium at school, listening to a concert.

It wasn't until after breakfast the next morning that someone else spoke up about it.

"Does anyone else hear that?" It was Boris.

A few people mumbled, shrugged. Emilio tilted his head to one side, listened intently a second, and said, "Yeah, I think so. Maybe?"

"Oh, for God's sake. There's an easy way to figure this out," Mitsuko said. She pushed herself out of her chair and went to the intercom. "SLH to Houston," she said. "This is Mitsuko Pinuelas. Question for you."

Crackling on the other end. "Go ahead, SLH."

"Are we hearing music in here?"

There was a pause. "Confirmed."

Mitsuko waited for an explanation. When one wasn't forthcoming, she rolled her eyes and hit the button again. "Houston, confirm *this* for me: What is the purpose of the music?"

Another long pause from Houston. "Don't want you kids getting bored in there."

Mitsuko shook her head and mouthed something I couldn't understand. "Thanks. That's all."

The music wasn't the last surprise NASA had in store for us, and it was probably the best one we were going to get. Giorgia ran out of the bathroom later that day complaining the hot water had gone out. Nothing but lukewarm came out of the shower from then on, no matter what anyone did.

The air was too cold, then too hot. The radioed instructions to fix it were purposely confusing, frustrating, and the radio kept cutting out. The toilet stopped flushing for an entire seven hours. Dinner was late, and then my shrink-wrapped plate contained a turkey sandwich, which I didn't eat. Emilio and Mitsuko gave me bits off their plates.

By the end of the second day, Giorgia had left the SLH, and the program, for good. Didn't discuss it with anyone, just walked up to the hatch and hit the red button. Gone.

Getting woken up in the middle of the night became kind of routine. It was always something. Lights coming on at midnight, unexplained noises, "emergencies" that we had to get out of bed and fix with instructions from the intercom. Night missions where we had to do repetitive tasks until someone nearly fell asleep standing up. One morning the lights never came on and we spent our day mostly in the dark, doing paperwork by the glow of the emergency floor lights.

Then we were tested: Mountains of paperwork came in through the port, each with a time limit for us to complete. Exams based on topics we'd discussed in classes the week before. History tests comprised of previous space missions: what had gone wrong, what had gone right, what lessons we could learn from them. Personality tests, which I started out enjoying and quickly came to hate.

No mail came for anyone, which wasn't a surprise. There

was also not a second where we did not have music pumped in through the speakers.

Ironically, the music became the thing that kept me sane. It changed often, sometimes the same pieces repeated, but almost always orchestral. Classics like Rossini, Tchaikovsky, Handel, and Bach mixed with relatively modern works like Sousa and Yo-Yo Ma and even a few experimental and modern pieces that were brand-new.

At dinner, we ate together at a table bolted into the floor while string quartets played quietly in the background. The strings lent an air of elegance to our artificial, shrink-wrapped meals that I enjoyed. I happened to catch Luka, sitting at the head of the table, his fork poised in midair like he'd forgotten it. Grimacing. The muscles in his jaw worked like he was quietly grinding his teeth, like he was in pain.

I wondered if I should say something.

Someone else beat me to it. "You don't look so good," Anton said. Anton was a genuinely nice guy—he really looked concerned. "You feeling sick?"

Luka seemed caught off guard for only a second. He pushed himself upright and the distaste left his face. "No. I'm fine."

Pratima twisted around to look at him. "Something wrong with your food?" She seemed less concerned, more intrigued, as if she was hoping he'd been poisoned.

Luka shook his head as everyone turned to look at him. Something was wrong with Luka, the man who hadn't left first place since day one? We watched and analyzed his every move.

But he looked fine now. Then there were a few shrill strokes from a violin, and Luka winced as if the sound physically pained him.

Forks dropped onto trays.

"You got a headache, man?" Emilio asked, putting a hand on his shoulder. "There's ibuprofen in the cabinet."

Luka shrugged it off immediately. "I'm fine, thank you."

The music, I realized. That was the only variable that had changed.

I said nothing. But I began to watch him a little more closely.

"There's just something weird about him," Mitsuko whispered to me later, during our hour of free time. Luka had disappeared to his bunk right after dinner without a word to anyone.

"So it's weird that he's good-looking, tall, athletic, foreign, and doesn't like classical music? God, it's just too bad he isn't perfect."

She didn't seem to notice the sarcasm. "Of all people, Cass, you're defending him? I admit, he may be hot, but who hates classical music? Especially you. I thought you played, like, four instruments."

I fisted then stretched my fingers. It'd been so long since I'd played, I hardly felt like a musician anymore. "Piano and violin. I tried trumpet but I was no good. You have to do weird things with your mouth."

"Whatever. You get my point. There's something off about him, that's all. I can't believe you don't see that."

I had to poke her to make her lower her voice. "So what? People have quirks. I don't like him for it, but it doesn't matter." I sighed. "Music or not, he'll probably be the one they pick."

Mitsuko snapped her head toward me and grabbed my shoulder. "Don't say that. If they wanted him they would have picked him by now. And he is not perfect. He's too . . . calm."

"I don't see how being *too* calm works against him."

"Like, he must bottle up his emotions. People like that are unstable."

I inhaled deeply, looking toward the bunk where Luka was. I didn't get that vibe from him at all, but how much did I really know about him? Next to nothing, despite our time in the wilderness.

Mitsuko's dark eyes bore into me. "I'm serious. Don't throw in the towel just yet."

The lights dimmed for the five-minute warning before lights-out, and we went to bed.

FIFTEEN

NINETY-SIX HOURS IN, seventy-two to go.

I kept meticulous count, but even so I couldn't believe it had been only four days. Sleep deprivation gnawed at the edges of my sanity. I walked around in a constant state of tension, my jaw tight and my hands clenched.

The eight of us left developed a schedule for showering so that we each got one shower per twelve-hour period of "daylight" while still allowing breaks in between so people could use the toilet. We imposed a ten-minute limit on ourselves, not to save hot water—that was gone for good—but to keep the toilets free as much as possible. Then there was a schedule for exercise. There was no worry about who would make dinner or do dishes—that was all done for us—but there were scuffles over whose turn it was to play with the sole deck of cards, who took longer than their allotted time to shower, who had left the bathroom a mess or left their dirty clothes on someone else's bed.

True colors began to show. Boris, who the week before was only aggravating, became a bully inside the SLH. Even Pratima, usually even-keeled, snapped at me when I reached across her at the breakfast table, and Mitsuko could jump on anyone if she was in the wrong mood. Emilio and Anton, the peacemakers, were constantly trying to put out the little fires that erupted between people pushed to their breaking point.

Luka kept to himself and remained cordial. I tried to follow his example.

The sleepovers centered around my bunk stopped. I was glad. It was the only way I could deal with never having any privacy except for ten minutes a day in the shower. Each of us drew farther apart, becoming little islands unto ourselves.

It was surprisingly easy to forget about the outside world. Before long, I stopped even thinking about it.

During the day, we were so busy, I could distract myself with the work; even if it was mind-numbing and often pointless exercises, it was complex enough to need my full attention. I dreaded the nights. I would lie awake listening to the combined sleeping sounds of all the people I was stuck with, trying to force my tired brain to stop churning, waiting for the midnight disturbance that was sure to come. It seemed useless to try to sleep when I knew at any moment we might be jerked awake.

Mitsuko, Emilio, Luka, and I agreed to take turns responding, but eventually Mitsuko stopped getting up, and Emilio was so out of it when he woke that he was useless. So it was me and Luka, mostly, taking turns dragging ourselves out of bed.

I fought to stay awake, knowing as soon as I closed my eyes the alarm would blare, but it was late in coming that night. Mission Control had established a pattern and then had broken it. One more thing that was getting under my skin.

I couldn't stand it anymore. I got out of bed as quietly as possible and made my way toward the kitchen. There was no food there, only packets of water you had to suck out of a plastic pouch. But I took one and sat at the kitchen table, my bare feet already tingling cold.

I sat scrunched with my knees to my chest, keeping my toes off the metal. Beethoven was still playing in a whisper over the intercom, a piece so mournful it was as though all four instruments were crying in harmony. I felt numb to it all by now, with only a vague sense of homesickness.

Bleary-eyed, I hardly noticed the shadows moving in the other tube until a human shape emerged out of the living quarters.

I jumped to my feet. The shadow stepped forward, over an emergency light, which illuminated him from below.

Luka.

He just stood there, quiet, looking as surprised to see me as I was to see him. "Can't sleep?" The words escaped like a breath, unintended. "Everything okay?"

"Yes." His voice was a baritone murmur. And just when I

thought that was all the answer I'd get, he added, "And you?"

"Yeah. I'm fine. Just waiting, you know. For the . . ." I spun my finger in the air, indicating the sirens. "You know. The 'emergency.' What are you doing up?"

A corner of his mouth tightened, like he was considering whether or not to tell me. "Pacing," he admitted. I flashed on what Mitsuko had told me sometime before—that Luka was the type to keep his emotions bottled up until they exploded. Was I witnessing the foreshock? His whole body seemed tense as a violin string. Even his fingers drummed against the top of the metal chair in a restless cadence.

I gave a nod, and the silence between us was filled with the music of mournful strings and a shared understanding. We were both trying to cope with the stress in our own ways.

He gestured toward the empty living quarters, and we sat side by side on the couch in front of the screen, shrouded in darkness.

Then he turned his eyes full on me and it felt like everything froze. "I never thanked you for saving my life. Back in the wetlands, when I fell into the creek—you pulled me out. I did not thank you then, but I have been grateful to you ever since."

For some reason I stood up, like I meant to do something in response, but wasn't sure what. "You would've done the same."

"Yes, I would." His eyes held an unreadable emotion. "But not for that reason."

"For what reason?" I was too tired to be dealing with this.

"If you had gone into the water instead of me, I would have

also tried to save you. But not because I had expectation of help in return."

"What? You think I saved your life so you would owe me a favor?"

His face changed suddenly, shadows rearranging, light reflecting the whites of his eyes. "No. Not at all. I'm sorry, my English . . . I'm sorry. Please, forget I said anything."

"Is that what's bothering you?" This was as close as I'd come to piercing the veil around Luka. As I tried to understand, wishing my enhanced eyesight was just a tad bit more super-human so it pierced the darkness and read all the details of his features, he broke his intense gaze and looked away. And even in the shadows I could see how open his countenance was—more vulnerable and raw than I'd ever seen, well, anyone.

His voice was so quiet, the music nearly covered it completely. His tone changed, his words coming slowly and hesitantly. "Do you ever feel, even when entirely surrounded by other people, that you are utterly alone?"

A cold hand clenched around my heart and squeezed. "You're not the only one," I said quietly. And then, because it didn't feel like it was enough to simply say the words, I reached out and put my hand on his shoulder.

He glanced up at me, seemingly taken aback. I let my hand drop. But then his face changed into an almost-smile, grateful and surprised, and I felt better for having done it. "Thank you, Cassie."

◐ ● ◑

I awoke in my bed with harsh pseudo-sunshine in my eyes, startled and disoriented. The others were ambling around their morning routine, getting the breakfast trays, waiting on the bathroom.

I couldn't even remember going back to bed, and yet somehow I'd overslept. Even with all the commotion and the lights on. Nobody had even tried to wake me.

Not until I zombie-walked into the kitchen did I realize there had been no alarm last night. Unless I'd slept through it. Which also didn't seem possible.

Had last night even been real?

The memory of reaching out in the darkness to touch Luka's shoulder felt too real to be a dream. And it was definitely not something *I* would ever dream.

At breakfast, he gave no outward sign of our midnight meeting. No acknowledgment, not even a smile.

Maybe I really was losing it.

As the day wore on, I convinced myself that the midnight conversation with Luka had been a figment of my imagination. He was pleasant but polite to me, not overly friendly.

The remaining time passed in a blur of routine, until we were a day away from freedom. I hardly slept at all. Sometime tomorrow they were going to let us out, and it seemed like every fault in everyone in this tube with me had been magnified a hundredfold. I hated every snore and grunt of every sleeping person. I hated the air I had to share with them. I hated their breathing noises and their combined body heat drifting over me, which may have been a construct of my own imagination but was annoying anyway.

My impatience was a living, breathing, *seething* thing.

The thought of that hatch door opening, running out of there and breathing fresh air, was both wonderful and awful. I couldn't let myself think about it very long.

SIXTEEN

BREAKFAST. THE LAST day.

No one was talking.

Oh, we were all civil on the surface, maintaining the illusion of cordiality. But inside, we were all counting down the seconds until the hatch door opened again. Which should be any minute now. Eating, chewing, waiting for the magical hour that we would be released.

It seemed our last test was one of boredom.

There were no tests today. No instructions sent through the radio or the video screen.

Absolutely nothing to occupy our minds except for the card games and exercise, which we were all sick of.

Hours passed—or so it felt like. My jaw ached from grinding my teeth.

What was taking them so long?

I paced up and down the two tubes. I passed Emilio and Mitsuko holding up cards but not really playing; they were staring at the hatch more than their cards. Anton was doing push-ups while Boris lifted weights. Luka appeared to be packing his clothes, folding them meticulously. Pratima, cleaning a kitchen that was already spotless. Kendra in her bunk, staring at the ceiling.

And then the fire alarm went off.

I met Mitsuko's gaze and we shared the same incredulous expression. *Really? This old trick again?* We'd done so many fire drills it was basically routine. This was their last big test?

Still, everyone rushed to the kitchen just as Mission Control opened the radio channel. "SLH, your system is showing a fire in the oxygen garden. I repeat, a fire in the oxygen garden. The fire has been contained but the ventilation system has automatically been shut down. You will need to manually restart the ventilation system within one hour or life support systems will fail. The oxygen garden has been sealed to prevent the fire spreading. You must use the ventilation shafts and the tools in your kit to repair it."

Now this was more like what I was expecting. The grand finale.

Mitsuko hit the return-call button. "Mission Control, what do you suggest for our plan of action?"

"Stand by for instructions. Over." The connection went dead.

Tense, we waited, frozen in place. It seemed no more than six rapid-fire heartbeats went by before Mitsuko hit the button again. "Mission Control, do you read me? Over."

She took her hand off the button and we heard nothing, not even static.

I became very aware of the blood rushing through my ears.

"Houston, do you read me?" Silence.

Her voice took on a higher pitch. "I repeat—do you read me?"

As if in response, a high-pitched wailing shriek began to blare, terrifying as a tornado siren from back home. It wasn't the fire alarm—by now, everyone knew that one by heart.

Everyone covered their ears. "What is that?" Boris yelled.

I searched the control panel. A tiny red light was blinking above a gauge. The thin white dial was just starting to touch a field of red.

I had the best vantage point. I leaned in close, studying the near-empty dial, and called up my memory. We'd studied the meanings of all the buttons and dials, but I'd assumed the read-outs were fake, or at least measured things that didn't apply to our simulation. I mean, we were on Earth, with food and light and gravity—99 percent of these things didn't apply to us. I'd never paid much attention to the readings before now.

Tiny white letters below the gauge gave me the answer. *Oxygen.*

My muscles tensed.

"What?" Boris asked.

I pushed the flashing red light and the siren cut off, leaving an echo ringing in my ears.

"It's oxygen," I said, still not totally comprehending. I focused on Mitsuko's worried eyes. "That's the low-oxygen alarm."

"But . . . the alarms go off all the time. They're simulations," Anton said.

I pointed to the empty gauge. "I don't think this is faking."

Everyone craned in close to see. Then four hands hit the radio call button at once.

Mitsuko glared at the other three and shouted into the mouthpiece. "Houston, this is SLH. We're showing danger- ously low levels of oxygen. Please verify the situation and issue instructions."

Mitsuko tried again. And again.

There was no one on the other end.

"They cut us off," Luka said, his face grim.

We looked at one another, all of us wearing the same incred- ulous expression. Would they really do this to us?

Then almost as one, we looked at the hatch door.

Boris and Anton were closest—they dove toward the door. The red button that was supposed to release the hatch—the red button that had opened the hatch for Giorgia just days before— didn't respond.

Anton stepped back and gaped at us, stunned. Boris shouted a curse in Russian and kicked the hatch, resulting in nothing but another shout, this time of pain.

"That's impossible," Anton said. "This—the hatch—the radio—it's all . . . it's impossible!"

My mind flew to the *Apollo 1* disaster. Three astronauts,

trapped on the launchpad during a simulation, burned to death while surrounded by people who couldn't get to them in time. Just like us.

My lungs seized up.

"It's not impossible because it's happening," I said, my voice pitching into hysteria. I had to be rational. Force myself to reason it through. "Whether this is a test or not, we have to do something; we can't just sit here. We might have less than an hour of oxygen left."

"But *how*?" Emilio muttered. "How do we not have air? We're on Earth!"

I knew the *how* didn't matter. What mattered was *what do we do about it?*

My mind raced. What tools did we have? Precious few. There were no windows to break. Only steel between us and the outside. There was another hatch door in the kitchen where our meals arrived three times a day, but it was about three inches high and locked until our meals were ready. Maybe there was a hidden way out that we didn't know? If we were trapped, our only other option was to do what Mission Control had instructed and climb through the air shafts to turn the vents back on. But in all our tests, there had been no scenario like this. We had no manual, no instructions, nothing. I didn't even know how to get into the ventilation shafts.

Luka met my gaze. I read in his face the same thing I was feeling: desperation.

"We need schematics," I said. "We need a map. Who has that

packet they gave us the first day, with all the diagrams?"

"That one with a thousand pages?" Emilio said, his black eyebrows creased together. "I—I still might. Let me go look." He raced to his bunk on long, flying strides.

"Tools," I said. My breath was coming so fast now it was almost hard to catch it. "Where are those?"

"Somewhere in here," Luka said. Anton and Pratima were already moving, opening drawers and cabinets.

"Got it," Pratima said, holding up a black fabric case.

Emilio came flying back to the kitchen, trailing loose papers. He slammed the packet down on the table, a textbook's worth of technical specs they'd given us as study material. We each dove into the pile, spreading papers around the table, trying to find something, anything.

Then the radio crackled to life. "SLH, this is Mission Control. Do you read me? Over."

It wasn't just Mission Control—it was Pierce! Joy surged in my chest. I had never been happier to hear that man's voice.

Everyone's hand went to hit the reply button at once but Mitsuko got to it first. "Yes!" we chorused.

"Listen, kids." Pierce spoke quickly; his voice had an edge. That was what made my skin prickle. He'd never, ever called us kids before. "Something's gone wrong. A computer glitch or some horseshit, we don't know exactly yet, but the hatch is sealed tight and we can't get to you. We're working on getting you out but it's going to take longer than you've got. The fire was simulated but somehow the computer thinks it's real. Your oxygen vent has been sealed off from the outside air and we can't override it. You'll have to work fast—get to the oxygen garden and to the control panel there." He paused and added, "This is not a test. I repeat, not a test. You have less than thirty minutes."

Every inhalation felt suddenly strained. Every lungful of air, not enough. Epinephrine flooded the synapses between cells, skyrocketing my heart rate, blood pressure, breathing. I glanced over my shoulder and locked eyes with Luka. His pupils were dilated, lips pressed together, bloodless and pale.

Pierce continued. "Listen close, I'm gonna go fast. There's an opening to the ventilation shafts at the rear of the sleeping quarters. Find the toolbox under the meal hatch in the kitchen, unscrew the vent cover, and send some people through the shaft to the mechanical room. The oxygen tanks will be there, and once you restart them you'll have plenty of air until we can get through the hatch. But you need to do it now and you need to do it *fast*."

Survival instincts kicked in.

Orders received, we raced to the end of the sleeping quarters. Anton and Boris together took off the vent cover, revealing a pitch-black opening in the wall about two feet across and three feet high.

"No way am I fitting through there," Boris said, shaking his head. And he was right: at six feet and some change, neither Boris nor Anton, and definitely not Luka, were going to get very far through that shaft. A quick survey confirmed it: even with my designer genes, at five foot seven I was still the short-est person there.

"I'll go," I said quickly. "No one else can fit."

"I can," Emilio said, stepping up. He gave me a reckless grin. "I'm about as tall as you, Cass."

I gave him a dubious look. "It'll be tight, with both of us."

He shrugged, the grin never fading. "Can't always let you have all the fun. I'll be your backup." He shot a look to Luka, as though asking if that was a good idea. Luka had been in the lead for so long, I guess it was kind of expected he would know what to do. "Just in case."

"Fine, just do it fast," Luka said. To me, quietly, he said, "Don't let him slow you down."

Anton scrambled around in the toolbox for a minute before pulling out a handful of items. A screwdriver, a wrench, a crow-bar, a flashlight, and finally, a couple of walkie-talkies.

No tool belt in sight, Emilio and I shoved the tools through our belt loops, and Emilio clipped on his walkie-talkie.

"We'll relay instructions from Pierce through the radio," Luka said, holding up the other walkie-talkie.

"As long as the connection holds," Mitsuko said darkly.

Luka stepped close, putting his hand on my shoulder. "Good luck," he said.

"Don't need luck," I said, adjusting the crowbar and screw-driver for maximum portability. "Just need time."

"Good luck," he said again, with emphasis.

I crawled in first on my hands and knees, leading the way

with the flashlight held in one hand. The light jerked and splayed with each movement, but for now I needed it only so I wouldn't run headfirst into any sudden stops.

The shaft was hot and airless. I ignored the sweat trickling down my back and the hair falling in my eyes, thinking only of moving forward to the oxygen garden.

By the time Emilio and I were fully ensconced in the dark recesses of the shaft, we'd already used about ten minutes of our thirty-minutes-give-or-take oxygen allowance.

"I know this is a life-or-death situation" came Emilio's halting, huffing words from behind me, "Which is why I am not going to make any jokes about staring at your ass."

Only Emilio could make me smile in a situation like this. "Try to get Luka on the radio."

A few seconds later, the static gave way to Luka's calm voice. Just hearing it made my heart slow, if only for a few seconds.

"Pierce says the shaft will go slightly uphill until you reach an impasse. At this point you should be directly above the mechanical room."

Above? But I'd worry about that later.

The slightly uphill section was, in fact, like trying to climb a steep metal slide. After the third attempt ended in me sliding back into Emilio, I made myself stop and take off my shoes— bending like a pretzel to reach them in the narrow confines and then kicking them back past Emilio, despite his protestations.

My bare feet found better purchase than my knees did on the slippery metal, and I shimmied up the incline like a spider.

But halfway up, my sweaty hand slipped and dropped the flashlight. It banged and reverberated all the way down until I heard Emilio shout, "Ow!"

After a few seconds of scrambling where I was held hostage by the impenetrable darkness, the flashlight beam found me. "Go on, Cass, I'll spot you."

I climbed the rest of the way until I came to a small landing. I was blind without the flashlight, but my bare feet told me that I was crouched over a metal grate. I put a hand out, testing, and made it only a foot or so before hitting another grate. We'd come to the dead end.

Emilio scrambled up behind me with his shoes tied by the laces and dangling around his neck—why hadn't I thought of that?—and the flashlight in his mouth, rescuing me from the darkness.

The two of us were huffing and puffing now, our breaths commingling. How long had it taken us? I had been too distracted to count the seconds.

I did a quick self-check: a little breathless and light-headed, but whether that was exertion or oxygen deprivation, I couldn't tell.

In the bobbing light of the flashlight, I could finally see that the wall we'd dead-ended into wasn't really a wall: behind the grate was an industrial-size fan, about as wide as I was tall, blades still and silent. Over our heads was its twin, also dead.

"Ready?" Emilio asked, a reckless grin spreading across his face. He'd aimed the light straight down, revealing the grate that I'd felt with my bare feet. His brown eyes shone wild in the darkness, his Mohawk a haphazard and sweaty mess. "Only way to go is down."

The grate was unlocked. All it took was some uncomfortable maneuvering to make enough room to lift it. The dark hole it revealed was even less inviting than the opened grate back in the sleeping quarters: round, pitch-black, and only slightly wider than my own body. I'd have to tuck in my arms and slide down the vent feetfirst.

"Just like a waterslide," Emilio said. "Like those big loopy ones at water parks. Only without the water. And with a little extra terror."

"I hate water parks," I muttered, and, hoping against hope that this would lead to where I needed to be, I clenched my jaw and pushed myself down the rabbit hole.

SEVENTEEN

I LANDED ON my feet but, unprepared for the shock, immediately fell backward with a painful thud. Back up, I hopped aside. Not a moment too soon, because Emilio came sailing down the chute behind me, crashing to a stop in the same space I'd occupied a second before.

The flashlight clattered to the ground and broke open, useless. But we didn't need it anymore. This room was lit with brilliant sunshine.

For a second we were both motionless, staring in awe at the windowed ceiling. Warm and buttery sunshine filtered in from the outside world, from the room where the SLH was parked. It was the most beautiful thing I'd seen in a week.

Then I looked down and realized where we were: on top of

one of two tanks, each easily twelve feet tall, so massive they took up half the room.

I spared one last glance upward at the glass ceiling. If only we could reach it—break the glass. Thinking quickly, I took the heavy iron crowbar from my belt loop and threw it with all my strength upward at the glass.

The crowbar bounced harmlessly off the glass, and a metallic clang echoed in the small space as it fell to the floor somewhere below.

I should've known. That ceiling could probably stop a meteorite.

"Cass . . ." My attention was diverted. Emilio was still prone, one hand cradling his side, groaning. "I think I broke something."

He'd landed worse than I thought. I knelt at his side, gave him a once-over. No bleeding, but he groaned louder and sucked in a breath when I tried helping him to his feet.

No time!

"I'll live," he said, but his voice was weak. "Go do what you gotta do."

Hesitating only a nanosecond, I left him, taking the walkie-talkie with me. I found a ladder built into the side of the tank and climbed down into the small room. A few rows of bare metal tables filled the small space. There was a door on the far side, but it was locked.

My foggy brain tried to piece the scene together. The functions of the SLH had been in one of the million manuals they'd given us to study. This was a mock-up, a practice habitat. But in the real one—the one designed for humans to live on Mars—they would grow their own oxygen here. The tanks held water, both potable and to use as a backup source of oxygen. But ours had been modified for use on Earth. No need for plants or electrolysis of water. Instead, a vent drew in air from outside.

"Cass, what's happening? Where are you?" Luka demanded over the walkie-talkie.

"I'm here," I said, my voice weak. Talking suddenly required a lot more effort. My lungs were working hard to draw out every molecule of oxygen they could.

"You have to manually open the valve to let in the air. Should be on a wall near the tanks."

Fighting hard against the dizziness, my unfocused eyes wandered around the room before finding an orange control panel and beneath it, a hand-wheel crank. That had to be it.

"Give me a minute," I said into the walkie-talkie, and then dropped it with an unspeakably loud *clang* onto a metal table. Emilio groaned again from the top of the tank.

I grabbed the crank and pulled with both hands. It didn't budge. Not enough air to fuel my muscles. They were hypoxic, useless.

I breathed quickly in and out through my mouth, purposely trying to hyperventilate, hoping to infuse my blood with as much oxygen as possible. If this didn't work, then using up my air quicker wouldn't really matter.

I gritted my teeth and put every ounce of strength into my arms.

The crank groaned, released. Gasping, I spun it open as fast as I could, spots dancing before my eyes.

Nothing was happening. I reached for the walkie-talkie, missed, stumbled and fell to my knees. My vision was going gray. My head felt like a helium balloon, floating above my body.

I reached up to the table with both hands and felt around blindly. *Yes!* My fingers hit hard plastic, wrapped around it. "Opened," I gasped into the radio. "Didn't work."

There was a moment's pause. I laid my head against the metal table and listened to my heart struggle to keep going.

The metal was pleasantly warm from the sunlight.

I closed my eyes.

"Pierce said you will need to open the control panel and turn the ventilation system back on. Cassie? Do you hear me?"

His voice sounded different. Distant.

I was so tired. Maybe I could lie down on this table and just rest for a few minutes.

"Cassie? Stay awake, Cassie! You have to turn on the ventilation system! We are almost out of oxygen!"

Oxygen. Right. That's why I was so sleepy.

But Luka, he was still awake. This exertion might kill me before the others. But I was their only shot.

A picture bubbled up through the fog of my brain. Mitsuko strewn like a discarded doll on the floor. Luka, back in the kitchen, slumped down in his chair, the radio fallen at his feet. Emilio, who'd gone quiet on top of the tank.

Without me, they would die.

I dragged myself to my feet. My heart pounded painfully in my ears as I felt my way back to the control panel.

"I'm here," I whispered into the radio. "What do I do?"

He recited a code to access the vent system. I punched the numbers dutifully, following his instructions, utilizing every bit of brain activity I had.

For a long time nothing seemed to happen. I collapsed into a heap, my legs unable to support me anymore. Blackness took over my vision, and briefly the world went away.

But not before a mechanical whir reached my ears and I felt a cool breeze rustle my hair.

EIGHTEEN

"A COMPUTER MALFUNCTION," Krieger was saying. Her voice was high and nervous, her hands doing almost as much talking as she was. "Improbable accident. We are most definitely going to find out what happened."

Krieger's flitting hands settled as she crossed her arms in front of her chest. Her fingernails, painted into pink, sharp tips, dug into the sleeves of her silver brocaded suit jacket.

I sat perched on the edge of a cot in the medical wing. Mitsuko sat beside me, her warm presence a comfort even as we shared dubious expressions. They'd insisted on everyone being evaluated by a doctor, so despite the fact that I felt fine, I was stuck there until the white-coat had finished with Emilio and made her way over to me. And since Emilio was the only one with an actual injury, the rest of us were going to be there awhile.

I could see them, way over in the far corner—Emilio shirtless and prone in bed, wincing, as the doctor palpated around his ribs, where a dark red bruise had begun to form.

Krieger had come rushing in not long after we'd arrived, with Pierce hot on her heels. They both stood at the end of the cot where Mitsuko and I sat. Luka stood beside me, Boris and the others clustered on the opposite side of the bed.

"That was no accident." Pierce froze her with a look that seemed to physically shut Krieger's mouth. He had his arms crossed, too, but his short-sleeved T-shirt revealed ropy-muscled arms. I'd never seen him in casual wear. He was actually wearing sweatpants. "Someone hacked into the system and put it into total lockdown. The simulation was never supposed to involve an actual oxygen-deprivation scenario, and the hatch door should never have been locked. These kids—who are under NASA's protection, by the way—were in real danger, Ms. Krieger. Your boss and I are about to have some words."

Pierce turned his gaze to us, the mottled and sad-looking former crew of the SLH, and it softened considerably. The fact that he'd just said all of that in front of us meant he was either too pissed off to care, or thought we deserved some measure of truth.

After the oxygen had come back on, I'd been able to make it back up to Emilio on top of the tank, but from there we were stuck. The ventilation shaft had been too high to reach, so we were the last to be "rescued." Emilio had had to be carried out of the hole they'd cut into the side of the living quarters with a blowtorch.

Pierce had been the one to carry him.

I was starting to soften to the old jerk.

"You kids sure you're all right?" he asked. Mitsuko and I shrugged and nodded. I could tell Boris was about to speak, but Mitsuko glared him into silence.

Luka stood behind us and the bed, refusing even to sit. "We are unharmed, although someone intended the opposite."

"Believe me, I'm no more happy about what happened than you are," Pierce said, his voice grave. "You'd better believe I'm going to find out what really happened." He sent a pointed look Krieger's way, unfolded his arms, and left.

Not till Pierce was out of sight did Krieger relax. "Well, now," she said, putting on a shaky smile. "Aren't we glad that's over?"

"How could you let this happen?" Mitsuko pressed. "We could've been killed!"

The pasted-on smile grew bigger, Krieger reaching a hand toward Mitsuko as if to comfort her. Mitsuko batted it away, and Krieger pretended not to notice. "Rest assured, we'll launch a full inquiry into what happened. But, my brave young souls, space travel is inherently dangerous. You knew this before you began."

They definitely weren't telling us everything, and it was

clear they weren't going to. I just wanted to get back to my room, away from all the people I'd seen entirely too much of, and be unconscious. For a long, long time.

"You'll have the rest of today to do as you please." Always the optimist, Krieger switched tacks. "A nice day to rest. Catch up on your beauty sleep!" She bit her lip in a rare show of uncertainty. "This may change how we proceed with the rest of the competition," she said, as though she was thinking aloud. "I will have to discuss this with Mr. Crane. He will not be pleased." Then, as if she remembered she was surrounded by a gaggle of tired, bruised, and very unhappy people, she put her happy face back on. "I'll have the cooks prepare a marvelous spread for you all. We'll pull out all the stops."

We were dismissed.

Finally, after a hot shower, I was in my bed, with a full belly of the decadent breakfast food that they'd delivered straight to our rooms. I closed my eyes and waited for sleep to take me. I hadn't had a full night's sleep in a week, and even though it was barely noon, I fully expected to be unconscious in seconds.

But I stared at the ceiling for twenty minutes, sleep eluding me.

Probably because Mitsuko seemed unable to stop pacing. And ranting, oblivious to the fact that I was trying to sleep.

"That *woman*," Mitsuko began. "Emilio has a broken rib and all she can say is 'Oops, sorry, you knew what you were getting into!' We almost *suffocated*. During a routine *simulation*."

"I know," I muttered. "I was there."

"Pierce seems to think something's up. So what's with Krieger and this cover-up bullshit? I'm telling you, Cass, if I don't get some straight answers—"

I sat up. There was no way I'd get to sleep now, anyway. "You're right," I said. "Let's go talk to Pierce. If he's correct that this was deliberate, we have a right to know."

Her mouth formed a hard smile. "I knew I liked you, Cass."

We met Emilio and Anton in the hall, carrying a tray of food to their room. "Hey, where you going?" Emilio asked.

"To get some answers," I replied.

Confusion knitted his brow. "Do I even want to know?"

"If you do, you'll come with us," Mitsuko replied.

He hesitated, looking down at his tray. There were two plates piled with pancakes, eggs, and bacon, which wasn't weird for Emilio, but also two cinnamon rolls at least the size of my fist.

"Didn't they bring food to our rooms?" Mitsuko asked with a raised eyebrow.

"I wanted seconds. Hey, I earned it," he protested. "Anton has to carry my tray because I can't."

"You fell down and bruised some ribs," Mitsuko said. "Big whoop. Cass just about died trying to save us."

"Hey, I helped!" He hesitated a moment, looking between Anton and the plates of food he held on the tray. "Okay, fine," he said to Mitsuko. He pivoted on his heel to follow us. "Just— leave me some pancakes, all right, Antonio?"

"No promises," came Anton's voice as he and the food disappeared into their room.

At his office, Colonel Pierce appeared haggard, and about

as annoyed as I'd expected to see us all appear at his door. But to my surprise, he stepped aside and invited us in. Mitsuko stormed in, clearly ready to demand some answers. Emilio and I filed in quietly behind her.

His utilitarian office was unchanged from the last time we'd been here, except for the narrow fold-up cot wedged in across from the desk. The makeshift bed was much smaller even than our own, with obviously slept-in bedding. Copeland had made a point of telling us the RAs didn't sleep here. Maybe Pierce had made an exception.

"You sleep here?" Emilio asked, bluntly stating the obvious.

Pierce merely sighed, a long and tired sound, and I felt suddenly bad for intruding on his personal space. He sat at his desk facing us, leaned back, and steepled his fingers. "I take it Krieger provided very little information."

That put Mitsuko off balance. "Well, yeah."

"Figures. She's all about PR, and this could rain shit down on her company if the public finds out. Which they will not. We have this place locked up tighter than a nuclear submarine." He looked grim. "At least, I thought we did."

"Was it a malfunction, sir?" Emilio asked.

Pierce shook his head slowly. "I do not believe so."

Emilio lowered his voice. "Sabotage? Do you have evidence? Should we be worried? Is someone trying to derail the mission?"

Pierce gazed steadily at us, expression unreadable. "Someone who knew what they were doing wanted to make it look like an accident. But there was no way that hatch locked on its own. No way the radio went out by accident. Someone would have had to hack into our simulation computers and override our fail-safes. Look, I'm going to level with you kids." He leaned forward on his elbows. "It will take a lot of time and manpower to comb through our code to trace the origin of the hack. We can't guarantee your safety. We're going to try. But whoever did this might try again."

Pierce leaned back. "We've locked down this wing to only those closest to the project: me, Krieger, Crane, Felix, and your instructors. Tomorrow you kids will have a day off while we figure out how to proceed."

I looked at Mitsuko.

"That's all?" Mitsuko asked.

Pierce's mouth twisted to one side and he shrugged. "Best I can do. You know where the door is."

"Thanks for nothing." Mitsuko clenched her fists, huffed loudly, and stalked out the door.

The two of us lingered, unsure whether to follow.

"We appreciate your candor," Emilio said, surprising me with his formality.

With Mitsuko gone, Pierce became almost gentle with us. He heaved another sigh and looked suddenly tired, his age showing. "Is there anything else I can do for you kids?"

"Thank you," Emilio said. "You saved our lives. If you hadn't told us where to go . . ."

Pierce lifted his chin, and for a moment I saw a glimpse not of the hero I'd worshipped for years, or the cranky taskmaster, but of the man who'd left the first human footprint on Mars and survived to tell the tale. "Your safety is my responsibility. But you kids saved yourselves. I expected no less."

"That was weird," I said as we walked back to our rooms.

Emilio gave a snort of agreement and paused by my door. "You want to hang out with us? It's just me and Anton. I'm gonna try to see if they'll let us watch TV or something. Play the sympathy card. Worth a shot, right?"

I offered a smile. "Thanks. No offense, but I think I need some time alone."

He shot me one back. "Yeah, yeah." He glanced up and down the hall, then leaned in closer to me. "You did good. Back . . . there. Sorry I screwed up and left you to do it all alone."

"You didn't screw up. You were wounded in the line of duty; they should give you a medal." That made him laugh, then wince and grab his side. "How are your ribs, anyway? Mitsuko never even gave me the chance to ask."

He shrugged and lifted a corner of his shirt to show me the wicked purple bruise stretching over his side. "Maybe a hairline fracture. Gave me a shot so I won't even notice how much it sucks until later."

There was a moment of awkward silence between us. "I couldn't have done it without you," I said quietly. "Thank you."

He gave me a smile and squeezed my shoulder, then went back into his room.

I lingered in the hall. And before I could question what I was doing, I was knocking on Luka's door.

He was lying on top of his made bed, reading from a small,

well-worn paperback. I wasn't surprised to find him alone. He hadn't had roommates since before wilderness survival.

It was strange how normal he looked. Why we had all regarded him as a god for the first two weeks, I didn't know. He was just like the rest of us. Maybe a little stronger, maybe a little luckier—but that's all.

"Hi," he said, sitting up and marking his page. He seemed mildly surprised, but not uncomfortable with my intrusion. "Come in."

"I was just . . ." Why had I come? *Think of a reason, quickly!* "Wanted to see if you were up for a run. I can't . . ." I gestured vaguely toward my room.

Luka stared at me for a second, then sprang up soundlessly. "I could do with some fresh air."

Maybe it was some lingering effect of the hypoxia, or the exhaustion that had sunk into my bones, but I just couldn't muster enough energy to actually run. Instead, Luka walked with me around the track at a leisurely pace. A cool breeze hinted at the coming fall, and I almost wished for a jacket.

His quiet company was welcome. Silence had been hard to find inside the SLH.

Soon, though, he gave me a sidelong look and asked, "Are you all right?"

"I'm fine," I replied. "We all survived without any lasting effects."

"Thanks to you." He stopped, and so did I. "We were relying on you."

"I was relying on *you*," I retorted. "Your voice? On the radio?

It was the only thing that kept me moving. My vision was going. I was . . ." I shook off the memory. "By the way, how were you so calm and composed? I was so close to blacking out."

He shrugged both shoulders, eyes focusing out into the black night beyond the fence. "You were in a small space. Less air. And I did not have to do anything more exhaustive than speak into a radio."

"I'm glad it was you," I said quietly as we headed back inside. "Anyway. You know what I mean."

The corner of his mouth perked up. "You would have done the same."

Hearing my words echoed back to me, my cheeks flared hot. "So we're even now."

He shook his head. "No, no. This is twice you've saved my life."

"It's not a competition."

"Isn't it?" He smiled to show he was joking.

There was a subtle shift between us. A mutual understanding. *He's your competition*, a voice in the back of my head reminded me. *You still have to beat him.*

"Thanks for walking with me," I said as we neared our respective doors. "I think I might be able to sleep now."

He hesitated; then he took a few steps back toward his room. "See you later."

I went back to our room, where Mitsuko had gone to take a long, and I presume very hot, shower. I turned out the light, crawled under the covers, and was asleep in seconds.

NINETEEN

TRUE TO KRIEGER'S word, they left us alone the rest of the day. And the next morning, she was waiting for us in the cafeteria. Her pantsuit was a subdued gray, her face a little pale. She wasn't wearing as much makeup as usual, and her hair wasn't teased in her usual glamorous updo, but pinned at the nape of her neck in a little bun. And for the first time, she was wearing a set of glasses, brown plastic with rectangle frames.

Once we had all gathered, she said, "I just want everyone to know that we are taking what happened yesterday very seriously. We are still deep in discussions about how to proceed with the program. Classes are suspended today." She touched her glasses self-consciously. "Let me reiterate that there are inherent dangers in a mission such as this, even in training.

And that you are all free to go home, should you choose to do so. There is no shame in it."

I found myself looking at Emilio's profile, but his face gave away nothing.

An entire day off was a luxury I hadn't thought possible. We spent it lounging outside on the grass under a blue sky studded with pearly clouds, lounging in the sunshine. Mitsuko and I brought out a handful of bath towels from the empty rooms and spread them out on the grass. Emilio and Anton were right behind us, balancing plates heavy with mounds of finger foods, all stolen from the cafeteria. We soaked up every second of sunlight we could.

Luka joined us, which surprised me. He sat apart, as he usually did, reading the same book he'd been reading last night. Up close, in the light, I realized it was *The Count of Monte Cristo*, in the original French. Unbelievable.

"God, I forgot how amazing the sun felt," Mitsuko said, leaning back on her elbows and tilting her face up to the light. She was wearing aviator sunglasses and had her long black hair loose down her back.

Anything we asked for in the RA office, they provided, save electronics. The guys had requested a football and were playing in the field in front of us. I'd stopped by there to see if I had any mail from home, but they told me no. I didn't believe them, but it wasn't like I could do anything about it.

"Hey, Suko?" I asked.

"Mm?"

"You get any mail lately?"

"Haven't checked. Why?"

I shrugged and lay back, using my hands as a pillow. "No reason."

Mitsuko turned to her side and squinted at me. "Waiting for something from home?"

"Yeah, actually. I haven't heard from anyone in a long time."

"I'm sure they wrote you. NASA is probably just holding all of our mail until the selection so we don't get distracted. I wouldn't worry." She turned back around and adjusted her sunglasses.

Emilio, huffing and red-faced, dropped to the grass in front of us and downed a bottle of water. Anton came trotting up behind.

"You guys should come play football with us," Emilio said.

Mitsuko waved him away vaguely. "Mm, no thanks."

He turned to me. "Lola?"

I wiggled my fingers. "Musician."

Emilio rolled his eyes. "Girls!"

Kendra stood up and brushed off her shorts. "Football? I'll play."

"Different kind of football, Kendra," Mitsuko said without opening her eyes.

"Ah. American football. Never mind." She sat down again.

Somehow everyone else was able to enjoy themselves. I smiled at the appropriate times, but there was a coldness inside of me that wouldn't thaw. I'd dreamed about the SLH in the night. I couldn't stop reliving it. Going over the details. The valve, the hatch, the radio. Had someone really hacked all of these things, set it all up with the express purpose of locking us in a metal tomb with no way to call for help?

And why?

Mitsuko went inside, citing the sun and something about her complexion. The weather was pleasant, and we had plenty of food and bottled water, so the rest of us stayed until the sun grew too hot.

When I finally went back to our room, Mitsuko was standing over her bed, facing away from me. She didn't turn when I came in. I took a few steps and realized what she had been doing.

Her suitcase lay open, partially packed on her bed. She hadn't heard me come in and she was bent over a pile of clothes on her bed, folding and packing them. Her hair was a curtain, concealing her face.

"Why?" I already knew. But I wanted to be wrong.

Mitsuko looked up at me, and her eyes were filled with tears. "Hey, Cass," she said, her voice breaking like glass underfoot. "I'm going home."

I felt suddenly unsteady. My hand reached for something to hold on to.

She smiled sadly. "I want to. After what happened back there? I just really, really want to go home to Michael. I got a clear understanding of the risks they're asking us to take, Cass. I want to go back and live a normal life. Even if it's boring in comparison. I'm okay with that."

I tried to say something. I don't know what. My eyes were fiery hot.

"Oh, don't do that. You're so close, Cass. You're so close." She came and pulled me into a hug. "I think you can make it. You're a good one. One of the best. Be braver than me, okay? Promise me you won't give up."

I shook my head. "I won't."

"Good."

"You . . . ," I began, forcing speech around the lump in my throat. "Thank you. For all your advice. For looking out for me." The words I was saying weren't the right ones. They weren't nearly enough. If I'd just had more time to think, I could've done this good-bye so much better. "You and Emilio . . . you're like the first real friends I've had."

She smiled sadly. "That's like the sweetest and saddest thing anyone's ever said to me." Then she nudged me with her shoulder. "Right back at you."

"When . . ." I took a breath to steady myself. "When do you leave?"

Mitsuko looked hopelessly back at her suitcase. "Now. Whenever I finish packing. I want to get it over with, you know? Like a Band-Aid. Rip it off and get out of here and on a plane home. But I can't seem to concentrate. I just keep . . . *standing* here . . ."

"I got it," I said. I picked up one of her shirts and started folding. "I'll help you."

Mitsuko gave me a teary smile. "One of the best, Cass."

When she was finally packed—I didn't realize how many skin-care products that girl had brought—Mitsuko said, "Don't tell the others. Not right away. Wait till I've left, okay? Wait as long as you can."

I nodded, swallowed hard. "You'll write me? Promise?"

She smiled and tousled my hair like I was a kid. "You know it."

It was all I could do just to say, "Thanks. Thank you."

She smiled, tears spilling into the creases in her cheeks. "Good luck."

I shook my head. "Do you . . . do you want me to walk with you?"

"No. I'll be okay."

One last hug and she walked out of the room and down the hall. Then she crossed the red paint, through a door I was holding strong not to follow.

I sat on my bed in my empty room—my *private* room—and looked at each empty bed. The one beside me, which had belonged to Giselle for one night only. The places where Hanna and Mitsuko had slept and complained and studied. How had all of this happened in only a few weeks?

I'd expected to outlast them all, and I had. I'd had so much hubris. That I didn't need friends or want them.

I'd been wrong. And not for the first time.

If I made the cut—if I, somewhere down the line, was launched into space on a journey that would take me out of the sight of Earth, it would be the most alone I'd ever be. I'd have to be okay with that. With being alone. Maybe forever.

And it was harder now than I remembered it being.

A couple of hours later, probably around dinnertime, some-one knocked on the door. Emilio, come to check on us, since we hadn't shown up for dinner. Only there wasn't an "us" anymore.

"Hey." His face was carefully neutral as he peered into the room. "Is Mitsuko here?"

Then I realized he had a backpack on his shoulder. "Oh my God. You too?"

"Too?"

"Mitsuko left two hours ago. She dropped out. Voluntary withdrawal."

He covered his face with one hand. "Oh, shit, Cass, I'm sorry. I didn't know." He dragged his hand down his face, cupping his mouth. "Please don't hate me. But I was just coming to say good-bye. I'm going home." At the look on my face, he smiled. "It's okay. It's what I want. And once I'm gone, you'll hardly remember I was here."

"Liar."

"Hey, buddy. Don't cry. I'm not, see?" And he didn't seem upset. Tired, maybe. But there was a ghost of a smile on his face. "I get to go home and see my folks. It's good news."

"Not for me." Then I remembered. "That night on the track—you were saying good-bye, weren't you? I just didn't realize it."

He gave a sheepish look and a shrug. "I knew I wasn't cut out for this place, but that shitstorm in the SLH just confirmed it. I guess Suko felt the same. It's not like I'm giving up on my dream, either. Turns out, this just wasn't it."

I put a hand over my mouth and nodded. Tried to rein myself in.

"Just like her to forget to say good-bye to me." He took hold of my shoulders, studied me. "Come on, kid. Buck up. Look on the bright side—you're down two competitors."

I shook my head. "I never thought of you as competition."

"Gee, thanks." He grinned. And as I tried to explain myself, he waved his hands to brush it off. "It's been fun, up until that last part. But I'd break my ribs all over again if I had to. For you, and all the others. Well, except maybe for Boris."

"I'm going to miss you." It sounded so lame, and yet I had to say it, had to, because when was I going to get another chance? This was the good-bye with Mitsuko all over again. "So much. You don't even know. You're . . ." I struggled to find a single word that could sum him up, and instead the only thing that came to me was, "Honestly, you're the first genuinely good guy I've ever met. You know, I didn't come here looking to make friends. But I'm really glad I met you." I swallowed around a growing lump in my throat. "You . . . you make me want to be a better person."

Emilio seemed taken aback, his face full of some emotion I couldn't read. And then he touched his chest, over his heart, and motioned me toward him with his other hand. "Come 'ere, Cass."

I took a step closer cautiously, and he hugged me. I hugged

247

him back automatically, being careful of his broken rib. My heart thudded, thinking this was all happening way too fast. I wasn't prepared for him to disappear, too.

He kissed my cheek before pulling away, a gesture so sweet and brotherly it sparked tears in my eyes. "Good luck, buddy. I'll see you when you get back. From outer space."

Only Emilio could make me laugh when I was trying not to cry.

He smiled, backed up into the hallway. I followed him to the doorway but no farther. I watched him walk down the hall, as he held his hand up in a wave. And then he turned his back to me and headed for the exit.

I watched him walk away because watching was all I could do. I waited for him to stop or turn around, but he didn't, of course.

I watched my last true friend and ally disappear through the red door.

Then I went back to my room. Closed the door. Sat on my bed and surveyed the empty space around me. I was truly alone now.

I needed to get used to it.

TWENTY

"WE'VE DECIDED TO move up the selection," Krieger said. "To today."

Pierce and Krieger dropped that news on us before anyone had even finished breakfast. Four of us sat at a table together: Luka, me, Kendra, and Anton. Pratima and Boris hadn't showed. Kicked out or left voluntarily, I'd never know.

"When you're finished here, go back to your rooms and pack. We'll call you when it's time." Pierce gave us each one last look. "Either way, you'll be on a plane out of here by tonight."

I packed my bag feeling robotic and distant from everything. With everyone else gone, it felt eerie to be in my room alone, to walk through an empty hallway.

They made us wait in a hall outside the auditorium where

we'd convened the very first day. It was fitting—ending where we began.

I glanced at the faces beside me. Kendra, her stare burning holes into the opposite wall. Anton, tapping his toe. Luka was a marble statue, unreadable. Why should he worry? He was a shoo-in.

Not once had I been ranked number one. I'd been so sure of myself—so sure that I was the best of the best. Why *wouldn't* I think that? I'd spent most of my life being number one. Selection into the top private high school in the city? Impressed the pants off *that* selection committee. First-chair violin, all-state orchestra? I threw myself into practice. I neglected social events, hobbies. I earned my place. A coveted internship at NASA? Please. My father may have put in a good word for me, but I hadn't needed nepotism. I'd worked for it, for everything. And I'd always gotten what I wanted because of it.

But this was different.

Luka Kereselidze was the first and only obstacle I hadn't been able to overcome. And I couldn't even hate him for it. He could have turned out to be an ass, but he'd never said an unkind word to me. He'd been cool under pressure in the SLH. He'd been a good guy in the wilderness. He'd been almost, in a way, my friend. He'd earned my respect, at least.

I couldn't hate him. Even if he was about to be crowned victor over me.

But then again, who knew? Luka hadn't aced everything. He'd never gotten his brain-wave patterns right. He hadn't really made friends the way Anton and I had. I'd saved his life in wilderness survival. And I'd clawed my way up from the bottom of the ranks. Some people liked underdogs.

But only one of us could be number one.

They called us individually onto the stage of the auditorium. Anton first. He was in there for maybe fifteen minutes, and then my name came over the loudspeaker.

I rose, my legs shaking. Even if I was wrong, and all my dreams were about to be smashed into smithereens, I would survive.

Probably.

I walked where they directed me, onto the stage, where our instructors sat behind a panel with the colonel, Ms. Krieger, and Felix. All eyes were on me.

Anton wasn't there. They must have taken him out a side door.

I stood in front of the people who would decide my fate and choked down bile, hoping I wouldn't throw up in front of them. I kept my eyes on the wood floor at my feet, concentrating on each breath. The house lights were on, casting harsh shadows on everyone's expression.

I tried to find a sympathetic face on the panel. Ms. Krieger was incapable of frowning; I couldn't trust her. Bolshakov looked severe and judgmental. Jeong had a nervous half smile on her face. Dr. Copeland was impassive, though her eyes were kind. Shaw gave me a reassuring smile.

"Cassandra Gupta." The colonel spoke my voice like it was heavy, made of stone.

I didn't know if I was supposed to speak. My gaze locked on his square, grizzled face.

"Your performance has been steadily improving since you got here. You began near the bottom of the pack, but quickly rose to the increasing challenges. Your classroom performance was impressive. Your physical endurance is commendable. Your dedication is to be praised. You showed good judgment in the face of stress, adequate social skills, and the best mental control we saw among the candidates. You are well rounded and impressively committed for being the youngest. However, you were not the strongest candidate overall."

I felt my knees buckle.

The colonel met my eyes and seemed to smile without breaking his stony facade.

Ms. Krieger smiled brightly, like I wasn't hearing the worst news I'd ever gotten in my life. "All is not lost, Cassie! We've chosen you as the alternate." She seemed to hear how weak that sounded and overcompensated by pasting on an even broader smile. Her hand swept over the rest of the panel, gesturing to my instructors. "You already know your future crewmates: Logan Shaw, flight engineer; Dr. Harper Copeland, medical officer; Michele Jeong, copilot; and Dominic Bolshakov, who will be your crew commander. All of them are experienced astronauts. We had our crew help choose their newest member, and they all spoke highly of your abilities."

I nodded. Plastered on a grateful smile.

"You'll train with them for the next few months in preparation for launch. And then, we'll see! Things happen, Cassie. You never know. You may yet go into space."

Her cheerfulness grated. I was getting the consolation speech.

I'll never go into space. I'll train with them and study with them, and then they'll go without me.

This was almost worse than not being chosen at all.

They were waiting for a response. My mouth was dry as gravel, but I murmured the expected response and hoped it didn't sound like garbled nonsense.

My eyes scanned one last time over my teachers. Copeland didn't show any emotion, but Shaw's sad smile and misty eyes behind his glasses almost broke me, right there in front of everyone.

Shaw stood and offered me his hand to shake. I wasn't aware of moving toward the panel, but somehow I found myself shaking hands with my instructors. "We'll see you soon," Shaw said. "Harper, Michele, and I are very proud of you."

"Admirable performance," Copeland said, her voice grave but approving.

"You did well," Jeong said, her short black bob tucked neatly behind her ears. "Looking forward to working with you."

I found myself looking into Dominic Bolshakov's steel gaze, frozen. He said nothing, but nodded once, slow.

I was excused.

I walked off that stage as fast as I could on legs that felt like they belonged to someone else. Someone backstage led me into a room with a digital display board and a few chairs around a conference table and a sofa, like some kind of greenroom.

I pressed my forehead against the dusty floral wallpaper and closed my eyes.

Not the strongest candidate.

FAILURE. That's what it meant. That's what I was.

I wanted to punch something. But if I damaged my hand, I'd probably be disqualified from training. So I paced, uselessly. After all that? Everything that had happened, it had been for nothing. I'd let everyone down. I'd never get into space now.

There was a pillow on the couch. I snatched it up and hurled it at the door.

The door swung open, revealing Luka, just as the pillow hit the door frame beside his head. He looked at me quizzically.

"Of course it's you," I said, throwing up my hands. "Of course."

"I suppose I am lucky it was only a pillow," he said, coming inside and closing the door. There was a moment of silence as he regarded me. "If it's any consolation, I am sorry."

I grimaced. It wasn't *his* fault he was perfect. "You don't have to apologize. It's just—*second place.* You're going for sure. I'm just here in case you get the flu. Which you won't. Because *look* at you."

I collapsed into a chair and buried my face in my hands.

Luka knelt in front of me. Pried my hands off my face. His

steady eyes bore into mine as my spine straightened at his nearness. "Why are you being so hard on yourself? They would not have picked you if they thought you could not do this. You and I are going to Florida together to train for a mission the likes of which has never been attempted before. That in itself is an honor."

"You don't understand," I said, too angry to think about how weird it was that Luka was holding my hands in his. "This was my first and only chance, okay? They don't do missions like this anymore. Maybe this is the last one they'll *ever* do. Coming this close and not making it? Almost worse than not making it at all." I ran out of steam, pulling my hands out of his to secure my ponytail, which had come loose. "And if the funding falls through, neither of us will be going."

Luka didn't waver. "The funding won't fall through."

I narrowed my eyes. "What do you know?"

The door opened again, and this time our instructors filed through. Surprised, both Luka and I stood. They seemed as confused as we were to see them.

Bringing up the rear were Pierce and Crane. The room was now full; we were all facing Pierce and Crane with matching expressions of expectant confusion.

I wavered on my feet, exhausted. So much had happened in the past couple of days, it felt like a lifetime. Luka shot me a sidelong glance, concerned. I ignored him.

The colonel cracked his knuckles, like he wasn't happy with what he was about to say. "Due to what happened two days ago during the SLH simulation, it has been decided that in the interest of safety, our timetable will be moved up. I've been given permission to brief you all on the particulars of the mission we're calling Project Adastra." His gaze, for the first time, didn't make me want to crawl into a hole. Then he turned and locked the door, trapping us all inside, and I suppressed a shiver. "You're about to learn what few others in the world know. I suggest you all take a seat."

I felt a spark of anticipation. Finally! We all obeyed, taking seats around the table, while Pierce and Crane remained near the door.

The colonel hit a few buttons on the table. The room's lights dimmed and a field of stars glowed to life in the air above our heads. "As we all know, life on Earth is fragile. Climate change is dramatically altering our daily reality. The growing problem of human infertility could be another symptom of a planet that is losing its ability to support life. We aren't sure when the tipping point will come. Some experts say it already has. If that's the case, humanity needs to find alternative solutions if we want to survive."

My muscles tightened in anticipation, urging him silently to get on with it. Nobody in this room needed anything spelled out to us.

He took a moment to survey the room. "Brace yourselves, everyone. Our goal on this mission is to send humans beyond our solar system."

There was a collective, quiet intake of breath. I'd been

expecting something like this, but nothing could have prepared me for actually *hearing* it.

Unprecedented was selling this short.

The general field of stars hovering over the center of the table organized itself into our Milky Way galaxy. We zoomed in to the familiar Sol system, to the blue marble of Earth. The stars became our own night sky, and we all looked up.

"Your destination is the star system of Kepler-186." The screen zeroed in on a previously dark square of sky, and a dim sparkle of light magnified on the screen. We zoomed in, farther and farther, until a blurry white dot enlarged on the screen. "Kepler-186 is an M-class red dwarf star approximately four hundred and ninety light-years from Earth and believed to harbor at least five planets. One of the planets, designated Kepler-186f, has a mass similar to Earth's and is within the star's habitable zone. Ladies and gentlemen, the objective of Project Adastra is to discover the habitability of the planet 186f, and perhaps more importantly . . ." His voice slowed, as though unwilling to speak the words out loud. ". . . whether life already exists there."

I couldn't focus on the details of what he was saying because my mind couldn't get away from the word *impossible*. The technology we had could only send us on a very long, very slow, one-way trip. *Voyager 1* had taken fifty years to reach the outer edges of our solar system. My father hadn't even been born when that thing was launched, and it was still just inching across interstellar space, in the dark places between stars.

The technology to take us five hundred light-years away simply didn't exist.

Unless it did, and it had been kept secret until now.

The field of stars above was now a close-up of an unfamiliar star system—Kepler-186, the red dwarf, surrounded by five orbiting spheres. One in particular twinkled helpfully as it orbited the farthest from its sun. That was it. Kepler-186f. Our destination.

I felt, suddenly, how small I was. Could almost feel Earth beneath my feet spinning freely, untethered to anything but laws of physics. Vulnerable. Alone.

I felt us as we were, on a grand scale—Earth and the sun and all the planets rocketing through space together like a comet—and experienced a moment of vertigo.

"I know what you're all thinking." The colonel's skin looked gray, his voice subdued. "Suffice to say, we are not knowingly sending you on a one-way trip. There is something else you need to know."

Mr. Crane materialized from the darkness to the front of the room near the projector, and I jumped almost out of my skin. He stood beside Pierce and didn't waste time with pleasantries. "On October eighteenth, 2024, SEE radio telescopes positioned in orbit around the moon picked up an unusual radio signal. Something unlike anything we'd ever received before. Its origin, we discovered, was Kepler-186."

2024. The year before I was born. I noted it dully through a haze of disbelief.

The hologram blinked out, and instead a series of fractal patterns grew in repeating circular patterns, repeating and building into infinity. "This is the beginning of the message we received. A universal constant, the Fibonacci sequence—which, as all you know, is a numerical pattern repeated over and over again in nature, from the shapes of universes to the smallest seashells. This pattern was followed by another, and another. In case you had any doubts, you're looking at the indisputable sign of an intelligent alien species trying to communicate with us."

I heard someone gasp. I raised my eyebrows at Luka, shocked, but he was stoic. If he was surprised, he hid it well.

Mr. Crane plowed on without giving us time to adjust. "It took our best people years to decipher the entire message. Such an incredible amount of data." Mr. Crane continued, as though he were commenting on the weather. "The first part of the message was just a hello—an intergalactic handshake, if you will. To show us that they are intelligent, and expected us to understand them. The second part was a mathematical designation of Kepler-186. Perhaps showing us their location. But the third part of the message was the truly amazing thing—and the reason why you are all here."

The air around us was now inhabited by ghostly mechanical 3D shapes rotating like tiny planets. Right in front of my face hung a familiar capsule, shrunk down to the size of my hand. The Human Hibernation Module.

At Crane's command, the hundreds of doll-size pieces

zoomed around the room, assembling themselves in a complex dance until they became one completed structure: a three-dimensional model of an alien spacecraft, its white bones transparent like the skeleton of a bird. A long, thin ring structure encased a snub-nosed, spherical craft, all smooth edges like a toddler's toy airplane. But elegant. Beautiful, even. I couldn't take my eyes off it.

"This is the product of fifteen years decoding the radio message, and the combined work of the best engineers in the world," Crane said. "A gift to humanity from a benevolent alien race. They have granted us the technology to travel faster than light. By showing us how to build a true Alcubierre drive-enabled spacecraft."

There were no words, not from any of us. My universe had inverted on itself as though I'd been swallowed by a wormhole. I realized I was pressing a hand against my chest as if to keep my heart from jumping out, though surprisingly my pulse was calm.

"This is absurd," Shaw said. The color had drained from his face. "This is ridiculous. You're telling us we have a way to travel faster than light? And no one's thought to mention this before now?

"Why did you think we were here, Logan?" Jeong's voice was quiet, her eyes steely.

He sputtered, unable to answer. "How long are we supposed to be gone?"

"A year, perhaps two," Crane said. "One year there, one year on your return. With this technology, there is no time dilation."

"That's impossible."

"Our simulations have run this mission, Mr. Shaw, innumerable times. One year each way, plus or minus six months."

Shaw's face was still ashen. He swallowed, his throat bobbing, as he seemed to begin to accept it. "Good lord, that message took almost five hundred years to reach us—whoever or whatever sent it, they're long gone now."

"That's a good point," Copeland said.

"You misunderstand," Crane replied, unruffled in the least. "The message did not come *from* Kepler-186. It, in fact, came to us from near one of Mars's moons."

"Oh my God," I whispered before I could stop myself. They had been so close. Were they still there? Watching us? Had they landed on Earth?

"Can this be possible?" Jeong asked, her eyes creased with worry and awe.

"Here is one hypothesis," Crane began. "The alien intelligence has sent probes, just as we have, to various places in the galaxy. With their superior technology it would not be out of the range of imagination that they could reach us here. Perhaps they discovered we may be intelligent, and have sent this message, and this ship, as a test. Perhaps it is an invitation to join them for an interspecies summit. You will find out when you arrive, I suppose."

He let us marvel on that a little while.

"My company has built this ship. I've named it *Odysseus*, and

I'm allowing NASA to use it. You were all chosen for this purpose. Not to be sacrificed—no, believe me, we intend to bring you all safely home long before I'm dead and buried."

We all watched the spinning hologram in silence, absorbing the knowledge of what this meant. I tried to quell my racing heart. *Not a death sentence. We'll be coming home. I'll see my family again.*

Assuming everything went perfectly according to plan. Assuming this alien intelligence was, in fact, benevolent. Assuming all of our experimental technology functioned as it should.

Assuming.

The lights came back on.

Nobody looked especially happy. Rather, the faces of my instructors were full of concern. Doubt.

"Each of you has been training precisely for the task we have set before you. Each of you has been chosen for the special skill set and experience vital to this mission. Believe that I am not about to waste billions of my dollars and the last fifteen years of my life sending you unprepared into the unknown." He leaned his knobby hands on the table. No wedding ring, I noticed. I realized I knew little to nothing about this man. "But it is your choice. Now that you know the truth in its entirety—will you stay?"

Silence, heavy. I felt it as though it were sitting on my chest.

Bolshakov had his hands pressed in front of him, eyes closed, as if in prayer. Finally, he broke the silence. "If all you say is true . . . how can any of us refuse?"

"You're right," Dr. Copeland agreed. "I can't walk away from this now. Could any of you?" No one said anything. Then Jeong shook her head.

"No, indeed," Luka said quietly beside me. He was looking down at this hands, lost in thought.

Shaw was staring straight ahead, as if he hadn't heard. He spoke in a nervous murmur. "Five hundred light-years. *Light-years*. Five hundred light-years from Earth."

There was another Earth out there, orbiting Kepler-186. A benevolent alien race. A world of things unknown and unknowable. Humanity's hope for the future.

To discover something like that, I would do anything.

"I don't want to leave." I pushed strength into my voice, trying to differentiate myself from Luka. I had to remind myself I was still an alternate; he was still my competition.

"Have we heard anything from these"—Dr. Copeland cleared her throat, as though she couldn't physically say the next word—"*extraterrestrials* since this transmission?"

"No," Mr. Crane said. "Regardless, we have this technology and it is irrational not to use it. We have the means and the opportunity. We have a destination that is likely habitable. We're going to find out who sent this transmission."

"Why not send probes first?" Jeong asked again. "Why a crewed mission?" The unasked question: *Why risk our lives for this?*

"This transmission gave us a means to possibly send living humans to a planet that may be habitable. Who sent it? Why? A probe can't ask those questions. And it may even be perceived as a threat, as a weapon."

"It goes without saying," Pierce broke in quietly, "that this information has not and will not be shared with the outside world. There will be no press, no media attention. All of you will be under strict monitoring and on communication restriction. The government is adamant that word of this mission not reach the general public. Under any circumstances."

"If you are all in agreement to stay," Crane said, "pack your bags. You'll be flying to Florida in the morning."

We were dismissed.

I walked out of that room a different person than when I'd entered. The universe had been irreparably altered. And we were the only ones who knew it.

Nothing, nothing would ever be the same again.

Luka walked beside me without a word. He had been quiet the entire presentation. Perhaps later I'd have time to talk to him about it, but for now I needed to absorb it on my own.

Technology that allowed us to traverse the universe. Physical evidence that intelligent life existed beyond Earth.

And we were going to meet them.

I had to prove I was more worthy of that honor than Luka.

TWENTY-ONE

ALMOST AS SOON as we landed in Florida, they subjected us to throat swabs and blood tests. If all the petri dishes came back clear after forty-eight hours, Pierce told us, we'd be quarantined—no contact with anyone other than the rest of the crew—until launch. Lessen the risk of us taking a virulent disease on board a cramped spacecraft.

Luka and I were moved into a small set of living quarters that was basically an old motel on the astronaut training campus. The rooms were definitely from days gone by: cinder-block walls, white paint turned yellow with old tobacco stains, the scent of mildew permeating every fabric, pillows that collapsed like bags of tissue paper.

But I was there, in the place where astronauts lived and

trained. Where *I* would become an astronaut. That was enough for me.

Time was a luxury we weren't afforded. We had time only to drop off our luggage before our first lecture.

It took only ten minutes for me to realize I was in the big leagues now. And I was *not* ready.

Our crewmates were older than my parents and they had collectively logged hundreds of hours in orbit. Among them, they had faced all the spaceflight problems that were possible to walk away from. For them, these classes were only a refresher; for me, they were a crash course in astrophysics and mathematics that most people need multiple graduate degrees to properly learn.

Luka and I were attempting to learn in a matter of weeks what most experienced astronauts learned in two years.

My hands were cramped from typing notes on the government-issue tablet, but Luka seemed to take it all in stride.

"What's wrong?" he asked.

I'd taken a seat by myself at a table in the café during our lunch break. The rest of the astronauts sat together and socialized at lunch. I didn't have that luxury—I needed every spare moment to catch up.

I was hunched over my seat, eating a limp cheese quesadilla with one hand while trying to solve a set of complex calculations with the other. I must have looked frazzled for Luka to stop on his way to get his own lunch.

I hesitated whether to tell him. It might show weakness. But

I had no other friends here. And he looked more cheerful than last night, a friendly smile on his face. "I . . . can't figure out how they got the solution to these equations."

"But in class—" he started.

"I pretended like I got it," I said quickly. "But I don't totally understand."

He slid into the seat beside me, eyes on my tablet. "It's just calculus."

"Yeah, well, it's a little more advanced than I'm used to." My face burned.

He wasn't looking at me, but at the numbers. "You're only a little off. Can I show you?"

I didn't want him to teach me, to know the extent of what I didn't know. But I needed the help. "Yes."

As he adjusted my calculations, and the numbers fell into their rightful places, I began to feel the tension in my chest ease. He never gloated, never treated me like the ignorant child I felt like.

In our class after lunch, I was finally able to show off the real advantage I had over Luka. When our instructor, Dr. Murray, a woman in her forties with thick round glasses that magnified her already large eyes, rolled in the EEG, I clasped the bottom of my chair so I wouldn't leap out of it to volunteer.

"Now, you veteran astronauts don't need to worry about this EEG," she said. "This is just for Cassandra and Luka. But I would like a volunteer or two for a little demonstration."

Dr. Copeland raised her hand. Her EEG never wavered.

Bolshakov was able to get into alpha for less than a minute. The older astronauts, it seemed, were inflexible in their brain-wave patterns.

Our instructor confirmed my hypothesis. "This is why we need a young, flexible brain. Now let's see what happens when we put Cassandra under."

Finally, I was able to let go of my chair and join our teacher at the front. I felt the familiar sticks of the electrodes snake through my hair and onto my scalp. I no longer needed any coaching; I closed my eyes, breathed from my diaphragm, and found Beethoven's "Für Elise," a sentimental favorite from childhood, and played it like a recording in my memory. My consciousness faded into a peaceful gray place.

When I opened my eyes, everyone was staring at me— Bolshakov with newfound respect.

"Good job," Luka whispered as he passed me on his way to the chair, and I felt like I was glowing from the inside.

"Well done," Dr. Murray said, her large eyes sparkling with excitement. "This is exactly what we want. This is the exact reason we need you two. Your brain-wave patterns are best suited for interfacing with our monitoring computer. Now, Luka, let's try you."

So that was one mystery solved, at least.

Luka didn't do nearly as well. He remained in alert beta the entire time, except for a few bizarre blips where he slipped into theta. I watched the readout with growing confusion.

Our instructor was obviously a little abashed when it was

over. "Well, that's—that's not quite . . ." She adjusted her glasses and reread the outline.

Luka actually seemed embarrassed. "It's difficult for me to achieve a meditative state."

Her mouth twisted uneasily. "You all have been under tremendous stress lately. We'll try again tomorrow."

He sat back in his seat, caught my eye, shrugged one shoulder, and smiled ruefully. The one thing I could do better than him, and he was a good sport about it. I couldn't believe I'd ever been annoyed at his supposed arrogance, when he didn't seem to have any pride at all. I'd misjudged him just as much as I'd misjudged Emilio and Mitsuko.

As everyone filed out of class later, I pulled him aside. "Hey, are you okay?"

His lips pressed together, his eyes watching the retreating backs of the other astronauts as they disappeared down the hall. "No. I'm having some trouble focusing, that's all. I'll work on it." His face looked drawn, his eyes red-rimmed and distracted.

"Let me know if I can help," I offered, though I had no idea how I could. "You helped me earlier. I'd like to return the favor."

He gave me a tired smile. "Thank you. But it is something I must do on my own. Come, let's go get dinner, before they turn off the lights."

By the end of the first day, my mind was a fog of mathematical equations and schematics, a mantra of endlessly repeating formulas hopefully carving itself into my brain. I fell onto my bed, hardly able to believe I'd woken up that morning in Houston.

But my brain wouldn't turn off.

So I laced up my tennis shoes and went off in search of the track they'd shown us on our brief tour. Our quarters had doors facing an open-air courtyard lined with a crumbling sidewalk. Across the courtyard was another building, lined with floor-to-ceiling windows, where the cafeteria and classrooms were.

Almost as soon as I left my room, I ran into Luka.

"Sorry!" My hands had latched on to his upper arms when we'd collided. He steadied me with hands on my shoulders as I pushed myself out of his way, carefully unclasped my hands from his arms. "Didn't see you there. Somehow."

Still holding on to my bare shoulders, he looked me up and down. "Running away already?"

I smirked, despite the pulse thrumming in my neck. "Antsy. Too much going on—I can't sleep. Was gonna go for a run. What about you?"

He offered a smile that didn't seem particularly happy. "The same." He looked me over again, seemed to realize his hands were still holding my shoulders, and released me. "Would you mind company?" Then he added, almost shyly: "That is, unless you'd rather run alone."

I thought about it. Remembered the times we'd run opposite each other those nights during selection, following each other around and around in comfortable silence and in our separate orbits. No explanations needed. Just me and Boy Wonder. "It'd be nice to have company," I heard myself say.

He smiled, grateful, and I was glad I'd said yes.

The whoosh of air as he passed me smelled clean and fresh, like he'd just showered. My skin was still remembering the feel of his hands.

That smile of his. It'd brightened his entire face. I wanted to make him smile like that again.

The facility and grounds were completely empty. Once we left the housing wing, only a few lights were on in the halls. We passed through a hallway lined with locked doors on one side and floor-to-ceiling windows on the other. We relied on moonlight through the windows to guide us.

"Do you think we'll get in trouble?" I whispered, even though there was no one around to hear.

"What will they do, kick us out? We are not children. They have chosen us to go into space; surely they must trust us within the walls of our own enclosure."

He had a good point.

"Bolshakov said the track was on the south side of the building. There should be an outside door near the café we can use."

"What if it locks behind us?"

He shot me a mischievous glance. "Then we sleep under the stars. Not like it would be the first time, yes?"

I remembered sleeping beside him in the lean-to and shivered. "I should've packed warmer clothes."

Without warning he reached around me and ran his hands up and down my upper arms, quick, as if to warm me. I nearly jumped out of my skin. "Better?"

"Y-yes." I hadn't been cold, but now my skin was flushed even warmer.

A turn left, then right, and Luka confidently led us into a large circular common area filled with tables covered with upside-down chairs. A metal grate was closed over an empty food stand, under an unlit seventies-era fluorescent sign reading "Star Café." The stench of Lysol, with an earthy undertone of mildew, permeated the air.

"Wow, where was this sense of direction when we were lost in the boonies?" I asked.

He smirked. "Come."

He pushed open a door and a rush of cool night air greeted us. The track was a desolate thing, weeds growing up in cracks between the faded lanes, a lone yellow streetlamp at the far edge of the grass the only light. In the murky distance I could just make out a stretch of empty parking lot. The fresh air was cool and muggy. Not quite fall, but getting there.

He was already circling the track, a slow warm-up jog. I followed suit. We fell into a rhythm and maintained a friendly distance. The night air grew cooler, more damp, but I grew warmer, until my muscles were loose and well used and I felt put back together again.

I waited for Luka to finish, picking out what constellations I could from the light-polluted sky. We walked back inside together, but now our pace was unhurried. The dim interior seemed less forbidding and more cozy, like we were the only two people awake in the entire facility.

A warm, relaxed fuzziness had descended over me like a drug. Maybe I could sleep now.

"So," I ventured, my voice low as we neared our rooms. "What do you think about . . . all this?"

As I side-eyed him, his jaw locked and then released—lips pressed together, and then relaxed. I had the feeling he didn't want to share, but then he said, "I assume you mean that they plan to send us four hundred ninety light-years away to rendezvous with extraterrestrials? It still hasn't quite sunk in, I think."

My voice lowered further. Now that we were alone, I wanted to ask him something that had been bothering me. "Do you think whoever sabotaged the SLH will try again here?"

His eyes grew dark. "I do not know what happened at Johnson. We are supposed to be the only ones who know this mission's objective. Perhaps it was nothing more than a disgruntled employee. One hopes that the circle of trust here is smaller."

"You're not worried?"

"You can worry about sabotage, or you can worry about the ship exploding on the tarmac. Worry doesn't do any good. I am cautious, but that is all."

"Don't you have reservations, though?"

"Do you?" he asked, giving me a quizzical look.

"A little," I admitted. "I was just wondering if I was alone in that. Do you think the rest of the crew is worried at all?"

"I think, as it is for either of us, any chance at space is reason enough. The reward is worth the risk."

I chewed on that awhile. "I suppose you're right."

He paused outside my door. "Feel better? No longer . . . what you say, antsy?"

I smiled. "Yeah, I feel better. Thanks."

He gave a nod, like a miniature bow. "Any time. Thank you for inviting me."

There was really no reason for us to continue standing there in front of our rooms, but it was like neither of us wanted to walk away. We were standing really close. I could see the pulse jumping in his neck. My eyes focused on his face. His cheeks pink from the run. The arched cupid bow of his lips, slightly chapped.

There was a growing roar in my ears.

"Well, good night," I said quickly, backing away.

His eyes followed me away; his voice sounded disappointed. "Have a good night, Cassie."

I escaped into my room, surprised to find how much my heart was racing.

I'd never felt flustered around anyone like this before. I'd always assumed I just wasn't made that way. But whatever was causing this reaction to Luka, I had to get over it. Now.

I was so close. This was my opportunity, and I wasn't going to squander it. Not for anything. Not for anyone.

TWENTY-TWO

THE SECOND DAY of class was even more intense than the first. They weren't expecting Luka and me to be on the same level as the rest of the crew, of course—but Luka seemed to be keeping up just fine. I was the only one floundering.

These were basic, general concepts I needed to know. It'd be irresponsible of NASA to send us unprepared into space. But these were only basic, general concepts for someone who'd already earned a degree or two. Not a rising high school senior.

Now that I was getting to know Luka a little better, I couldn't blame him for being perfect for this place. Not only did he absorb the information more readily, he even got along more easily with the other astronauts.

My own experience with making friends started and ended

with Mitsuko and Emilio. And these four were not only astro-nauts, but our former instructors. I could hardly remember what words were in their presence, much less talk to them as if we were equal.

At the end of the second day, I was heading back to my room after an unsuccessful attempt to outrun my stress on the track when I intercepted Luka in the quiet hallway off the cafeteria.

He wasn't dressed for running. But when he saw me, he smiled. And a little knot in my chest started to loosen. "Feeling better yet?"

I swiped a sweaty lock of hair away from my brow. "Actually, no. Running lets me forget a little while, that's all."

He cocked his head toward the direction he'd been heading. "Would you like to join me?"

"Where are you headed?"

"Follow and see."

At the end of an abandoned hall was a carved oak door com-pletely unlike the industrial metal-and-glass ones everywhere else on the compound. He opened the door for me and I stepped inside, not knowing what to expect.

It was a chapel. Small, narrow, barely wider than a janitor's closet. A few rows of decoratively carved wooden pews led up to an altar, over which a half circle of stained glass bled a rainbow mosaic of color on the floor. It was empty of people and mostly bare of decoration, save for a low cabinet covered by a drape behind the pew. A soft scent of roses and the deep, earthy aroma of polished wood permeated the air.

It was the most aesthetically pleasing place I'd seen in the entire compound. More knots in my chest and stomach began to ease. It somehow felt easier to breathe, like an iron band that had encircled my ribs was now gone. My hand went to the curved spiral decoration carved into the end of the pew, tracing its round shape, feeling the slippery-smooth polished wood beneath my fingertips.

Something that sounded suspiciously like Christmas hymns played on an old speaker at such quiet volume that you had to sit completely still to hear it. Had we missed Thanksgiving, or was someone here a little overeager for Christmas?

"I didn't know we had a chapel," I whispered. Whispering seemed appropriate in a place like this.

He motioned me into the pew and sat beside me, leaving a polite space between us. "I come here sometimes," he said, his voice quiet. "It's calming."

It struck me as odd that I had never considered Luka being religious. "Catholic?"

"Georgia has its own orthodox church," he said, a bit of smile in his voice at my ignorance.

"Oh."

He craned his head a little to smile at me, and then looked up at the stained-glass window. "It's not all that different. To me. So many names to worship the same God."

I nodded, my breath catching in my throat. I'd joked about Ganesh and Ram, but in reality I didn't put much stock in the Hindu pantheon. They were stories from my childhood, little symbols sprinkled through my house, a thread connecting me to my history. Not my present.

"My grandma's Hindu," I said, venturing out into the subject like an ice-skater on the rink. "The rest of my family is basically agnostic. We still celebrate Christmas like most people do. My mom puts up a little nativity scene on the fireplace mantel for when her sisters come over. And every year, we catch my grandma sneaking a blue figurine of infant Krishna as a substitute for the baby Jesus."

Luka smiled. He really was handsome up close, with eyes that looked like they understood everything they saw, a sheen of blond stubble on his square jaw. The soft light from the stained glass gave him an ethereal glow. "So what is it that you believe?"

My lips parted, but nothing came out.

I'd never thought too much about it. I figured if there was a God, he was kind of like the moon: up there watching, possibly affecting life on Earth in subtle ways—but otherwise something that I would never fully understand or see up close.

"You miss your family?" I asked, changing the subject.

Luka turned away from me again, bowed his head. For a long time I thought he was going to ignore me. "I've never been away from them for so long."

"Me neither." Thinking of them was like a physical pain in my stomach.

"It's odd, isn't it? To be so far from home, surrounded by strangers. To feel like an outsider." His eyes went far away and I wondered what he was talking about. He looked like any other white American kid, and he hardly had an accent. What reason could he have to feel like an outsider, either here or back where he came from?

I stayed quiet, unsure if it was ruder to ask him about it or not ask him.

In the quiet that followed, my eyes alighted on the draped cabinet beside the altar. It suddenly hit me, the familiarity of its shape.

Forgetting myself, I jumped to my feet, lifting the drape to see if I was correct. I was rewarded with the polished walnut gleam of an upright piano. It was an old one, and cheap, but when I lifted the lid the expanse of black and white ivories still made my heart dance like fingers on the keys.

The bench had been pushed underneath the key bed. I brought it out a little with my toe and sat, fingertips grazing the cool surface of the keys.

I turned back around to Luka, unable to keep the smile from my face. "I haven't touched a piano in months. Do you mind?"

He nodded politely. "Please, go ahead."

I touched the first key experimentally, and a rich, satisfying tenor note broke the solemn silence of the chapel, hanging in the air a few seconds before reverberating into nothing. My fingers, remembering their old patterns, played a few notes in a made-up melody, getting back into the feel of it. I started playing snatches of some melancholy waltz whose name I couldn't recall. It felt good, and proper, like stretching after a long flight.

I snuck a look over my shoulder at Luka. He'd closed his eyes, leaned forward over his knees, fists against his mouth.

Sad? Or tired, maybe? I couldn't tell if he enjoyed the tune or not.

Then I hit a sour note and pulled my hands into my lap like it had bitten me. "It's a little out of tune," I said sheepishly.

He opened his eyes. "Sad melody."

I shrugged a shoulder. Then I put my hands back onto the keys, because now that they'd had a taste, my fingers were itching for more. I began "Clair de lune," a sentimental favorite that pretty much everyone in the world recognized.

The familiar calm descended on me. Even though I could play this blindfolded and probably in my sleep, the mental exercise and the music itself always put me in kind of a trance.

I stopped. Luka had been having so much trouble getting into the semiconscious state lately. He hadn't made any progress. Maybe music could do for him what it did for me. If it could help, even a little, I owed it to him to at least try.

"Hey, come here," I said.

His eyebrows knitted momentarily, but he complied, getting up from the pew and then sliding onto the narrow bench beside me.

"This is how I get into the right mental state," I said. "For the EEG tests. I play music in my head—pretend like I'm playing piano. Maybe it could work the same for you. Here." I grabbed his balled-up hands without thinking, and smoothed his palms out.

"I don't know how to play," he protested.

"You can't get in the right place mentally if you're tense. Just relax." My fingers released his and found their former places over the keys. "Close your eyes. Don't think about anything else. Concentrate on the music."

I started "Clair de lune" again, taking it half as fast as I normally would and hoping he didn't notice the sharp, off-key middle C too much. That was a good, generically tranquil piece, at least in the first movement.

I watched his profile as I played. With his eyes closed, he was an open and up-close study. I watched the blond tips of his eyelashes flutter, wondering what was going on behind those eyelids. I felt the air move in and out of his chest in a steady rhythm. Let my eyes take in the finer details of his face: the stubble on his cheek, the texture of his skin, the planes of his cheekbones. It was impossible to tell if my plan was working.

I stopped at the end of the slow first movement, and observed as his eyes opened.

"Well?" I asked.

He took in a long breath and let it out. "It is something I will have to work on. But thank you for trying. I can see how this method works for you."

"Sure." My hands slipped from the keys, though my fingers still itched to finish the piece. "What do you say we . . . practice? If you want, I mean. I miss playing, and if it helps you . . ."

I was close enough to see that his smile was more for my benefit; he didn't think the piano playing would help. "Thank you. That would be nice."

The silence filled with the distant, generic babbling of Christmas music again.

Luka shook his head, smiling ruefully. "Americans play Christmas music far too early in the season. And the songs are different from those at home. But I like it."

"Me too." I nodded, leaned back on my hands. "Even though it's cheesy. It's so . . . I don't know. Hopeful."

One corner of his mouth perked up in one of the first genuine smiles I'd seen on him. We sat next to each other, our legs touching, listening to the rise and fall of the verses until they faded away.

"Thank you, Cassie," he said, his voice so low and sweet in my ear that I couldn't look at him. "I will try your method next time. Perhaps it will help."

I bit back a smile, savoring the warm glow in my chest that was starting to burn off the chill of loneliness. "It was purely selfish. I just wanted an excuse to show off my musical skills."

TWENTY-THREE

"WHAT'S HAPPENING?" I whispered to Luka, sliding into the chair next to his. I'd spent half the night cramming, overslept, and had barely made it in time.

Luka just shook his head.

Our instructor from the last two days was absent. Pierce was an imposing presence at the head of the room, arms crossed like a bouncer. His eyes followed me as I slid into my seat, the last one in.

Instead of our usual instructor, Mr. Crane entered the lecture hall. Everyone shifted in their chairs, sitting up straighter. "A few announcements," Crane said, without so much as a greeting. "Everyone's swabs came back clear. Tomorrow morning, all of you will move into quarantine in preparation for launch.

Tonight, there will be a short cocktail party for some of our investors. Gupta, Kereselidze, you are excused from this event. In fact, Gupta, directly after this lecture, report to Exam Room 2C for an individual assessment."

I furrowed my brow at Luka, wondering what new surprise they could possibly have waiting for me. But before Luka could offer any hypothesis, the door opened, and the last person I ever expected to see again walked into the room.

Hanna Schulz looked different than when I'd last seen her, pale and shaking in the locker room. She sported the same sleek ponytail, but now she was wearing makeup and a black blazer over a white button-down and black pants. She faced us serenely—almost defiantly—her shoulders square and chin high. She looked ten years older. Nothing of that defeated girl remained.

"You all remember Hanna Schulz, one of our more promising candidates from the selection phase." My mouth gaped, but Mr. Crane continued. "I plucked her from the competition because I believed her skills could be put to better use on the ground crew. She'll be observing you while under quarantine and reporting your progress directly to me. Our accelerated training schedule means we have much to do in little time. It is imperative everyone is performing at their peak in time for launch."

So she hadn't been kicked out because of her claustrophobia? What sort of skills could Hanna possibly have that were so valuable to a man like Crane, who could afford the best of the best in every field?

"When will that be?" Bolshakov asked.

Crane turned steely eyes on him. "When you need to know that, commander, I will tell you."

With a brisk nod he left. Hanna stayed put. She surveyed us all coolly, and then slid into a seat in the front row.

Luka and I took our turns on the EEG, as usual. For the first time, Luka appeared to have some success with it. I flashed him a little thumbs-up and a smile. Maybe I'd actually been able to pay him back for all the times he'd helped me.

But he didn't appear as happy as I expected. He returned my smile politely, but still seemed troubled.

Hanna stayed for the entire class. When it ended, she stood by her chair and waited for the rest of us to file out.

I paused in front of her. "Nice to see you again," I ventured, though that was stretching the truth. "I guess we'll be working together."

There was almost a smile on her lips. "Don't worry, Cass, I'm not here to compete for your precious spot. Mr. Crane needs me on the ground."

"Why?"

Now the smile brightened; she had clearly been hoping I would ask. "That's on a need-to-know basis," she said, brushing past me toward our instructor, who seemed to be waiting for her at his desk. "And you don't need to know."

"Close your eyes."

I did. The chill tickle of electrodes slid through my hair as the tech fitted the helmet over my head. She checked to make sure the helmet was secure, the electrodes placed correctly.

Exam Room 2C was a nondescript gray box of a room, with what I was fairly certain was a two-way mirror on one wall. I was reclined in a dentist's chair beside a large, whirring machine, my pulse thumping in my wrists, goose bumps breaking out across my skin.

The tech assisted me with the helmet, specially fitted with dozens of tiny wires just like the one I'd wear during our voyage asleep in the HHMs. The helmet directly connected me with the computer that would monitor our vitals during flight.

I was given little instruction. Only that I was to go into my meditative state and attempt to make connection with the computer. When I asked how, the tech only shook her head.

"This is a new area of science," the tech said. "The brain is a complex organ, and each has its own unique makeup of neural connections. You must discover your own way to connect to the computer."

Over the speaker, Pierce's voice: "Whenever you're ready, Gupta."

Inside the helmet my hearing was deadened, my peripheral vision gone. With my eyes closed, it was actually easier to disconnect from physical sensations—the cool steel of the chair, the heavy weight of the helmet over my head, the sound of my own breathing echoing inside the helmet, the vaguely electric smell of plastic—and went to the now-familiar space in my mind. I heard only the distant mechanical whoosh of the machine, until that, too, became nothing.

The place I went to in my meditative state was bland and quiet, a void with little else beyond a distant consciousness of melody that blended into a constant refrain that ebbed in and out of focus.

But this time when I faded away, I didn't go *entirely* away. I felt a thin connection to conscious thought, an awareness of being watched. The awareness of something else aware of me.

Something else was there in the quiet of my consciousness. I searched for it but it kept away from me, always at the edge of my awareness, making me wonder if it was really there at all.

I stopped chasing the feeling. It didn't go away. Instead, I formed a thought, aimed it, as though I were calling out hesitantly to an empty room: *Hello?*

The awareness flickered. Strengthened. Its attention focused on me like a laser. There was no response, but had I really expected one?

Instead of trying to communicate again, I simply tried to make myself more visible, more open. *Here I am. See me.*

I repeated the mantra as long as I could maintain the openness of my mind, to no response. But the awareness was stronger now, more of a concrete presence. It was also somehow *closer*. If this wasn't all happening in my mind, I could've sworn I might have been able to reach out and touch it.

But then it was gone, a pulled plug, and even in my reduced state I felt the nauseating swoop of failure.

"That's enough, Gupta. You can come out of it now."

I swam back to the surface of consciousness. The electrodes retracted and I shivered at the removal of my helmet. Cold white lights suddenly brightened the room, blinding me as I realized the tiny lab was now full of people.

Blinking away the spots, I eventually recognized the stern outline of Colonel Pierce and the smaller, only slightly less stern figure of Hanna. A tech was removing the heart-rate monitor and unstrapping the various other devices that had been monitoring my vitals. Four or five others in white coats were looking at the digital readouts from the computer and whispering to themselves.

"You did well, Gupta," Pierce said. There was disbelief in his eyes.

Hanna was watching me with curious concern, her tablet poised on her arm as if she were a reporter taking notes. "How do you feel?"

"A little groggy. But fine."

"Do you remember being aware at all?"

"I remember being aware. I remember something being aware of *me*."

Hanna's stylus froze above her tablet. The white coats stopped their whispering and looked at me.

"Is . . . that bad?" I asked, a worm of anxiety twisting through my chest.

The white coats smiled.

"No. It confirms what we saw on our end," Hanna said, touching her stylus to her tablet a few times, then looking back at me.

She actually looked happy. "It's exactly what we had hoped."

One of the white coats explained. "This is the first time you were connected to the supercomputer. Your semiconscious state must have felt the connection and relayed it to you as a sense of being watched. Your brain was, in fact, directly connected with the computer. It interfaced with your bioelectricity."

Someone was slowly clapping, the noise quieting everyone in the room. Crane strode through the crowd, the sea of white coats parting for him like repelling magnets. "Congratulations, Cassandra. You've just shown us you're able to form a direct neural link with the computer. Something that precious few test subjects have achieved."

The words *test subject* made me narrow my eyes. "It didn't feel like I did much of anything."

"It's good news," Hanna assured me. "It's just what we wanted to happen. This is only the first step, making the connection. You have no idea how many thousands of trials haven't been able to get this far. Cassie, this is the reason why we need you. Older people, even our established astronauts, they can't form this type of connection. Not to the level you've shown today."

"No, they cannot." Crane's closed-mouth smile was tight. He was thrilled—triumphant, even, but trying not to show it. He addressed a group of scientists to his left. "It's too early to tell if this was a complete success. We'll need more attempts. Gupta will need time and practice to refine the connection. And we have exposed her only to the beta version of the software. The full potential of the neural link may not be known until she interfaces with Sunny in her whole form."

I gave Hanna a "what the hell is he talking about" glare. She waited for visual permission from Crane before she answered. "Sunny is the nickname we've given to PROPHET, the supercomputer that will be installed aboard the ship. There's only one, and she's on board *Odysseus*, so you're practicing with a less powerful version—an earlier prototype. She will monitor the crew while in flight as well as perform a multitude of other functions: autopilot, recording scientific data, and so forth."

"Our little joke," Crane said, not at all looking like a man who could tell a joke. "Sunny is solar-powered. Well, photon-powered, to be precise, as solar power will have little importance on an interstellar journey."

"You calling a computer *she* is a little disconcerting."

"Sunny is as intelligent as a young human child," Crane said. "Theoretically, of course—intelligence is such a difficult thing to measure. We don't typically think of children as intelligent; the lack of impulse control, attention span, and basic knowledge of the world tend to cloud their true potential. But in the capacity to learn? The ability to process data and extrapolate it into new conclusions, to solve problems? Sunny is as near to human intelligence as we have yet achieved."

I tried to find the sense of triumph and elation everyone around me seemed to feel. And there was a sense of accomplishment. But it was overshadowed by apprehension. What was I getting myself into, directly connecting my brain to a supercomputer? A *prototype* supercomputer. Nobody else had done this before—that meant no one knew the risks. What might happen to me when they finally connected me to the real Sunny?

Everything about this felt rushed. Research half finished, hypotheses half tested, results unknown. I was their experiment.

I reminded myself I was *already* a product of human experimentation, from my very conception. Science had given me life. Maybe this was my turn to give to science. Was I really going to let untested science keep me from my lifelong dream?

Maybe this was my destiny.

My reservations shifted into resolve.

Two techs helped me to my feet. I took one step on my own. "I'm fine," I told them.

They released me, and I promptly lost consciousness.

TWENTY-FOUR

INCESSANT POUNDING ON my door. I roused, groggily, finding myself alone in my quarters, the lights off.

I stumbled out of bed, pulling open the door just to make the noise stop.

Krieger was in my room before I could fully process her existence. She was in a metallic cream jacket and glittering gold dress that nearly blinded me. High-heeled shoes added to the considerable inches of her hair, making her taller than me.

As Krieger brushed past me to the closet, reality slowly filtered back into my brain.

I'd briefly regained consciousness as I'd been carried back to my room, during which someone had explained what'd happened to me. Apparently the process of forming and maintaining the neural link was so incredibly taxing on the brain that mine simply shut itself off. A hard restart. Not uncommon, they said. I'd been told to sleep it off.

According to the clock beside my bed, that had been seven hours ago. The slice of sky I'd glimpsed out the open door was black. I'd missed the entire day.

I watched her flit around like a wild bird that had accidently flown into my room. She was examining every article of clothing in my closet, giving each a brief moment of scrutiny before impatiently shoving it aside. A few items she flung onto the bed beside me. "Mr. Crane is pleased with your success today," she said into my closet. "He's decided that you and Luka are to attend the party tonight."

"The party?" I repeated. I struggled in vain to remember what the hell she was talking about.

"Mr. Crane is hosting cocktails for his investors and wants to celebrate your success from this morning." She finally turned and eyed the articles of clothing she'd thrown onto my bed disapprovingly. "A bit short notice, but we'll make it work. The entire crew is going to be there, as well as a few key investors and some higher-level people from NASA. We need you looking respectable."

So it wasn't just a celebratory party—it was Mr. Crane trotting his crew out for inspection like so many prize horses. I stopped dragging my feet.

Whether or not I was actually guaranteed a spot on the ship was still up in the air. If the rest of the crew was going to be there to schmooze, I would, too.

I dressed without complaint. The nicest clothes I'd brought were a businesslike black skirt and a slightly wrinkled gray blouse with buttons. I had two pairs of shoes: a pair for running, and the brown clogs I wore every day. I picked the clogs.

I twisted my thick hair—wild from not having been properly brushed in days—into a messy bun, and glanced at my reflection. I looked like a librarian headed to a funeral. Who had bad taste in shoes.

But it wasn't bad for five minutes' notice.

She clucked her tongue disapprovingly but said nothing as I followed her next door to Luka's room. She rapped on his door, and he joined us on the sidewalk, already dressed.

He must've had prior warning about this party, because he looked good. He was wearing a white collared shirt with a gray suit jacket and pants, looking every bit the *GQ* model, Russian edition. I felt a twinge of . . . something, maybe jealousy, that he looked more put-together than I did.

We barely had a chance to greet each other in mutual confusion before Krieger escorted us across the courtyard. The "party" was being held in a conference room on the training campus, a few minutes' walk away.

The room was only just large enough for the amount of people in it, but dressed up for the occasion with a bar and bartender set up in the far corner and a poker table on the end near us. A few tables and chairs were scattered around the perimeter of the room, a buffet table lining one wall.

"Well, you two, get to mingling. Make us look good!" She left Luka and me stranded by the door.

"Tell me you were given more notice about this than I was, so I don't feel so bad," I said.

To my surprise, he laughed. "My apologies. We were given strict instructions not to disturb you after your collapse. And apparently, until this afternoon, neither of us was actually invited. But Crane wanted to celebrate your success." He shot a furtive glance around the room and lowered his voice. "I want to say congratulations. But . . . are you sure you're all right?"

Triumph mixed with some gray emotion filled me. "Just groggy. It hardly felt like anything at all," I said, affecting nonchalance. What was *wrong* with me? I *was* proud of myself. But when my breakthrough threatened Luka's hard-won place on the crew, it felt like I was lording it over him.

Bragging had never bothered me before.

"Apparently it was quite something. Certainly much more than I had achieved."

My heart twisted. "Luka, don't . . ."

But his eyes were already roaming the room, and he nodded as he spotted some familiar faces.

The others of the crew were here already. I saw Dr. Copeland, in a silver dress with dangling earrings sending sparkles dancing across her ebony skin, sipping wine at the bar beside Bolshakov, who looked gruff but handsome in a dark suit. Jeong and Shaw were at a round table socializing with a few people I'd never seen before, each dressed more expensively than the next.

Jeong herself was in a formal gown, deep blue, with a dramatically steep neckline. I'd never seen any of them like this before. Dr. Copeland was always in polo shirts and khakis, and Jeong was dowdy at her best.

I attempted in vain to tug out the wrinkles from my department-store blouse.

"So," Luka said, crossing his arms and looking out over the intimidating faces. "Mingle. What does this word mean again?"

"It means we should probably split up," I said, dreading it. "Make small talk with strangers. Impress them with your wit and intellect and accent."

He smiled warmly, grasping my elbow for only a moment. "Thank you for the clarification." He made his way to a group of bored-looking scientist types in bow ties and glasses standing idle by the buffet.

I scanned the room again and spotted Hanna at the bar, where I was surprised to see the bartender pour amber liquid into a scotch glass without even asking for ID.

I came up behind her. "Pretty sure you're not twenty-one."

"Pretty sure I don't care." She motioned with her head to the far corner, where in the dim light I made out the tall, well-dressed figure of Clayton Crane. "He's hosting this party, and he swore to the bartending company that everyone at this party was of legal age. And where I come from, I've been legal for years." She took a sip, ice cubes tinkling in the glass, and sucked in a breath. "If we're old enough for space, we should be old enough for a drink."

She motioned to the bar. The bartender, unbidden by me, had poured a glass of something dark and bubbly and put it in front of me.

"I'd rather not," I said.

Hanna's expression went from carefully cultivated boredom to that laser-focused intensity I knew so well. Her voice dropped an octave, lips barely moving to conceal her words. "Before the month is over, you may or may not be leaving Earth on an experimental spacecraft, which may or may not bring you back. Live a little."

Point taken. I tipped back the glass before I could let myself think about it too much. "Wait—is this Coke?"

Hanna flashed a wide grin. "With a splash of rum. Now give me a minute. I just need a little liquid courage before I go introduce you to Crane's friends."

I didn't like the sound of that, but I left her in peace, drifting around the room and sipping from my cup. It just tasted like Coke, syrupy sweet, with only a warm tingle down the back of my throat that betrayed the alcohol entering my system. The rush of sugar and cold carbonated liquid was like a kick in the mouth, and I realized how long it'd been since I'd had anything stronger than tea.

"I didn't take you for a drinker" came a voice behind me, and I felt a rush of relief at seeing Luka at my elbow again. "An underage one, at that."

"Hanna is a bad influence," I said, shrugging and looking into my glass. "But really, I think it's mostly Coke."

Maybe it was the alcohol—at least, I was going to blame the alcohol—but my heart was thumping a little harder than usual, and my hands felt oddly warm and tingly. "How was mingling?"

"Fair," he said. "Though you don't seem to have made any new acquaintances."

"Hey, I'm just the alternate," I joked, even though the truth of it stung. "No one cares much about me."

His face lost its mirth. I bit the inside of my lip, regretting the words. With this breakthrough, the scales were tipping in my favor. And possibly risking the last friendship I had left.

We made our way over to the table to say hello to Jeong and Shaw. I nudged Luka, whispered, "Mr. Crane is over there. Hanna said something about introducing us to his friends later." His friends were all serious-faced men, and they seemed deep in quiet discussion in the corner.

We joined the conversation with Jeong and Shaw. Correction: Luka participated, and I nodded at appropriate intervals, sneaking glances at the men gathered around Crane.

"Okay, you two," Hanna said, her voice flinty and sudden in my ear. "Come on. Mr. Crane wants to officially introduce you."

We rose as one from the table, my legs feeling surprisingly weak as Luka excused the both of us. Hanna's anxiety put me on edge. I shot a sideways glance at Luka. His jaw was clenched, eyes focused on the men in the corner. If *Hanna* needed a drink before talking with these guys, and Luka was already steeling himself, I knew for a fact I wasn't going to enjoy the encounter.

Hanna led us across the room. Mr. Crane didn't even acknowledge her presence beside him for five solid minutes, but Hanna seemed to expect that.

When he finally did acknowledge us standing there awkwardly outside the tight circle of men, Mr. Crane gestured to us with an arm and the circle split open to accommodate us. "Ah, gentlemen, here are the exceptional young people I wish you to meet. You already know Hanna Schulz. These two here are our top contenders for our fifth crew member. I'd like you to meet Luka Kereselidze and Cassandra Gupta."

The men—one stout and bearded with a sweating glass of scotch in one hand, one with thick eyeglasses and bushy brows that were constantly furrowed, making him appear permanently concerned, the third pale and stern and gaunt-faced, all of them old—did not smile. They did not give their names. The bearded one inclined his head slightly, acknowledging only Luka in his greeting.

Crane continued. "I believe you are familiar with Mr. Kereselidze's qualifications, as they were furnished in my report. He has continued to impress here on campus, and I think his knowledge of the mission-essential skills rivals even mine. But both of these young people have shown remarkable fortitude and maturity for their age, and each has their own special skill set that would prove invaluable to our mission. Just this morning, Ms. Gupta successfully formed a direct neural link with our testing computer. She possesses an able mind with abilities we know are exceedingly difficult to find. Which is why, gentlemen, we are considering increasing crew manifest to six, and including both of these talented individuals on our mission."

My breath caught. Both of us? *Yes!* I wanted to shout, but I kept my face impassive. I snuck a glance sideways at Luka to see if he was happy for me, too. His eyes widened in surprise, but he allowed no other emotion to surface.

"The craft is built for five," the gaunt man said. His voice was as heavy and plodding as steel boots.

I let the air deflate from my lungs, slowly.

"It is not a critical change, Yeltsov," said the man with the glasses. "One extra module, a few calculation changes for the extra weight and oxygen. It can be done."

"Not without extra cost," said the bearded man. "And added risk. The simulations must be run again to account for the changes. You would be looking at a launch delay of at least a year. To be conservative."

He spoke as if we weren't standing right there, like we didn't matter at all.

"She formed a neural link with the *test* computer, you say?" said the man with the glasses.

I drank the rest of my rum and Coke too quickly; the burn provoked a cough I couldn't suppress. The men glanced at me as though they'd only just noticed I was there.

Hanna stepped in. "The test computer is simply a scaled-down version of Sunny, possessing all the same capabilities at lower processing speed—a way to test candidates cheaply. The neural handshake—the ability to make the connection—that is the difficult thing, and that is what Cassie has proven she's capable of achieving."

I appreciated her defending me, but even in its best light, my "success" sounded insubstantial. I tried projecting an air of unaffected genius. As though I weren't a teen girl unable to handle alcohol.

Hanna's words actually provoked an impressed raise of the eyebrows and a few nods from the men—except for pale Mr. Yeltsov, who did nothing.

"And Luka cannot perform to the same level," said the man with the glasses. "The board will not sign off on yet another redesign of the craft and spending years testing it just so you can add an additional crew member, Crane. You want to have your cake and eat it, too."

"We need to see a return on our investment. Now, before any more unfortunate accidents occur." The gaunt man's voice was grave, and with the way the other two leveled their eyes at Crane, they were in agreement.

Luka and I both startled. Crane had told them about the sabotage? Or could they be talking about something else?

"The solution seems quite simple to me," agreed the bearded man.

Crane's schmoozing facade broke only for a second, his annoyance showing through. "That is not quite—"

"This supercomputer," Mr. Yeltsov began, apparently changing the subject. "This is the project you reported as being over budget, yes?"

Crane's eyes turned hard, and he flicked his head almost imperceptibly at Hanna. She put her hands on our shoulders and pushed us away. "Time to go, kiddies," she muttered under her breath. "Daddy and his friends have to talk privately now."

Luka was still having trouble with his EEG tests.

Crane's investors were doubling the pressure to launch.

Something was going to give. Soon.

We went to the bar, where Hanna immediately got another drink and I let the bartender refill my glass as I slipped onto a bar stool between her and Luka, my body still wound with tension.

Crane wanted both of us on the mission. Crane was trying to convince his investors to allow us both without compromising a quick launch date. But it might not work. As much as SEE professed to streamline the process of getting into space, bypassing politics, there seemed to be plenty of politicking going on behind the scenes.

I don't know why I was surprised when Luka motioned the bartender over and immediately downed half the amber liquid the bartender poured him. The drinking age in Georgia was probably eleven.

"So that part's over," Hanna said. "I've fulfilled my official duties, and you two are on your own. I'd avoid that happy little foursome for the remainder of the night, though, unless Crane asks to see you. And even then I'd probably try to get out of it."

"He's been having money trouble? I thought the guy was loaded," I said.

"It isn't money trouble, and it isn't any of your business. Or mine," she added, almost as an afterthought. She slipped off the bar stool and grabbed my arm. She said nothing, but her eyes flicked meaningfully to Luka, then back to me.

Confused, I allowed a quick glance at Luka, who was intently staring into his glass.

Luka hadn't said a word since meeting the investors. He was still lost in thought, eyes focused on the amber liquid in his glass as he swirled it slowly in a circle.

"Hey, you okay?" I asked. Maybe Hanna thought Luka could use a pep talk, and thought it'd better come from me.

He looked up as though he'd forgotten I was there. Then he nodded. Took a sip. "Yes, of course."

His voice was hard. The words clipped. A lie.

I watched him a moment, studying his profile, trying to read him.

Then it hit me: Luka, despite all the work he put into this, despite his consistently high scores, had failed on one crucial element, and now they were considering bringing me in, too. That'd hurt even the most humble person.

"Your EEG tests haven't been improving," I guessed out loud. "Even after . . ."

"No." He didn't seem eager to discuss it. I was probably the *last* person he wanted to see right now.

He downed the rest of his glass and rose from his chair. "I don't wish to be here any longer. Would you like to join me in an escape?"

A corner of my mouth quirked upward of its own accord. "We'll have to be quick. Before Krieger or Hanna can catch us."

We slipped into the empty hallway. Emergency fluorescents lit the linoleum in patches every fifteen feet or so. It was otherwise shadows and stillness, a welcome relief from being in a room full of tense strangers.

We strolled slowly, nowhere in particular to go, only wanting to be somewhere *other* than where we'd been. Luka occasionally glanced sideways at me, as if he meant to speak, but never did.

"Something's wrong with you and I don't know what it is," I finally said. "Can I . . . help? Can I do anything?"

He just shook his head.

"Did I do something wrong? If I did . . . I'm sorry."

He stopped, his voice emphatic. "No! No. I'm happy for your success. It's simply that . . . I've been reconsidering why I am here. Perhaps it is dawning on me, the finality of our mission. The ramifications. I am not . . ." He stopped, shook his head, and looked up at the dark sky. "I am not sure I want to be so far from my family. Perhaps this is why you have succeeded where I have failed. Perhaps I have not found within myself the sufficient desire to succeed."

Hearing him say it, the tide of my own homesickness crested over me, barely kept at bay.

His eyes were so blue in the too-bright light of the sole fluorescent above us. They were pleading with me. "How do you manage the possibility of never seeing your loved ones again?"

"I don't let myself think about it." It was the truth.

"Don't you? That is brave."

"Brave?" I huffed, skeptical. "More like willful ignorance. I'm very good at compartmentalizing my feelings."

He considered me, eyes still locked on my face, as if searching for some answer there. "What is it that makes you so driven? To give up your family, your home, potentially your life, to leave behind the known for the unknown? What . . . drives you to this?"

My heart was beating faster, my breath coming a little harder. "That's just it," I said, willing myself to remain calm in the face of some rising emotional storm in Luka. He'd always been the stalwart one. Now his calm sea was becoming a tempest and I didn't know how to navigate it. "The unknown. I'm so *curious* about the universe—we know so little and I want to learn it all, *see* it all—I always have—there are so many wonders out there that humans have never dreamed possible. I want to help us get there. I want to discover and I want to learn. I want to *know*. Don't you? Isn't that why you're here?"

"Yes," he said with a little smile.

"And this?" I added, dropping my voice. "*Meeting* an alien civilization? They would have so much to teach us. It's so cheesy, but—this is the dawn of something entirely new. I want to be right there when it happens. I've dreamed of it my whole life."

Luka was smiling with only half his mouth.

"What?" I asked, self-conscious.

He just shook his head, as though he was trying to discourage something.

I was about to push him further into revealing it—he'd somehow gotten me to reveal more of *my* inner thoughts without giving away much himself—when we both heard, at the same time, the sound of voices down the hall behind us.

Everyone we knew to have clearance in this part of the facility was at the party.

Luka and I shared a confused glance, and then silently crept back the way we'd come. I was glad for my ugly, quiet shoes now. High heels would have announced my steps like a snare drum.

We found the occupied room easily. The door had been left open a crack, like someone had forgotten to push it closed, a narrow rectangle of yellow light spearing the darkness between the emergency lights.

A raised voice met my ears, and Luka held out an arm to stop me from going farther to see its source. But I recognized the deep, plodding words of the gaunt-faced man. "The board cannot and will not abide further delays, Mr. Crane."

Mr. Crane's voice was, in typical fashion, calm and aloof, but the words were quiet and their meaning lost to me. A note of aggravation in his tone told me this was an escalating argument.

Whatever Mr. Crane had been saying, he didn't get a chance to finish. "Christmas," said the louder voice, the word final, like the pounding of a gavel. "The launch must happen before Christmas. Or it will not happen at all. Make your decision."

Luka and I looked at each other.

Shadows danced on the floor; someone was moving inside the room. Coming closer to the door. Luka and I flew backward, turning and ducking through the first door we saw, out into the chill of the night air.

Momentum carried us farther in the darkness of the courtyard, until there was enough distance between us and the door that I no longer felt in danger of being discovered.

A spot of moonlight had broken through the clouds, like a narrow spotlight on the grass. I stopped there to read Luka's face. His expression was grim.

I didn't know what to say about what we'd overheard. How many weeks till Christmas? I wasn't sure.

What did this mean for Luka? For me?

Luka took a half step closer to me. "You're shivering."

In the adrenaline of the moment I hadn't noticed the chill of the air. My limbs were quivering. "I'm from Alabama. I'm not designed for the cold."

He slipped out of his jacket and held it open for me in offering.

"Oh, you don't . . ." But the offer was tempting, and it seemed rude to refuse, so I turned and allowed him to help me into it.

His jacket was soft, warm, and suffused with the smell of him—fresh and sharp, like aftershave; I felt at once both comforted and electrified. I turned back toward him, holding the jacket tight around myself. The sleeves were so long that only my fingertips emerged from them. The grim set of his mouth and around his eyes had softened somewhat. "You didn't have to . . . but thank you."

He took another step closer, and I heard him exhale quietly. Watched his face lose more of its tension, lose its guardedness—the facade he'd worn inside. "Cassie . . . Cass. I never asked. Which do you prefer?"

Nobody had ever asked me my preference. "Cass is fine," I whispered.

"Cass." His hands were on my elbows now, an almost-embrace. A chill breeze rustled through the courtyard, making goose bumps break out on my bare calves.

My head was full of the smell of his jacket. Such an alien, *boy* scent.

I started taking shallower breaths. It didn't diminish. It blocked out every other thought.

"I've enjoyed this," he said. "The competition. Getting to know you. I'm glad you're here with me. I'm glad it was you."

His tone was suspiciously final. "You're not giving up, are you? Nothing's changed, Luka. You're amazing. You're the obvious choice. Don't act like this now—we're so *close*."

A ghost of a smile. "No, I won't give up. And neither will you. Agreed?"

I breathed a little easier. "Agreed."

He shook his head with a huff of rueful laughter, like he hadn't expected my reaction. And then he came out with it, his face open and sincere and genuine. "I like you, Cass."

It wasn't a throwaway line, something you said to a friend, like something Emilio would say. It wasn't casual.

"I like you a lot more than I expected to," I answered honestly.

He laughed, surprised and genuine and true, and it wrung out my heart.

I didn't know if he was trying to say his good-byes now, while we were still friends. All signs pointed to one of us going and the other one staying. At this moment, either scenario was unthinkable. I'd glimpsed the tenuous hope that we'd both be able to go, together, and it had been a heady thing.

I desperately wanted that hope again.

And then his mouth was right there—*right there.* I found I couldn't look away from his lips, thin and pale pink and a little chapped. They parted as though he meant to say something, and then closed again. And I realized with a glance he was also looking at me in the same way I was looking at him.

All the blood went rushing to my face. And with it, the realization of how much I really did like him. I'd meant it when I'd said that. I respected him. Enjoyed his company.

He inclined his head and I realized, with a jolt of fear, that I knew exactly what he meant to do.

I took a step backward, breaking out of the gentle grasp of his hands.

His eyes flashed hurt only a moment before the facade came over his emotions again. He held out his hands, open and empty, meaning no harm. "I apologize. I overstepped."

I closed the short distance I'd made between us in my moment of panic. I struggled for a way to make him understand

without pushing him farther away. "No. You didn't. I just . . .
I'm not a big fan of kissing, I don't think. I . . . don't have much
experience in that area. With someone who actually wants to
kiss me. And who isn't drunk."

"Of course. I understand." He was putting distance between
us, putting up his guard again. His voice dropped an octave.
"But I'm not drunk."

The scent of alcohol on his breath seemed to contradict those
words, but he was as clear-eyed as I was. Probably more.

I'd closed this door hastily, a fearful knee-jerk. Luka was
holding it slightly open for me, just in case I decided I actually
did want to step through.

This may be my last chance to ever kiss a boy I like.

I'd never thought that would matter to me, but suddenly it
did—making me wonder if I knew anything about myself at all.
I'd never wanted, never even had a *glimmer* of wanting to do
this with someone else before.

My mind rapidly ticked off explanations. This was supposed
to be the big, formative teenage experience, wasn't it? I didn't
want to leave Earth with regrets. Maybe it'd be different this
time. It certainly couldn't be as bad as last time.

And I was genuinely *curious*. It could be nice. It was *supposed*
to be nice, wasn't it?

I stepped close enough to him that the backs of my hands,
still holding his jacket closed, bumped into his sternum. "But
maybe my hypothesis is wrong. Maybe I should . . . test it again.
Under different . . . experimental conditions."

He gave me a hesitant half smile. "Are you sure? Or are you lying to spare my feelings? Because—"

"How often have you seen me lie to spare people's feelings?"

His smile broke into a grin as he took my face in his cold-chapped hands and brought his mouth down to mine.

A star burst inside my chest at the contact. I was surprised at the intensity of it; how he kissed me without hesitation or fear, with *purpose*. As if it'd been something he'd wanted to do all along. As if he knew how this was supposed to go.

I tried to match him, to return his enthusiasm, but I had no idea if I was failing or succeeding.

It was an entirely different species from the drunk half kiss from the kid I'd never wanted to kiss to begin with. It was even pleasant. His nearness. His warmth. His hands holding me with a touching gentleness. But I found that when his lips broke from mine, I had no desire to keep going.

We stayed, hovering, close, catching our breaths.

I had no idea what came next.

But then he did the most amazing thing: he smiled.

His mouth still inches from mine, eyes still closed, hands holding my face in his hands, he grinned. He didn't know I was watching him. He smiled for himself only.

And then he opened his eyes to mine and laughed an incredulous laugh. I felt it vibrate through me, joy leaping into my chest and escaping me in giggles.

"I hope that was a better experience than last time," he said, his voice low and tender.

"So much better."

Luka wrapped his arms around my shoulders, pulling me into his solid form so tight I couldn't move. I closed my eyes and let my head rest against his chest. Let our inhales and exhales synchronize, find a rhythm.

"One of us may go," I said finally, hating myself for darkening the bright light that was still warming me from within. "And leave the other one behind."

I felt, rather than heard, the heaviness of his next breath.

"It seems that way." His voice rumbled through me, more feeling than sound.

What else was there to say? It was simply the truth. There was no changing it.

"Promise me this changes nothing," he said, his voice muffled and surprising. "Promise me you will not give up your spot for me." He pulled back from me to search my eyes, his gaze tense and reflecting moonlight. "That neither of us will do anything to jeopardize the mission."

"The mission still comes first," I agreed. "And you had better not entertain any stupid ideas of dropping out so I can go instead. Nothing like that, you hear me? I don't need you to give me a leg up—I can earn it on my own. No martyrdom. Promise me."

He nodded, then took my face in his hands again. "Nothing stupid. Understood." We shared a smile. "But, Cass . . . even if it means leaving all of this behind—your family, Earth . . ." He trailed off, as if unwilling to rank himself among the things that mattered most to me. "Think of all those things that motivate you. Don't forget them."

"Hey," I said, reaching a hand up to the side of his face. I didn't know what he meant by those words, exactly—there was too much going on in my head for my brain to process it all accurately. I don't know why this felt like good-bye. Why it felt so important to take advantage of this moment. "You never told me why you're here. What motivates *you*? You've come such a long way—you're so far from home."

For a second, I thought he might be about to cry. And then he was pressing his hand against the one that cradled his cheek, and drew it down. He smiled, but it was only an echo of his earlier one. "One day I hope to tell you. But it is a long story." He lifted my hand, kissed the back of it, and let go. "Come, let's go inside, before we catch a cold and they disqualify us both."

TWENTY-FIVE

THE NEXT MORNING the sky was a cheery blue but for an ominous, towering white thunderhead on the horizon, trailing a dark curtain of rain falling somewhere far away.

"Take a good long look," Bolshakov said, surprising me. He pulled along a small rolling suitcase made of battered leather. "We will not see the sky again until launch."

The crew was gathering in the courtyard, readying our move to quarantine quarters. I'd been watching Luka's door in my peripheral vision, but it still hadn't opened. Anxiety roiled in my stomach; I'd been waiting to see him again, waiting to know what would happen between us when I did.

There was still a glow inside me, but it had died down to a flickering flame—something easily hidden and fragile.

Luka had never been late, but Bolshakov, Jeong, Shaw, and Copeland had all filtered out of their rooms with their luggage and Luka was still absent.

My eyes were drawn again to the storm clouds.

When Pierce and Crane came personally to ferry us to our next destination, I should have known. Luka's door remained closed.

"Wait," I said. "Where's Luka?"

Pierce stopped short. Regarded me. He appeared tired. His head tilted slightly to the side, either mocking or confused. He pointedly did not answer.

Crane took his time before he spoke, surveying each of us in turn. He prolonged the silence just long enough to turn the atmosphere solemn and expectant, like an orchestra director boosting the anticipation before the music. "We are about to move into the final phase. I need each of you, at this moment, to search inside yourselves and ensure that you are committed to this project. I am offering you a chance that precious few humans in history have been given. You must put earthly concerns behind you. Look only to the future. Four of you have lived full lives, have families, reached the pinnacles of your careers." His cool, intelligent eyes focused on me and my spine straightened. "But you, Cassandra, you are young. Your life is yet unlived. I cannot have a last-minute change of heart from you. *Odysseus* must launch, and it must launch with you aboard."

I saw, as though through a distorted lens, how the other astronauts looked at me now with renewed interest. Copeland didn't hide her surprise. Shaw and Jeong gave me congratulatory smiles.

I didn't meet any of their eyes, didn't feel the shock I should have. Nothing registered.

Pierce clarified. "Luka Kereselidze is no longer a part of this program. He flew home this morning."

"What?" It was *still* morning. How early had they sprung this on him? Had he just walked past my door an hour ago, saying nothing? Did they not let him say good-bye, or did he not want to tell me himself?

Colonel Pierce kept his voice steady, but there was a hint of an apology in his eyes. "He could not fulfill the mission requirements. There was no longer a place for him in Project Adastra."

Crane continued as if Pierce had never spoken, the full intensity of his eyes locked on mine. "Cassandra Gupta, you are needed. You are the fifth member of this crew. There's no alternate who can take your place." Now he turned from me to the others. "You, each of you, must decide at this moment. Will you commit to give all, for the good of all mankind?"

Each of them, in turn, murmured their affirmations.

Now all eyes were on me.

"Yes," I said, and was proud that I had not hesitated.

Bolshakov was still beside me. He offered me his hand. Numb, I slipped my hand in his, and had the impression of shaking hands with a grizzly bear. "Congratulations, Ms. Gupta. It is an honor." He seemed grim. They all did. I didn't understand it. Even though Shaw patted me awkwardly on the shoulder and

Jeong squeezed my forearm encouragingly, the smiles were all tight and lifeless.

This was a job to them. A dangerous, experimental, completely unprecedented job, but otherwise one they'd done time and again. Maybe they thought I shouldn't be here. Maybe they didn't like that it turned out to be me.

"Congratulations, kid," Copeland said as we started trudging after Pierce, weighed down by various pieces of luggage. Her voice was quiet and tense, her gray eyes scanning me up and down as if to evaluate my worthiness. "You've earned it." And then, a moment later, when she'd dropped back behind me, she spoke in a hushed voice to Jeong that she probably thought I couldn't hear. "This is so shitty. She's just a kid. It shouldn't be someone with so much to lose."

And then I understood.

I followed the others out the door, trying and failing to reconcile the two warring thoughts in my brain: *Luka's gone. I'm going into space.*

I looked around me, at the astronauts I was now a part of. This was my job now, too.

And it was time to get to work.

The downpour started just as I was getting settled into my new quarters inside quarantine. It was a windowless shoe box compared to my last two rooms—more wall alcove than living space—but I didn't care. It wasn't like I was going to be here long.

I took a few long, steadying breaths. *Get ahold of yourself.* Why was I suddenly so afraid?

The grim mood that had fallen like a cloud of smog on the rest of the crew had afflicted me, too. A tug-of-war was happening inside me.

Luka was gone. I was going into space. I might never see him, or my family or my friends, again. I was going to leave Earth until it was not even a pale blue dot in the rearview mirror. I was going to see amazing things. Alien planets. Faraway stars. An entirely new species. Everything I'd always wanted.

But there were suddenly other, new things I wanted, too.

Was my lifelong dream worth losing everyone I'd ever cared about, all the wonders and creations and humans on Earth, my *life*? Even if everything went solidly according to plan, it would still mean giving up prime years of my life, spending years I'd never get back semiconscious in a cryogenic tube and hurtling through space. Something could happen to my parents. My dadi might not live to see me return safely home.

I weighed them in my heart. Everything I was, would ever be—a life wrapped up in love and friendship and long happy years on a green-and-blue planet—against many lonely years adrift in a cold, endless, lifeless black void. A fervent, lifelong, heartfelt dream and the promise of unimaginable experiences.

I wanted to push that boundary even further. I wanted to be a pioneer. To dare mighty things. What was out there would forever call to me, and the things I could do for history were more important than my one little life.

I collapsed onto the thin mattress.

This is my dream come true.

I repeated that over and over again. And slowly, the distorted carnival mirror of my thoughts shifted. The universe reordered itself, and suddenly I felt lighter, my way clear and vision unclouded.

The girl I'd been before I'd come there—the one who was willing to sacrifice everything to get to this place—would have never believed I'd have doubts once there. But I was still that girl.

I put everything else—everything that might make me doubt myself—into a box in my mind and sealed it off.

I took another breath. Saw myself promising Luka that I wouldn't let anything stop me. And then erased the memory, because Luka belonged in that box of things I was leaving behind.

I imagined my body turning to steel. My stomach, full of butterflies and bad omens, replaced with a core of strength. I thought of the person I'd been before coming to Houston: friendless by choice, driven only by ambition and determination. Tethered to Earth by only a gossamer thread. Head constantly tilted upward, skyward, eyes on the prize. I'd been the unstoppable girl before.

I was still that girl.

TWENTY-SIX

THE FOURTEEN DAYS we spent in quarantine were like this: claustrophobic, tense, and fraught with anticipation.

Our quarantine quarters were hardly larger than two double-wide trailers, sealed off from the rest of the compound, with their own air and water-filtration system. In one wing, we slept. In the other, we worked.

No fresh air. No outdoor time. No running.

It reminded me of the SLH.

This was the home stretch. Every moment of every day reminded us of that. Every day was one day closer to launch.

The knowledge that I would soon be leaving Earth behind, and all the preparation required in order to do so, was enough to keep that box in my head firmly sealed.

At least, while I was awake. But whatever dreams I might have dreamed were quickly wiped away by the frantic pace of my last days on Earth.

While Bolshakov, Jeong, and Shaw were busy learning all there was to know about our new ship and how to pilot it, Copeland worked to help me acclimate to Sunny-Lite. Hooked up, brain-to-circuit-board, I practiced each day interfacing with the computers.

As flight surgeon, she had taken over my neural interface training. She sat beside me in a metal folding chair in the closet-size room allotted for my practice, barely big enough for the two of us and the computer equipment. "To go straight to Sunny herself would be too much, too overwhelming. We want to ease you into it."

I learned how to send commands to Sunny-Lite. She was synced wirelessly to a small robot. With a little practice, I eventually was able to make the robot turn on, off, and move in the general directions I specified using only my thoughts, which Sunny-Lite read and responded to.

It felt powerful, this potential—but it was hardly groundbreaking. Thought-controlled prosthetics had been around for a long time.

I also learned how to receive input from the computer. As a test, Copeland hooked a heartbeat monitor to her finger and linked it to Sunny. I calmed my mind and let the sensation of my own body fall away. After a few seconds, I heard—or felt—a soft, repeating pulse, like the thumping bass of faraway music in a steady rhythm. With a start, I realized I was actually connected *directly* to Copeland's heartbeat monitor.

"Fifty-five beats per minute," I said.

Copeland's lips parted slightly. "That's incredible," she breathed. "Goddamn."

These exercises were designed for my brain to become accustomed to an external link. It was like muscle memory; new nerve endings had to grow where they had never gone before. That way, when I was connected to the real Sunny, I'd be prepared.

Once the connection was established, Copeland told me, the drugs would take over and allow me to rest in semiconsciousness without having to maintain the mental state on my own. But I couldn't make the connection while sedated. So we practiced that more than anything: finding the tenuous connection between my brain and Sunny, and latching on.

Copeland told me to imagine it like I was looking for Sunny in a hall filled with doors. She knocked so quietly that it was almost impossible to hear unless I was able to filter out as much external stimuli as possible. Once I found the door, all I had to do was open it and let her in. And she'd take care of the rest.

My lessons tapered off to independent study. The takeoff procedures and flight mechanics would be taken care of by the experienced astronauts; my job, my entire focus, was to learn to interface with Sunny.

I'd hoped to get to know the others like I had with my roommates during selection, but everyone was subdued, focused, and carefully polite under the cramped circumstances. The atmosphere was tense, quiet, contemplative. Everyone spoke little and in hushed voices. We were all hanging by the thread of anticipation, living carefully in a pressure cooker.

But unlike the SLH, this was the real deal.

I barely slept. All of the cells in my body felt like they were vibrating. I never felt like I was standing still. Apprehension and sheer adrenaline shook me at a molecular level. I spoke only when necessary. I ate the food they gave us. I did my work and went to bed and tried in vain to sleep. I tried not to remember my dreams.

T-minus forty-eight hours to launch. Visiting day.

The last time I would see my family before leaving Earth.

When the intercom called me into the visitors' room, I wasn't sure what to expect. How it would be to see them after so long.

I certainly wasn't expecting Mitsuko, in a stylish black trench coat and knee-high boots, with flawless makeup and a multicolored silk scarf tucked around her neck. She looked like a model. She was grinning and waving through the plexiglass.

A tall, broad man with a buzzed head and an expensive-looking leather jacket sat in a chair behind her. He had a handsome, blocky face that made me think of a Latino Captain America. He stood when I entered. And then I could see Emilio, sitting on the other side, leaping to his feet and grinning like a puppy.

Mitsuko was still grinning when I sat down in front of the

plexiglass window and grabbed the telephone.

"You can wait your turn, that's what you get for being late" were the first words I heard from her mouth, and they weren't even directed at me. Instead of backing down, Emilio crowded into the booth next to Mitsuko and hopped up onto the narrow table on their side.

"Cass, I can't believe I'm looking at you right now." She put her hand against the glass and tapped her manicured fingernails against it, like she couldn't keep her excitement to herself. "Michael came with me, so you could finally meet him—kind of. This is so awesome. How freaked out are you?"

I didn't know what to say. I just looked at her. How long had it been since selection? She was like a relic from someone else's life. Like a friend you hadn't seen since freshman year. So much had changed. For me—maybe not so much for her.

Mitsuko's smile fell away. Her voice lowered. "Cass?" She shot a worried glance up to Emilio, who shrugged. "Cassandra Gupta, you tell me what's wrong *right now*, or so help me I will reach through this phone—"

I tried to smile. "Just nerves. I'm really happy to see you." She looked at me so long I had to avert my eyes. How could I tell her? That I was about to strap into an alien machine, hook my brain directly to a blindingly intelligent computer, and travel farther and longer than any human alive had ever traveled?

"I might be a little scared." The words released from me like a confession of guilt.

"Cassie Gupta," she said again, and her voice was like a call to action. I sat up straighter. "I'm jealous of you right now. Actually jealous. That doesn't happen to me much." Her voice went softer. "You earned this. Own it."

I closed my eyes, just for a second, letting her words wash over me. I wished I could take them inside me, etch them on my rib cage.

She tapped on the plexiglass and smiled. "Brought you a present." She clicked open the box inside the partition and dropped in something small with a light *ting*. Ten seconds of sterilization to remove any virulent germs, and the light on my side turned green.

I picked up the tiny metal thing, examining it. It was a thin silver cuff, a ring, stamped with a pattern of dots and stars. In a moment, I recognized it, and felt a grin nearly split my face. "The constellation Leo?" On the back was a tiny black stamp of Leo's symbol, a circle with a little tail coming from the top.

Mitsuko looked pleased with herself. "For you, my little lion girl, to remember *who you are*." She said it low and spooky.

"How did you know my birthday?"

"I'm sneaky like that. Or I looked you up when I got home."

I slipped the ring onto my finger and shouldn't have been surprised that it fit snug. "How did I get so lucky to have met you?" I asked.

Mitsuko winked. "Michael's always saying that."

She and I shared a smile.

"I'm so glad you came. I didn't think you would. I thought . . ."

Mitsuko inclined her head, conceding the point. "Yeah, well.

I didn't want that stinking astronaut job after all. Pay's shit anyway. Turns out I'd rather eat empanadas at home with the hubby and watch that shit on the internet."

I laughed and it hurt. Those muscles were underused these days. "No hard feelings?"

"Cass. Would I have *flown* here at the last minute if there were?"

Thankfulness filled me to the brim.

Emilio had taken to shoving her lightly on the shoulder with the toe of his sneaker, apparently impatient for his turn. She sent him a dirty look and stood. "You'd better come see me when you get back, or I'll hunt you down." She pressed her palm against the glass, waved, and then she was gone. Nothing left but a fading handprint.

Emilio grabbed the handset and held it up to his ear. He wore a red T-shirt and ripped jeans, and he still had the single stripe of hair down the middle of his scalp. He'd gelled and spiked it, dyed some of the tips red. To look at him, you probably wouldn't think he'd been chosen as one of the elite minds of his generation. You'd probably be telling him to stop skateboarding on your sidewalk.

He cradled the phone in the crook of his shoulder. "Funny, I always knew I'd see you like this one day" were the first words out of his mouth.

"What have you been up to?" I asked, eager for some taste of a life outside these walls.

"Oh, you know. Got a new job." He paused for effect. "At

NASA. A contractor job in Houston, actually. Should be fun. Might even get to work behind the scenes on your mission at some point."

Doubtful, but I widened my smile anyway. "Reassuring. So you'll be close to Mitsuko?" I felt a little pang. They'd all be together, and I'd be lifetimes away.

"Yeah, same town, not far away. We came down here together. We've been so busy that we don't get to hang much, though."

Jealousy began biting at the heels of all those good feelings.

And then, over his shoulder to Mitsuko but loud enough for me to hear: "Shit, you got her a gift?" Emilio sent her a wounded look, then shot me a wicked grin. "Just kidding. I got you something, too."

He fished a small pouch out of his pocket and dropped into the box in the wall something so light it hardly made a sound.

A souvenir patch from the STS-87 mission—Kalpana Chawla's first spaceflight. Shaped like a space helmet, it was half earth, half space, with the *Columbia* shuttle forming the border between them. I traced her name along the edge of space.

"I saw it at the gift shop," Emilio said, a little sheepish. "I thought it might be something sentimental for you to have. I don't know if that's, like, stereotyping you or whatever."

If I'd looked at Emilio right then, I might have cried. "No, it's perfect. I love it."

"I hoped you would." His voice took on a rare note of sincerity. "Take that up there with you. That way I can feel like maybe a part of me is going, too."

"That all of us are going," Mitsuko added loudly.

I nodded, hugged their gifts between my hands. "I will. I promise."

There was silence. I collected myself and found him gazing at me, his forehead against the glass. Since he was sitting on the counter he was above me, looking down. "I promise this isn't me being weird or anything. But I love you. I know we're not, like—you know, whatever. I just want you to know that. As a friend. You and Mitsuko, too. We went through some shit back there, and I'll never forget it. Just—you know what I mean?"

I knew what he meant.

My parents' flight had been delayed, and they arrived a few hours after Mitsuko and Emilio had gone.

Saying good-bye to them—for the second time—made me feel empty and smarting, like my soul had been ripped out from the inside.

I didn't know how to say good-bye to my family. I feared it might just kill me.

My parents entered side by side, obviously fresh from the red-eye to Florida. Then Dadi, the lines of her face deeper than I'd remembered, her hair seemingly more gray. My uncle, hair standing up from where he'd messed with it, one cheek still red from where he'd fallen asleep in the plane. Both my parents looked drawn and tired, as though they hadn't slept for weeks, their clothes wrinkled.

They'd come straight from the airport. Hadn't even stopped at the hotel to change.

"Hi, Mom," I said into the phone. That's as far as I got.

My mom cried. I cried. Not for myself, but because I realized what she had gone through to let me go.

She'd walked through fire to bring me, her only child, into the world. Only for her to leave it, literally. And possibly forever.

My mom couldn't even speak. She just cried into the phone until Dadi took it from her, gently, and held it to her ear.

"I'm sorry," I said, choking back sobs.

"Cassandra Harita Gupta, you do not apologize to anyone for following your heart," Dadi said, her rich voice strong and steady. "Your mother understands. We all understand. Now you listen. You will be safe. You will go into the universe and you will come home to us again. Understand?"

I nodded, tears trailing down my cheeks and prickling in my throat. I could not let myself look at my mother and her tearstained face. If I did, I would walk away from everything I had worked for and never look back.

Dadi placed the handset gingerly on the table, and with her spindly brown fingers reached up to her neck and unclasped the necklace she wore. She dropped it into the receiving bin that crossed the barrier between us. After a flash sterilization procedure, the box opened on my side.

Confused, I reached in and retrieved the necklace my grandmother had been wearing, still warm. My hand closed around the charm. The warmth from the stone made it seem alive in my palm. Her pendant of Ganesh, carved in alabaster soapstone.

The familiar elephant-head god smiled at me with enigmatic black bead eyes. His twisting trunk curled up around his head, human hands held out, open at his sides, welcoming.

The remover of obstacles.

It was as much a part of Dadi as the smell of her hair.

Dadi's voice was tinny and narrow over the old phone line, and I longed to crawl through it and bury my face in her shoulder, like I had when I was a kid and life overwhelmed me. "My mother gave that to me when I got married," she said. Her eyes were shining. "From her hands, to mine, to yours." Her knobby finger jabbed upward. "Now to the stars." Mom, beside her, had mostly stemmed her own tears but was pressing her lips hard to keep them at bay. They both gazed at me fiercely, as though trying to memorize my face.

I smiled tearfully and squeezed the pendant in my palm.

Uncle Gauresh leaned over Dadi and said, "See you when you get back home." Then my father finally lifted the phone to his ear, gazing at me silently behind his old-fashioned glasses. He tried to speak but only swallowed thickly, over and over.

My mother leaned in close to hear my voice and my father held it out for her to share.

"Why didn't you guys write me?" I hadn't planned to mention it, but the words escaped anyway.

"Oh, Cassandra," my mother said, taking the phone. "We did, we did. I never received anything back. I thought that you were just too busy to respond."

I swallowed back a fresh wave of tears, not letting them surface.

"I can't believe I am letting this happen," she said.

"You know this is what I want," I whispered.

My mom nodded, her eyes swollen.

"This is ridiculous. Everything's going to be fine," I said, though my quavering voice betrayed me. "This is the best thing that's ever happened to me. You'll see me in the news. In history books. No one will ever forget our name. Don't worry. You're going to be really, really proud of me."

Those were the words I'd practiced saying in the mirror in the bathroom four hours ago. But now they just felt rehearsed and ominous.

My mother's expression was a wreck, but her voice was steady. "I was already proud, my darling. Always proud."

"I'm coming back," I promised, meaning to be unafraid and confident, and almost pulling it off. "Don't cry, Mom, you're making me cry. This is happy, remember?"

I tried to drink them in, all crowded around the phone like that, loving me so much that they'd hopped on a plane with almost no notice in order to see me, behind glass—not even able to touch—for less than an hour. Hunched over a phone for a last chance to hear my voice.

They had made me who I was—literally. Wherever I went, there they would be, too.

When they left, I felt lighter. Unbalanced. Like I'd been carrying a heavy weight for so long, I didn't know how to drop it. I felt unmoored, unstable, like gravity had become treacherous.

Now I could truly put all earthly things behind me. No unfinished business. No good-byes unsaid. No regrets. This was what they'd told us, anyway—the NASA experts, the psychologists.

If only it were true.

I was already in my pajamas when the intercom buzzed again. Another visitor? At this hour?

Luka, I thought, with a spark of nervous hope. But that spark quickly died.

Hanna stood in the visitors' room, wearing a cardigan and khakis and holding her purse with both hands like a shield. It was way after hours. She should've left for home ages ago.

I hadn't seen Hanna since entering quarantine. Hadn't expected to see her. Had thought her part in this to be over. We shared a long look through the glass.

She picked up the phone on her end and motioned for me to do the same. Up close, I could see the heavy makeup that she'd used to hide dark circles under her eyes. Mr. Crane must be working her to the bone. Or she was working herself.

I could hear the soft puffs of her breath hitting the receiver. Her eyes locked with mine as she kept me in suspense. "Luka wanted me to tell you something."

An iron fist grabbed on to my stomach and tugged. I had to try twice to get my voice to come out. "What? When did you talk to him?"

"That last day, after the party for the board members when you interfaced with Sunny for the first time. He could see the writing on the wall. Wanted me to pass on a message, in case they didn't let him say good-bye. Guess they were in a hurry to get this show on the road."

"And . . . ?" My entire chest cavity was being crushed now.

"That he doesn't regret anything, and neither should you. And to keep your promise." Her eyes glinted, trying to read meaning in my reaction. I gave her nothing.

"And there's something else. Something he wanted you to have. God knows what it is." She opened up her purse and dropped something in the sterilization box between us.

I opened the box and pulled out a warm piece of black ivory. It took me a moment to place what it was—familiar but strange on its own, a thin rectangular prism the length of a finger, mounted in silver as though it were a paperweight or some other decoration.

A piano key. Where would he have even gotten something like that?

My throat closed around a sob.

I pressed my lips together.

"I'll be watching out for you on this end," she said. "Good luck. Godspeed."

"Thank you." Then, as she was about to hang up the phone: "Could you do one thing for me, maybe?"

Her hand stilled, waiting.

"If there's any way you could find Luka—I mean, if he's left the country it's probably impossible to track him down now. But if SEE has kept up with him, maybe, could you get him a message for me?"

Her eyebrow perked up. "I can try. What do you want me to tell him?"

"Just that I . . . I kept my promise. And I intend to tell him that in person, when I come back."

I couldn't sleep. How could I?

NASA astronauts had usually been allowed to take a small bag, called a Personal Preference Kit, of keepsake-type things with them into space. I was allowed less than a pound and a half for my PPK, and nothing electronic.

I hadn't brought much in my luggage that I'd want to take into space. I'd already put in a picture of my family and a scrap of paper with Beethoven's Sonata op. 106 I'd jotted down from memory.

I held the Ganesh pendant in my palm, feeling its little but significant weight. Felt the echo of my great-grandmother—a woman I'd never met, but whose blood ran in my veins—and imagined the familial line of my ancestors, the mitochondrial DNA that stretched in an unbroken chain of the women who'd made me, all the way back to the beginning of human life. I carried the echoes of the past with me and within me.

Emilio had been the first person to befriend me—not just the first person here, but the first ever. He'd sat down beside me by chance, and hadn't left my side since. My first impression of him had been so awful. Luka, too, I realized. And Mitsuko. Maybe Hanna most of all.

I'd made snap decisions about all of them and been wrong.

I had thought I was above them. That other people would distract me, compete with me, get in my way. Without my friends, I wouldn't be here. I had fulfilled the promise to my mom after all.

I brought the pendant up to my lips and kissed it. "Thank you," I whispered. Emilio had been right—he was the remover of obstacles, but Ganesh also placed obstacles in the paths of those who needed to be made humble.

I put Ganesh and the piano key in my PPK, along with the rest of my mementos from home.

Finally, there was nothing left to do but wait. I lay awake for hours, counting each as it passed.

I closed my eyes and tried to remember what it had been like to kiss Luka. Had that actually happened? It had been over so quickly, and I'd never gotten a chance to talk to him after.

Luka was my only regret, the only question left unanswered. Where was he? Was he thinking about me? What *did* he think about me? I imagined him in some faraway room, sitting awake like me, tortured by what he didn't get to say. I hoped he didn't blame me for taking his spot. Somehow I didn't think he would.

But why didn't he come say good-bye?

I was never going to find out.

I checked the clock.

T-minus twenty-four hours.

TWENTY-SEVEN

"ALL SYSTEMS ARE go for launch. Over."

Strapped in, on my back, looking straight up into the sky—if the sky were a curve of metal instead of atmosphere, and the twinkling status readouts from the instrument panels were stars.

We'd been sitting here for two and a half hours already, going through endless rounds of safety checks, but to me it had felt like nothing. I had no fear, just an urgent desire for liftoff.

Okay, so maybe there was a little fear.

The official line was that we had only a certain window of time for the launch, to coordinate with local weather patterns and the gravity well of the moon—that was the reason for the night launch. The launchpad was lit by so many stadium lights it was like a hundred miniature suns bearing down on us, but outside of the pad was utter darkness and quiet.

Night launch meant secrecy. Obviously they weren't going to be able to keep the noise a secret, but as long as no one saw the ship, they could pass it off as a routine satellite launch.

I'd been to a few launches as a kid. This time there were no crowds in lawn chairs and bleachers to watch. No press conference. No press at all. Only one picture of the crew before takeoff. The official photographer showed it to us after he'd taken it, and no one was smiling. There were no mission patches, no names on suits.

In all the launches I'd ever been to, the mood had been excited, jubilant. Command and crew spoke over the radio conversationally, spoke as friends, used nicknames and call signs.

This was entirely different. No one was joking to try to lighten the mood. Everyone was somber, resolute. Maybe they were summoning their bravery.

We pulled up to the launchpad. I saw the ghostly white form of the *Odysseus* for the first time, lit like a massive metal angel in the darkness.

It was shaped roughly like the old space shuttle—aerodynamic, like a plane or a bird. But these wings were short, stubby, rounded. The hull was smooth and unblemished except for a few NASA insignias on the wings. The middle was elongated and bloated, like a huge egg that the ship had swallowed whole. That was the habitation module, where five HHMs waited to insulate us for the long journey. The egg could detach and become an escape pod in an emergency.

The entire ship was encircled by a thick white ring, like a halo of steel. The Alcubierre drive. Which, according to hypothesis, could bend reality and take us to another star.

It was glowing faintly, the shining surface reflecting the bright lights of the launchpad. White vapor was emanating from the boosters like the breath of a sleeping dragon, shrouding *Odysseus* in a veil of dissipating fog. It looked mystical, magical. Like something from another world.

It *had* been designed on another world, I reminded myself. And when I woke, I'd be there.

Or maybe that ship was about to be our grave.

I'd stared at it until my eyes unfocused. *Odysseus* was my destiny. And whether my destiny called for me to make human history or to die trying, I realized it didn't matter. Either way, I was meant to be on board. Everything from my birth until now had led up to this.

When it was finally my turn to crawl into the launch module, I wasn't scared anymore.

The voices of multiple levels of command quipped back and forth in my ear, but I had trouble focusing on what they were saying.

In between the preflight checks, a voice would cut in to announce the time remaining. T-minus ten minutes and counting. T-minus five minutes. My limbs were shaking uncontrollably inside my suit as I could do nothing but listen and wait as the rockets below us roared and churned to life. I couldn't help but think again of being strapped into a living dragon.

Voices in my radio checked and rechecked and confirmed and double-confirmed, endlessly, over and over again, until finally . . .

"T-minus fifteen seconds." The voice in my comm was male, absurdly calm.

How many times had I watched videos of this online? The last time humans had taken off to a faraway destination, I'd been eight years old, in my pajamas, and watching it live on TV. Sitting in my grandma's lap while my mom made popcorn in the kitchen.

And now it was happening in real life. To *me*.

I was strapped in tighter than a race-car driver, wedged in the second row behind Jeong and Bolshakov, pushed against the curved bulkhead on my right, with Copeland and Shaw on my left.

The bright orange, modified Advanced Crew Escape Suits we wore in case we needed emergency ejection were like puffy, extremely expensive exoskeletons. Outside the tiny round window to my right there was nothing but black night and some white drifts of condensed air floating upward from the idling engines below. I did a breathing exercise and I tried to relax. Mission Control was watching our heart rates.

"Ten. Nine. Eight."

I tried to think of the faces of my family. My friends. Everything I loved on this planet I was about to leave.

"Seven. Six. Five."

Inside my head was quiet. Inside my chest my heart was stuttering wildly, adrenaline surging in my veins.

"Four. Three. Two."

The *Odysseus* began to shake. The dragon roared violently to life.

"One. Liftoff."

WOOOOOOOMPH!

Four rocket boosters roared with the intensity of thousands of tons of fuel, lifting us off the launchpad with a wall of fire. I was shoved into my chair as if an elephant had dropped onto my chest. My stomach jumped from the turbulence that shook us from side to side.

The rattling was so intense it felt like a separate earthquake inside each of my limbs. I exerted all my energy on inhaling and exhaling, forcing the air in and out of my lungs.

The voices in my ear gave status updates, but it was hard to hear over the roar. In twelve seconds, we'd exceeded a hundred miles per hour. In thirty seconds we were two miles off the ground. Six and a half minutes to reach orbit. I tried not to think of how many things could go catastrophically wrong at any second. But in spite of the danger, my heart swelled. I wanted to laugh from the sheer joy of it. *We were doing it.* What I'd always imagined, always dreamed, it was happening!

We were already going faster than I'd ever traveled. Higher than any plane I'd ever flown in.

A boom shook the entire craft as we broke the sound barrier. Now I couldn't lift my arms. Breathing got difficult. The g-forces tripled. My ears popped; my vision spotted.

But I'd practiced this. I knew what to do. I concentrated on my breathing, pushing with my diaphragm, forcing my lungs to open against the multiplied press of gravity. In and out. In and out.

The pressure steadily eased back to normal. We were still speeding away from Earth, but we were escaping gravity, fighting less resistance and needing less forward thrust.

I watched the numbers on the control panel fly upward as we pierced the sky. Thousands of miles per hour and still going up. So unbelievably fast.

Forty miles above Earth now. Nothing below me but a massive column of fire and smoke, a deep ocean of air.

Breathe. Breathe.

The cabin was strangely quiet. We could have been sitting on the tarmac except for the eerie silence that meant we were no longer fighting the atmosphere.

The shaking subsided. The g-load relaxed. I could expand my lungs a little easier.

"*Odysseus*, negative return," came the voice in my radio.

Bolshakov responded. "Roger, negative return."

We'd passed the point of no return. There would be no abort to the launchpad in case an engine failed.

There were a few short back-and-forths from Bolshakov and command, confirming everything was nominal.

And short minutes later, an engine cut off, completely emptied of its tons of fuel. There was a gentle jolt as the booster separated and began its slow fall back to Earth.

We'd done it. We were in space.

My restraints felt suddenly loose. I checked to make sure they were still connected, and realized I was floating a few inches above my seat. Zero-g.

Then Bolshakov again. "Ladies and gentlemen, the captain has turned off the seat belt sign. You may now move freely about the cabin."

There were some combined chuckles over the comm as Jeong and Shaw unbuckled beside me. This was like a walk in the park for them. Just another day at work.

"Easy as pie," Jeong said.

I was frozen in my seat, disbelieving, my body still in shock. That had just happened. It'd been over in minutes. Less than ten minutes. That was all it took to leave Earth below us. It had taken less time to leave Earth than the flight my parents had taken to see me one last time. Less time than it usually took me to drive to school in the morning.

We flew for what felt like ages and, simultaneously, no time at all. The cabin was almost utterly still. We were beyond turbulence now. The forward momentum of the boosters still carried us, even though the boosters were long gone.

"Come on, Cassie. You won't get this chance for very long," Shaw said.

I couldn't get my sausage-glove hands to work. I'd been gripping the armrest so tight my fingers had gone stiff. Shaw had to help me jimmy open the latches. And then I was flying free in the cabin in a rocket far above Earth.

I'd done this before, of course, but only for forty seconds at a time. And the cabin was so much more cramped than the Vomit Comet. I constantly bumped into something or part of somebody else. But what did it matter? I was floating!

I had only a few minutes to enjoy it, before the second set of boosters powered up to send us in the trajectory of our destination—away from the light of our sun, into the vast dark places between the stars.

Then we'd transfer to the habitation module, change out of our protective launch suits into our black honeycomb Space Activity Suits, or SASs, and climb into the HHMs. And once we slept, once we were far enough from Earth to put a buffer of safety between us, the Alcubierre drive would initiate.

And then human history would be made, and laws of physics rewritten.

"Houston, everything still looking good down there?" Copeland asked over the comm.

There was a second of silence where I imagined her voice traveling the many miles down below. "*Odysseus*, flying beautifully. All systems are go. Second booster separation in three hours. Have a nice flight."

"Cassie, look." Shaw was floating over by the bulkhead on the left, motioning with his arm. "You've got to see this."

I pulled myself hand over hand with the grips built into the bulkhead and floated over to see out of the small plexiglass window. We were still so close to Earth that all I could see was a curve of blue that seemed to go on forever, a sea of planet that we were falling into, filling up the entire half of the window. I could see daylight dawning in some part of the world, dazzling sunlight brighter than any light I'd seen in my life. Unfiltered by atmosphere, the sun was pure white, a blinding spotlight in the deepest dark.

The night side of Earth was not dark, but lit with artificial light. The mark of the one planet we knew that held life. But there was another out there, somewhere far, far away—and the five of us would be the first humans to see it. And maybe the last.

For a long time I couldn't say a word. I could only stare and stare until the image of our world burned into my retinas.

The light from the sun traveled eight minutes to brighten the horizon of our slowly rotating world. I could see the pale blue fuzz where life ended and dead space began, the fragile envelope of atmosphere that protected us from the void. It seemed as thin as a fingernail. My breath caught in my chest and I found myself sending waves of gratitude to whatever miracle had allowed life to flourish in relative safety all these centuries.

Beyond that edge of blue, darkness stretched endlessly in all directions. A thousand lifetimes wouldn't be enough to explore all that was out there.

"Houston, *Odysseus*," Bolshakov said. "Scheduled separation in ten. Nine. Eight."

Back into our seats, strapped in, still in our bulky escape suits. The last boosters were about to drop away, our last chance to redirect our course in a land without edges. A strange euphoria had come over me. I was feeling light-headed, impervious to danger, impatient for the booster separation to get over with so I could get out of this seat belt again.

". . . two. One."

Odysseus trembled as it broke away from the boosters. I was already fumbling with my seat belt latch, ready to be free of it, when the ship rocked, a metallic clang echoed, and the interior lights and holo panels flickered.

My mortality came rushing back to me.

The booster separation in low gravity was so much more dangerous than in the atmosphere—the release mechanism had to push the canisters away from us with enough force that they wouldn't just hover there beside the ship, unanchored. If they didn't drop below us, they'd remain in an unstable orbit until eventually falling to Earth.

Or they'd hit us.

"Maneuvering," Jeong said, her voice taught like a bowstring. Her fingers descended expertly over the controls, twisting the *Odysseus* using the tiny army of auxiliary boosters—little more than mini shots of air used for fine-tuning our movements.

Nothing I could do except hold my breath and watch the exterior monitors.

The cabin tilted to the right. The exterior cam showed the left booster hadn't properly disengaged and was hovering exactly where it had been connected. We were moving away from it, but slowly. This ship wasn't designed to make small, precise movements.

For a few minutes I didn't breathe, watching the booster inch away. Finally the computer blinked green, showing the booster had cleared.

Everyone seemed to exhale at once.

"Damage?" Bolshakov demanded.

"Minimal," Jeong said. "Doesn't look like any critical systems were affected."

"Let us be more careful in the future," Bolshakov said, his voice heavy like my father's when he was upset with me.

"View screen up," Bolshakov said. The holographic field of instruments over our heads temporarily thinned and became transparent, giving way to a live transmission from the exterior cameras. "Everyone, look. This is the closest humans have been to the moon since the 1970s."

"Hello, old friend," I heard Jeong whisper over the radio.

I couldn't help the smile on my face. The view screen was dominated by a pale disc straight ahead, immeasurably huge and bright. But it wasn't a disc anymore; it was a giant sphere, a real 3D object. We were so close! The moon had never filled my entire field of vision before. I couldn't believe how many details I could see from here that were impossible to view from home. It was like I had been nearsighted my entire life, and now I could finally see.

I'm sure Mission Control was taking note of my increased heart rate.

"It's gorgeous." The first words I spoke in space. Even my own voice sounded different, not weighted down by gravity.

But we didn't have all the time in the world. We had forty-five minutes to hang suspended, orbiting Earth, before the ship computer took over and turned on the experimental engines that would take us far away. A few minutes of moon gazing, that was all I got.

"Come on, Cassandra," Jeong said, her overlarge head bobbing in front of the port toward the habitation module. "Time to go."

Reluctantly I took one last look at the moon. Bolshakov still sat in his pilot's chair, gazing at it. He'd remain there as everyone else entered the HHMs one by one, until he was finally all alone. He'd pilot the ship until the last second, when he'd turn it—and all of our lives—over to Sunny, the computer.

We would all be asleep. I guess that's a good way to die, if you had to choose. Asleep, hanging in space between Earth and the moon.

Not that I planned on dying.

I followed Jeong through the hatch, pulling myself along with conveniently placed handholds. Through the narrow passage, just wide enough to accommodate our bloated, suited selves, and then it opened up to the habitation module. Five silver tubes, seven feet tall, stood in a solemn circle like some new-age Stonehenge.

I felt a stab of cold anxiety. "Is it time? Already?" I asked, even though I knew full well.

"What, you want to go to the bathroom first?" I heard Shaw's laughter over the comm and thought momentarily about flying over and kicking him. "This is the easy part."

"You're not scared, are you?" Copeland asked, floating in behind me. "You were always the best one at this. That's why you get to go first."

I sighed. This was where I'd spend who knew how long asleep and floating in muck while a computer controlled whether I lived or died. Who wouldn't be excited?

No going back now. "Okay, let's get me out of this thing, then."

Copeland and Jeong helped lift me out of my suit. No need for it now. If we had to jettison—if, for some reason, the computer found it necessary for us to leave the ship after we'd entered hibernation—the HHMs would be our life support. They would keep us alive as long as Sunny had access to any measurable amount of light.

I shivered as I emerged from the crumpled white cocoon, like a caterpillar in reverse. The air in here was kept in a survivable temperature range, but we were still on the night side of Earth and it was about as cold as a winter basement.

I floated, finally free, in a flight suit that was the only thing keeping heat against my skin. "Okay, I'm ready."

I stripped off the flight suit, as fast as possible, eager to spend the fewest number of seconds with my arms and legs bare.

Jeong and Copeland helped me into the skintight SAS and I was instantly warmed. The material fit like patterned silk against my skin. The suit moved with me, stretching when needed and snapping back into place, allowing me almost perfect dexterity.

Copeland nudged my back gently, sending me careering toward the nearest HHM. I caught myself and eased backward into the upright pod. I tried not to think the word coffin. Copeland settled the narrow helmet over my head and tested the seams to the suit. The oxygen kicked on with an industrial stale scent, like airplane air-conditioning.

"All right so far?" she asked, doctorly concern etched into her knitted brow.

"So far," I murmured.

She patted my shoulder encouragingly. "You've got this."

Inside the helmet, the neural network descended and threaded through my hair like spaghetti fingers, tickling my scalp. In practice I'd worn a breathing mask and goggles, but now the helmet provided my oxygen and my protection. Sensors inside the HHM monitored and controlled my temperature, heart rate, oxygen saturation, hormone levels. Together with the neural network, the computer would be able to know everything that was going on inside the tubes. So many variables. So many things to keep in check to maintain homeostasis.

So many things that could go wrong.

The others would get to sleep through it. They would be completely sedated. But I would hover somewhere in between, in a gray space that humans weren't supposed to live in. Their welfare would be my responsibility.

"Breathe deep and slow," Copeland said. Her comm was linked to my ear. Her voice was warm and strong, and I took comfort in her composure. "Your heart rate is a little high."

"Of course it is," I muttered, hating the way my voice fell flat and full inside of the helmet. Like being locked in a box. "Isn't yours?"

She smiled without showing teeth. Tense. I saw beads of sweat on her brow. We were all sweating. From excitement, but from fear, too.

Right now there was a fine line between those two emotions.

"All right, looks like you're good," Shaw said. He was hovering across the room, looking into the control console. The computer inside had the processing power of a five-year-old human brain—though not the maturity, I hoped—and enough backups and solar batteries to make it effectively immortal, so long as we weren't stranded in deep space. It would directly interface with my brain through the neural network and keep me updated on the stats of the others. It would watch over us while we slept.

Hopefully, it would keep us alive.

Shaw's helmet rotated an inch so he could look over his shoulder at me. "Nothing's gonna go wrong, Cassie. We'll be awake a few minutes after you go under while we finish setting up the autopilot. We're here if you should need us."

"But you won't," Copeland said, with finality born of confidence.

"Use this time to try to get acclimated to Sunny," Jeong said. "I know you've worked with her to some extent before, but the longer you're interfaced, the more you and she will both learn. She adapts to your brain waves over time."

I flinched as Copeland stuck a needle into my arm—the first of the tubes that would be my umbilical. My digestive system wouldn't quite work the same way when I was under; the drugs would slow peristalsis to barely more than a ripple. My heart would go sluggish, my conscious brain dim. The things I needed to stay alive would come directly into my veins.

"I'm so ready," I said, forcing bravado. In reality, I felt like I'd been kicked in the stomach. "Let's do this."

Jeong smiled, a gesture that was supposed to reassure me. "See you soon." She closed the door with a soft, permanent click.

I was prepared for the gel filling the tube. I had done this already on Earth. What I wasn't prepared for was the lack of gravity. The gel didn't sit at my feet and rise; it floated up all around me—solid bubbles, shifting and changing like life-forms.

It was fascinating and strangely beautiful; the light catching, glinting, in the gel bubbles, throwing miniature rainbows that lasted milliseconds. For a few minutes it was like I wasn't alone in the tube, but accompanied by a few members of a lovely alien species.

Aliens. That was who we were going to meet, why we were taking such risks. I could only hope they were as benevolent as Crane believed.

Eventually the gel bubbles formed conglomerates, until they filled every inch of empty space between me and the cushioned walls. The drugs began to seep into my blood, and as much as I wanted to stay awake and watch the blurry shapes of my human caretakers move about and check on me, I couldn't fight the cocktail of psychoactives for long.

This is it, I realized, as one by one partitions of my brain signed off. *This is what I've wanted, what I've worked for. I made it. It doesn't matter what happens after this; I'll go into eternity with the image of Earth imprinted on my soul.*

I tried to call up the image of a friend, of a familiar face, to ease me into sleep. I saw my family, crowded around the phone back at quarantine, smiling with happy tears. Mitsuko, basking in the sun with those giant sunglasses. Emilio, laughing. He always seemed to be laughing.

My eyelids grew as heavy as stones, and finally I let them fall. I heard music in my head, an instinct now as I descended to the place I'd worked so hard to find. Sinking down into the dark, deep ocean. Reaching out with my mind—out to the outer reaches of my conscious self, the nerves firing across synapses and into electrodes, to find the other awareness waiting to be let in.

Sunny. The real Sunny. Full-powered intelligence embedded in the most powerful ship built by humans.

She was there waiting, just on the other side of the door, just beyond the reach of my brain.

I opened the door and let her in.

My mind blinked out like the last light in a window, and it was quiet.

But then a voice—unfamiliar, distant, stilted. Like an echo from the end of a long hallway. The sound wasn't in my ears. There was a voice in my head that wasn't my own.

Neural handshake initiated. Loading.

Connection established. System initialized.

Then—

Hello, Cassie.

TWENTY-EIGHT

I WAS FLOATING underwater. Bobbing, like a boneless jellyfish, in water that was clear and warm.

Sunlight filtered down from someplace above. No matter how hard I tried, the silvery boundary between my world and whatever was above did not break. But I didn't need to surface. Water filled my lungs as easily as air.

My ears were full of seawater. I heard only the *thud thud thud* of my heartbeat, beating and beating like sea grass in the current. The rhythm lulled me. I fell in and out of dreamless sleep.

Always, always a pinging in my ear. It was soft and distant, a single burst of sonar at a steady, slow rhythm. Like a faraway lighthouse with its rotating beam of light.

I closed my eyes.

Cassie. Cassie.

That voice again. Something from a long time ago, from a faraway memory.

When I opened them again, something was different. There had never been anything in my sea and now there was. Something small and white like a speck of sea foam in the distance.

Curious, I swam toward it. The thing grew larger. Closer.

It was something that should not exist.

It was the size of a large dog. A white elephant's head perched in the center of a shapeless, almost octopod body, surrounded by too many arms, which undulated gently in the waves. Ivory white, the elephant eyed me coolly, its black eyes blank and enigmatic, a peaceful expression on its face. It was like some strange amalgam of my grandmother's Ganesh pendant and a sea creature. Something dredged from my memories and pieced back together all wrong, my mind trying to force some logic to the situation.

A word—a name—surfaced in my mind like a half-remembered dream. *Sunny.*

Sunny was a computer program. Inside my head, inside my dream.

Whether this was a form she'd chosen, or one my brain had projected to make sense of her, I did not know.

We stared at each other.

Maybe I could talk to her. *Hello. I'm Cassie.*

Hello, Cassie. The response was instant, the voice female and calm, though I could not explain how I knew either of those things.

What a strange dream this is, I thought. Then, *Where are we?*

We are here.

Couldn't argue with that.

What are we doing here? I asked.

Watching, she replied.

What are we watching?

One of Sunny's many waving arms gestured for me to follow her. I obeyed.

We swam with almost no effort past unchanging scenery; or perhaps the scenery swam past us, I could not tell. Sunny led me to the bottom of the sea, to a place I had not been able to go on my own. A sheer cliff of white rocks emerged to my right, an impenetrable wall, the first solid boundary I'd encountered in my ocean. And at the bottom of the sea was a metal Stonehenge, alien and out of place.

Four smooth silver tubes standing in a circle, like upright coffins, each half buried in white sand.

Tubes?

No—no, this wasn't real. This was a dream.

But no, this was a piece of reality within my dream.

A shock of recognition, and the truth emerged from its murky depths in the sleeping zones of my brain.

The ship. I was aboard the ship. An image of the pale *Odysseus* bathed in artificial light on a launchpad filtered through my consciousness like a picture from another life. I saw myself, sleeping under the influence of drugs and floating in gel like a lab specimen, dead to the outside world aside from the regular pinging of my crewmates' life support systems. Four steady, slow heartbeats in the dark.

The drugs in my veins kept hormones balanced and my emotions to a minimum. I was almost entirely asleep. There was no panic, no fear.

How long had we been traveling? How long had I floated in this endless ocean before remembering myself?

Were we still on course to our destination? How much longer would I be alive, floating in an endless dream?

Those thoughts drifted away like a bubble on the waves. Inconsequential, out of reach. *Pop.*

It did not matter. Nothing outside my ocean mattered. I was warm and I was safe, and here I would sleep while keeping watch over the others.

Sunny was staring at me, tentacle arms waving idly as though she didn't care—she had all the time in the world. She waited. She watched. Time was nothing.

My mission was to stand guard over the other sleeping astronauts. Sunny and me, together. For as long as it took.

TWENTY-NINE

THERE WAS NOTHING behind me and nothing ahead but more of the same endless blue, the same incessant heartbeats, the same four metal tubes in the sand, and Sunny's black shark eyes and undulating tentacles. The world behind my eyes drifted between blue sea and dreamless sleep.

I did not sleep, but sometimes I closed my eyes. And when I closed my eyes I heard a voice calling my name, as though carried by the wind from far away.

Cassie. Cassie, do you hear me?

Old memories. They did not matter here. I opened my eyes.

The voice came again, but louder now. *Cassie, do you hear me? You must listen.*

The voice was not coming from my memories. It was coming

from Sunny. But it was not the voice I had come to associate with her presence.

I looked at Sunny, but her black elephant eyes showed no recognition.

I am listening, I thought, curious.

Cassie, you must make me another promise.

Okay, I thought hesitantly.

Promise me that you will remember why you dreamed of space. And when you wake, I hope you can forgive me.

An earthquake trembled beneath the ocean floor.

I jerked out of drifting and looked to Sunny, questioning. Her blank gaze never wavered. *We have arrived.*

A shiver ran through me.

No—that was impossible. My body didn't shiver. I couldn't be cold. My sea was warm like a tropical lagoon. Drugs kept my body in homeostasis, my body paralyzed. The gel insulated my body heat. I couldn't even remember what it was like to be cold.

The edges of my vision turned from soft blue to sickly gray. A harsh, metallic edge formed around my world, shrinking my endless sea.

Time to wake, Sunny said.

My eyes flew open. My real, physical eyes, and it felt like my eyelids were ripping apart. My warm, safe ocean sizzled away in the harsh light of reality.

My eyes, unpracticed, unfocused, saw blurry shapes, washed out like an overexposed photo through a watery lens. At first I didn't remember I was wearing a helmet, and what I saw made no sense. Light filtering through bubbles in gel, vague steel-colored shapes in the distance.

Gradually my brain discovered the rest of my body. Face, covered. The helmet's weight against my shoulders. Arms and legs, dangling, numb and useless.

Small electric pulses raced into my limbs, making them twitch erratically. Pain arced up my nerves like strings of fire. Sunny, helping to stimulate my muscles. A low, guttural groan tore from my throat, and the sound was so foreign I didn't recognize the source. My body writhed and tried to arch away from the pain, but there was nowhere to go to escape it.

A harsh sound scraped against the inside of my ears: the last of the gel being sucked out of the tube. There was a sickening tug under my skin as the tubes retracted, followed by a sound like a hair dryer, the vacuum removing the last of the gel from my suit so that it would not escape into the cabin.

The door hatch released with a hiss of air. Unable to so much as put my arms out to catch myself, I was about to slam into the floor.

Instead, I fell into a pair of arms.

I felt myself being lowered gently to the ground, which was impossible for two reasons: I was supposed to be the first to wake. And we were still supposed to be in space.

Those impossibilities would have to wait. I couldn't lift a single muscle off the floor.

I gasped for air like a stranded fish, the muscles around my ribs straining with disuse. Everything ached, every muscle and tendon. My skin tingled with hot needle pricks as the nerve endings groaned awake.

Slowly, the more I blinked, the more the world came into focus. The pain in my muscles eased, and I was able to shift until I sat slumped against the bulkhead. My head, however, was still entirely too heavy in its helmet, and I couldn't lift it. I had no choice but to stare at the steel floor.

The snaps on either side of my helmet were released. It was pulled gently from my shoulders. My long black braid tumbled free over my shoulder.

I was finally able to lift my head to see who had caught me. My eyes traveled slowly up from his legs, kneeling on the floor in front of me, to his torso, all clad in the same skintight black honeycomb suit I wore, and finally up to his face.

His face. The one that had been tempting my dreams.

My lips moved, but no sound came out.

". . . Luka?"

THIRTY

HIS FACE WAS etched in concern. Hair longer than I remembered, messy and dark gold. Lines by his eyes. Looking older than I remembered.

He held a packet of water up to my lips. One of the pouches from *Odysseus*'s stores. The liquid soothed my parched throat.

I pushed away his hand so I could speak. "Luka?" My voice was harsh, gravelly. "What . . . how?"

"Please, save your voice."

I tried to shake my head, but I only succeeded in losing the delicate balance I'd gained. My head slumped uncomfortably to one shoulder.

Gingerly, Luka cradled the back of my skull and held me upright.

"You're not real," I whispered. My voice was broken like it'd been run over by a truck, more scratch than sound.

"Do I not look real?" A ghost of a smile, one corner of his mouth perked up wryly.

"You could be . . . not you. Something else, data mining my memories. Showing me a friendly face to . . . gain my trust." That had been too many words. I swallowed a few times to moisten my throat. "Tell me it's you."

The smile dropped away. "It's me."

"Prove it."

"Okay. I'll tell you something only I know. Something you couldn't make up."

He released the back of my head, and to my relief I managed to hold it up without his help. His gaze locked with mine, steady and grim and resolute. "I knew I was never going to be selected for this mission. My entire aim in participating in the competition was to monitor the other candidates. From the moment I saw your skill at manipulating your brain waves, I knew it was going to be you." His voice dropped. "From the beginning, I had hoped it would be you, Cassie."

My lungs were working extra hard to bring in oxygen. My voice was more breath than sound. "What the hell are you talking about?"

"Cassie. That message that Crane's satellites received? The blueprints for *Odysseus*? We sent that message. My father designed this ship. *We* invited you here. This is our home planet." His jaw clenched. Then he added, with venom so unlike

363

him it made me shiver, "What's left of it."

I squeezed my eyes shut, wanting him to stop. Unwilling for this to be reality. Unable to digest it.

When I opened them again, the world hadn't even begun to make sense. I couldn't look at his face. Instead I scanned the room, looking for some semblance of normal, something that would make this okay.

Around us stood the four silver pods, each of my crew members still fast asleep within, their heart-rate monitors beeping peacefully from the control pads. They were all still there. Still breathing. Copeland's shorn hair had grown at least six inches, floating around her skull like a dark halo. Bolshakov's face had a scruff of grizzly beard, where he'd been clean-shaven the last I'd seen him.

I reached a hand up to my hair. It'd been long to begin with, but now it came down nearly to my waist.

I turned my eyes back to Luka. He was waiting for me to accept it, his expression bleak. Like he expected me to take this badly.

My eyes blinked away what felt like many months' worth of sleep, and the details of his face came into high-definition focus. The ruddiness of his cheeks. The perspiration at his hairline, hinting at some exertion. All impossible, impossible.

"How long has it been?" I whispered.

"Six months. Please forgive me for being blunt," he said. "I know you are still recovering from the stasis. But there is much I must tell you, and we have little time. The rest of your crew will soon begin their waking sequences."

I gaped at him.

I couldn't understand what was happening. If it wasn't for the fact that my muscles obviously hadn't been used in months, and the impossible fact that Luka was sitting in front of me, on a spacecraft presumably five hundred light-years from Earth, there would have been no way for me to believe it.

The months I'd known him flashed before my eyes.

He'd never been anything but number one, ensuring he lasted until the final round. He understood every concept in class better and faster than I did. He'd never been able to alter his brain waves. He'd always been a little set apart from the rest, a little awkward. I'd attributed that to him being a fish out of water—being foreign.

He took a breath and began to speak, quickly, more words than I'd ever heard him say at once. "When the rest of your crew awaken, you'll learn that you are in an underground bunker. The planet above our heads is empty and barren and long abandoned. The surface is too irradiated for life to exist. Right now, we're the only living things in this entire system. My people have returned here only to show you that we mean no harm, and that we are telling the truth. Cassie, we are here because we need your help."

He was speaking fast, as though forcing himself to say everything as quickly as possible. I could only stare at his moving mouth, watching him form the words that fell like so many discordant piano notes in my ears. Noise. Random, nonsensical noise.

My brain was still stuck on the first impossible thing. "You're not . . . Luka, you look human. You speak English!"

He sighed in frustration and ran his hand through his hair, mussing it up even more. "Yes. As ambassadors, we have chosen to appear human. We took on your form, permanently, to be recognizable and nonthreatening. We wanted to assimilate."

"Why were you at the competition to begin with if you had set this all up? What were you even doing there?"

His face was grim, but he answered dutifully. "My job was to monitor the progress of the candidates, attempt to discern who among them would be most amenable to our proposal, and try to sway the selection in our favor."

"You . . ." I coughed, sat back away from him, as my emotions twisted from disbelief to realization to anger. "You were trying to tip the scales in your favor." Then, as realization fully dawned: "You were trying to get me on your side! The whole time, everything you were doing, you were trying to win me over so I could . . ." Something nagged at me. "Is this why someone tried to sabotage the mission? Could someone on Earth . . . know about you?"

A dark cloud passed over his face. "I don't know. It could have nothing to do with us, or everything."

I was so angry I couldn't even find words to finish my thought. Memories of kissing him washed over me. All our time in the wilderness, in the SLH, every moment now flashed in my mind with a new and sinister angle. My mind struggled to process. "You deliberately tried to make me . . . *like* you? So I'd try to convince the others that you were trustworthy. You played me like a chess piece."

Hurt filled his eyes. "That was not my intent."

"Oh, yes, it was." I tried to move away from him, but slipped and fell on my knees. He reached forward to help and I twisted away. At the first hint of my resistance, his hands released me. "Don't. Don't presume that we're friends. You aren't . . . I don't know who you are."

"Cassie, what could I have said?" There was a note of exasperation in his voice. "I had no choice. How could I have told you the truth?"

"Just—stop." I was hurt, furious, unreasonable.

He reached out to me, holding my forearms gingerly. "Let me tell you why you are here. And then I will leave you alone."

I met his eyes. Gave him a nod.

"It was a surprise to you to discover you were not alone in the universe. It was not so for my people. One of our moons was, in fact, as teeming with life as our own planet. It was our failing that we did not deduce the intelligence of the dominant species. It was, in fact, our downfall. We underestimated them; their intelligence, their intentions. These aliens—the vrag— they turned against us. They killed our scientists, stole our spacecraft, and within no time at all were rampaging across our planet."

I opened my mouth to say something, but he shook his head and went on.

"I was not alive to witness this. My family just barely escaped the destruction of our planet. Our only chance at long-term survival was to find a livable planet to colonize. They traveled for years upon years, despairing at ever finding another. Until Earth."

I was beginning to see where this would lead. "But it was already inhabited."

He nodded, releasing my arms. "My people are desperate. We were willing to share our knowledge, come to humans in good faith, and ask for refuge."

"You want to . . . *share* Earth?" And then I realized. "You're using past tense."

"Our numbers are few; it could have been done. We planned to invite you here, giving you *Odysseus* as a show of good faith and to show what we had lost. To meet here in a neutral place, where we would not risk a volatile response."

I narrowed my eyes. "What do you mean, it *could* have been done? Aren't we here? Wasn't this exactly what you wanted? You hold us hostage until we agree to your terms?"

His eyes went wide in alarm. "No, no, not at all." His eyes darted over to the pods and back again. "Cassie, circumstances have changed. The alien species that destroyed my planet and my people—they have found us. They have discovered Earth. And we fear it is only a matter of time before Earth shares in our planet's fate." He held on to my shoulders. "My people escaped because we had the means to disappear into the galaxy. There will be no such escape for humanity."

The bottom dropped out of my stomach, a black hole forming where it had been.

I thought of Earth, the only color in the black void. Alone and vulnerable.

"What can we do?" I whispered.

Luka squeezed my shoulders, his handsome face resolute. "My family believes there is a weapon hidden somewhere inside this bunker that may challenge the vrag. Something my people never got a chance to use. We plan to retrieve it, and to return to Earth, with you as our allies, to defend the planet."

His hands fell away, putting space between us. "By the time your crewmates awake, I will be gone. You need to regain your strength, and they will need time to recover. But you're safe here, for now." He glanced down at a screen embedded in the suit at his wrist, then met my eyes. "When you're ready, we will meet to discuss our mutual survival. I ask only that you consider what I've told you. Take what you know of me, Cassie. I never lied except to protect myself. I have only ever tried to help you. Please, help me now."

My voice was a cautious whisper. "What do you want from me?"

He took half a step closer, his voice going soft. "I want you to be on our side."

I considered him. How I'd misjudged him so severely in the beginning—how I'd misjudged everyone, really, on sight, and how I'd been proven wrong each and every time.

He was right. He'd only ever been a friend. And now he needed me to trust him.

"One last thing." I cleared my throat. "What . . . what's your name?"

He tilted his head, as though confused I would choose that question out of the infinite others. "You know my name."

"Your *real* name."

He took a step closer. We were now breathing the same air. My heart pounded in my ears. "I have always been Luka. I was born on Earth. I have been human since my earliest memories." He smiled distantly. "I believe I told you once—that I understood how it felt to feel like a stranger in your own land."

I blinked at him, remembering.

"But my people, my family, we call ourselves megobari."

Despite everything, despite knowing the truth beneath the surface, he was still Luka. The planes of his face were so familiar and so dear to me. And beneath the anger and confusion and fear, I still cared about him. Still trusted him.

A beat of silence. And then one of the pods began to beep.

"My people wish to help yours," Luka said, backing slowly away, leaving me propped against the bulkhead. "I ask only that you help convince your people that we are telling the truth. There's no time to waste with arguing."

Looking into his eyes, I saw no deceit. "I'll do what I can. But I want to know all the details first. Everything. No more deceit."

"Agreed." He smiled. The hatch opened into the airlock. He glanced out at it and then at me. "It was . . . good to see you again."

If I hadn't been dehydrated, my eyes might've filled with tears. "I didn't know if I ever would."

"It won't do for me to be aboard when your crew awakens. But when they do, we'll be waiting." A loud vacuum sound broke the silence as Bolshakov's pod began to empty of gel, and Luka shot a quick look back before meeting my eyes again. "Remember what we promised."

I sat straighter, finding my body's strength returning. "Yes."

With a solemn nod, Luka exited the hatch, the door closing behind him.

We'd promised each other—a long time ago now, but recent in my memory—that no matter what, we would not let anything that might be between us jeopardize the mission.

I understood that now.

Think of all the things that motivate you. My family. Earth. And now, my friends. This was why we'd come. This was why we were here.

My job wasn't over because we'd arrived safely; it had only just begun.

I faced the pods of my crew as, one by one, they began their waking sequences. I squared my shoulders and forced air into my lungs until the pain was only background noise. Time to be strong.

Time to get to work.

ACKNOWLEDGMENTS

RARELY ARE DREAMS achieved alone. This book began, literally, as a dream. I truly never thought it might become anything more than that. But thanks to the support of a legion of incredible people working behind the scenes, it became the book you hold in your hands. I'm going to try to express my gratitude to all of those people here.

First, to my wonderful editor, Jen Klonsky, who understood this book and what it needed, and carried it every step along the way. Anytime I had an idea I was iffy about, you always responded with enthusiasm. Thank you for that. And thank you for always encouraging and supporting the diversity in this book.

Thank you also to everyone at HarperCollins who helped

make this book a reality, including Catherine Wallace, Sarah Kaufman, Alison Klapthor, Alexandra Rakaczki, Sabrina Abballe, and anyone else who I may have left out: I think you're all wonderful.

To my amazing superhero of an agent, Kristin Nelson: Working with you is another impossible dream come true. I'm unbelievably proud to be part of the NLA family. Thank you for your laser-sharp editorial eye that whipped this book into shape, for loving it as much as I do, and for finding it a perfect home. You changed my life.

A special thank-you is due to astronaut Randy "Komrade" Bresnik, who took the time to answer my questions about astronaut training and what it truly feels like to see Earth from a distance. I hope I was able to express a fraction of your experiences through Cassie. (Though, please don't check my math too closely.) Also, a big shout-out to NASA in general, for being the inspiration not just for me, but generations of kids who looked up at the stars and wondered. Thank you for letting me be a part of #NASASocial and touring the facilities at Marshall. I hope I've done you all justice. Keep fighting the good fight and chasing that horizon.

Thank you to Ayesha Patel, Mathangi Subramanian, Sangu Mandanna, Urvi Patel, Katie Slivensky, and AdriAnne Strickland for their advice and assistance, helping me portray, hopefully, a more sensitive, accurate, and respectful representation of the different facets of Cassie's character. Your insight was invaluable and much appreciated.

To my library ladies, past and present: Carrie, Barbara, Brenda, Pam, Martha, Sara—and Nate, who isn't a lady but still counts—thank you for being the best coworkers a girl could ask for, and for all your wholehearted and enthusiastic support of me and my writing. It's rare to have coworkers who are also friends, and I thank you for making each day pass in relative comfort. Also, thanks for all the cake. Special thanks to Sara for reading rejection emails out loud to me so the blow would sting a little less, and for beta reading. And to Barbara, for making my pie-in-the-sky hopes of finding an astronaut to interview a reality, leading to one of the coolest emails I've ever received hitting my in-box.

To my critique partners, Alexa Donne and Emily Neal: You guys are my rock. I'm so lucky to have found you and so grateful for our friendship. Five years of this publishing journey and I don't know that I would've made it without you by my side. I quite literally wouldn't be where I am today without you. Extra-special thanks to Alexa, for your constant and unwavering support. She encouraged me to send out the query I was too afraid to send that ended up changing everything. You guys were my life rafts in the treacherous query seas, and this book owes its life to you both.

Big shout-out to my various circles of writing friends who have all lent me support and advice somewhere along the way! To Roshani Chokshi, for your mentorship and advice, and for gracing me with your goddess-like wisdom. To the Epic Book Club of Love (even though we never seem to read any books):

Jilly Gagnon, Anna Priemaza, Chelsea Sedoti, Kristen Orlando, and Kayla Olson; the Lucky 13s: Mara Fitzgerald, Austin Gilkerson, Rebecca Caprara, Julie Dao, Kevin van Whye, Jordan Villegas, Jessica Rubinkowski, and Kati Gardner: I can't wait till we can all pose in front of our published books with our matching T-shirts; and finally my fellow 2017 debut authors who have become friends, especially Elly Blake (for being the best roommate ever), Sarah Tolcser, Misa Sugiura, Sarah Henson (for navigating Darcy Miller and me safely through the Smoky Mountains and back!), Sandhya Menon, Tanaz Bhathena, and Axie Oh (I promise I'll work more on that Secret Other Book now!). And to anyone and everyone who read early versions of this book before it was any good, I thank you.

To my sister, Kayla, who was the very first person to read this book, sent in emailed chunks straight from my brain—you were its first cheerleader, and the reason this book was ever even finished. Your excited flailing was the best motivation. I'm glad we were able to keep your favorite title! Thank you for being my sister—I know that it wasn't always easy. But it is a very reassuring feeling to have someone who always understands you, the way only siblings do. Love you.

To my parents: You sacrificed so much to make everything in my life possible and paved the way for me to succeed. Despite not being readers yourselves, you made sure to read to me so that I would always love books. You assured that I grew up in a loving, supportive home. You are the best second set of parents for my child I could ever ask for, and I'll never be able to repay you for the years of free babysitting. (Sorry about that.) I feel so lucky and blessed to have you both. Love you always.

To Nick: Thank you for working so hard for our family, and for all the solo parenting required for me to finish this book. I'm so lucky to have found my partner in life when I was sixteen. Thank you for putting up with me these past twelve years, and for always doing the dishes.

To my Rosie: This book existed before you did, but I am more proud of you than I'll ever be of anything else. I'm sorry for all the times my work has taken me away from you. (Hopefully you won't remember very much of that.) Thank you for choosing me as your mom. I hope you learn that you can do anything you aspire to in life. (But please—just for me—please don't go off on a dangerous mission into deep space. Anything else is cool.) I love you more than all the stars.

To anyone and everyone who has read this book and passed it along to a friend—librarians, booksellers, bloggers, readers—I thank you from the bottom of my heart. There is no better champion of a book than a friend who says to another friend, "You HAVE to read this."

And thank you, reader, for picking up this book and giving it a chance. I hope it inspires you to take a chance on your own dreams, too. Even if nobody else does, know that I believe in you.